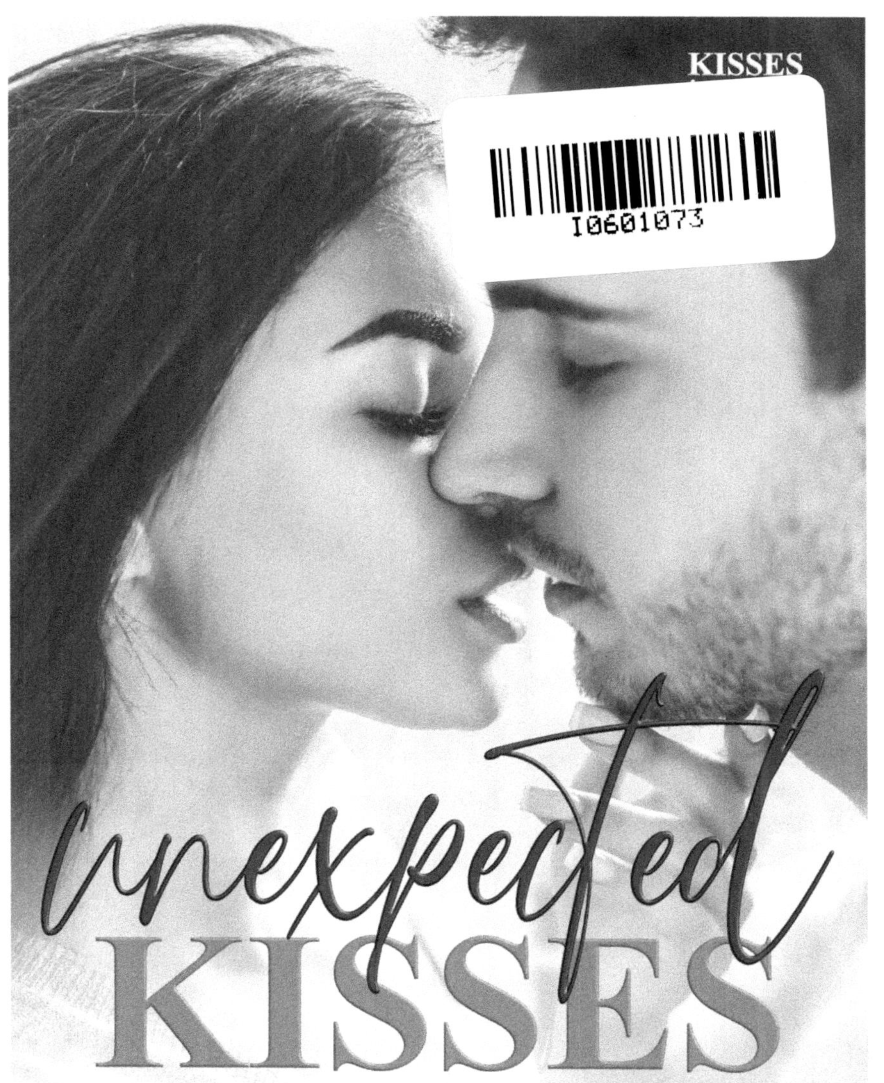

KISSES
I0601073
unexpected
KISSES
DEBRA ST JAMES

Unexpected Kisses

KISSES — BOOK THREE

DEBRA ST JAMES

Website: www.debrastjamesbooks.com

Email: debrastjamesbooks@gmail.com

Published by: Debra St James Author

Edited by: Cruel Ink Editing and Design

Formatted by: Debra St James Author

ISBN: 978-0-6457395-3-4 [Paperback]

ISBN: 978-0-6457395-4-1 [Discreet Edition Paperback]

ISBN: 978-0-6450483-8-4 [Ebook]

inspiration

This story was inspired by the lyrics ...

—> *Adore You by Harry Styles* <—

playlist

Adore You … *Harry Styles*
Slow Hands … *Niall Horan*
Terrified … *Katharine McPhee/Jason Reeves*
Everything Has Changed … *Jasmine Thompson/Gerald Ko*
Still Falling for You … *Ellie Goulding*
Once in a Lifetime … *Landon Austin*
Natural … *THE DRIVER ERA*
Beautiful Soul … *Boyce Avenue*
Like I'm Gonna Lose You … *Meghan Trainor/John Legend*
I Love You Always … *Betty Who*

You can check it out here:
https://tinyurl.com/unexpectedkisses-spotify

—sarah—

JANUARY

Drawing in a deep breath, I take the final step up the porch of my childhood home. I've promised myself that today I'm going to break the news of my plan to my family since I have my first interview with the fertility clinic this week. Actually, I think I'll refer to it as an agency. It doesn't sound so … so clinical. My family is always supportive, and I know they always have my best interest at heart, so I'm not worried they'll disapprove of my decision.

Oh, what the hell? If I can't be honest with myself, who can I be honest with? I'm terrified they'll think I'm making the wrong decision. That they'll try to talk me out of it and encourage me to wait until I meet the love of my life. *Ha!* I thought I'd had that with Michael but I was sorely mistaken. Every time I think about the day he came home with his news about the promotion he'd accepted without considering me, I'm taken back to the years of misery when my heart was a pile of mush and barely functioning.

Balancing Emma's birthday cake with one hand, I open the

screen and front door to step inside with a shiver. Warmth immediately greets me, wrapping me in a familiar embrace and taking me back to a simpler time. The house smells delicious—inviting me farther in. "I'm here!"

Mom steps out of the kitchen, drying her hands on her apron and wearing a wide smile. "Hiya, Honey. Oh, that cake looks amazing. Emma's gonna love it!"

"I figured she deserved a great cake for her last year in her thirties." I step into the kitchen and place the cake in the middle of the counter. Once my hands are free, I hug Mom. We're about the same height and pretty much the same shape; I have her eyes, as do Em and Max. Apart from the few grays that have snuck in, you wouldn't think Mom was old enough to have an almost forty-year-old daughter. "Where's Dad?"

"He's drying Archie," she huffs. "That naughty dog rolled in mud on his morning walk, so your dad thought he'd better give him a bath before the kids arrive."

"He's always getting up to mischief." I chuckle and Mom rolls her eyes. "Anything I can do to help?"

"Would you mind making the salad?" She points to the salad vegetables sitting on the counter.

"Of course not." I set about doing as Mom asked and before long, I have the salad ready to complement the feast I'm certain Mom's prepared. She loves feeding us and always makes a big fuss about our family's Sunday lunches.

Archie comes sprinting through the kitchen, bouncing around like a gazelle. He's funny when he has a bath, it's like he gets a new lease on life. "Oh, who's this handsome boy?" I crouch down to give him a rub around the scruff of his neck. His back end wriggles like crazy with the wagging of his tail.

Dad chuckles as his feet come into view, so I stand. "Dad."

He wraps his arms around me, pulling me in tight and landing a kiss on top of my head. "Baby Girl. How are you?"

I draw back, still holding him. "I've had a good week. I hear you've been rolling around in mud puddles."

We both chuckle, but he points down at the family dog. "That troublemaker there, not me. I'm innocent." He holds his hands up in surrender.

The front door opens, and the sound of little feet running on Mom and Dad's hardwood floor, along with little girl giggles, fills the house. Kenny bursts into the kitchen. "I'm here!"

Mom sweeps forward, collecting Kenny in her arms. She holds her tight against her body while Kenny's little feet hang loosely. "Hello. My, don't you look pretty today."

Kenny smiles wide at Mom's compliment then wriggles down to greet Dad.

Em, Theo, and the boys follow close behind and we all greet each other with our usual boisterous happiness. I'm not sure if all families are this close or demonstrative in their affection for each other, but ours is, and I'm thankful for it. I love spending time with Mom and Dad, my brother and sister, and my niece and nephews.

I step out to go to the bathroom. While I'm here I may as well practice the news—*for the millionth time*—I'm going to share today. Butterflies erupt in my stomach as I study myself in the mirror, then I draw in a deep breath and head back to the kitchen, which is filled with loud laughter.

"What's funny?" I ask as I step into the room, moving straight to my brother to wrap my arms around his waist. He embraces me in return, kissing the top of my head. God, I love my brother; he's so steady and strong.

Emma turns the T-shirt she's holding around to show me the front. I read it out for everyone. "I'm a proud sister of a freaking awesome brother (and yes, he brought me this shirt)." I can't hold back my laughter. Only Max!

"It's perfect, right?" Max asks the room as Emma twists the shirt around for everyone to see.

Dad claps Max on the shoulder and chuckles. "Only you, Max." *Right!*

I spin around, pushing away from my brother, and point my finger at him. "Don't even think about getting me one of those." I can't hold in my grin, which probably gives away that I'm not all that serious. I honestly don't care what he gets me for my birthday, as long as I get to spend time with him.

Everyone settles, and we prepare the table for lunch. Theo helps Emma with the kids, careful to ensure Lachlan's food isn't touching. I don't think I've ever seen my sister so happy; Theo has been so good for her and the boys. The first few moments are silent as we serve ourselves and take our first few bites of food. *Mmm.* Mom's cooking is the best.

Our regular chatter strikes up once the eating slows, and Mom places her silverware down to study Max. "You said you've been busy at work. When are you going to employ someone to help?"

We've been nagging him for quite some time to get help at his workshop. He does too much on his own with the actual mechanical work and the restoration of old muscle cars and trucks, as well as the business management side of things. It takes up all of his time.

"You'll be happy to know that I have an office manager starting at eight a.m. on Monday," he proudly announces.

We all cheer. This has been a long time coming.

"Finally!" Mom raises her voice to be heard above the noise. I glance across to check if Lachlan is okay, but he's covering his ears. I smile inwardly at him, proud of how far he's come.

Hang on a minute. He's suddenly found an office manager? He never said he was advertising *or* interviewing. "How did you find this office manager, and are you sure they're qualified?"

I can see the cogs turning in Max's head, and I know my brother well enough to figure out he's hired some random person. "She *is* qualified, right? You didn't just hire anyone off the street?" He leans his elbow on the table and rubs his thumbnail across his bottom lip in thought. His action tells me that's exactly what he did. "Oh, my gawd! You did. Are you an idiot?" I roll my eyes at him and Emma snickers.

"I'm not an idiot, Sarah," he snaps. "She's highly competent or I wouldn't have hired her," he adds more calmly, then proceeds to tell us how Molly came to be employed and I have to admit, she does sound competent. Perhaps I'm worrying for nothing. We all tend to be a little overprotective of each other.

Discussion ensues regarding Molly's knowledge of the city since she's new here as well as where she's staying. I get the sense that Max hadn't given it much thought before now, but his concern for his new employee is obvious. This could be interesting.

"How are things going at your office, Sarah? Any news on Eric's retirement?" Emma asks.

I blow out a heavy sigh and slump in my chair. "Something happened and delayed Adam's move to the west coast. I'm not sure when things will change."

Emma gives me a sympathetic smile. "Well, on the positive side of things, it means you get to work with Eric longer." My mood improves at the thought.

"That's true, and it's something I'm cherishing." I tuck my hair behind my ear. "I love working with Eric, and you guys know how I feel about change."

"Eric's grandson might be a lot like him. You never know, it might be a seamless transition," Max adds.

I nod and place my silverware down. It's now or never. This is the perfect opportunity to talk with my family about my plans. I swallow the lump in my throat. "I have something I wanted to talk with you guys about."

Everyone gives me one hundred percent of their attention and my stomach rolls. Maybe I shouldn't have eaten. "What is it, Love?" Mom asks when I hesitate.

I blow out a breath, my nerves getting the better of me. "Please don't judge me. I've thought long and hard about this, and it's the right decision for me. I'm hoping you'll all be supportive."

Creases form between Dad's eyebrows. "Of course we'll support you."

Well, that's a good start. "Great." I blow out a long breath. Here goes. "I've decided I want to have a baby." The silence in the room is loud as I glance around the table. "I'm not getting any younger, and it's impossible to meet someone decent. Someone I'd want to raise a family with." I glance at Emma and the sympathy on her face tells me she understands what I'm saying.

Mom's hand rises to fidget with her necklace. "Oh. Well … uh … that's unexpected news. How will you make this happen?" I'm going to take this as a positive sign. She's asking for more details, not telling me I shouldn't do it.

"There are agencies that help women like me. I complete a whole heap of paperwork, give them a whole wad of money, and they give me sperm from a baby daddy of my choosing." A simplified explanation, but sometimes simple is the best approach.

"My sister, Anna, did that." Theo looks at Kenny with eyes full of love and adoration for his niece-slash-daughter. "That's how we ended up with Kenny."

That's right. I remember Emma telling me about it. Maybe that was the conversation that triggered my urgency to have a baby; knowing there was a way I could do it on my own. If things don't work out with the clinic I'm interviewing with this week, then maybe it would be a good idea to have a backup. Just in case.

"Do you know which agency she used?" I ask.

Theo thinks for a moment. "I don't, sorry. Dad might know, though. I'll ask him and let you know."

I smile gratefully at him. "Thanks."

"This isn't the way we expected you to be having a baby, but we'll support you in any way we can." Dad reaches across, patting my hand with love and support. Some of the tension I've been holding in my body releases, and I relax a little.

Everyone offers their support to me in any way they can as I find a baby daddy, through my pregnancy, and then into motherhood. I'm not sure why I was so worried. I should have known they would support me in any way they could. They always want the best for me.

We clean up from lunch, then I place the chocolate birthday cake I made for Emma on the table. We sing "Happy Birthday" in our usual, terribly off-key fashion and enjoy the delicious cake. I'm so thankful I got the chance to bake yet another birthday cake for my sister and that she's healthy after her brush with cancer.

Once things are quiet and the kids are playing with Archie in the backyard, Emma, Mom, and I have a few moments on our own. Emma slides her fingers through my hair and whispers, "You know I'll help you in any way I can once you have the baby." I smile and wrap my arms around her.

"Thanks, Sis. You're the best."

We separate and Em's eyes widen. "I still have the crib from the boys and some other stuff. Would you like it?"

Excitement fills me. "Absolutely. Thank you so much. I'll take whatever you have."

"I'll get everything out and bring it over. This is so exciting." She squeezes me tight, and I know she's genuinely happy and excited for me.

Mom catches our attention. "You're one hundred percent positive this is what you want to do?"

I nod. "I've thought about it a lot ever since Michael left. I know this must seem like it's come out of the blue, but I promise it hasn't. I've weighed up my options carefully, and I truly think this is what will work best for me."

Mom steps toward me, wrapping me in her motherly embrace. "I completely understand, Baby Girl." She smooths my bangs out of my eyes. "Once the baby's born, don't forget your father and I can help out with babysitting. That way you can go back to work at least part-time."

"Thanks, Mom. Your support means the world to me. I'll admit, I was nervous breaking the news to you guys."

Creases form between her eyebrows. "Why would you worry? You know your father and I try our best to support you kids however we can."

And now I feel like a shitty daughter because I *do* know that. "I'm sorry, Mom." I hug her close, attempting to show her how sorry I am.

CHAPTER 1
—sarah—

JUNE

Melanie's name lights up my screen with a text.

> MEL
>
> I'm waiting …

Trust her to know my cycle. It only makes sense since we've known each other since kindergarten; we know most things about each other, and she knows how much I want this to work. The problem is that I'm not ready to tell anyone I failed again. Not even my best friend. After my second attempt to get pregnant, I'm still no closer to becoming a mom. The disappointment weighs heavily on my heart, and I'm terrified my dream may never become a reality. I blow out a heavy breath and pick up my phone.

> ME
>
> I got my period

I drop my phone back to the cushion beside me and take a sip of my wine. I'd been staying clear of the sweet goodness, but I needed something to help me commiserate my failure. Staring off into space, the doorway to the second bedroom mocks me. I don't know when it became essential to me that I needed to have a baby; I just know it's all I can think about. I've always wanted to be a mom. As a kid, I would always play mommies and daddies with my dolls, and watching Em with her kids makes me realize I have this gaping hole inside of me. Sighing heavily, I blow out a long breath and sink into the plush cushion. My phone lights up again, and I read her messages without picking it up.

> MEL
>
> I'm sorry. I know how much you want this

My nose tingles and I swallow the lump in my throat.

> MEL
>
> I'm taking you out dancing tomorrow night. No arguments

I don't want to go out dancing. At thirty-four, I feel so old when we go to clubs. I grab my phone, ready to make up some excuse when it rings. I press the green button and hold it to my ear. "Mel—"

"Don't say it, Sare. No excuses. We're going dancing. There's a new club with an over-thirties crowd." Her tone is no-nonsense.

"I'm really not feeling it. I just want to wallow. Let me wallow. Just this once," I whine like a child.

She chuckles. "What sort of friend would I be if I let you wallow? Besides, you'll be a mom before you know it, and then you won't be able to go out and have fun with your bestie."

I know she won't relent, so I may as well save myself a whole lot of arguing and simply agree. "Okay. But I don't want to be out late. I have my shift at the hospital on Saturday morning."

"I know, I know. I have my shift too. I promise to get you home before you turn into a pauper!" My long-time friend giggles. "See you tomorrow night. Mwah!"

I can't help but chuckle too. She's infectious. "Tomorrow night, Mels Bells."

We end the call, and I take a long sip of my wine. I guess I should have dinner and finish crocheting the beanies I need to take with me on Saturday since I won't be able to finish them tomorrow night. Climbing to my feet, I head to my poky kitchen, pull out the container labeled Thursday, and pop it in the microwave. As I wait for the timer to go off, I check whether the cupcakes I baked as soon as I got home are cool enough to pack into Tupperware. They are, so I quickly transfer them, then top off my wineglass and grab a fork out of the drawer. With my butt leaning against the counter, I allow my gaze to wander around my small apartment. Even though the space is compact and it's not in the swanky part of town, I feel accomplished that I saved up enough money to buy it. I've always been great at saving money and working toward a goal. Even when I was a kid, I would save my birthday and pocket money until I had enough to buy something special. Which reminds me, I need to start saving again for more treatments. Not getting pregnant is going to set my plan back, but what else can I do?

The microwave dings so I grab my chicken masala and head back to the couch. I smile to myself, grateful that I didn't have to cook dinner tonight with the way I'm feeling. The hour of meal prep I do every Sunday morning saves me a heap of time and money because I'm not tempted to grab takeout when I'm tired or work late or just feel blah. A little planning goes a long way, and it helps me to keep on track with my financial goals, too.

I had saved enough money for two rounds with the clinic in the hopes I would get pregnant, but no dice. Now I need to start all over again—another eight grand for two more attempts. If I don't get pregnant by the end of those rounds, I'm not sure what my next step will be.

My tan patent heels clack across the stone floor as I make my way toward the elevator that'll take me up to the forty-fifth floor. I balance the two dozen cupcakes I baked last night as I walk toward Joe.

"Morning, Sarah," Joe calls across from his post near the elevator, ready to press the button for me.

I smile at him. Every day, he's here to greet me with his warm smile and a friendly hello. "Hi, Joe. How are things?"

"Never better." That's always his answer as he presses the button to my floor on my behalf.

I hold the container toward him and raise an eyebrow. "Would you like one before I take them upstairs?"

"I'll never say no to your baking." He reaches across, lifts the lid, and makes his selection. "Mmm, smell that lemon."

"There's a treat hidden inside." I wink at him. The lemon curd filling is always a hit.

"Nice. I'll look forward to it when I take my morning break. Thank you. Mr. Wainwright hasn't arrived yet."

That gives me pause. Eric is always in the office before me. Well, he used to always be in the office before me; now, not so much. "Thanks, Joe. Have a great day."

"You too," he says as I step inside the elevator with a stone-tiled floor and stainless-steel walls, which match the lobby. I don't have to share the space with anyone this early in the morning.

The building is incredibly stylish and classy, and I love that I work in one of the most iconic buildings in the city, *Stone*

Tower. It doesn't hurt that, on occasion, I manage to lay eyes on the one and only owner of the building, Oliver Stone. That man is all sorts of hot! His wife is gorgeous too. I've met them both a couple of times over the years because Emma works with her and we crossed paths when Emma was in the hospital and again at her wedding. Even though I know Kate is really down to earth, I can't believe the wife of a billionaire businessman still works in an elementary school. I shake my head.

Using the polished stainless-steel walls as a mirror, I adjust the collar of the navy sleeveless dress I'm wearing today. Nobody would even guess the dress I'm wearing only cost thirty-nine ninety-five, including postage—such a steal. I love dressing up and finding outfits that accentuate my assets— which are on the curvier side—not that there's anyone to impress in the office, but I like to look nice.

The reception desk is empty when I step off the elevator, which is normal because Lucy doesn't usually get here until she's dropped her teenage kids off at school. I start her computer, then head toward my desk, located outside of Eric's office. As I pass by the research and development cubicles, I raise the Tupperware container of cupcakes so the guys know to grab one each before they all disappear. Evan and Jordan always start early on Fridays so they can leave early and hit the bars. Eric's always been generous with his staff, allowing us to start and finish whenever it suits us as long as we work our designated number of hours in the week. I was lucky to land this job over ten years ago.

I tuck my purse in the cupboard behind my desk and turn on my computer. Glancing at Eric's darkened office, I mentally run through his calendar, searching for an early appointment I've forgotten but come up blank. His behavior has been worrying and uncharacteristic as of late. He's been stressed about his grandson, Adam, taking over his position within the company. Eric's ready to retire, and it shows in the considerable decline of his enthusiasm over the last twelve months.

Adam's been reluctant, making Eric understandably upset. I consider the situation from Adam's point of view as I turn on the lights and computer in Eric's office. Glancing at the old black and white photograph of his daughter and her family he keeps on his desk, I study the little boy, Adam, closely. I guess it takes time to pack up your life and move across the country from New Jersey, but it's been over eighteen months and the delay is impacting Eric's health. Apparently, Adam moved there straight from college for a job and hasn't been home since, but surely he knew he'd have to take over from his grandfather one day. I'm not even sure he's capable of taking over such a large company; he's never even set foot in this building. Would he even know how to run *FutureTech*?

I drop the cupcakes off in the kitchen, turn on the coffee machine, then move through the rest of our floor, switching on the lights and printers. Once I've made myself a coffee, I pop my head in to say hello to Evan and Jordan. "Morning. Are you guys ready for your presentation with Eric this morning at ten?"

"Morning, Sarah. Yeah, we're ready, but where is he?" Jordan asks.

"I don't know. I'll give him thirty minutes, then I'll try calling him. Don't forget to grab a cupcake. I made the lemon ones this week."

They both nod. "Thanks, Sarah. Your cupcakes make Fridays bearable."

"You're welcome." I head back to my desk. Taking my seat, I work through the emails in my inbox, forwarding them where needed, and double-checking Eric's calendar for today. He leaves at lunchtime to play golf on Fridays; it's something he's always done. More often than not, by three p.m. on Friday afternoons, our office is almost completely empty. I love it because it affords me the quiet I need to prepare for the following work week.

Eric wanders toward me, looking a million miles away. "Good morning, Mr. Wainwright." I smile at him.

He glances up as though he's only now realized where he is. "Good morning, Sarah. Please cancel the presentation this morning. Move it to the first available time next week. I need to make an important call."

"Sure. Is everything okay?"

He waves over his shoulder as he disappears through the door to his office. "Of course."

Puzzled at Eric's uncharacteristic behavior, I check his calendar for next week and move the presentation, then head down the hallway to tell the guys. I'm sure they'll be disappointed. They seemed excited about showing Eric the new chip they've been working on.

I make Eric's pot of tea, pop a cupcake on a plate, and head back to his office, catching him before he makes his call. "I've changed the presentation to your earliest available time next Tuesday. Here's your tea, and I made lemon curd cupcakes this week."

His cloudy eyes meet mine, and he offers me a genuine smile. "What would I do without you, Sarah? Thank you."

"Oh, I'm sure you'd get by, but I'm glad I can help." I tip my lips up. "Do you need anything else?"

"No, thank you. Please ensure I'm not disturbed."

"Of course." I spin on my heel, closing Eric's door behind me.

CHAPTER 2

—aj—

I END THE CALL AND LEAN BACK IN MY LEATHER CHAIR, BEYOND pleased with the outcome. After my disastrous phone call this morning, I needed this. Dylan already knows the outcome is positive from listening to my side of the conversation, but he sits opposite me with his eyebrows raised and an expectant look.

"We got it!"

He jumps out of his chair, pumping his fist in the air. "Fuck yeah!" He wraps his hand around my bicep, pulling me to my feet, and we embrace in celebration. "I knew we had it in the bag, but I don't like to celebrate until the deal is sealed."

I chuckle at his enthusiasm. "This is an incredible opportunity for us. We'd better not fuck it up."

"We won't. We've got this. Everything we've done up until now has led us to this point. We're ready." He's always supremely confident in our abilities. I know he's right, but I hope we haven't taken on more than we can handle. It is only the two of us after all, and this is a big deal—it's the biggest contract we've ever had. The company, *booknow.com*, is listed in the top twenty tech companies in the US. If we can impress them, who knows where it might lead?

"Mr. Noble's going to send over the final contract for our lawyer to look at, then we can sign on the dotted line. This is huge for us." Excitement bubbles inside me. This is the break we've been working toward. Taking smaller jobs and edging our way closer to the bigger companies that will put us on the map has finally paid off. "He said he wants to keep the project between the three of us. He's even using his personal lawyer, so no one in the company knows what's going to happen. *He* doesn't even want to know when we're going to take the company down."

Dylan raises his eyebrows. "Makes sense to do a stealth attack." I nod in agreement as he claps his hands together. "This calls for a celebration."

"Yep, it sure does. Let's try out *Club Rumors*. It's a new club for the over-thirties crowd." I'm sick of the younger chicks. Most of them have nothing going on upstairs, relying solely on their looks. Dylan doesn't mind the lack of conversation because he's only looking to get laid, but I need more than a wet pussy.

He screws up his nose. "We're only thirty, man. I'm not sure I want to age up just yet."

I slap him on the back. "Haven't you heard how horny women are in their thirties?"

His eyes light up. "Oh yeah?" I knew that would pique his interest. "Okay. I'm down for that. Let's grab dinner first."

"Sure. We'll meet at *Cristo's* at seven-thirty. I'll book us a table."

"Cool. See you there."

The door closes behind him and I make a booking at our favorite Greek restaurant. As I end the call, my phone lights up with my sister's name.

"Unca AJ!" Colton, my three-year-old nephew, squeals down the line.

"Colton, my man." This isn't the first time he's picked up my sister's phone and called me. "How are you doing, buddy?"

"I good. I love you, Unca—" His words stop abruptly, and I'm guessing my sister's discovered him using her phone again.

"AJ? Is that you?"

I chuckle. "Yeah, it's me. I'm guessing you need to find a new hiding place for your phone?"

"Yeah. How'd you guess?" Hayley laughs. "I'm running out of places. I had it on top of the damn fridge! He pulled a chair over to the counter, climbed up, and then used a wooden spoon to drag the damn phone within his reach," she huffs out.

My heart races. "Shit! Lucky he didn't fall."

"I know. We can't take our eyes off him for a second. Lisa's not home from work yet, and I was in the bathroom." She sounds frustrated, and I can imagine her running her fingers through her dark-brown curls. I hear her draw in a deep breath. "Anyway, I was going to call you. How did your call go? Did you get the contract?"

"Yep!"

"Woohoo!" she sings across the line. "I knew you would. I'm so damn proud of you and Dylan! You've done incredible to build your reputation as quickly as you have."

Her praise means the world to me since she and Lisa run their own successful business creating and designing educational games. Lisa's an ex-teacher and Hayley is a game designer. That's how they met. Lisa had an idea for an educational game to help teach kids grammar, so she contacted Hayley. They started working together on the project and one thing led to another and they've been together ever since. From that initial project, the two have created a whole slew of educational resources which are being used worldwide. What they've built over a short period is truly inspiring. It also allows them the flexibility to work from home or in the office, which means they can take turns being home with their son.

I hear Colton squeal in the background. "Hey, I've gotta go. Lisa's home. Congratulations again. We'll have you over for dinner to celebrate."

"Sure. Bye, Sis." The call disconnects and I check the clock on the wall. I have time for a quick workout before I need to get ready for dinner.

"ID please." The woman at the door holds out her hand, a bored expression on her face.

I dig into my pocket. "We're over twenty-one."

She pops her bubblegum as her eyes scan us from head to toe. "I can see that. I need to check that you're at least thirty."

Fuck! I didn't think they'd be checking our ages. Dylan glances at me with a smirk. "Sure." I hand over my driver's license and so does Dylan. It was only two weeks ago that he turned thirty.

With a level of boredom I haven't seen since high school, the woman studies our licenses, then hands them back to us. "That'll be twenty-five each." I hand over my credit card and she scans it, then stamps our wrists. "Have a good night, boys." She winks at us, then directs her attention to the next people in line.

As soon as the doors open, a thumping bass beat hits me square in the chest. Oh yeah! I can't stop my body from moving as we make our way through the crowded space to the bar. We can't help but press up against women of all shapes and sizes who check us out in return as we pass by. I'm not being big-headed when I say that Dylan and I are good-looking guys. We generally don't have trouble gaining the attention of the ladies, particularly Dylan with his naturally flirtatious personality. He's the light to my darker features, with his blond hair, blue-eyed surfer look. He comes across as laid back, but he takes life seriously where it counts.

Skating my eyes around the darkened space, lit by random purple strobe lights, I'm already mentally patting myself on the back for my decision to come here tonight. The place is filled wall to wall with women who ooze confidence that younger girls just don't have. It would be great to finish the day by sharing a drink and interesting conversation with a beautiful woman. I mean, I wouldn't say no to getting naked with said woman, but I don't want to push my luck. My day's already been successful beyond my imagination.

Dylan leans in close to my ear. "You want a beer?"

I glance up at the drink menu, spotting my favorite craft beer. "Sure. I'll have a Crusoe." He nods and moves closer to the bar, which is three people deep in places, to order our drinks so it's going to take him a while. I tuck my hands into my pockets and step toward the dance floor to watch. It doesn't take long before a particular woman catches my attention. She has a banging body, all curves, dips, and valleys—just the way I like my women. Her black lace dress hugs her body as she shakes her delectable ass to the music. She spins around, finally facing me, and the front is as spec-tacular as the back. Her smile is contagious as her blonde friend grinds her ass against hers. They're too caught up having their own fun to be trying to impress anyone, and it's sexy as fuck.

Dylan steps beside me, handing me my beer. I take a drink and then tip my head toward the women. "They look like they're having a good time." He glances to where I'm pointing, then smiles at me with raised eyebrows. Where the brunette is everything I look for in a woman, her blonde friend is Dylan's perfect woman come to life.

"I think we're in for a good night, my friend." He taps his glass against my bottle and takes another drink.

I smile at my long-time friend, then take a drink. Both of us turn toward the dance floor to watch the women enjoying themselves. As many times as I tear my eyes away from the stunning brunette to peer around the room, they instinctually find their way back to her.

Six pillars topped with silver cages, rise out of the floor at random intervals around the room. Each has a woman inside wearing a barely there shimmering outfit. My eyes momentarily lock on the dancer closest to me as she moves her body to the music, but she can't hold my attention for long as my eyes fight to find the sexy brunette again. I snap my head around to seek her out but she's not where she was a moment earlier. Scanning the area, I come up empty. I shift my position to see if I can locate her, but she's vanished into thin air. *Fuck!*

Dylan leans into me. "Who are you looking for?"

I point to the spot where my girl was. "The brunette who was dancing with the blonde."

He nods, then lifts his chin in the direction of the large, raised booths facing the dance floor along the side. "They went that way."

I relax and Dylan leads the way, making a path through the crowd as purple lights strobe across the room in time with the music. Someone pinches my ass as I follow behind. I turn to lay eyes on the offender to be greeted with a wink and a wide smile surrounded by bristles. I raise my eyebrows and tip my head, but keep moving forward. He was decent looking if I swung that way, but I don't.

I spot the women in a circular booth toward the back, the farthest from the speakers. How fortuitous … the other half of the booth is free. Walking directly toward them, I lean closer to the blonde, who's sitting closest to the edge. "Mind if we take the other half of the booth?"

Her eyes skate down my body and across to Dylan, then she returns her attention to me. "Be our guest." She waves her hand out toward the empty side.

"Thanks." I slide into the other end of the booth first, then Dylan follows in behind me. His eyes catch on the blonde and stay there for a long moment. I try to catch the eye of the brunette, but it's not happening; she's too busy watching the action on the dance floor. I press my back against the cushioned chair and stretch my legs out, playing with the coaster on the table.

"How are you feeling?" I look beside me, knowing full well the space is empty. The voice is as clear as if the woman it belongs to was sitting right beside me. I lift my gaze to the women at the other end of the booth.

The brunette blows out a breath. "Disappointed, but I'll survive."

The blonde rubs her friend's arm, her face full of compassion. "Have you got enough money to do another round?"

"Nope. I have to save again, which will put me behind schedule, but what else can I do? I want a baby."

A baby. I'm certain my eyebrows are touching my hairline and my eyes are as wide as saucers.

"I know." The blonde sighs. "Why don't you try picking up a hot guy and taking him home? There are plenty here to choose from," she suggests. "And it would be cheaper than going through the clinic."

"You know I can't do that, Mel."

"Why not? He would never have to know."

"Uhhh, because it's unethical. Plus, there's that little tidbit about my personality that you're forgetting."

The blonde pauses for a moment; her eyebrows scrunch down, then her eyes widen and her lips spread. "Oh, right. I forgot. You know, you can have sex for fun without being involved?" She nudges her shoulder playfully into her friend's.

"I know *you* can do that, but I've tried it. I wish I could do what you do, but I'm not built that way."

Thank fuck for that. The relief filling my body is swift, knowing she's not the type of woman who hooks up for the hell of it. I'm being completely unfair because God knows when I was in college, I hooked up with my fair share of women only for sex.

"I know you're not, Sare. So how long will it take you to save?"

"Another twelve months if I'm careful. This will have to be my last night out for a while."

Shit, she must really want a baby.

"Doesn't the clinic offer a payment plan or something?"

The brunette huffs out a breath. "I wish. Waiting another twelve months puts me on the cusp of needing to change to IVF, which is even more expensive."

"I wish I could help you." She rubs her hand along her friend's back in comfort. "How about I get us another drink?"

The brunette, Sare, maybe short for Sarah, smiles and nods at her friend. The blonde stands and heads to the bar, leaving Sare on her own. I glance down at my bottle, noticing it's empty.

"I'm gonna get us some refills. Be back in a minute," Dylan says and I nod, digging into my pocket for my card, but he waves me off.

I glance at the brunette and decide this is my moment to chat with her, so I close the four-foot distance between us.

CHAPTER 3

—sarah—

"Hi." I turn slightly to face the owner of the deep voice. It's the guy who asked to share our booth. "I'm sorry, I couldn't help but overhear your conversation with your friend." He gestures with a tilt of his chin toward Melanie as she heads to the bar.

I blush. Shit, I really should learn to keep my voice down. I thought our conversation would have been muffled somewhat by the music. How embarrassing that the guy I was checking out earlier overheard such a personal conversation.

He shrugs apologetically. "Sorry, I guess it's because the booth is curved; your conversation traveled. Honestly, I'm not a creeper or anything." He raises his hands in surrender. "I wanted to say how much I admire that you know what you want and you're going after it."

I blow out a relieved breath, and the tension across my shoulders disappears. I don't want people to think I'm some desperate woman. Well, I sort of am, but I don't want other people to think I am. I tuck a lock of hair behind my ear. "Thank you. I'm not getting any younger, and I really want to have a baby."

His eyebrows tilt down over his rich brown eyes surrounded by thick, dark lashes. What is it with guys always having the best lashes? "Which fertility clinic are you using?"

I swivel my body around so I'm facing the guy directly. "I'm using *Eastside Fertility*." He nods as if he's familiar with them. "They've been great, but it's a lot of paperwork and medical tests, not to mention expensive. But it will all be worth it if I have a baby. Though there are no guarantees, obviously. I've already had two rounds of the procedure with no luck." My stomach sinks at the verbal reminder as to the reason we're out tonight.

He twists his body so he's facing me, raising his knee onto the seat and pressing against my hip. His arm rests on the back of the curved booth, bringing his hand close to my head. "Is there a way you can do it without all the expense?"

"Afraid not. I haven't met the right person, and even if I met someone now, by the time I go through the dating process, get to know the guy, and figure out if the relationship will be successful … it all takes time. Time I don't feel I have." I shrug. "It would be a little weird on the first or second date to say … *oh, by the way, I want to have a baby. Would you mind knocking me up?*" We both chuckle. "I can't imagine it going down well. He'd probably run a mile. And with good reason." I take the last sip of my drink, then add, "And most guys don't stick around long-term anyway. They're generally not reliable so I'm happy to do it on my own." Well, that's what I tell people anyway.

"What if you found a guy who would be happy to help you?"

I wave my hand in front of me, brushing off his comment. "That's never gonna happen. If I want a baby, I have to take matters into my own hands."

He leans forward slightly, and his fresh citrus scent wafts around him. I move in slightly to inhale more of the fragrance. He smells so freaking good. "What if I said I'd be happy to help you?" The deep timbre of his voice vibrates through my body as he poses the question. He pulls back slightly with a smirk and my heart stops. *What?*

"Pardon?" Surely he didn't offer to get me pregnant.

He leans back in and I mirror him. My eyes lock on his and the warmth in his chocolate gaze invites me to get lost. I do love a bit of chocolate occasionally. "I said I would be happy to get you pregnant." He raises an eyebrow, and I swallow down the extra saliva that's suddenly pooling in my mouth.

I chuckle uncomfortably. "It's very kind of you to offer … your … uh … services." Geez, Louise. This took an awkward turn. "But I don't know you and you don't know me. It's a little weird." Make that a lot weird.

"How much do you need to know? It's not like you know the donors from the clinic." He shrugs as if this is an ordinary conversation. He has a point, but at the clinic, I get to choose my baby daddy based on the extensive information they collect. "You only need my semen, right? You don't actually *want* a guy to stick around?" He raises his eyebrows as he waits for my answer.

Well, I *do* want a guy to stick around, but I've run out of options, and I feel my body's running out of time, so that was taken off the table. I want a family like the one I grew up with; a mom and dad working together to raise happy, healthy kids. I never imagined I'd be going down this route to have a family. The whole idea would have been preposterous to me in my twenties, but here I am. "I'd at least need to know your medical history and if your semen is viable, and that you're clean. Would you be prepared to do the necessary tests?" I can't believe I'm even entertaining this stranger's absurd offer.

"Of course. No point if I'm shooting blanks, right?" His answering smile is wide. He has beautiful teeth, straight and white. I scan the rest of his features. Tanned skin, thick dark hair. He looks healthy enough. He seems tall, but it's hard to tell while he's sitting down.

I shake my head. "No point." I ponder his offer for a few moments. He doesn't seem like a psycho, but I'm sure some psychos are good at hiding their true selves. Would it be any different from a hook-up? It's not like you know anything about the guy you take home for a night. But this is different. I *want* to get pregnant. This is a big freaking deal, and he's offering it to me like it's of no consequence. Who does that? "This is a big deal. You know that, right?" He nods and a grin slowly slides across his perfect lips. "I'd pay for all the tests. It wouldn't be fair to expect you to fork out money for my cause."

He waves off my offer. "I can afford to do all of that. Don't worry." Is he for real right now? He's incredibly nonchalant about his life-changing offer.

I drop my eyes to my glass and twist it by the stem. "I guess we'd need some kind of contract?"

He lifts one shoulder and drops it. "If it would make you feel better, but I don't think it's necessary. I'll give you my swimmers until you're pregnant, and then we'll go our separate ways, never to see each other again."

And why does my heart squeeze tight at the thought of that?

I tuck my hair behind my ear, glancing toward the bar, looking for Mel. Suddenly, I'm incredibly hot. His gaze is locked on my face, and I swallow my nerves. "Uhm, I'm not sure I feel comfortable. The clinic vets its donors. When I make my selection, I have a file I can read through to find the match that suits me best."

He shifts in his seat and taps his fingers on the table between us like he doesn't have a care in the world. "If you want to make up a questionnaire, I'll answer your questions. I don't have anything to hide."

I blow out a breath. This guy seems happy enough to do anything I ask. "Are you positive?"

"Yeah, I'd be happy to do whatever makes you comfortable." Even though his superficial body language is trying to portray this as no big deal, I can see the tightness around his eyes and across his shoulders. It's contradictory to his words and obvious actions.

"Why? Why would you help a complete stranger have a baby?" Why would someone offer to get a stranger pregnant? I can't help but question his motives.

He blows out a breath and glances around the club. When I follow his eyes, I notice Mel is still talking to his friend at the bar. Their conversation looks a lot lighter than ours as she throws her head back with laughter. "I like to help people where I can. It's not like you need a kidney, it's just sperm. I make new sperm every day." He chuckles, his eyes sparkling in the low light. He digs his hand into his pocket and pulls out a black business card, handing it to me.

Jackson & Baker is all it says on the front in stylish silver block letters. It gives no clue about what type of business it is. I flip it over to find an email and phone number.

"What type of work do you do?" Not that it's my business, it has nothing to do with his semen health or count.

"My friend and I"—he points his chin toward his friend at the bar, still chatting with Mel—"hack computer systems for companies to test out their security. Then we help them fix any issues they may have to secure their system."

"Oh … that … that sounds … uh … like you're very smart." Geez, Sarah, could you sound any more juvenile?

"We're pretty good at what we do." He doesn't come across as cocky or boastful as he says it, more like he's simply stating a fact.

"What made you get into that line of work?"

"It was fun. We met in college doing computer science, and

in our spare time, we messed around to see if we could hack into big corporations. Then we would send them an email explaining the issues we found in their system. Once we worked out companies would pay us to test their system, we decided to start taking it more seriously and it sort of grew from there."

"Wow. That's incredible. Congratulations on making a fun hobby work out for you."

"Thanks." He pauses as if thinking about something as he glances around the club. "Would you like to dance?"

"Sure." I smile at him and then slide out of the booth, him following behind and before I can stop myself, I add extra sway to my hips. His warm hand takes up residence on my lower back, sending goosebumps racing over my body.

Don't get attached, Sarah. He's just gonna give you his sperm. No big deal.

We make it to the dance floor, the upbeat music fills my body, and I have no choice but to move. There's not a lot of room on the dance floor, so … shit, I don't even know this guy's name. I chuckle and he gives me a puzzled look. I lean in close so he can hear me, my breast grazing his arm. "I just realized I don't know your name. I'm Sarah, by the way."

He chuckles, then moves his mouth next to my ear. His hot breath hits the crook of my neck as I draw in a breath soaked with his citrus scent.

So sexy. *Stop it, Sarah!*

"My family and friends call me AJ. Since I'm going to be your donor, I'll consider you a friend." He draws back and winks at me. His soulful eyes melting my insides.

This is never going to work if I get attached to this guy. I've known him a whole thirty minutes and I'm already feeling things I shouldn't. Sure, he's attractive. Physically, he's everything I look for in a guy: tall, dark, *and* handsome. It seems unfair that I've met him under the circumstances I have. The song changes to a slower-than-usual version of "Slow Hands," the bass thumping heavily, pulsing through my body.

AJ moves in closer. Landing one hand on my hip, he spins me around. The front of his body molds to the back of mine, his strong thighs against my butt. Heat races up my spine, and I can't stop myself from pressing back into him. *What is wrong with me?*

Bodies press in on us from both sides, and his other hand comes around my front, holding me to him with firm pressure. Dragging my hair away from my neck, I reach up, moving my arms to the music. His hands slide up my body, trailing over my exposed flesh, sending flames licking through my blood as his hands tangle with mine above us. The chemistry between us is potent. Using his hips, he moves his body and mine in time with the sensual rhythm, and I get lost in the music—in the moment—with this handsome stranger who may well end up being the father of my baby.

CHAPTER 4

—aj—

I'M DOING EVERYTHING IN MY POWER TO KEEP MY HARD COCK away from her delicious ass so she doesn't think I'm some kind of perverted asshole, but the way she moves her body is so damn sexy. She has a confidence about her that is rare, and it's sexy as fuck.

Shit! She presses back into my body, and she has to feel exactly what's happening in my pants. I try to pull back to put more space between us, but she drops her hand and grabs my hip, holding me in place. Well, if that's the way she wants to play it, I'm happy to oblige. I guess I'll be getting more intimate with her than this soon enough. Maybe she wants to start tonight? My cock expands at the thought. She turns her head to the side and glances up at me, a sexy smirk on her face.

I lean down. My mouth is so close to hers that her breaths cast lightly across my lips. I run my tongue across mine and glance up into her eyes. I can't quite tell their color in this low light, but they appear dark. I move closer still but am shoved to the side by a woman doing some type of crazy, over-the-top dance move. I tighten my hold to keep Sarah from falling, twisting my body to protect her from the crazy woman's moves.

The lady is spinning around all over the place as though she has the entire dance floor to herself.

Sarah giggles and I turn her around to face me, her gorgeous smile brightening her face. "That was a close call." She swipes her hand across her forehead as if she's wiping away sweat.

Does she mean it was a close call that we were almost knocked over? Or does she mean it was a close call that we almost kissed? She grabs my hand and leads me from the dance floor, back to the booth we were sharing. Dylan and Mel are already there … making out. Sarah's steps pause momentarily.

"It looks as though our friends are getting along."

I drop my eyes to hers and nod. "It seems so." Not a surprise for me because Dylan gets along with anyone, particularly those of the female persuasion.

We drop into the booth, disrupting their moment. Sarah takes a sip of her wine, and I watch as her throat moves with her swallow. Peeling my eyes away from her, I take a drink of my beer. We spend the night talking over the music, drinking, and dancing. It's impossible to have any further meaningful conversation with Dylan and her friend sharing the booth with us.

"Well, I need to get home. I have an early start tomorrow," Sarah tells us, giving Mel a pointed look.

The girls climb out of the booth, and Dylan and I follow them through the club. I hold the door open for everyone and we step onto the sidewalk; I'm sad our night's come to an end. While Dylan and Mel lock lips again for a lengthy period, I study Sarah. What I would give to kiss her like that but I don't feel Sarah and I are at that stage. She's more reserved and I respect that about her.

I tuck my hands into my pockets and lean closer to Sarah's ear to keep our conversation private. "So, uh, about the baby thing. When did you want to get together about that?" I really want her to take me up on my offer. It'll give me an opportunity to spend time with her, to get to know her better, because the little time I spent with her tonight has made me want more.

She chuckles and tucks a lock of silky-looking hair behind her ear. "I figured you weren't serious."

I frown. "I thought I was pretty clear about my offer to help you. As I said, I'm happy to answer any questions and get any tests done. Just say the word."

She drops her gaze, looking at the dirty sidewalk beneath our feet, then raises her eyes to me. "Can I think about it? I have your number. I'll text you and let you know. Maybe we can catch up for a coffee and talk about it some more."

I'm not sure what she needs to think about. I'm offering my services, free of charge, so she can have a baby. I try to play off my enthusiasm with a shrug. "Sure." Leaning in, I place a chaste kiss on her soft cheek and her cheeks flush. I want to do so much more than that. I want to see her whole body flush. Out here, I can smell her subtle scent of spring flowers and I draw it into my lungs. "Do you mind texting me your decision either way?" That way I'll have her number and maybe I can at least coax her out on a date or something.

"Of course. And … thank you." She rests her hand on my forearm, her heat searing through the fabric of my shirt, and I flex the muscle. "I appreciate your offer to help." Sincerity shines in her eyes. She turns around and grabs her friend's arm, tugging her away. "Come on, Mel. Let's go."

Mel and Dylan mumble something to each other with matching grins, then Mel turns to Sarah. "Okay, okay. Let's go! See ya, AJ."

I raise my hand to wave goodbye to the girls, like the lame guy I am. "Yeah, see ya. Nice meeting you both." *Could I be any more pathetic?*

"What's up with you? You've checked your phone at least a dozen times in the last hour." With my mind a million miles from here, Dylan's voice seems loud in the quiet of our office.

"Nothing."

"Don't lie to me. I've known you for too long. What's up?"

Instead of answering and risking his judgment, I'll distract him with a question of my own. "What's up with you? You didn't take Melanie home on Friday night." I raise my brows and rest my ankle on my opposite knee, trying to appear relaxed.

"She shared a ride with Sarah and didn't want to leave her friend. I got her number, though. So we'll see." He taps his phone with two fingers. "How about you and Sarah? You seemed to be cozy."

"She's a cool chick. I … uh … actually offered to help her out with something. That's why I keep checking my phone. I'm expecting her to text me." He nods and turns back to the computer, his hands flying over the keys. "Do you want a coffee? I'm going to make a fresh one."

"Nah, I'm good. Thanks."

I grab my phone and head toward my kitchen; one of the perks of having our office in my home. I'm annoyed with myself that I didn't insist on grabbing Sarah's number. I would have followed up by now, but I have to wait for her. I'm unsure what it was about her that made me want to help her with her baby predicament, apart from the fact that my proposition means I'll have the opportunity to get to know her better. A nice side benefit will be that I'll be getting laid on the regular for the foreseeable future. And doesn't that bring a smile to my face. I can't wait to get my hands and mouth on her body. *Those curves!* I bring my fist up to my mouth and bite the knuckle. She's my dream woman come to life. Everything about her, from the color of her hair to her smile to her sweet, sweet curves, is utter perfection. Then, on top of all that, she's easy to talk with and kind to boot. When she told me how she crochets hats for premature babies in her spare time and how she loves spending time with her sister's kids, I think I fell a little in love with her. Her entire being almost vibrated with joy as she spoke about them.

I need to remember she only wants me as a donor. She wants a baby, not a partner. Cool your jets dickhead. Maybe with a bit of time, I can convince her I'm partner material. Fuck, the way her eyes lit up whenever she spoke about becoming a mom convinced me I'd made the right decision to help her.

As I pour coffee into my cup, my phone lights up with a text from an unknown number. I snatch it up and unlock the screen.

> UNKNOWN
>
> Hi, this is Sarah. I'm not sure if you remember me from Friday night at Club Rumors, but I'm the woman you offered to help

As if I wouldn't remember her, or our conversation. I roll my eyes at no one.

> UNKNOWN
>
> If your offer still stands, I was hoping we could meet and discuss it further

Fuck, yeah! I barely restrain fist bumping the air. I settle myself so I can respond. She's being formal in her messages, so I need to keep that in mind.

> ME
>
> Hi, how could I possibly forget you?

Of course my offer is still on the table. Happy to
meet wherever and whenever you're free

Shit. Does that sound too eager? I mean, I am, even
though my motives aren't purely altruistic—I want to give her
more than my swimmers—but I don't want to sound desperate.
I save her number in my phone.

SARAH

Would you be free Saturday morning? We could
meet at The Bistro over on Fourth Avenue at 10

ME

Sounds great. See you then

It's gonna be a long week. I'll be counting down the days
until I see the woman who consumed my thoughts all weekend.
I blow out a breath, collect my coffee, and head back to work.
The best thing I can do is get lost in our current projects.

"I'm getting close to breaching the firewall," Dylan informs
me as I step back into the office.

"That was quick." I take my seat and a mouthful of coffee.

"Yep. Scarily so. I'm surprised hackers haven't sunk these
guys already." He taps his keyboard a few more times. "I'm
in!" He pushes away from the desk, rolling back a few feet in
his chair, wearing a smug smile.

"Good job, man. Now we need to detail exactly what you
did and what they need to do to secure their site."

"Yep. I made notes as I went. It won't take long to put my
report together."

"Great." I turn back to my project and get to work.
Saturday can't come soon enough.

CHAPTER 5

—sarah—

Nope, this outfit isn't any good either. Why is it so hard to choose a damn outfit to wear today? It's not like I need to impress the guy; we're not dating or anything. He's only giving me his semen, and then I'll never see him again. Simple. I sigh heavily. Just my luck to meet someone who seems to be perfect. Life is unfair sometimes. But looking on the bright side, I've hopefully found a solution to my problem, depending on how our chat works out today.

I huff as I pick up my jeans again. Maybe I can pair them with my off-the-shoulder top and my tan sandals. Yeah, that'll work. Glancing at the time, I fly into a panic. I don't want to be late, but at the rate I'm going, I will be. Dressing quickly, I apply a little makeup and tie my hair in a high ponytail. I check my appearance in the full-length mirror behind my bedroom door and smile—my butt always looks fabulous in these jeans.

Collecting the paperwork from my small dining table, I slide it carefully into my purse and check to make sure I have everything I need. Butterflies fill my stomach as I head toward the elevator. I have the distinct feeling that today is the beginning of a new chapter for me. I'm hoping he doesn't think I'm too neurotic and rescind his offer to help.

I finally find a parking space after driving around for fifteen minutes, my frustration growing by the minute, along with the sweat beneath my armpits. I'm definitely late now. It's a trait I don't like, so I get annoyed with myself when I'm late somewhere. If you say you're going to arrive at a certain time, then damn well be there on time.

Quickly, I climb out of my car, ready to race across the street when the handle from my purse gets trapped in the closed door, spilling the contents all over the street. Sheets of paper escape and I hastily stomp on them to prevent them from flying away. When I bend down to pick them up, they're all crinkled and imprinted with the dirty print of my shoe. Dammit, this is not how I wanted to present myself. Because as much as I'm looking at him and his genetics under the microscope, I want to make a good impression. I don't want him to think I'm not good enough to become a mom. He might change his mind about being my donor, and I don't want that. I scoop everything up and draw in several deep breaths, calming myself before I have a panic attack in the street. I drag my purse straps over my shoulder and take purposeful strides toward the café, fifteen minutes late. I can't do anything about it now, so I try to put the shit show of the last twenty minutes behind me.

Pausing outside the door, I calm my mind ready to meet with my possible baby daddy. The door opens and when I move to clear the doorway for whoever's exiting the café, I spot AJ holding it open with a warm smile.

Great. He probably saw everything.

His smiling eyes connect with mine and the last twenty minutes disappear. I don't know what's wrong with me. He has some magnetic force that draws me to him, which I'm trying hard to fight. He's only interested in sharing his semen, not his life. I must remember that but I always struggle to keep my heart locked away. It's why I could never risk Mel's suggestion of sleeping with some random guy to get pregnant. My heart doesn't know the difference between having hot sex and falling in love. It thinks sex means love. My brain knows that's not the case, but the damn muscle in my chest can't separate the two.

He leans forward to kiss my cheek, sending sparks shooting through my body. My heart tries to engage—nope, not happening—I push it down and pull away from his touch. His eyebrows sink low, but he quickly catches himself and smiles at me. "Hey, Sarah. It's great to see you." He waves his hand toward a table by the window. "I already have a table for us."

"Hey. Thanks for meeting me today. I'm sorry I'm late." He guides me forward with his hand at the base of my spine and those same sparks erupt again. I drop to the seat, placing my purse next to me and he sits opposite. "How's your week been?" Good one, Sarah. You're not here to make small talk and his week is none of your damn business.

"Pretty good, thanks. We cracked a couple of firewalls, which is always a great feeling. Did you want to order a coffee and then we can chat?" *See?* He just wants to get straight down to business.

We each order a coffee, and AJ quickly scans his card to pay for mine. "You don't need to pay for my coffee, I should be paying for yours since we're here because of me."

"Don't be ridiculous. A coffee and a slice of banana bread aren't going to break the bank. It's ingrained in me to pay for the lady. It's how I work." He shrugs and one side of his mouth rises. It's a half-smile but it looks oh-so-good on him. *Stop it, Sarah.*

We return to our booth and I drag out the paperwork I brought with me along with a pen. Placing them on the table, I press out the creases, giving AJ an embarrassed smile. He's watching me closely, and I think he's hiding his amusement behind his hand, but I can still see the crinkles around his eyes. "Sorry. I dropped them when I got out of my car."

"That's okay. What are all the papers for?"

"Uh, well, this is a questionnaire"—I hold up one set of papers—"for you to complete. And this one is a little information about me." I hold up the other set of papers.

His eyebrows rise. "Can't we just chat? Does it need to be so formal?"

I shift in my seat. I was worried he would say that. "We can do that, but would you mind completing some parts of the questionnaire? They're related to your genetic and health history. I tried to remember the information that was provided through the clinic, and I replicated it as best I could. I just want to be sure." I lick my suddenly dry lips.

God, has the temperature risen? Suddenly, it's incredibly hot and uncomfortable in here.

"I get that." He holds out his hand for the papers, and I place them in his palm.

His eyes drop to the document, and he holds out his hand for the pen, which I quickly hand over. I started with the most straightforward questions—age, blood type, height and weight, history of drug and alcohol use, and his level of fitness—so he's working quickly. His eyes rise to mine and a smirk lifts his lips.

A server delivers our food to the table and once he leaves, AJ asks, "Why do you need to know how many sexual partners I've had?"

Uh, I just added that one out of curiosity. I skate my gaze around the café and shift in my seat. "To make sure you won't be hooking up with other women while I'm trying to get pregnant. If you're used to taking home different women every weekend, then that would be unacceptable for me." It's not like we'll be having sex, but I don't want to worry about him contracting an STD while I'm trying to get pregnant.

Lines form across his forehead as he shakes his head. "I'm

not like that. And while we're trying to get you pregnant, I won't see anyone else. I promise."

At his genuine answer, I blow out a relieved breath, and the tightness across my shoulders releases. I don't know why the idea of him giving me that level of commitment was so important to me. It's not like we're going to be in a relationship. I smile. "Thank you. That's … that's a relief."

He drops his eyes back to the paperwork, and I take a shaky sip of my coffee. Even though I ordered a slice of banana bread, I'm not sure I can eat it. My leg bounces nervously beneath the table, and I drop my hands to my thighs to stop the action. While he quietly completes the form, I stare out the window watching people pass by. Pregnant women and women pushing strollers. Men and women holding hands and couples with babies. It's like that's all I ever see around me and I desperately want that.

AJ clears his throat. "I … uh … actually helped my sister and her wife get pregnant about four years ago and again about three months ago. So I guess, technically, I already have two kids … well one, with another on the way."

My eyebrows rise with surprise. "How exactly did that work? That seems a little weird."

He chuckles. "Oh yeah, I guess it does. Hayley, my sister, and her wife, Lisa, went through a fertility clinic. Lisa's the one who carries the babies, and by using me as their donor it meant our family's genetics were passed on to their child."

Well, that makes sense. I had this weird vision of him impregnating his sister. "Oh, right. That's amazing. I would never have thought of doing something like that." I drop my eyes to my banana bread and break a piece off. "So does their child call you Daddy?"

"At the moment Colton calls me Uncle AJ because that's the role I play in his life. When he starts asking questions about where he came from, we'll sit down and explain to him that

I'm his biological father in terms appropriate for his age. It's never going to be a secret. If he chooses to call me Dad from that point on, then so be it. It will be his choice at that time. The girls and I discussed it at great length before we went ahead with the donation." He rubs the back of his neck. "Is that going to be a problem?"

"No, not at all. Do you think your sister and her wife will want their children to have contact with this child?" I didn't really think about what would happen if he already had kids. I could still be tied to AJ and his family for life through this child —*if* it happens. "Actually, do you need to check with them if they're okay with you doing this?"

He leans back in his chair with a sigh and brushes his hand through his hair, messing up the strands, his bicep flexing. And what a bicep it is. *Stop looking at his bicep, Sarah.* I internally roll my eyes at myself. "I hadn't considered that. Maybe I should have a chat with them about all this before we move forward. Make sure they'll be okay with it and what their preference would be. I'm sorry. I hadn't really thought about this fully. I tend to be a little spontaneous sometimes." He releases a deprecating laugh.

Oh shit! Did he even think this through at all? He *was* very quick to offer his … uh … services to me last weekend. "Look. Maybe this is a bad idea." I place my hand on the papers to draw them back toward me but AJ places his warm hand over mine, stopping me in my tracks. His hand is so much bigger than mine with a tan that only comes from spending time outdoors. He squeezes gently and I lift my eyes to his.

"What did I say to upset you?"

His expression is open and genuine, curiosity evident. "I wondered if you'd thought this through. You were quick to offer to help me last weekend and maybe you should have taken time to consider all of the ramifications of such an offer." I swallow past the lump forming in my throat because if

I walk away today, I'll have to go back to my original plan and it'll be at least twelve months before I can afford to try again. The backs of my eyes sting and I blink to keep my emotions in check. "I don't want you to rush into something that requires a significant amount of thought and consideration. You'll probably meet the woman of your dreams one day and want to start a family with her. This could end up being an issue for you."

He leaves his hand resting on top of mine, and I take comfort from his warmth, even though I shouldn't. He glances out of the window for a moment, then brings his eyes back to mine. "I know I was quick to offer my help, but that's because I've already gone through this process and I know how happy it's made Hayley and Lisa." The love for his sister is clear. "Had I ever thought I would do the same for a stranger? No. I can't say I had ever considered the possibility. After leaving you on Friday night, I went home and gave the whole idea some serious thought, and I decided to follow through with my offer if you reached out to me. The only aspect I hadn't considered was how my decision may impact my sister and her family. I'll talk with Hayley and Lisa, but I don't think there'll be a problem. Would you want this child to have regular contact with his or her half-siblings?" Creases form between his brows.

"To be honest, I hadn't considered this possibility. I knew when I was going through the fertility clinic that the possibility of half-siblings was inevitable, but it's a little different because I never met those donors face to face. There's a level of anonymity. The thought of family connections hadn't crossed my mind." Now I feel like a hypocrite for accusing him of not thinking it through when I've pretty much done the same thing. "If you don't mind me asking, how will it work for you when you eventually settle and want to start a family? How will you deal with the half-sibling issue?"

He shrugs. "I don't see it as an issue."

Hmmm. I'm not sure how I'd feel knowing a prospective partner offered to be a donor to a complete stranger. Hang on a minute. That's exactly what the guys who donate their semen to the clinic do. Why am I making such a big deal about AJ doing it?

"So, how did things work with your sister and her wife, exactly? Did you sign anything?"

"As I already told you, they went through a fertility clinic. They used my donation to do it, which reduced the cost somewhat, but they still had to pay the fees. I had to sign the documents the clinic requires a donor to sign." I nod as he explains. "I assumed we would skip the clinic, but is that how you want to do this?"

"I was hoping to do this without the clinic because it would mean I can try again sooner. But if you would feel more comfortable doing it that way, I can wait." Fingers crossed he's happy to skip the clinic.

He shakes his head. "Not at all. I'm happy to work it out between the two of us. I don't foresee any issues."

"Are you sure your sister and her wife will be okay with this? Their children will be related to this one," I remind him again.

He shakes his head. "I don't think they'll have any issues with it but I'll ask what level of involvement they would like, and we'll see if we can come to an agreement. You didn't answer me before, would *you* want the kids to know each other?"

I ponder his question for a moment. Since this will probably be the only child I'll have, it might be nice for him or her to know their half-siblings. My child wouldn't have this opportunity if I was using an anonymous donor through the clinic. I'd be crazy to refuse. I nod. "I think I would. But only if your family agrees."

He nods, then leans forward slightly, pulling something out

of his back pocket. "I brought my paperwork. It's from six months ago when I went through the process with Hayley and Lisa for the second time, but if you want me to get a more up-to-date semen analysis and sexual health check done, I don't mind. I haven't … I haven't uh … been with anyone since these results." A slight blush stains his cheeks as his eyes drop away from mine. I'm not sure why he'd be embarrassed about that. I'm happy to know he doesn't sleep around on the regular.

He slides the results across the table, and I dig my glasses out of my purse to read them.

Concentration: 285 million. *I raise my eyebrows, that's fantastic.*

Motility: 85%. *Another fantastic result. This is promising.*

Morphology: 90%. *This guy's sperm is like the high achievers of sperm according to these results.*

I take off my glasses and glance up at AJ. He's sitting there like he got a perfect score on his SATs, and he *should* feel proud. These are outstanding results.

"Wow. Your sperm are real go-getters." I chuckle as I place my glasses on the table and slide the paper back to him. Did I think I would ever say a sentence like that in my life? Nope. But here I am sitting opposite a man who has one of the best semen analysis results I've seen.

He chuckles. "Thanks." He points at my glasses resting on the table. "You look cute with your glasses on."

I glance down at them and my cheeks heat at his compliment. "Thanks. I only need them for reading. Do you wear glasses at all?"

"Nope. I have twenty-twenty vision." He relaxes back in his seat. "About that last question." He points to the questionnaire.

I straighten. This is important. "Yeah."

"I'll stick with your pregnancy plan for as long as it takes, Sarah." He leans forward, placing his elbows on the table, looking intently at my face. "And I won't be seeing anyone during that time."

I blow out a relieved breath and my shoulders drop. "Thank you. But what if you meet someone?"

He shrugs. "I haven't met anyone yet, and I'm not actively looking at this point."

"Well, let me know if you do and we'll re-evaluate where things are at." He nods and I remember the paperwork I brought for him about me. I gather it together and hand it over. "Here's some information on my background. I figured it was only fair you had an idea of the type of person you're helping to get pregnant." I chuckle awkwardly. "Is this the weirdest conversation you've ever had?"

He tilts his flattened hand from side to side with a grin. "Maybe. How about you *tell* me a little about yourself? Like how did someone as gorgeous as you end up having to go down this path to have a baby?" My light mood slips a little and I drop my hands to my lap to fidget. I glance out of the window and watch the people passing by while I gather my thoughts. "If it's too personal, you don't have to tell me. It has no bearing on whether or not I give you my jizz."

I give him a grateful smile, but I feel as though he deserves an explanation since he's being so generous. I lick my dry lips and take a sip of my coffee. "I was dating my high school sweetheart. We did all the things you normally do in a long-term relationship, we moved in together, bought a dog, he proposed, and I said 'yes.' Then one day he came home from work and said he had accepted a promotion within his company. I was so excited for him until he told me it was in Perth, Australia." AJ's eyes widen and his mouth drops open a little. "I was settled and happy in my job, and I didn't want to leave my family and friends to travel to the other side of the world, so he left and I stayed. He took our dog and moved to Australia." AJ moves his hand to cover mine, and I soak up his kindness. "It all happened so fast. I couldn't believe he accepted the promotion without even discussing it with me. I thought our relationship was stronger than that ... I thought I was more important to him, but I was wrong."

"I'm sorry, Sarah. That's tough and the guy's an asshole."

I shrug. "His dreams were different to mine, I guess. Anyway, I was thirty when that happened and by the time I recovered emotionally, I was thirty-two. Over the last two years, I've had some short relationships which were headed nowhere fast ... and here I am." It sounds trivial when I lay it out in simple terms but my heart was shattered when Michael so easily chose the promotion over me.

"Thank you for sharing your story with me. Time moves fast, and I get that you feel like you're running out of time. I think you're incredible for taking matters into your own hands and going after what you want."

CHAPTER 6

I REACH TOWARD THE NEXT PINCH HOLD, PUSHING UPWARD WITH my legs, straining and pushing my body to the limit. Sweat trickles down my temples and my spine making my tank stick to my body. One more crimp and I'm at the top. My hand makes contact with the button to stop the clock and I glance down at Dylan with a grin.

"Zero point five seven seconds. That's gotta be your best time yet."

"Yep. I'm pretty happy with that." I glance up at the time, pride filling my chest. "Take," I call down to Dylan who's belaying for me today. I get myself into the seated position, my feet shoulder-width apart, ready to be lowered.

"Are you ready to lower?"

"Ready to lower."

I keep my feet high and push into the wall as I'm lowered to the pads below. I like coming to the gym a couple of times a week to maintain my muscle strength and endurance, so I'm climbing fit for whenever I decide to do an outdoor climb. When my feet connect with the pads, Dylan provides enough slack in the rope and then holds up his hand. I slap my palm against his, creating a puff of chalk dust and he pulls me in for a back slap-come-hug.

"Congrats, man."

"Thanks." I tilt my chin toward the wall. "Do you wanna see if you can beat my time?"

"Nah. I need to get going. I promised Mom I'd cut her grass this afternoon." He disengages from the belay rope, removing his harness, and I untie my knots to remove mine, then reach down for my hand towel to wipe away the sweat and remove the excess chalk from my fingers.

"Thanks for belaying for me today. Say hi to your mom for me."

"I will." He collects his bag. "See ya on Monday."

"Yep. Bye." He turns and heads out, and I decide to do some bouldering for a bit before heading to my sister's place. I need to chat with her about a possible half-sibling for Colton and the bubba. I hadn't really thought about the impact my decision would have on my sister's family.

I started climbing as a way to practice mindfulness. When I'm climbing, my thoughts and focus have to be solely on what I'm doing, planning my next hold, and my path up the rock face. I can't think about work, family, or anything else that's going on in my life. I've found since developing the skill, my work focus has also improved. I'm better at being focused on a singular task and planning the steps I need to take to see a job through to completion.

The lactic acid in my muscles is building, and they're beginning to shake, meaning it's time to call it quits for today. I do some cool-down stretches and head home to shower and get ready for dinner with my sister and her family.

"Knock, knock!" I call out through the screen door. The handle won't budge, which is a good thing. Hayley and Lisa started taking their safety seriously after a home invasion two doors down from them. Prior to that, they often left their doors and windows unlocked, even though I regularly lectured them about their personal safety.

Lisa walks toward me with a smile as she rests Colton on her hip, her very slight baby bump only now beginning to show. "Hey, favorite brother-in-law."

I huff out a chuckle as she unlocks the door to let me inside. Colton immediately reaches for me, climbing from Lisa to me. "I'm your only brother-in-law, so that doesn't make me feel special."

She waves off my comment and leans in to kiss my cheek. "You're still my favorite."

Colton presses his little hands on each of my bristly cheeks and rubs my nose with his. "Hello, Unca AJ!"

"Hey, little man." I kiss the tip of his nose. "Have you been a good boy for your mommy and mama?"

He nods vigorously. "I have."

I glance at Lisa and she nods at me, gently smoothing Colton's hair down with eyes full of love. "Mostly. You just need to stop climbing on everything."

"I want to be like Unca AJ!" He bounces up and down in my arms.

"Well, if you want to be like me, you have to stop climbing on the furniture and counters. I don't do stuff like that. I only climb where I'm supposed to." I make sure my tone is serious to ensure he understands the importance. If he keeps climbing the way he does, I'm worried Hayley or Lisa will suffer a heart attack.

His little eyebrows scrunch together over his brown eyes and his expression turns serious as he nods. "Okay, Unca AJ. I'll stop."

Maybe I should commission a climbing wall to make climbing safer. I'll talk to the girls about it when he's out of earshot. We head through the house to the backyard, where Hayley's standing at the grill. I place Colton down and go straight to her, wrapping my arms around her waist and lifting her off her feet.

She giggles and as I drop her to her feet, she spins around and engulfs me in her embrace. "AJ! It's so good to see you. It's been too long."

I kiss her cheek. "It has. I'm sorry. Work's been busy and Grandfather has been breathing down my neck." I roll my eyes at the last part of my sentence. "How have you guys been?"

"We're doing great. I don't know why Grandfather won't let it go when Mom's dying to step into the role."

I give my sister a pointed look. "You know exactly why."

"Yep. He's old-fashioned. As much as I love him, it's time he dragged himself into the twenty-first century." She huffs, rolling her eyes. She lifts the chicken from the grill to check it. "Dinner's nearly ready."

Lisa's setting the outdoor table, so I head over to help her. We work together to bring out the salads and drinks. "How are you feeling?"

She strokes her abdomen. "Still struggling to keep food down for most of the day. I'm hoping it will settle down for the second trimester like it did with Colton."

"Unca AJ. Look at me!" Colton calls out from his swing set as he climbs up the slide. I glance across at Lisa who's shaking her head at her son.

"Hold on with two hands!" I call back to him. While he's busy, I lower my voice. "How about I look at getting him a climbing wall for the backyard? I've seen them online. They don't look that hard to do. I could get a carpenter to build the frame and I can attach the holds."

"That'd be fantastic and maybe it would stop him from

climbing everything in sight inside." Lisa sighs as Hayley places the tray of chicken onto the table.

"I'll get onto it."

Lisa and Hayley give me grateful smiles. "That'd be great. Thanks, AJ."

"No problem."

Lisa and Hayley lay out the food, placing small portions on Colton's plate while I retrieve him from the slide and take him inside to wash his hands, then he eagerly leads me back to the table. "Unca AJ, sit next to me."

He climbs into his booster chair, and I take the seat next to him. We all dig into the scrumptious barbecue. "This is delicious. Thanks for the invite."

"You're welcome. We meant to invite you last weekend but Lisa was too sick." Hayley smiles at her wife and tucks Lisa's hair behind her ear with affection. A pang strikes the muscle in my chest. I want what they have but I can't seem to find someone who wants the same thing. Even Sarah, whom I know I have a connection with, doesn't want a committed relationship. "What have you been up to?"

Even though the girls already know about the huge contract Dylan and I landed with *booknow.com*, I tell them a bit more detail about it. "This could put us on the map. It's a huge coup."

"Congratulations. I'm so proud of what you guys have built. You deserve all the success," Lisa says, mirroring Hayley's words when I initially told her about it.

"Thanks." I'm not sure why as a grown-ass man I need my family's approval, but it seems I still do as pride fills me with her praise. Maybe it's because everyone in my family runs a successful business, and as the baby of the family, I want to be considered successful in their eyes too.

"We had some good news this week too." Hayley glances at Lisa and matching smiles break across their faces. "My application to adopt Colton was approved. I'm officially his mama."

"Congratulations. I know how important it was to you." I stand from my seat to hug my sister and sister-in-law.

"Thanks. It was such a relief to have the official paperwork."

"I bet." I'm thrilled for them. Who knew that the non-biological parent would have to formally adopt her own child? It's ridiculous. We finish eating and I stand to collect the plates. "Why don't you two put your feet up and Colton and I will clean up." I give Colton a wink. "Are you ready to help me?"

He throws his little fist into the air. "Yeah, Unca AJ. Let's do this!" Colton climbs down from his chair and heads straight toward Lisa and Hayley. Taking each of their hands, he tugs. "Come on, Mommy. Come on, Mama." They both chuckle as they stand, following Colton's lead to the living room. I set about clearing the table, carrying everything inside to start the dishes as he ensures his moms are comfortable with enough cushions to sink a small boat. He lifts each of their feet onto the ottoman, then hands them the TV remote. He walks toward me with a look of accomplishment as his moms sink into the couch with matching grins as they watch him walk toward me.

After carefully packing away the leftovers, I wash all of the plastic cutlery and plates for him to dry. He stands proudly on the small step the girls have at the sink for him and he carefully dries each item, laying them on the counter. I notice the items aren't completely dry, so I'll have to wipe them over later so I can put them away. He's used to helping his moms, so we make quick work of the dishes.

I want to talk with Hayley and Lisa about my discussion with Sarah yesterday, but I need to have all of their attention when we discuss it, so I bathe Colton and offer to read him a bedtime story.

"This one, Unca AJ!" He waves a bright green book over his head as he runs back to his brand-new big-boy bed. He had been sleeping in his crib, minus one side but the girls decided to get him a bed so the crib was free for their next baby. He climbs into bed, handing me the book and I tuck him under the sheet. It's too warm for anything more than that; this summer has been unseasonably hot. I get comfortable beside him and scan the cover.

"By Crikey? What does that mean?" I look at my nephew.

"It's a book from Aus-tray-li-uh. It's something they say. It's really funny. Read it!" His little chocolate-colored eyes—exactly like mine and Hayley's—are sparkling with delight. "It's my fav-rite."

I chuckle. "Okay, okay." I read all about the sheep called Doug who lives on an Australian farm. He doesn't want to be shorn and his antics to avoid the experience at all costs are detailed with humorous illustrations. I take note of the author, Jodie Reeder, so I can check if she has any more books. I might have to get Colton the next book for his birthday.

"Can you please read it again? I promise to go to sleep if you read it again." How can I deny him when he gives me his puppy dog eyes? So I read it again, chuckling each time Doug the sheep manages to escape the shearer's clutches. When I close the book to place it on his nightstand and glance at my nephew's angelic face, his eyes are heavy with sleep. "Thank you, Unca AJ."

"You're welcome. Sweet dreams, little man." I dip down to kiss his forehead, brushing my fingers through his silky hair. I'm not sure if the strong bond I share with him is because I'm his biological father or if it's because we usually spend a lot of time together. I carefully climb from his bed and make my way to the living room where I find Lisa lying across the cushions with her head in Hayley's lap. Hayley's eyes are locked on the television as she strokes Lisa's hair, a look of contentment on her face.

They both notice me and Lisa pushes to sit up but I stop her. "Stay where you are. You look comfortable. I won't stay for long, but there was something I needed to speak with you both about."

Hayley responds, creases forming between her brows. "Sure. Sounds serious."

Now, where do I start? Suddenly, I'm nervous. What if they say no? I don't want to tell Sarah I can't help her. It wouldn't be fair but I need to consider my family first. I rub the back of my neck and start. I explain how I met Sarah and what she's hoping to achieve.

"Good for her." Hayley's quick to show her support. "Did she want to use the same fertility clinic we did? I have their details on my phone."

"Uh, no. She's already had two procedures without success with a clinic. She's going to do it independently or else she'll have to wait for another twelve months while she saves enough money." Both women nod. They understand the expense of trying to get pregnant. They were lucky that some of the costs were reduced because they had me as their donor.

"What's she going to do then?" My sister's eyes widen and a slow smile graces her face, which is so similar to mine and Colton's. "You're going to help her, right?" She wriggles her eyebrows up and down.

"Well …" I shrug. "Yeah."

"You're so sweet," Lisa chirps.

"More like he knows he'll get laid on the regular with this arrangement." Hayley chuckles. "Am I right?"

I get up to pace. "Well, a little of both. I wanted to help her out. I think what she's trying to do is admirable and I know my"—I wave my hand down around my groin area—"swimmers are viable. Plus, it won't hurt that I'll get to spend extended time with her. She's pretty cool."

"Good for you. Are you going to be able to do this without getting attached to her? I mean, you're going to have to spend a fair amount of time with her. It could take months for her to actually get pregnant." Hayley points out.

"Well, I can't get attached. She doesn't want a partner. Just a baby. I'm sure I can do it." I sit back down. "But I need to ask you two how you feel about it because her baby will be a half-sibling to your kids. She was wondering how the two of you would feel about it. If you would want the kids to know each other and spend time together?"

They glance at each other. They always seem to know what the other is thinking, it's quite weird. "We're fine with it. Honestly. I think it's great you're going to help her fulfill her dream of becoming a mother. It's the best thing. As for the kids being in contact, it would be nice, but it's up to her. We're absolutely open to the idea, but it's whatever Sarah feels most comfortable with."

I blow out a breath and a smile breaks across my lips. "Thanks. I knew you'd be cool with the whole thing." Lisa sits up and Hayley climbs to her feet to embrace me.

"Anytime." She lays her hand over my heart. "Just be careful, AJ. I don't want you to get hurt. You already seem to like her."

I brush off her concern. "I promise I'll be okay. She's really sweet and I think we'll be able to keep the lines of communication open if anything changes."

CHAPTER 7

—sarah—

"Good morning, Mr. Wainwright," I say brightly from my perch behind my desk. It's weird being here before him because he's usually here long before anyone else.

Eric stops at my desk. "Morning, Sarah. How was your weekend?"

"Busy as usual. Got to hang out with the family yesterday." A smile tugs at my lips at the memory of Kenny and Austin chasing poor old Archie around Mom and Dad's backyard.

"Great," he says distractedly as he steps into his office, and I head to the kitchen to make his pot of tea.

It's obvious to everyone in the office he's lost his desire to be here. He's been passing more and more of his tasks over to Tony, the Vice President, who happens to be a dick. I only hope his grandson takes over sooner rather than later.

With Eric's tea in hand, I head back to his office with a smile, ready to go over his plans for the week. "Thank you, Sarah. I have a face-to-face call with Adam in ten minutes, so we'll do our planning after that. Please shut the door on your way out."

"Sure thing." I step out and quietly close the door behind me, returning to my desk to update the database. We changed to a new system and some of our information got lost in the transition, so I have the delightful task of cross-checking everything. It's an enormous job and tedious to boot.

Lost in the task, I jump at the sudden shout which bursts from Eric's office. I glance across, but he's closed his blinds, so I can't see inside. In all the time I've worked here, not once have I heard Eric raise his voice, and there have been times when the guys from development and testing have tried his patience. I strain to hear more of the conversation, my body leaning toward his office, but his words are muffled.

"Sarah. Can you let Eric know we're ready for the second round of testing for MicroE19?" Evan raps his knuckles once on my desk and heads back the way he came.

"Sure," I call to his retreating back and make a note in an email to Eric.

Eric's door opens and slams closed. With angry steps, he strides down the hallway carrying his briefcase. I quickly jump to my feet to follow him. "Mr. Wainwright. Is everything okay?"

He stops suddenly and I almost run into the back of him. He spins around, wearing a tight smile, his face flushed in anger. "No, Sarah. Everything is not okay. I've decided to go home for the day. I'll start fresh tomorrow." He spins on his heel and I struggle to come up with what to say. I've never seen him like this.

"Uh, okay. I'll see you tomorrow. Please take care."

He nods, waving over his shoulder, and the elevator doors close him inside the metal box. As I arrive back at my desk, my phone vibrates, so I quickly snatch it up.

AJ

Hi

> I spoke with Hayley and Lisa and they don't
> have any issues with us moving forward
>
> I'm ready to start when you are

I squeal inside, dropping my head back to gaze up at the ceiling in relief. I instantly feel lighter. I actually started ovulating yesterday, I wonder if it's too soon to ask him to start.

> AJ
>
> When do you start ovulating next?

Wow. He's perfect.

> ME
>
> Hey. That's awesome news
>
> As good fortune would have it, I started
> ovulating yesterday

Straight away my phone lights up.

> AJ
>
> Perfect. I'm free tonight

My heart rate accelerates and my hand shakes. Tonight! I guess it's great he's eager, but am I ready? I mean, I know I'm ready, but this feels fast. I deliberate how to respond. I need to plan this. I didn't think he'd talk with his sister so soon. I thought I had time to work up the courage to do this with a complete stranger. Well, not a complete stranger, because we got to know each other a little more over coffee, but he's still a stranger compared to people I've known for a long time.

What if he's been luring me in with his nice guy act but he's really a creep? I didn't get that vibe from him, but I have been wrong in the past. Shit! Why is this so hard? He's offering me my dream and I still need to think it to death. I grasp my hair on either side of my head and tug on it in frustration.

My phone rings in my hand and I jump. Glancing at the screen, AJ's name is there clear as day. Shit! I don't know what to say to him. He's going to think I'm some crazy woman if I can't get myself together. It rings and rings while I try to gather my thoughts but they won't cooperate. My mind's a mess. This is everything I want. This man is offering to make my dream come true with no strings attached. But for some reason, I didn't think it would happen this month. I figured it would happen next month and I'd have time to plan things properly.

This is not following my plan! Ugh!

The device in my hand goes quiet, the screen going dark. Then the missed call message shows. I blow out a frustrated breath.

What the hell is wrong with me?

I drop into my chair and swivel around to stare out of the window, not really seeing the city skyline I normally adore. My phone buzzes again.

AJ

Sarah? Everything okay?

How do I tell him I had a momentary internal crisis? He's going to think I'm crazy. And I definitely don't want him to think that.

ME

Yeah. Everything's great, just overthinking everything as usual

I delete the last part of the message and change it.

ME

Yeah. Everything's great, just busy atm

AJ

Okay. Let me know if you want me tonight

Oh my, what an offer. Under any other circumstance, his offer would be totally hot. But for my overthinking brain, it's too much, too soon. But the sooner we get started, the sooner I'll get pregnant, right?

ME

Sure

I make myself a coffee and head back to my desk. Only I don't make it that far.

"Sarah," Tony calls from behind his desk, so I stop and poke my head in his doorway. "Where did Eric go? I need to speak with him about these figures."

"He didn't say. He was in a rush. Said he'll be back in the office tomorrow." I shrug, as though it's nothing out of the ordinary even though it really is.

"Tomorrow!" he bellows. "What the hell is going on with him?" he mumbles.

My eyes are going fuzzy and the slight pounding at the back of my head is warning enough for me to take a break from the screen. I glance at the time and notice it's past lunch. I may as well take a quick break and eat my lunch in the break room, something I rarely do. Collecting my phone and water bottle, I grab my lunch out of the fridge. Because it's past lunch, the room is empty, and the low hum of the fridge is the only noise in the room. I sigh and take the lid off my pre-prepared salad jar, tipping the contents into a bowl. Now that I'm not focused on the database, my mind spins back to AJ's offer to start on my pregnancy plan tonight.

Maybe it's best to jump in and get started. We're both clear on our arrangement, and he seems genuinely interested in helping me achieve my dream. I need someone to talk me through this. I don't want to call Emma and interrupt her day. I double-check the time. Mel may be available.

ME

Have you got time to talk?

I return to my salad, my mind churning over AJ's offer so I jolt when my phone rings. Quickly, I pick it up and accept the call. "Hey, Mel. Thanks for calling me back."

"Anytime, Sare. But this is unusual for you to be calling me in the middle of a workday. What's up?"

I blow out a heavy breath and spill everything about AJ and how I'm overthinking everything as usual. She listens to my rambling thoughts, as she always does. "It feels too fast."

"I hear what you're saying, but this is what you wanted. He's giving it to you on a silver platter. Book a hotel, it'll take you five minutes, and then text him the place and time. You don't need to overthink this, Sare. You've already thought of everything."

Thank God for my best friend. "Okay. I'll do it. Thank you."

"Have you got everything you need?"

"Yeah, I ordered everything I needed as soon as he offered when we first met. It arrived on Friday, so I'm ready."

"No excuses. Go forth and get knocked up, my friend." She chuckles. "If you need me, I'm off tonight."

"Thanks, Mels Bells. You're the best."

"I know. Mwah! Good luck."

We disconnect the call and I locate the number of a hotel not far from my place, make the damn booking, and message AJ.

ME

Hey, it's me

God, Sarah. He already knows it's you. Your name probably shows up on his damn screen.

AJ

Hey you

ME

Are you still available tonight?

AJ

Of course. My sperm is ready and waiting! I made a fresh batch today

I chuckle. I'm glad he finds this whole thing funny.

ME

Would you be able to meet me at the Como after dinner?

I hold my breath as I wait for his answer.

AJ

We could have dinner together

Shit! That would make it feel like a date and I'm not sure if I can keep my emotional distance if we share a meal before doing what needs to be done. I need to keep the lines clear and defined or my heart may get confused.

AJ

Or we don't have to and I'll meet you at the hotel. Do you have a room number?

ME

Thanks, I'm not sure what time I'll finish here and then I need to get home. Room 743

See you after 7

Thank you

AJ

No problem

CHAPTER 8

—sarah—

I don't think I've ever been this nervous before. My legs are shaky, and I'm worried I'm going to tip over because I'm off-balance. I check in at the front counter and collect my key to the room. I didn't want to do this at my apartment, because well, I don't know AJ. I didn't think it was prudent to invite him into my home. I tighten my hold on the strap of my purse as I step into the elevator, pressing the button for my floor. As the doors are about to close, a couple enters and he whispers something to her. She glances across at me, then giggles. He pulls her incredibly close and nuzzles down into the crook of her neck and my chest tightens because I want that. I lock my eyes on the numbers above the door, so I'm not tempted to watch their interaction. Nothing good can come from wishing and hoping for something that's never going to happen for me. I have different priorities now and I need to remember that.

The doors finally open on my floor, and I scurry out after wishing the couple a mumbled good night. I'm sure their evening will be completely the opposite of mine. Though, if everything goes as planned, I'll be on my way to being pregnant! Yay me! Stopping outside my room, I scan the card with a shaky hand. Geez, Sarah, get yourself under control, girl. I'm a little early, but I wanted to set up before AJ arrives. He's been extremely accommodating, offering to meet with me at such short notice, so I don't want to waste his time.

The hotel isn't fancy and the room is basic, but it has everything I need. A clean bathroom and a bed. I drop my purse on the dresser, then fish out what I need. Bending down, I take off my shoes and pad into the bathroom, the tiles cold underfoot. I diligently wash my hands with soap and then lay out what I need on the vanity.

When I glance into the mirror, I pause, studying my reflection carefully. My life could possibly change tonight. I fiddle with my hair and smooth my hands down my clothes, twisting this way and that in the mirror.

Now, what do I do while I wait? Peering out of the glass doors to the small balcony, I think some fresh air is in order. The sounds of the city greet me as I step outside and draw in a deep breath. I love this city. I love the skyline at night, and I love the sunsets on the beach. I love spring walks along the river and hikes in the fall. This city has everything I need, which is one of the reasons I didn't want to leave when Michael got his promotion.

A knock sounds and I jump. *Shit! Calm down, girl.* My foot connects with the soft carpet as I step back inside to answer the door with a racing heart. I pause for a moment, my hand on the knob, and take breaths to calm my nerves. AJ's been cool and laid back throughout the entire process so far, and he's happily gone along with every request I've made. I shake out my hands while I draw in and blow out a long breath, put on my best smile, and open the door as though I'm not a nervous wreck.

My eyes connect with AJ's, and then dart around his face, taking in the five o'clock shadow he's had every time we've met. I then skim down his fit physique and the navy Henley, which hugs his torso like a second skin to the black ripped jeans, clinging to his defined thighs. He definitely has great genetics. Physically, he's my ultimate in every single way. I wonder how he stays in such great shape when his job keeps him tied to a desk. My eyes make it back to his face and the smirk he's wearing, his eyes crinkled in humor. My cheeks heat having been caught admiring him so blatantly.

"Hey." *Good one, Sarah.*

"Hi." He leans forward, laying a chaste kiss on my cheek and sending heat racing through my body, then bends down to collect a bag as if his kiss was of no consequence. When he steps over the threshold, I take a step back to allow him to pass through the doorway. I'm not sure why he needs an overnight bag, his part will be over and done with and he'll be able to go home shortly.

He places his bag on the luggage rack and glances around the room. AJ walks over to the bed and presses down on the mattress, then turns to me with a sparkle in his eye. "Are you nervous? Because I'm nervous and I really hope I'm not alone in my nerves." He chuckles, rubbing the back of his neck, and making his bicep bulge. My eyes follow the action with appreciation. "I've never had sex on demand before."

Uhm, what? His words jolt me out of my stupor and I snap my eyes back to his face.

What does he mean, he's never had sex on demand before? Does he think we're having sex tonight?

I can't have sex with him. Whenever someone sticks their dick in me, I fall in love with them. I can't separate my emotions from the act. My stupid hormones and heart think it's love. It's why I can't have one-night stands like Mel.

Well, this is awkward. I shuffle on my feet, glancing around the small space. Has the room shrunk? It suddenly feels too small. And hot. Is it hotter in here? My pulse pounds in my ears like a drumline.

AJ steps into my space, and this close I can smell his citrus aftershave. He smells so freaking good—his pheromones play havoc with my senses. I tip my head back, hoping he didn't notice me drawing in a deep breath of his scent. "Are you okay, Sarah?"

I nod, then bite my bottom lip, and his eyes drop to the action. His pupils dilate and his nostrils flare. I take half a step back, putting more space between us. "I, uh, think maybe there's been a … a … misunderstanding."

Creases form across his forehead and his eyes narrow. "In what way?"

"Well, uh, we don't actually need to have sex for me to get pregnant." I semi-chuckle awkwardly as I spin on my heel and head toward the bathroom. Collecting the sealed items I placed on the vanity earlier, I turn back toward AJ, bumping into him. "Uh, sorry. I didn't realize you were so close."

He glances down at the items in my hands, then up at my face. "What the hell is that for?" He waves his hand around the items I'm holding.

I hold one of the items up higher. "Well, you're going to collect your semen in this collection condom." I shake the pink packet in front of him. "Then you can go home. I'll use this syringe to get the sperm where it needs to go." I wave the plastic device around between us as I explain the process—I assumed he would be somewhat familiar with the collection process.

He studies the items as if he's never seen either of them before, then his eyes flick up to mine as his hands land on his hips. He opens and closes his mouth several times, then raises his hand to grasp the back of his neck, making his bicep bulge again. *Nice.* "You can't be serious."

"What do you mean? Of course I'm serious. I've never been more serious about anything in my life." I place the items back on the vanity.

"I figured we'd be doing this the old-fashioned way. You know … having sex." He paces away from me, shaking his head.

I cross my arms under my breasts and huff out a breath. Oh God, I hope he doesn't change his mind. I narrow my eyes and try to work out a way to keep him here. To ensure he follows through with our plan and our agreement. "You're not going to change your mind, are you?"

He spins around to face me, his eyes dropping to my breasts, then sliding back up to my face. "I said I'd give you my swimmers until you were pregnant. I don't go back on my word. Ever." He softens his voice, stepping closer to me. "Don't worry, I won't back out."

I blow out a long breath, my shoulders dropping from around my ears. "Oh, thank God. I was worried for a minute there. Well, if you want to get started"—I gesture with my head toward the bathroom—"I'll wait out here for you." I give him my best smile, trying to appear less frazzled than I feel.

He steps into the bathroom, studying me like he's investigating a science project and my body heats under his gaze. "So I wear this condom and do the deed in here, while you … you're on the other side of this door?" He points to the bathroom door.

"Uh, yeah. Do you need anything?" Maybe I should have brought some nudie magazines or something?

His eyes linger on me for several long moments before he shakes his head and begins to unbuckle his belt. I take the hint and pull the door closed. It's weird to be out here with a flimsy wall and door between us, knowing what he's doing in there. I glance at the door as I pace around the small room.

I can't believe he thought we'd be having sex. I *know* he didn't have sex with his sister-in-law to get her pregnant. I assumed he knew we wouldn't need to actually 'have sex.' I check my purse to make sure I have my handy dandy bullet and tuck it beneath the pillow.

I pace the room and I pace some more. Stepping closer to the bathroom door, I'm tempted to press my ear against it, but I resist—barely. As I'm pulling away, the door flies open and AJ is revealed. Shit, he nearly caught me about to eavesdrop. His hair is disheveled and his cheeks are adorably pink. He holds up the collection condom, the top pinched between his fingers. My heart gallops in my chest and I want to jump up and down on the spot with glee. He did it! My eyes snap to his and I hope he can see the gratitude I have for him.

"Thank you so much, AJ. You have no idea how much I appreciate this." I reach forward to take the condom from him but he drags it toward himself and away from me.

"You're welcome. What's the next step?" His voice is rough and slightly deeper than it was before.

"Well … uhm … I'm going to use that syringe"—I point toward the wrapped syringe on the vanity—"to draw up the fluid and then insert it inside me." My cheeks heat with embarrassment. It seems every conversation I have with this man is incredibly awkward.

He nods. "I guessed that much. Do you need any help?"

My head snaps up. "Uh, nope. I should be able to manage fine on my own. Thanks. Once you leave, I'll get straight to it to ensure your donation is as fresh as possible."

"Right." Only one word, but it comes out full of skepticism. "So …" He grips the back of his neck with his free hand. "I was reading up on all this and it says that you should *have sex*"—he raises his brows—"at least every second day while you're ovulating for your best chance." My heart pounds faster behind my ribs and my cheeks heat further. "Did you want to do this again on Wednesday?"

Could I be any more blessed to have found this guy? "You read up on the best practices for conception?" He simply nods as if it's not a big deal. "If you don't mind. I'd appreciate it."

He nods again. "Okay. Same time, same place on Wednesday. I'll uh … I'll leave you to it." He tips his head down to the condom he's still holding and passes it over.

I take it gratefully, swallowing my embarrassment, and give him an awkward side hug with my free hand. This stuff is as precious as gold, no it's even more precious, I don't want to spill a drop. "Thanks again, AJ. I'll see you on Wednesday."

I see him to the door and after a long pause, he presses the softest kiss to my cheek and leaves. My eyes drop to the condom I have pinched between my thumb and forefinger and my lips widen. This could be it! As I walk toward the bathroom to retrieve the cup and syringe, I squeal a little—giddy with excitement.

I grab the items and head toward the bed. Using the cup, I carefully balance the condom inside and remove my panties, hiking my skirt up past my hips. Reaching over to the nightstand, I unwrap the syringe and draw the plunger back, then press it all the way down as the website told me to do. I insert it into the condom, being careful not to touch the bottom. It's tricky keeping everything balanced but I manage and draw back the plunger, sucking up AJ's release. Lifting it closer to my face, I check for air bubbles and tap them out, careful not to let anything escape. I need every single one of those little suckers. Positioning a pillow in the middle of the bed I lay down with my hips tilted. The website said it wasn't essential to do this, but I want to give myself the best possible chance.

Dipping the syringe into my vagina, I position it where I think is best and slowly depress the plunger, hoping against hope I'm getting it in the right place. Then I grab my bullet. The website said it was best to have an orgasm to help push the semen where it needs to go. This whole situation feels so clinical, and I wonder how AJ managed to orgasm while standing in the bathroom with no stimulation. He's a guy, so it was probably no drama for him. I close my eyes and try to get in the zone but my mind won't quit. So many things have to go right for this to work. And I desperately want it to work.

With my eyes closed and my hips tilted, I try to clear my head and not think, just feel. Images of AJ in the bathroom stroking his cock come to the fore unbidden. My lids fly open as I try to push the images away.

I have no business thinking about him in that way.

He's helping me.

He's not in this for anything more than to give me his semen.

Don't fucking get attached, Sarah.

Think about someone else. Maybe Dean Winchester. Yeah, he's hot. That sexy smile of his and the shy way he tilts his head to the side. I relax into the moment, the buzz of the bullet against my clit beginning to work its magic when AJ's smile takes the place of Dean's.

What the hell?

My buzz wanes as I work to shoo him out of my mind, but he won't go. Damn it!

Dean's hazel eyes turn to warm brown and his light brown hair changes to dark brown in my mind. My clit pulses and I give up and go with it. AJ's handsome and has a body most men would die for. Every time he grasped the back of his neck tonight, his bicep bulged perfectly, and the obvious strength in his forearms is a real turn-on. Even his fingers as he held the condom pinched between his thumb and forefinger looked strong and capable, and my mind can't help but go *there*!

What would it be like to have his fingers working me over right now instead of this silicone device? My body builds and an image of AJ pressing his perfect lips against mine blinds me along with my orgasm. I huff out a moan as shudders rack my body and my vagina pulses around nothing. As strong as the orgasm was, it wasn't satisfying in the least.

Once I calm down, embarrassment floods me. I can't believe it took thoughts and images of AJ—*my donor*—to make me come. Luckily we didn't actually have sex or I'd be asking the guy to move in with me, for God's sake.

Now to lie here in my mortification for the next thirty minutes and let gravity work its magic while I try not to let my shame overtake me.

CHAPTER 9

—aj—

To say I'm disappointed my evening turned out like this is an understatement. I figured I'd be getting lucky; that I'd be having sex all night. I walked into this hotel with a pep in my step, barely able to hold in my smile, knowing I was about to get laid. When Sarah broke the news that we weren't having sex and instead using sterilized equipment, I almost walked out the door. But I made a promise and I never break my promises. *Never*. I pride myself on following through, even if the task isn't something I want to do.

But what disappointed me more is the top-of-the-line firewall Sarah's built between us. I understand we're basically strangers, but she must trust me to some degree to meet me in this hotel on her own. I'm not sure how I'm going to break through the barrier she's built around herself, but I'll steadily crack her code until she lets me inside.

Shaking my head at myself, I sweep past the hotel bar, conversation and laughter trickling through the doorway. What the hell? I may as well have a drink before I go home. I have nothing to go home to anyway. Stepping inside, the place reminds me of a social club I imagine at the local lawn bowls center. It's nothing fancy, with basic furnishings and fans moving the stale air around the space.

I was surprised when Sarah chose this particular hotel; I assumed we'd go to her place to do the deed. I guess it makes sense to meet in a neutral place since she doesn't know me all that well. Smart really. The hotel certainly isn't anything flashy; I guess it would be on the cheaper side and if we have to do this a few times, she needs to consider her budget.

"What can I get for you, sir?"

I'm dragged from my thoughts, not even realizing I've taken a seat at the bar. Man, she has my head in a spin. I glance along the bar and notice several beers on tap. At least they have craft beers, which are always my preference. Tipping my chin toward them, I tell the bartender, "A craft beer, thanks."

He nods and sets to work pouring my beer. I dig into my back pocket, drag out my wallet, and hand the guy my card as he places my beer on a coaster with *Como* printed in block letters across the outline of a lake. I'm assuming this place is named after the city on the border between Italy and Switzerland. I always loved geography in high school and I still enjoy watching travel shows in my downtime.

Lifting the glass to my lips, I take a sip and lift my eyebrows at the familiar flavor. Raising my eyes, I meet those of the bartender, who's waiting for my approval. I raise my glass to him and tip my head. "Very nice. Local Honey?"

He grins and nods. "Good pick. What gave it away?"

"The lavender and eucalyptus flavors finished off with a tinge of honey. One of my favorite beers." I smile at him and take another sip. Nice. Just what I need to wind down.

Keeping my eyes on my drink, I run my fingers down the condensation that's formed on the glass and blow out a long breath. I can't believe I had to jack off in the bathroom when I had a perfectly sexy woman in the room next door. Though, seeing Sarah in her tight skirt and silky blouse was enough to get me hard. It didn't take much before I was filling the condom to images of the woman with the sexiest curves I think I've ever seen; images of peeling that tight skirt up her shapely thighs, tearing her panties away, and plunging my cock so deep into her tight, wet heat flooded my mind. I barely hold in my groan as the images flash through my mind again.

So damn sweet.

I was itching to get my hands and mouth on her body. To explore every single inch. I shake my head and adjust my position, willing my cock down. She never said we'd be having sex to get her pregnant. I made an assumption. I mean, it's a fair assumption to make. *Right?* I frown at my beer and think back over our conversations. No. We never talked about the mechanics of getting Sarah pregnant. Maybe I should have specified that's how I would participate. No. That wouldn't be fair. I agreed to give her my swimmers. Not orgasms.

I roll my eyes and take another drink. I can't help but feel I've missed out on an amazing experience, though. I would have made it good for her *while* helping her out. It would have been a win for both of us. Now neither of us will be feeling satisfied tonight. I guess Sarah will be, she got what she needs.

I finish my beer, decide to call it a night, and head for my car. Walking through the dark parking lot, I glance up and notice several of the lights aren't working. I don't like the thought of Sarah coming out here and walking to her car on her own; assuming she'll be coming out here tonight and not tomorrow morning. Stopping at my Jeep, I dig in my pocket for my keys only to come up empty. I know I didn't put them on the bar. Shit! I left my overnight bag in the room. I remember dropping my keys into the side pocket before going inside.

I glance up at the hotel and blow out a heavy breath. I'm going to have to go back up there to get my bag so I can go home. This works out well if Sarah's not staying the night, I can walk her to her car to make sure she's safe at the same time. Yeah, I like that idea. I'll feel better knowing she got to her car without incident. Striding back to the hotel doors, I head straight up to Sarah's room. As I come to a stop at the door, I pause. What if she's still doing whatever it is she's supposed to do? I don't want to interrupt the process.

Pressing my ear against the door, I feel like a total creeper and glance around me to make sure nobody's witnessing my shady behavior. Everything's silent. I can't hear any movement from inside. I hope she hasn't already checked out. I raise my hand to rap three times and wait. Shuffling sounds from inside and I breathe a sigh of relief that she's still here.

The door swings open and I'm greeted by a disheveled Sarah. "AJ," she squeaks. Her cheeks are flushed and her eyes are bright. She tucks some messy strands of hair behind her ear and drops her gaze, stealing her unique-colored eyes from me. They were quite a bright green when I arrived earlier, but now they're almost brown.

"Hey. Sorry to bother you, but I forgot my bag and it has my keys in it." I use my chin to point to where I left it.

"No problem." She opens the door wider and I step inside, my eyes tracing their way to the bed and the pillows resting in the middle. A pair of teal-colored lace panties sit on the bed covers, and I close my eyes, shifting my attention to my overnight bag.

"Did you, uh, did you manage everything okay?" I grab the handles of my bag.

She clears her throat. "Uh, yeah. Thanks. Easy as anything."

"Great. Are you staying the night?" This conversation is awkward, considering I just gave this woman my semen and she now has it inside her body.

"Uh, no. I'll head home."

"Good. Great. I can walk you down to your car. I noticed

several lights are out in the parking lot. I'd feel happier knowing you got to your car safely."

Her eyes finally snap up to mine. "Oh, you don't need to do that. You've already done enough for me."

"I insist." I plant my feet, so she knows I'm not going anywhere until she's ready.

Sarah chuckles. "Okay. Okay. Just give me a minute to gather my stuff." She turns, heading toward the bed in a rush.

Then I remember what she's just done. She probably shouldn't be moving around so much. Dropping my bag, I move into her space. "Hey. How about you sit and I'll sort everything out? You should be taking it easy."

"Oh, you're sweet to offer. I think I should be okay, though."

"I insist." With my hand pressed to her lower back, I guide her to the bed and gently push her down to sit at the edge. I move around the room, collecting the used condom in the cup and the used syringe.

Sarah notices the items in my hand. "I have a plastic bag in my purse to put them in. I'll dispose of them at home."

I peek inside her purse and find the empty bag sitting on top, so I place the items inside and drop it back in her purse. Then I collect her lace panties and hand them to Sarah. She takes them with a pretty blush, her eyes dropping to the floor. "Thanks."

I nod and continue with my check. I drop her shoes on the floor next to her feet and double-check the bathroom to make sure there's nothing inside. When I step out, I spot Sarah tucking her panties inside her purse and raise my eyebrows in question.

"I can't put them on with you in the room. I'm driving straight home, so it doesn't matter." My pulse races with the visual of Sarah's bare pussy beneath that skin-tight skirt.

"Fair enough." I collect the pillow from the middle of the

bed to toss it where it belongs and discover a small silicone bullet. I can't help the smile that tugs at my lips. I read online that an orgasm helps to move the sperm up to where they're needed, that's why I figured we'd be doing this the regular way. I wonder if we read the same article? With Sarah's back to me, she hasn't noticed my discovery so I pick it up, and before I know what I'm doing I take a whiff of the device, closing my eyes to get the full impact of her scent.

Mmmm.

Shit, that probably makes me a creep!

I hand it to her and the flush that spreads across her cheeks is sexy as hell. She quickly snatches it from me, hiding her eyes as she drops it into her purse. Clearing my throat I ask, "Are you ready to go? I think we have everything."

"Uh, sure. Thanks again." She still hasn't made eye contact. Interesting. I wonder what *or* who she was thinking about when she came.

I hold out my hand to help her stand, then place it just above her sexy ass to guide her to the door, collecting my bag on the way. The walk toward the elevator and the ride down to reception is made in silence. The air is thick with tension and I'm not sure how to break it or even whether I should. We approach the reception desk and the woman behind it widens her eyes as she smiles at us.

"Can I help you with anything?" she asks.

"No thanks. I'm just checking out," Sarah responds as she slides her keycard across the desk.

The woman's eyes skate between us and I can tell she's working to school her expression. It must look suspect that Sarah checked in a couple of hours ago and now she's checking out with a guy in tow.

"Was everything to your satisfaction?"

"Yes, everything was great. Would I be able to make a booking for Wednesday night, please?" Sarah glances at me, giving me a timid smile, then returns her attention to the woman behind the desk.

The woman glances between the two of us again. "Sure. Would you like the same room?"

"If I can. That would be great. Thanks."

She taps some keys and then smiles at Sarah. "All done. We'll see you on Wednesday." She finishes with raised brows at both of us.

I return my hand to her lower back, and guide Sarah to the double doors, the heat of her flesh searing my palm through the thin fabric of her blouse. Once we're outside and out of earshot of the receptionist, I burst out laughing and Sarah joins me. "I was waiting for her to tell you this establishment doesn't rent rooms by the hour."

Sarah's giggles increase and she snorts, making her even more attractive. "Me too. I was so embarrassed." She wipes tears from her eyes. "I never once considered how it would appear if I checked in and out on the same night."

"I'm sure she sees all sorts of people and situations. It's probably nothing out of the ordinary for her." I try to reassure her, because even though I don't know Sarah all that well yet, I know she's not the type of woman to hire a room by the hour and I don't want her to be uncomfortable.

We make our way toward Sarah's car through the dark parking lot, Sarah still chuckling now and then. "Sorry, once I get the giggles, I find it hard to stop sometimes."

"No need to apologize. You're beautiful when you let your worries go and laugh." Damn. I probably shouldn't have said that because she freezes in place.

"You think I'm beautiful?" Her voice is unsure, and I don't understand why.

"Hell yeah, you're beautiful. You're stunning." I shake my head. "Why are you asking as if you don't know?"

She shrugs. "It's been a long time since anyone outside of my family has told me that. It's nice to be told now and then."

If she were mine, I'd be telling and showing her exactly how beautiful I think she is every day. She would never have any doubts. But she's not mine and she's not looking to be anybody's, so I should keep my mouth shut—I don't want to make things any more awkward between us. It's the last thing I want to do.

She wants to have a baby, dickhead, nothing more.

CHAPTER 10

—sarah—

Well, that was embarrassing. The receptionist probably thinks I'm a hooker, not that there's anything wrong with the profession, it just couldn't be further from the truth. Here I am trying to get pregnant and I'm not even having sex to do it. *Only me!* I barely refrain from palming my head.

When I opened the door to find AJ standing there after what I'd just done with thoughts of him invading every part of me, I couldn't look him square in the eye. And then he took care of me, cleaning up so he could walk me to my car to ensure my safety. Why couldn't I have met the guy under ordinary circumstances? Now we have this awkward connection between us, which I know can't go any further.

He doesn't want to be anything more than a donor. *I need to remember that.*

My car comes into view and my pulse speeds up. Sarah, get in your car and leave. You'll see the guy on Wednesday night. No need to prolong the evening and make things awkward. I'm sure he has plenty of other things he needs to do. "Uh, thank you for walking me to my car and for tonight." I tuck my loose hair behind my ear. "I guess I'll see you on Wednesday. Same place, same time." I do my best not to sound as awkward as I feel at this point.

He grasps the back of his neck, making his bicep bulge again. It seems to be something he does a lot, and I certainly won't be complaining about it. My eyes naturally drop to watch the action and I swear my mouth waters a little. For a computer guy, he has a great physique. "Yep. I'll come." He smirks at me and my cheeks heat.

"I see what you did there. Good one." I chuckle as I unlock and open the door, using the metal as a barrier so I don't do something stupid like kiss him goodbye. I mean I usually embrace my friends and kiss their cheeks, but we're not really friends. Are we? It's all so confusing. I throw my purse across to the passenger seat as AJ lingers. Is he feeling the same?

He winks and taps the top of my door frame. "See ya Wednesday, Sarah. Take it easy, okay?"

"I will. And … thanks. For everything."

"You're welcome." I close the door and he spins on his heel, walking toward his car. He tucks one hand in his pocket, pulling the denim across his tight ass. My forehead meets the steering wheel as I blow out a breath.

Stop staring at his ass. Stop noticing his muscles. *Just stop already*.

After a shower, I put on my most comfy pajamas and drop onto my couch to call my sister as promised. The phone rings twice, then her voice comes on the line. "How did it go?"

"Well, hello to you too, Sis." I chuckle.

"Sorry." She giggles. "Hey. How did it go?" she asks, impatience thick in her voice.

"As you know I won't know for a little while, but things went smoothly."

"Oh good. And the guy … he wasn't a creep? You felt safe?" Being the eldest, Emma always worries about us, even though she has her own family to worry about now. "You know Theo and Max would have happily stood outside the door to make sure you were safe."

"Oh, God. No way." I huff out a laugh. "Poor AJ. I can't imagine what his response would have been if he'd turned up to find my door guarded. I told you, he's a nice guy. He would have to be to help a stranger make her dream come true."

"I know you said he came across as a decent guy, but I worry. You know how many psychos there are out there."

"I know and I was careful. I promise. I wouldn't have taken things this far if I didn't feel completely comfortable with him." I pause. "Maybe too comfortable." My cheeks heat as my mind skips back to when I was lying on the bed trying to make myself come.

Her tone softens. "Sarah? What do you mean … too comfortable? You're not going to get attached to this guy are you?" Not that Emma would care if I did, so long as the feelings were mutual. She helped pick up the mess Michael left behind, and she never wants to see me hurt like that again.

"No. I won't. That's why I'm not actually having sex with him. You know what I'm like. I can't afford to catch feelings this time, and that's why I'm making it as clinical as I possibly can." I smile as I remember the look on his face when I showed him the collection condom and syringe.

I hear rustling in the background. "Oh yeah. Did he know that was the plan?"

"I assumed he did, but the look on his face suggested otherwise." He could have easily become upset and walked out when my plan was different from his, but he didn't. He's been completely accommodating from the beginning and I get the sense he'll always be that way.

"Oh God, Sarah. Was he okay with it all? He didn't try to change your mind, did he?"

"Nope. He was very amiable once he got over the surprise. He assumed we'd be having sex, so it was a bit of a shock to him. Honestly, it was a fair assumption."

"Well, I thought you'd be doing it that way when you told me about AJ." I can hear the smile in her voice. "So now you wait?"

I sink back farther into the couch, lifting my foot to rest on the cushion. "Actually. He did some research about trying to get pregnant and suggested we meet again in two days. We're going to repeat the process on Wednesday and maybe again on Friday but we didn't get that far yet." I can't keep the excitement out of my voice.

"Oh wow," she breathes. "He's serious about helping you."

"Yep. I can't believe how lucky I am."

"I'm so happy for you. I hope you're on your way to being pregnant as we speak."

"Me too." My heart twinges at the thought of not getting to spend more time with AJ. *Stupid heart!*

"You're going to be such a great mom. I'm proud of you, Sis."

Emotions clog my throat and I nod. "That means a lot coming from you, Em." I can only hope to be half the mom she is.

"I love you, Sare," she says, her voice soft.

"Love you, too. I'll let you get back to that sexy husband of yours. Talk soon. Mwah!"

"Mwah. Talk soon. Take it easy."

"I will." I press the red button, drop my phone to the cushion beside me, and stare at the doorway to the second bedroom. Maybe one day, sooner than I thought, I'll have a baby asleep in the gorgeous crib Emma passed on to me. I sigh at the thought. My phone buzzes.

MEL

I'm waiting

How did it go?

ME

It went really well. Everything was smooth and easy

MEL

He didn't mind that he had to use a condom
devil face

ME

Not at all. He was great about everything. Even walked me to my car

MEL

Awww, he's so sweet. I have everything crossed that you're pregnant

ME

Me too

MEL

Chat later, just got paged x

ME

Okay x

I drop my eyes to my stomach and run my hand over the area. Wishing and hoping.

I almost bounce out of bed as soon as my alarm sounds. It's my Saturday to spend time with the babies in the neonatal

intensive care unit where Mel works. Every second Saturday I get my fill of cuddling tiny babies, thanks to Mel. She's always known how much I love babies, so when she got the position there, she encouraged me to do the volunteer training to become a baby cuddler.

I move through my morning routine, ensuring I tie all of my hair out of the way and choose an outfit to help me stay cool while I'm there because the room is kept warm for the babies. Traffic is light this early and I make it to the hospital with time to spare. I grab the caps I crocheted over the last two weeks, toss the straps of my purse over my shoulder, and make my way inside the enormous building.

After I wash my hands thoroughly all the way up to my elbows, I put on the hospital gown provided over my clothes and secure it, then enter the NICU. The warmth of the room and the sound of machines buzzing and beeping greet me like an old friend, and I inhale the weird, but now familiar scent of antiseptic mixed with baby powder. I scan the room gauging how many babies are here this week. I look forward to my time here cuddling the babies when their families can't. As sad as it is that babies are born needing this additional care, I know they get the best possible attention here. I smile as my eyes land on Mel, and I head in her direction. I'm grateful she encouraged me to join this program, because as good as the cuddling program is for the babies, I get just as much out of it, if not more. In those moments when I'm sitting and cuddling a tiny baby, I'm quiet. My mind is quiet and so is my body. I'm calm and centered as I solely focus on the precious bundle in my arms while I give any comfort I can to the tiny human who needs a little extra love and warmth to flourish.

"Hey, Sare. How are you feeling?"

"Hey. I'm great and ready to get my cuddle on," I say enthusiastically.

She chuckles and leads me over to an incubator. "I'm glad

to hear it. We have baby Robert. He has neonatal opioid withdrawal syndrome. His mom's struggling at the moment with her own issues, so she can't spend as much time with him as she'd like."

My eyes sting as my heart cracks right down the middle. "Oh no. Poor baby." Mel nods. She reaches in and carefully collects him along with all of his tubes and wires, nodding toward the chair off to the side. I take a seat and get comfortable for my cuddle session. She places Robert in my arms gently and his weight is barely negligible. "Oh my gosh, he's tiny."

She nods. "Yeah, it's common for these babies. You'll notice he's a little yellow too. He desperately needs this contact."

I tuck him in close to my body and get lost in studying his little face. His fair eyebrows, which are almost invisible because they're so pale, to his long eyelashes, and his little cheeks. When I finally glance up, Mel's busy dealing with a baby on the other side of the room.

Another nurse comes over, checking his chart and then her watch, ensuring he's comfortable and everything is still connected properly. The nurses are always incredibly vigilant. They must go home from their shift beyond exhausted, I know Mel does. This job takes such an incredible amount of concentration. I don't know how they do it and not get attached to each baby who spends time here.

I rock the chair back and forth slightly, rubbing his back gently with steady strokes, keeping him tucked in close to make sure he gets the maximum possible benefit from me. I chuckle as tiny creases form between his brows, his little eyes moving from side to side beneath closed lids. "What are you dreaming about, Robert?" I murmur.

At the end of my time, I reluctantly hand Robert back to Mel and she places him carefully back inside the incubator.

"Thanks for coming today, Sare. And thanks for the new caps. They're so cute."

"Aww, it's always my pleasure. I love coming here, you know that."

"I know." She smiles at me.

I glance down at Robert—such a sweet baby—and wonder what his future holds.

I gently rub my finger over his soft downy hair, wishing him well with my whispered words. Then Mel closes the small window to help keep his environment stable, while my heart cracks as I say goodbye.

CHAPTER 11

—sarah—

I DON'T THINK I'VE EVER SEEN MY BROTHER SO HAPPY. IN FACT, I *know* I've never seen him this happy. Molly has been the best thing to ever happen to him, and I'm thrilled they found each other. It's been so much fun helping Max and Molly prepare for today; everything looks simply stunning with the late afternoon sun shimmering on the ocean as a backdrop. I can't wait to see my brother's face when he lays eyes on his almost-wife in her wedding gown. Em and I were with her when she chose it and she looked spectacular. I can't imagine how gorgeous she looks with her hair and makeup done as well.

Cristo sits beside me, kissing each of my cheeks. "Geia sas ómorfi kopéla."

"Hi, Cristo." I chuckle. "I have no idea what you just said."

He gives me his cheeky smile. "Hello, beautiful lady."

Heat rises to my cheeks. "Thank you. You're looking handsome today."

He pretends to dust lint from his dark pants, a proud smirk on his face, so much like Theo's. "Why thank you." He tips his head.

"I bet Kenny was excited today."

"Oh"—he raises his thick brows—"she was. She'll be the prettiest flower girl."

"Yes, she will."

"Can I please sit next to you, Aunty Sarah?" Austin asks sweetly.

I pat the empty seat next to mine. "Of course. I was hoping you'd keep me company."

He makes himself comfortable and then takes my hand. "Thank you. I wanted to say hello to Uncle Max, but Mommy said he was busy right now."

I chuckle as the music changes and Max's head snaps toward the sand dune. Kenny and Holly are the first to crest the top, looking as pretty as ever in matching blush pink dresses. As the girls reach the chairs, Kenny breaks away and leaps for Max. He catches her easily, his smile as bright as I've ever seen. The muscle behind my ribs tightens with a sense of longing so strong, that it's almost crippling. I suck in a breath to gain control and look back toward the dune waiting for Molly. My breath freezes as she crests the dune. She's beyond stunning on an ordinary day, but she looks like a goddess today. I glance back at my brother and I'm surprised his tongue isn't dragging in the sand at his feet. His eyes are locked on her in a way I could only dream of having a man look at me.

"Wow," I whisper, and Cristo nods.

"Panemorfi," he whispers with a soft breath. "Gorgeous."

I can't peel my eyes away as Max leaves his spot to meet Molly. As I would expect, he kisses her, and with matching smiles, they walk toward the celebrant together. As they exchange their promises, I wipe away my tears. First Emma and Theo blew me away with their beautiful love and now my brother has found his. I'm happy for both of my siblings but I can't help the thoughts that whisper to me that I may never have what they have. I need to make peace with it and stop hoping for something that's unlikely to happen. I had my chance, but I chose my family, friends, and job over it. I guess that says it all.

If I wasn't prepared to walk away from everything for Michael, then maybe the relationship wasn't the right one. Surely if I felt more for him—that deep, deep connection—I would have moved to Australia with him.

Cheers erupt and I'm startled from my thoughts. Molly and Max are kissing, and I'm pretty sure if there weren't an audience my brother would be doing a lot more than that. I rise from my seat, lifting Austin with me so we can cheer along with everyone else.

"Ewwww, why does everyone have to kiss all the time?" Austin scrunches up his face.

I chuckle and tap his nose. "Because they love each other so much."

"I love you and Mommy and Theo and Kenny and Lachlan and everyone else, but you don't see me kissing everyone like that. It's gross." He's quite appalled and I can't stop my laughter.

"One day, Austin, when you're big, you'll meet someone and you'll want to kiss them all the time."

He crosses his arms. "No I won't," he says.

"We'll see." I wink at him and place him on his feet. "Come on." I hope he does. I hope he finds a love as true as his mom has with Theo and Max has with Molly. Holding his hand I lead him forward so I can congratulate my brother and new sister. *New sister!* I'm ecstatic that we get to keep Molly in our family.

Austin and I join the line to congratulate the newly married couple. Max has Molly's hand in his, and I notice he's not letting go as each guest congratulates them. I chuckle as I reach my brother. "Are you going to let her go?"

He looks at me as if I've grown two heads. "Nope. Never."

"Okay." I wrap my arms around him, pulling him in as

close as possible. "I'm so happy for you, Max. So happy you found your forever love." I lay a kiss on his cheek and pull back, wiping a stray tear—damn emotions.

"You know it'll happen for you, Sare." I nod, ensuring he sees my smile because I don't want to put a downer on his mood. I squeeze his arm and move across to Molly.

"Welcome to our family, Molly." I almost squeal as I embrace her, careful not to crush her gorgeous dress. "I'm so happy to be able to call you my sister." I lean in and kiss her cheek, her free hand wrapping around me, holding me close.

"I'm so blessed to have joined such a wonderful family. Thank you for always making me feel welcome." We squeeze each other before I move away and let Max's soccer friends have their turn to congratulate the pair.

My phone vibrates in my purse.

AJ

How are you feeling?

A smile touches my lips. Each evening, he's messaged to check on me. He knows I won't know if I'm pregnant yet, but he still checks on me. I can't believe the guy's still single, to be honest. He seems quite the catch.

ME

I'm feeling just fine

Thank you for checking in with me but I won't have news for another 8 days

AJ

I know but I like to check on you

How's the wedding?

ME

Beautiful. My brother is so happy

The dots bounce, then stop. I wait and watch for a message but nothing comes, so I tuck my phone back inside my purse. It vibrates as I sit while Max and Molly sign the legal documents with Mom and Martin as witnesses.

AJ

Have fun

ME

Thanks. Enjoy your weekend

AJ

Are you doing anything over the weekend?

ME

Not really. Family lunch on Sunday

AJ

Did you want to catch up?

I almost drop my phone when I read his message. I already like him too much. If I spend time with him outside of trying to get pregnant, I'm not sure I'll be able to keep the distance I need to maintain between us. I'm already struggling and I haven't spent all that much time with him.

AJ

We could go to the beach or something. Let me know

I'll leave you alone to enjoy the wedding. Talk later

I blow out a breath. He generously gave me time to think it over.

"Is that the guy who's helping you?" Em's voice breaks into my thoughts.

I drag the phone to my chest to hide the screen, not that I need to, she already read the message. "Uh, yeah."

She raises her eyebrows. "He wants to catch up, huh?" She nudges me. "The beach." She wiggles her eyebrows and then spins around to Theo and the kids. "Who wants to go to the beach tomorrow?"

The kids cheer. "Yay. Me!"

She turns back to me, smiling. "Better text him back and invite him along." She finishes with an innocent look and spins on her heel to return to Theo's side. Damn Emma, stirring the pot.

"I'm not inviting him to the beach with the family." I rest my hands on my hips, I glance down at the kids. "He's just a *you-know-what* donor." I raise my brows at my sister.

She smiles at me. "If you say so. But I'd like to meet him. Invite him along."

I move closer to her and lower my voice. "Only if you promise not to invite Mom and Dad. You know how she gets, and I don't want to scare him off. I need his help. And you're not allowed to say anything either."

"I promise. Now text him. I want to lay eyes on him and make sure I get a good vibe." Her jaw is set in that stubborn line she gets when she's bound and determined to get her way.

I hold up my hands. "Okay, okay. I'll invite him to the beach tomorrow."

Emma smiles wide and claps her hands together as Theo watches on, shaking his head. He lays a kiss on top of her head and her lids drop closed for a second as he whispers something in her ear. She turns toward him, laying a chaste kiss on his lips and I return my attention to my phone.

"Usual beach, usual time?" I ask Em.

"Yep."

I nod and text AJ.

I'm going to the beach tomorrow afternoon with my sister and her family if you would like to join us

Immediately my phone vibrates.

Which beach and what time?

I tell him and he agrees to meet us there. I blow out a nervous breath and glance at my sister, who's watching me like a hawk. I nod and she smiles. She had better not embarrass me or I'll never forgive her.

—aj—

I FINALLY PULL INTO A PARKING SPACE AFTER DRIVING AROUND in the heat for the last fifteen minutes. I glance at my watch. I'm late. I hate being late. It's one of the worst traits. I always aim to be early rather than late. When I left home, I didn't consider how busy it would be at the beach today. I shouldn't be surprised—it's damn hot. I don't know how I'm going to find Sarah and her family among the hordes of people down here.

I tug on my baseball cap, grab my cooler and towel, and head toward the beach. The pavement is hot as hell beneath my flip-flops and the sun is already burning my skin. I hope Sarah's wearing sunscreen because her pale skin must fry. Now to find the red umbrella she said they would have. As I reach the edge of the sand, I shield my eyes and scan the area for a red umbrella. There are at least a dozen red umbrellas scattered from one end of the crowded beach to the other.

I take off toward the first umbrella, studying the people underneath, no Sarah. I continue until I get to the sixth umbrella and finally lay eyes on the woman who always seems to be on my mind. I'm not sure if it's because I was with her every second evening last week and haven't laid eyes on her at all this week, but I can't get her off my mind.

She hasn't noticed me yet because she's busy building a sandcastle in the shade with a little girl, while two boys, which look to be a little older, eat apple slices. They look as though they've been here a while already. Sarah glances up, spotting me and preventing further observation, so I step forward. She stands, brushing sand from her butt and thick thighs as she steps forward to greet me, her eyes skating around her sister's family. She's told me a little about them, so I at least feel I know who each person is.

She smiles at me. "Hey. You found us."

"Yeah. I had no idea it would be so busy. I'm sorry I'm late. I had trouble finding a parking space and then ..." I point to the red umbrella. "There are quite a few red umbrellas." I chuckle mildly.

She shields her eyes and peers around. "Oh. Sorry about that."

I step into her space and lean down to press a light kiss to her cheek in greeting, then glance around at her family. Her sister and brother-in-law are watching us closely. Emma's lips are tipped up slightly at the edges as she watches my interaction with Sarah, while Theo appears ready to land me on my ass. Shit, maybe I shouldn't have kissed her. Sarah pulls away abruptly, then turns toward her family.

"Uhm, this is AJ. This is my sister, Emma." I step forward to shake her hand, only she pulls me in for a hug while her husband continues to give me the evil eye.

"Hi, AJ. It's nice to meet you."

"You too. You and Sarah look a lot alike. I think I would pick you as sisters even if I didn't know you guys."

"Oh, you're so sweet! Obviously, Sarah's the beautiful one." She chuckles.

"Peaches," Theo growls, moving closer to us.

Sarah blushes but continues with the introductions. "This is her husband, Theo." I move to shake his hand. His roughened palm slides against mine and he squeezes—hard—as he tips his chin.

"Hi, Theo. Nice to meet you."

"We'll see." *Oh-kay* then.

Sarah clears her throat. "And these are their children, Lachlan, Austin, and Kenny." She points to each child as she introduces them.

The boys wave at me from their position, but Kenny jumps up and wraps her arms around my legs. "Hello, Uncle AJ!"

Sarah and Emma laugh while Theo glares at his little girl. I'm not quite sure what to do, so I pat the back of her head. She seems like a sweet kid. His glare moves up to me and then he glances at his wife, who smiles widely at him. He shakes his head and moves closer to her, landing a kiss on her forehead and I only wish I had the privilege to do the same with Sarah.

Kenny tugs my hand. "I want to go for a swim."

I place my cooler down and glance up at the others.

"We were about to head into the water. Boys, are you ready to get wet?" Emma asks.

"Yeah. Let's go!" The youngest boy, Austin, jumps up.

Theo grabs a pair of wings and heads straight for Kenny. "Not before you put on your water wings."

"I don't need them anymore, Daddy." His eyes go soft when she says his name, a marked difference from how he was just looking at me. "I'm a big girl now."

He turns toward Emma. "What do you think?"

"I think Kenny can go without, so long as she stays in the shallow part." She looks pointedly at the little girl. "There are four adults here to watch the kids."

Sarah and I nod as I drop my towel and remove my flip-flops.

"Okay." Theo relents, and Kenny jumps up and down with

the glee of a young child who's managed to get her way. She grabs my hand, pulling me forward.

"Come on. Let's go."

"Hang on, Kenny. Mommy and I need to take off our coverups and you need to take off your shorts," Sarah tells the little dynamo.

Sarah pulls her coverup over her head, revealing a teal bikini. It's the most exposed I've seen her, and as amazing as she looks dressed, this may be my favorite. I grasp the back of my neck as I scan her curves. I can't stop the images of my hands gliding smoothly up those thick thighs of hers, across her soft stomach, to her luscious tits which are almost spilling out of the cups. She adjusts the straps, making them jiggle, and I struggle to tear my eyes away.

Glancing around the beach, I decide I don't want every asshole to see what will hopefully be mine one day. I drag my T-shirt over my head and hand it to her. "Here, you need to cover up out there." I point toward the water. Theo and Emma burst into laughter, and I feel I've missed out on some family joke.

"I don't need it. Thanks." She scowls at me, then turns her angry eyes toward her sister and brother-in-law.

Shit! I need to come up with a reason so she'll cover those damn curves. "You'll get sunburned. I felt as though I was getting burned just walking from my car."

"I'm wearing sunscreen. I don't need to cover up, thanks." She snips, grasping Kenny's hand and heading toward the water, leaving the rest of us behind. I admire her shapely ass as she makes her way across the sand. Austin jumps up to follow, and Theo shakes his head at me.

"I feel your pain, brother." He slaps me on the shoulder and takes Lachlan's hand to lead him to the water.

I grasp the back of my neck and look at Emma. "Did I say the wrong thing?"

She chuckles. "Not at all. You were being … *thoughtful.* Right?"

Well, I wouldn't call it that exactly. But I'll go with that so I don't sound like the asshole I seem to have become. "Yeah. It's not fun being sunburned."

"And I'm sure that's all you were worried about." She laughs and heads toward the water, so I follow close behind.

Austin and Kenny are having a blast, splashing each other and the adults in the process. I notice Lachlan is on the periphery, avoiding the splashes, but he's watching Austin and Kenny closely with a half-smile and I can tell they're being careful not to splash him. Theo wraps his arm around Emma and pulls her in close, not taking his eyes from the kids. They talk and chuckle quietly together and I move closer to Sarah.

"Uh, sorry about before. I didn't want your pale skin getting burned."

She glances across at me. "That's okay, but I can look after myself. I've been doing it for quite some time now."

"I get that. But I do consider us at the very least … friends. What sort of friend would I be if I didn't look out for you?"

She smiles at me then, and I take a full breath. I didn't like feeling as though things weren't right between us. "Friends? Is that what we are?"

"I'd like us to be friends at least." I point to her stomach. "Even once you're pregnant, I'd like to spend time together. I … uh …" I grasp the back of my neck and her eyes snap to my bicep. I tense it and smile internally when her tongue darts out to lick her lips. "I like spending time with you." Maybe she's not as unaffected by me as she portrays.

I drop my arm and her eyes slide back to my face. "I'd like that too." She glances around, tightness building around her eyes and mouth. "Does that mean you want to be part of the child's life?"

I'm hoping I'll be part of both of their lives, but she seems averse to a relationship, so I shrug, playing off the importance. "Whatever works best for you, Sarah. I'm not going back on our agreement or anything like that. You're the one in charge here." She nods thoughtfully and some of the tightness dissipates. I need to lighten the mood. I don't want her to change her mind and look elsewhere for a donor. "So, do you guys spend much time at the beach?"

She glides her hands through the water at her waist. "Oh yeah. We usually try to get down here as a family as many times as our schedules allow during the summer. How about you?"

"Yes and no. I like to climb, so I sometimes wake early and head out to some of my favorite climbing spots when the weather allows, then I tend to take a dip in whatever water's close by to cool off," I explain.

Her eyes skim my body, pausing on my abdomen, then traveling over my arms. "Well, that explains how defined you are considering you spend your days behind a computer."

I chuckle and glide my hand down my torso, her eyes following the path. "Thanks for noticing." I give her a wink and her cheeks turn pink. A splash of cold water against my back breaks our moment, and I spin around to catch the culprit trying to run away as she giggles. I chase after her, pretending to fight my way through huge waves to get to her. When I catch Kenny, I lift her out of the water as she giggles and wiggles, kicking her feet. I throw her up in the air and catch her, her giggles growing louder by the second as I drop her gently back into the water and splash a small amount of water at the sweet girl.

She squeals as she runs away, dropping down to paddle through the shallow water. "Ahhhh, Uncle AJ got me but I escaped. I'm a superhero like Black Widow!"

"Well, that makes a change from her usual princesses." Sarah giggles, raising her eyebrows at her sister.

"Yeah, in the last week or so, she's been watching the Marvel movies with the boys. Normally, she leaves the room and plays with her dollhouse when the boys are watching the movies, but she's been staying. She's hooked!"

"I'm hungry, Mommy," Lachlan calls out to Emma, still keeping a safe distance from the action.

"Okay, let's get out and get something to eat."

We all head out of the water and back to our spot, Emma and Theo working together, along with Sarah to organize the kids. I readjust the umbrella to ensure the blanket and chairs are shaded, keeping up my ruse that I'm concerned about sunburn. As I watch Sarah with the kids; I know she's going to make a great mom. She obviously has a strong bond with her niece and nephews because there's a level of comfort between them that shows how much they love each other. Much like me and Colton.

After we've finished eating, the girls head to the bathroom with Austin and Kenny in tow, leaving me alone with Theo and Lachlan. As soon as the girls are out of sight, Theo's eyes snap to me.

"So, AJ, explain to me what sort of man offers to help a stranger in a club to get pregnant." His eyes bore into me and I swallow. The guy is freaking intimidating. I thought we had a moment before, but clearly, I was mistaken.

I glance around, then look him square in the eye. "Look, I'm going to be completely honest with you, but it has to stay between us. Do I have your word?"

He nods but keeps his lips sealed.

I grasp the back of my neck and then draw in a deep breath, hoping the guy doesn't think I'm some kind of psycho. "I saw her in the club and thought she was stunning. Not gonna lie, those curves drew me right in." He nods in agreement. Obviously, we have similar tastes because Emma has the same feminine body shape. "When I overheard her speaking with her friend about wanting a baby, I thought I'd take the opportunity to speak with her about it. Let's face it, the woman is way out of my league and I'm pretty sure she wouldn't look twice at me if it weren't for my …" I skate my eyes across to Lachlan and then down to my groin area, hoping he gets my meaning. "I helped my sister and her wife get pregnant, so I knew I could help her. And … well … I'm hoping if she spends enough time with me, she'll get to know me and want to stick around." I shrug as though my confession is no big deal.

Theo's entire body relaxes for the first time since I arrived and he nods. A slight tilt of his lips makes me relax too. "Just don't hurt her. Okay."

I hold up my hands in surrender. "Never. It's not even something I remotely want to do."

Emma, Sarah, and the kids return ending our chat and we spend the rest of the afternoon building sandcastles, getting wet, and having fun. It's possibly the most fun I've had in ages and as I get to know Emma and her family I think Hayley, Lisa, and Colton would like them too. I think our families would blend well together. Which reminds me.

"Theo, Sarah was telling me you're a carpenter."

He smiles. "Yeah. That's right."

I collect my phone and open the photo app. Turning it around, I show Theo the photo I have of the climbing wall I was looking at for Colton. "My nephew is three and he's a climber. He's driving my sister and her wife crazy, so I said I'd look into getting him a climbing wall for their backyard." He takes the device and studies the pic, showing it to Lachlan. "Do you think you could build the frame? I'll add the climbing holds."

He and Lachlan share a smile. "We sure can. This is an easy A-frame. We could use cedar and pine for this. What do you think, Lachlan?"

He nods. "Yeah, this looks pretty easy."

Theo returns my phone. "We should be able to build this for you. When did you want it? I have a couple of orders I'm working on at the moment."

"Whenever you can squeeze it in."

"No problem. I'll grab your number from Sarah when we're ready to start."

"Thanks. Appreciate it."

CHAPTER 13

—sarah—

A FAMILIAR, HEAVY FEELING FILLS ME WITH DISAPPOINTMENT. Slight cramps and pain in my lower back deliver the news that I failed once again. That my body is still completely my own and I won't be sharing it with another life for at least another month. With already two failed attempts through the fertility clinic and now this one, I'm wondering if my dream will ever become a reality. I head straight to the bathroom to deal with it and mentally prepare myself for worsening cramps later this afternoon and tonight.

As I sort myself out, I remind myself it takes time to get pregnant, that it can take up to two years, but I'm worried I'm running out of time. My inner voice reminds me I can't decide one day I want a baby and it'll happen straight away, but that rational thought doesn't stop the sheer disappointment and anxiety. Running my fingers through my hair, I drag the elastic band from my wrist and tie it up in a ponytail, then grab the next load of washing.

If I can't get pregnant, is that a sign from the universe that I shouldn't be a mother? I know I want to be a mom. I know I love kids and the idea of a biological child, a child that's genetically part of me is a yearning so deep in my soul, it's something I can't ignore.

My phone vibrates with a text. It'll either be Emma or Mel checking to find out if I got my period and I'm not ready to admit my failure to anyone yet, so I ignore it. I know they mean well and I'm thankful for their support, but I need time to wrap my head around it before I share the news with anyone else, no matter how well-meaning they are. It vibrates again, so without looking at the screen I flip it over and tuck it beneath the couch cushion.

Cramping in my lower abdomen increases as the afternoon wears on, so I grab the heat pack and throw it in the microwave to heat, take a couple of Midol, and grab the bar of chocolate I allow myself for such an occasion. My phone vibrates again, but I ignore it.

Making myself comfortable on my couch, I grab my supplies and begin working on another cap to build up a fresh collection for my next volunteer shift. Choosing the super-soft pink yarn, I get lost in the stitches and rows, nibbling on my chocolate in between. Before I know it, the cap is finished and I'm ready to fasten off. I leave a six-inch tail, cut the yarn, and pull it through the final loop, tightening the end. Knowing I'm helping a tiny baby who's struggling in his or her first few weeks of life gives me a sense of satisfaction each time I complete a cap. I'm sure it seems trivial to some, but I love that I'm helping even the tiniest bit.

A knock sounds on my door, startling me. I frown as I run through my plans for this weekend. I'm not expecting anyone unless Emma got sick of waiting for me to return her text. Mel's working, so I know it's not her. As I swing the door open, I start with my excuse. "Em—" My words die on my tongue as I lay eyes on the one and only AJ. He's holding up a bag of takeout which smells delicious as he gives me a sexy smile.

"Sorry. Not Emma," he announces as he steps inside,

pressing his soft lips to my cheek, his bristles a stark contrast against my skin. He wanders into my home as though he's my best friend and drops by all the time.

I shake myself out of my stupor to close the door and follow him in. "Uh, what are you doing here? More importantly, *how* do you know where I live?"

I narrow my eyes when I meet him in my kitchen as he opens and closes cupboards in search of something. "Where do you keep … oh, here they are." He grabs two plates and places them on the counter. "I'm a hacker, Sarah. Or did you forget? It took me all of thirty seconds to find you." He reminds me as he raises a single brow while continuing with his quest to serve dinner for both of us, as if it's no big deal he's turned up at my apartment completely unannounced and unexpectedly. So far I haven't picked up on any psycho vibes, but maybe I missed them.

I cross my arms and clear my throat. "Please tell me how you being a hacker explains why you've turned up on my doorstep on a Saturday night with dinner?"

"You didn't answer my texts. The fact you didn't, suggests you started your period. I thought I'd come and keep you company since I figured you're probably feeling disappointed." My heart stutters at his thoughtfulness. He scoops equal amounts of food onto each plate as I watch the play of the muscles in his forearms. *Tasty*. And I'm not talking about the food.

As sweet as his gesture is, this wasn't part of the deal, and I can't afford to spend additional time with him outside of our arrangement. It was bad enough sharing the afternoon with him at the beach. Watching him play with my niece and nephews as though he'd known them all their lives. Having his eyes caressing every single inch of my body. Yes, I felt them. He thought he was being discreet behind those aviators of his, but I felt the burn of his gaze as though he'd traced my flesh with his fingers. It was too much. My heart's already trying to engage. Then I had to deal with Emma swooning over how handsome he is and maybe I should reconsider my methods for getting pregnant.

I'm baffled as to how he thought I'd be okay with him knowing where I live. I thought I'd made it clear I wasn't prepared to have him in my space by using a hotel each time we met. "AJ, can you stop for a minute and look at me." I try to soften my posture, so I uncross my arms, dropping them to my side.

He collects the loaded plates as he looks at me. "Do you mind grabbing the cutlery?"

I huff out a breath but grab the necessary cutlery and follow him to my small dining table. "AJ?"

"If you want me to apologize, I'm not going to. I promised I would support you with your pregnancy plan. This is me supporting you."

The stiffness in my body evaporates and my lips fight to spread in a grin. I think my ovaries are swooning. "Thank you. Even if this is a little … unexpected." Crazy is the word I actually want to use, but he's being thoughtful, sweet even.

"I hope you like Thai. Eat up." He points to my plate with his fork.

My stomach growls at the delicious smell of lemongrass and chili, mixed with the sweet scent of jasmine rice. "I do. Thanks for all this. You really didn't have to. It's not part of our deal." He raises his hand, flicking his wrist as if to erase my words and I take a forkful of the delicious chicken curry with rice, moaning at the flavors. "It's been such a long time since I've had Thai takeout. I'd forgotten how much I love it."

"Good. I figured most people like Thai, and if you didn't like it, I'd just order something different." He takes a bite of food, chews, and swallows; I watch as his Adam's apple bobs. "How are you feeling?"

My mood instantly drops and my shoulders sag forward. "Disappointed would probably be the first word to come to mind, along with a few others. I've spent the day reminding myself these things take time and I need to be patient. That it will all be worth it in the end." I shrug. "I'm also very aware that the longer this takes, the more I'm imposing on your valuable time."

"Well, there's no need to worry about that. None of this is an imposition at all. I told you I'm with you until you get the result you're looking for. I meant it, Sarah."

I nod. *See, Sarah. Remember, he's only in this to get you pregnant. Lock that heart away, girl.*

I need to change the subject before I drown in my thoughts. "Did you go climbing today?"

"Yeah. I have this place that's not too far out of the city; I visit whenever I can. It has a couple of different routes that vary in difficulty, so it's a favorite of mine."

Vivid images of AJ, shirtless and glistening with sweat fill my mind. His muscles straining and shifting as he scales a rock face; the sheer masculine strength required to pull your body weight upward against the forces of gravity. My eyes drop to his sexy forearms and hands, imagining his skilled fingers working over my body. Heat fills my face and I push back from the table. "Uh, did you want a glass of water?"

AJ chuckles. "Sure. Thanks."

Placing a glass of water in front of AJ and one in front of my dinner, I take my seat again and try to block out the images of him reaching for his next hold, instead concentrating on eating my meal.

"This is a nice place."

I lift my eyes, glancing at AJ while he studies my apartment. "Thank you. It's small but it's cozy and it's all mine. Well, it mostly belongs to the bank, but it'll be all mine one day."

He grins and tips his chin toward my couch. "Are you making another cap?"

I glance across and smile. "Yeah. I delivered my last batch this morning during my shift. So now I have to start all over again."

He tilts his head. "Your shift?"

"Yeah, at the NICU."

AJ's eyebrows shoot up. "Really? I thought you were a corporate secretary."

I chuckle. "Yeah, I am. But every second Saturday I volunteer at the NICU as a baby cuddler."

"I had no idea people could do that. I bet it's incredible. I used to love holding Colton when he was a newborn. Not that I don't love cuddling him now that he's bigger, but there was something so special about holding him when he was tiny and fragile. He needed the adults around him to keep him safe and to provide for all his needs. It was really special to be part of his inner circle."

I nod as he shares his experience, my heart expanding at the obvious love he has for his nephew. "Yeah, it's amazing. The babies are incredibly tiny and all they need is a little extra help to get to where they need to be. Parents can't be with their baby twenty-four-seven because they may already have other children at home, or they may still be recovering themselves. So the extra hands, or should I say warm bodies, is a big help."

"You sound like you really love it."

"I do. As much as I do it to help the babies, I find I get as much from the experience. While I'm there with the babies, I'm not thinking about anything else. I'm completely in the moment with them." AJ nods. "There's a certain quiet that settles over me when I'm cuddling the newborns."

"Climbing does that for me. It centers my mind and my body. I can only focus on what I'm doing, the next hold, staying safe, and moving forward. It takes all of my focus. I find it helps me with my work, too."

I tilt my head to the side. "How so?"

"Climbing has taught me to plan out my steps and stay focused on the task at hand."

"Interesting. So, how long have you been climbing?"

AJ stands, collecting our empty dishes. "Probably about five years or so. It was a little while after I finished my studies when Dylan and I were getting our business up and running. I used to find it hard to stay on track with my tasks, always getting distracted by some other unimportant task that could wait. A friend was getting married and as part of his bachelor party, we did a couple of hours of indoor rock climbing and I loved it. I started going once every few weeks and my interest grew from there. Once I noticed the difference in my work, I made it a habit and built it into my schedule." He fills the kitchen sink and proceeds to wash the dishes like it's the most natural thing in the world to do.

"I can do the dishes since you brought dinner." I try to nudge him out of the way so I can take over but he doesn't budge.

"It's no problem, Sarah. There are less than ten items." He elbows me out of the way, so I scoop up some of the bubbles from the sink and flick them at him. His eyes widen and a mischievous grin takes over his face and I know I'm in trouble. "Oh, it's on!" He scoops out some bubbles and flicks them at me, covering the front of my left boob. His eyes drop to where the bubbles are disintegrating, leaving a wet patch on my white tank and making my nipples pebble. "Shit! Sorry." His wide eyes glance up to my face, then drop back down when I wipe the spot, making my breast jiggle. It's only then I realize that by doing so, I've pressed the fabric against my flesh, making my peaked nipple visible through the flimsy fabric.

I chuckle, turning my back to him. "Don't worry, I totally

started that. I'm just going to quickly change, so I'm not flashing you."

"I don't mind. You can flash me all you want." He winks and I head for my bedroom, chuckling. As I search through my drawers for a fresh bra and T-shirt, I can't help but wonder what it would be like to spend all of my Saturday nights like this.

CHAPTER 14

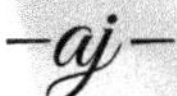

I'm glad I could make her laugh when she must be feeling crappy. I debated, for all of five minutes, whether it would be a good idea to turn up on her doorstep. I hoped she wouldn't think I was some creeper and that she'd let me inside. I figured it would be harder for her to refuse if I brought dinner with me and I was right.

I finish the dishes and make myself comfortable on her couch while I wait for her to change. I would like to say I'm a gentleman and I didn't take advantage of the view her see-through tank afforded me, but I'm not a liar. I pick up the pink yarn resting on the couch, running the strands through my fingers. It's so damn soft. I collect the cap she's left on the coffee table, fitting it over my fist. It's tight, reminding me how tiny a newborn is, and I would imagine the newborns in the NICU are even tinier than Colton was when he was born.

Movement out of my periphery has me glancing up. Sarah's standing just inside her bedroom door, watching me study the cap. "This is really something. How many of these do you make?"

"Depends on what I have going on and if I need to stay

back late at work. But anywhere from five to eight every two weeks. Each one takes me around two hours to make from start to finish. I usually make a little pompom to go on top. They look so cute when they're done."

"Are they hard to make?"

"They were at first because I had to teach myself how to crochet. I had quite a few failures as I mastered the technique. And even now, I'm not the fastest, but it's a great way to wind down and relax while I'm watching TV."

"Could you teach me? I think Colton would like one of these. Maybe I could make one for Hayley and Lisa's new baby too." Her eyes widen and her mouth drops open a little.

"Uh, sure. If you like. Fair warning, I'm not an expert, though."

I pat the seat beside me, soaking in Sarah's fresh spring scent as she sits. She collects a hook thing and some yarn, then spends the next forty minutes trying to teach me how to start, but my fingers are too thick and I'm finding it difficult to get my hands to do what they need to do.

"Hmph, I don't think crochet is for me."

Sarah laughs. "Maybe not. What's Colton's favorite color? I could make him a cap easily enough."

"He loves orange. The brighter the orange, the better."

She chuckles. "I'm pretty sure I saw some fluorescent orange at the store the last time I stocked up on yarn. I'll grab some next time and make him one."

And just like that, Sarah's burrowed herself in a little deeper. Not that she needed to, I'm already so gone for this woman. When she didn't respond to my texts this afternoon, I grew worried. I know how much this means to her and she must be disappointed. This is her third attempt and still no baby. I was going to camp overnight and climb again tomorrow, but as it grew later and I hadn't heard from her, I couldn't stay away. Having her phone number made it easy enough to reverse search for her address. I've put measures in place to ensure others can't find the information so easily. If people knew how much information someone like me can access from only having a phone number, they would be shocked.

"Thanks. He'll love that. Let me know how much everything costs and I'll reimburse you."

"You will not. I'll happily make him one. After everything you're doing for me, it's the least I can do."

I sit forward. "I want to make one thing very clear. You don't owe me anything. Nothing at all. I'm happy to help you."

Her stunning smile falls from her face and her eyes drop to her lap. "I *do* owe you. I owe you so much for your time and your"—she waves her hand around the general area of my cock—"your generosity."

I chuckle. "I'm happy to help." I drop my voice. "I'm sorry it didn't happen this month. We'll start fresh next month. You let me know when we need to start again, and I'll be there."

"Thank you, AJ. I'm not sure what I did to get so lucky." She glances away. "Would you like a cup of hot chocolate? I'm craving chocolate today." She points toward an empty chocolate wrapper on the table.

"Sure."

Sarah makes our drinks and I turn on the television. She pops her head out of the kitchen. "Would you mind leaving it on that channel? It's the finale and I want to see what they bake."

I drop the remote to the couch and Sarah returns with our drinks, her eyes locked on the television screen. "I love baking cupcakes. I bake them for everyone in the office on Thursday nights and take them in on Friday. Sort of a celebration that we've made it through the week."

Is there anything this woman does for herself? She seems to give a lot of time and resources to those around her.

"Oh yeah. I don't mind a cupcake now and then. What's your favorite to bake?"

She ponders my question for a moment. "I love making lemon curd cupcakes if I had to choose one. The smooth lemon center is to die for, especially when they're freshly baked." She smiles. "Though, I try to limit myself to only one cupcake a week."

We get caught up watching the show. The level of comfort and ease between us makes me wonder what it would be like to share every Saturday night with Sarah. What would it be like to watch her make cupcakes every Thursday evening, cleaning up the mess for her while she decorates the tasty treats? The fantasy of living with her plays on a reel in my mind and the idea is wholly appealing. I can't see a downside to sharing a place with her, which is a concept I never imagined I would find attractive. Watching her while she watches the final minutes of the show, riveted to her seat as she waits for the winner to be announced, I decide I want to make it happen. I want to have Sarah living with me. Probably in my space. As nice as her apartment is, it would be too small for a family.

The show ends and Sarah turns to me. "I think I'm addicted to baking shows."

I shrug. "There are worse things you could be addicted to."

"That's what I tell myself."

I peek at my watch. It's getting late but I'm not ready to give up my time with Sarah yet. "Did you want to watch another episode?"

"You don't mind?"

"Not at all."

We spend the next hour watching the first episode of the next season and as fascinating as it is to watch, I would rather watch Sarah's interest in the program. She yawns for what must be the fifth time, letting me know that my time with her is coming to an end tonight.

As the credits roll, Sarah turns to me. "Thanks for indulging me."

"You're welcome. I've never seen the show before. I had no idea there were cupcake-making competitions." I chuckle as I stand, collecting our empty cups and heading toward the kitchen to clean up. Once I've rinsed the cups and placed them on the dish rack to dry, I step back into the living room as Sarah stands. She's rubbing across her stomach with a grimace. "Are you okay?"

"Yeah. Just cramps. They're always worse the first night. I'll take some more Midol and heat up the heat pack before I climb into bed." She moves closer to me. "Thanks for coming over and keeping me company."

"No problem. Are you doing anything for the Fourth?" Maybe I can see her at some point.

"I'll be spending tomorrow with my sister and her family to help set up for a party on Monday with friends and family. You?"

Damn. I tuck my hands in my pockets to stop myself from tucking the loose strands of hair that have fallen out of her ponytail behind her ear. "I'll be catching up with the family on Monday, too."

She walks me to the door and my mood drops considerably, knowing our time has come to an end and I won't see her until she's ovulating. "Have a great time with your family. Bye, AJ, and thanks again." She opens the door and I shuffle through, not wanting to leave. I lean forward, pressing my lips to her cheek, inhaling her subtle scent as I do.

"Enjoy the rest of your weekend. Bye, Sare." I tip my head and give her a final wave, disappointed I can't do more than that.

CHAPTER 15

—aj—

"AJ!" M OM GUSHES AS SHE ALMOST RUNS TOWARD ME WITH HER arms outstretched. "It's so good to see you." I know I don't visit her as much as she'd like, but she's acting like she hasn't seen me all year, rather than the month since our last family dinner. I've been avoiding family events like this one because I'm tired of dealing with my grandfather.

"Mom." She pulls me in tight, kissing my cheeks.

"I've missed you so much." She pulls back, her hands on my biceps. "You're looking well. Healthy. Happy."

"Thanks, Mom. I'm making sure I eat better and the climbing helps me keep in shape." She nods, securing her hold on my arm and pulling me through my grandparents' home and out to the backyard which overlooks the bay. It's a stunning property, but Hayley and I could never just be kids and jump in the pool or run around the massive space inside. I mean they have a damn ballroom for God's sake. I'm not sure how my mother grew up here as an only child. I can't imagine she would have been allowed to have any fun. My earliest memories of spending time here always include the constant shushing and being told we weren't allowed to do this or touch that. We basically weren't allowed to be kids whenever we visited.

"Adam, look, AJ's here," Mom calls out to Dad as if he didn't already know I'd arrived, but Mom's being over the top today for some reason.

"Unca AJ!" Colton calls as he comes running for me. I crouch down to catch him before he's shushed or told to slow down.

"Hey, little man. How's my boy?"

Mom's hand flies up to her chest as she gives Colton a tight smile. "Oh, do you think it's appropriate to call him *'your boy'*?"

I frown at Mom. "What do you mean?"

"Well, he might get confused. You know with you being his biological f-a-t-h-e-r and all." She widens her eyes to make her point.

"It's just a phrase, Mom. Don't stress. But the girls will tell him who I am to him once he's old enough to understand. It's not going to be some big secret."

Colton claps his hands. "You're my bestest unca!"

I chuckle. "I'd better be your bestest! I'm your only uncle."

Mom chuckles nervously as Dad steps closer. I hold out my free hand to Dad. "Hey, Dad."

"Son. Good to see you. Life looks like it's been treating you well."

I readjust Colton, holding him more firmly. "Thanks. Life's pretty great at the moment."

"Oh yeah." He raises a dark eyebrow. "Why's that?"

"Dylan and I won the multi-million-dollar contract we were chasing." I desperately want to tell my family I've met the woman of my dreams, but I fear it's too soon—Sarah's still incredibly closed off. Who knows how long it'll take for me to break through her walls? But if I have the patience to hack into some of the world's most secure servers, I have the patience to break through Sarah's firewalls. I smirk at myself.

Dad's smile is swift. "Congratulations, AJ. I'm proud of you, Son."

"Thanks, Dad. We worked hard to position ourselves in such a way to even be considered a contender."

"Good planning is important. Congratulate Dylan for me, too."

"I will."

A hand drops heavily onto my shoulder and my muscles lock. "AJ. I'm happy you could make it. We need to talk."

"Grandfather. We do, but I'm sure it can wait until after lunch."

"No. I think it's best to get business out of the way. Join me in my study, please." I follow him with my eyes as he walks inside expecting me to follow.

I move my gaze back to my parents. Mom is chewing on her bottom lip, tightness pulling around her eyes. "I guess I've been summoned." I place Colton on his feet. "Why don't you go see if Mama will take you for a swim? I'll be back in a minute."

"Okay, Unca AJ!" He takes off toward Hayley, shouting, "Mama. I wanna go for a swim!"

Hayley waves to me and I return the gesture, then turn back to my parents. "What's going on? Has something been said?"

"Your grandfather is growing tired of waiting for you to make a decision."

I huff out a frustrated breath. "I've already given him my decision, but it doesn't stop him from harassing me about it at least once a week."

Dad sighs. "He's an old man, Son. Just humor him. Do what he asks and once he's gone, you can make your own choices."

"I don't want to do that. I have my own business with Dylan, which is growing by the week. I don't want to walk away from it. We've worked damn hard to build it up to where we are today." I wave my arm out toward Mom. "Mom is dying to get in there and take over. She's wanted to be part of it since she was a little girl—"

"It's his business, his decision," Mom says tightly. "Just go and get the conversation out of the way, so we can enjoy a pleasant afternoon as a family. Okay?" I don't know why she's happy to continue being overlooked for the position.

I roll my eyes heavenward. "Okay. But I doubt it will be a pleasant afternoon when I say what needs to be said."

I walk away before Dad can try to convince me to do otherwise. I'm sick and tired of being bullied into a role I don't want. A role I have absolutely zero interest in. My heart pounds and I strengthen my resolve as I close the distance to Grandfather's study—a place that was always off-limits when I was a child.

I blow out a breath as my hand connects with the heavy door to push it open. I'm taken aback when I look at his grand desk to find the chair behind it empty. Skimming my eyes around the spacious room, they land on him standing in front of the window, hands in the pockets of his shorts. It's odd to see him dressed so casually. From my earliest memories, even on weekends, he always wore a suit.

"Grandfather." I step into the middle of the room after closing the door.

He keeps his gaze out of the window. "I'm not getting any younger, you know, boy."

"I know."

"Exactly how long do you intend to make me wait."

As much as my body wants to move, to leave the room, I stay glued to the spot. "I've already told you, Grandfather. I don't want the position. It's something Mom has wanted since she was young. Give it to her. Your company will be in safe hands with her. In fact, she's probably better equipped to manage it than I could ever dream to be."

He turns around to face me, his features drawn tight in anger. "And I've already told you she won't be given the position. It *has* to be you. Stop trying to shirk your responsibilities, boy!" he shouts.

I keep my tone calm. He's been getting progressively angrier each time we have this same discussion, but I'm not prepared to budge. I guess I get my stubbornness from him. "I'm not shirking my responsibilities. I have my own company to run. I've built it from nothing and I'm not prepared to walk away from it or from doing something I love. Especially now we're hitting our stride. I don't consider that shirking my responsibilities."

He moves toward me. "Your responsibility is taking over the family company."

"And Mom is more than happy to take the reins. Give the leadership position to her." I want him to realize this is the twenty-first century and to make decisions accordingly, but we keep having this same argument. I could easily take the company from him and give Mom the position, but I want it to come from *him*. I think it's important that *he* makes that decision. I've seen how hurt Mom is each time he overlooks her and insists I take over. He needs to make it better.

"No."

I blow out a breath and grasp the back of my neck. "We're not living in the nineteen-fifties anymore, Grandfather." Though sometimes I wonder, with the decisions being made by the government. "Women hold CEO positions all the time. It's not uncommon. She would do a fantastic job. You know she would. You're being stubborn."

"Watch your tongue, boy. It's my company, my decision and you'll do as I say or so help me … you'll be out of my will," he snaps at me, spittle flying out of his mouth, reminding me of my place.

He wants me to take over his company but he still treats me like a child. He won't let Mom take over, even though she's been dying to do so since she was young, because, in his eyes, women don't run corporations, they run homes or do menial type work. It's infuriating.

I'm not going to win this conversation today. "Look, I think it would be best to have this conversation another day. This is meant to be a casual family barbecue celebrating the Fourth of July. I'll make time to come into the office and we can have this discussion where it belongs."

"It had better happen sooner rather than later, boy. I'm all out of patience. I want to retire at the end of this year. Do you hear me?"

"Yes, Grandfather. I hear you loud and clear."

CHAPTER 16

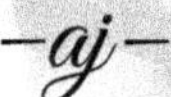

Dylan and I freeze as we step inside the *Cardinal Quarry Casino and Resort* lobby, our overnight bags in hand. Polished brown and cream marble flooring gleams beneath our shoes and I'm pleased we decided to wear suits for this meeting with Mr. Mitchell, the owner. I can't believe we were even on this guy's radar, but this opportunity is beyond our wildest dreams. If we can land this contract, it could open up a whole new world for us because this resort casino is one of many that come under the family's umbrella.

The twenty-minute drive from the airport to here in the complimentary limo sent by Mr. Mitchell to collect us was an unexpected bonus. The air conditioning was a welcome reprieve as we made our way through the city of Las Vegas toward the outskirts. The Mitchell family seems to be pulling out all the stops to impress us when it really should be us working to impress them. They even offered us the opportunity to stay in the hotel overnight free of charge and provided us complimentary chips for the casino. Dylan and I couldn't pass up their offer and opted to return home in the morning, even though our meeting will be well and truly over and done with this afternoon.

A man, much younger than I expected, strides toward us with his arm outstretched and a warm smile. "You must be AJ and Dylan. I'm Charles." I raise my eyebrows and glance at Dylan. "You were probably expecting my father, but he's handing more responsibilities over to me. I hope that won't be an issue."

"No, not at all. Happy to meet you, Charles." I grip his hand.

He shakes hands with Dylan. "Nice to meet you."

"You too. This is a stunning building." Dylan smiles at Charles.

"Thank you. We pride ourselves on offering a luxurious experience from the moment you step foot on one of our properties." He waves his arm out toward the front desk. "Katie, please ensure Mr. Jackson and Mr. Baker's bags are situated in their room."

"Certainly, Mr. Mitchell."

"Please, follow me." We make our way toward the elevator and enter the glass car which has a magnificent view across the desert, showcasing craggy outcrops I'd love to climb one day. When the elevator comes to a stop, we're guided into an office that is equally as impressive as what we've seen so far. "I thought we could get business out of the way first, then I'll show you around before we have dinner."

Floor-to-ceiling windows across the entire office wall overlook the view we just enjoyed in the elevator and I don't want to tear my eyes away. "How do you get any work done with this view?" I ask.

Charles glances out of the window as if to check what I'm talking about. "You know what. I've grown up here and I guess I take it for granted." He shrugs. "I don't even notice it anymore." If I had this office, I'd never get any work done.

He offers us a drink and we get down to business. Three hours later we've signed contracts and set up a schedule of events we'll implement to test the security of the casino's servers. Charles is concerned about the threat of hackers taking over the machines on the floor and the internal banking system they have in place for purchasing and cashing in chips. I can certainly understand his concern because a breach of their security could cost them millions of dollars.

With business out of the way, Charles takes us on a tour of the casino and resort. I'd love to bring Sarah here one day, perhaps for a weekend getaway. The pool area alone is something I've never seen before. The entire facility is tastefully designed and artfully decorated, which is very different from what I was expecting. From what I'd seen of casinos in Vegas, they tend to fall on the gaudy side.

"Well, I'll leave you two to explore." He hands us a keycard each. "I'll meet you in *The Quarry Restaurant* at seven for dinner. Enjoy, gentlemen."

"Thanks, Charles." We both say as we shake his hand in turn.

"This place is incredible," I say, my voice full of awe.

Dylan looks at me. "It's spectacular."

Deciding we want to celebrate our success, we stop at the *Cardinal Bar* and order a couple of local craft beers.

"To us and our success!" Dylan raises his glass, tapping it against mine.

I chuckle at his excitement. "To us, man. Who knew a couple of teenagers could make a career out of breaching firewalls!" We both take a long drink and the balanced salty and tart flavor bursts across my tongue, drawing a moan from me. "That's a nice blend of orange and blackberry."

Dylan nods and we recap some of the most significant points from the meeting and formulate a rough plan to get started.

"So, how are things going with Sarah's plan?" Dylan asks.

I wipe my fingers down the condensation of my glass. "We were unsuccessful last month. We'll try again when she ovulates this month, which I think should be any day now."

"Are you sure this is a good idea?" I give him a what the fuck look and he holds up his hands in surrender. "You seem to be getting attached."

"Yep, I think it's a fantastic idea."

He takes a sip of his beer. "If you're sure."

"I am." I take another drink and turn my head to check out the people around us. My phone buzzes in my pocket, so I grab it.

SARAH

I started ovulating today. Any chance you can come over?

Without thought, I turn to Dylan. "I need to go home. Will you be okay here to handle dinner?" We've finished the actual business part of our meeting, tonight's more about socializing.

His eyebrows scrunch over his eyes. "Why? What's happened? Is everything okay?"

"Yeah, nothing serious but Sarah's ovulating. I need to get home so I can do my part." I stand and finish my beer. Actually, I should check to see if I can get on a flight before I tell her I'm on my way.

"Can't it wait 'til tomorrow?" He's completely confused. And yeah, I probably could tell her I'm out of town and I'll be back tomorrow, but I don't want to. I've missed her and I want to see her.

"Nah. We need to act quickly. There's only a limited window of opportunity." I dig out my phone and call the airline. There's a flight leaving in an hour, then it'll be an hour and a half home, plus the drive; I won't be home for three hours. I check the time—five-thirty. That'll work. "All right. I'll see you when you get home. Have a good night."

"Good luck. What should I tell Charles?" Dylan asks.

"Tell him I had an emergency and I had to get home. It's not a lie," I tell him as I step away.

In the elevator up to our room, I message Sarah.

ME

I'm in a meeting, so I'll see you at 8:30

SARAH

If you're busy, it can wait until tomorrow

ME

I'll be finished by then, see you at 8:30

SARAH

Okay, thank you. Just come to my place

ME

Are you sure?

SARAH

You already know where I live. May as well

One side of my mouth tips up. Yes, I do.

ME

Okay

Arriving on Sarah's doorstep, I draw in a deep breath, then knock on her door. I hear shuffling inside before the door opens revealing Sarah in shorts and a tank, her feet bare with teal nail polish.

She's stunning.

Her smile is immediate when she sees me, so I lean forward and press my lips against her soft cheek, simultaneously dragging a bouquet of flowers from behind my back. As she pulls away from me, her eyes land on the peonies and her smile widens. Mine matches hers without delay.

"Oh, AJ, you didn't have to do this." She leans forward and pecks my cheek and it was worth every penny of the eighty dollars the arrangement cost me from the overpriced shop at the airport. "They're stunning." She drops her nose into the bouquet, drawing in a deep breath. "They smell gorgeous too. My apartment's going to smell fabulous! Thank you so much."

She steps to the side and I enter her cozy apartment, which already smells incredible. She has one of her cooking shows on the television and she was obviously crocheting while she was waiting for me.

"You're welcome."

"Have you had anything to eat?" Sarah asks as she steps into the kitchen, bending down to reach under the sink and giving me a spectacular view of her plump ass. She stands, holding a vase, and looks at me over her shoulder as she fills it with water. I snap my eyes up, but I'm not sure I've done it quickly enough to not get caught.

"Yeah. I had something on the plane," I tell her.

She spins to face me fully, tightness surrounding her eyes. "On the plane? Where were you?"

"Vegas."

"Oh. How come you were there?"

Full of pride, I tell her about our meeting with Charles and how we've secured him as a client, while she arranges the flowers to her liking. Sarah surprises me when she wraps her arms around me, tugging me into her lush body. My hands automatically rise to hold her waist, taking advantage of the opportunity to feel her curves.

"Congratulations! You should be out celebrating with

Dylan, not here with me." She releases me and grabs the vase, placing it on her dining table, then turns toward me with a smile. "Thank you. They're so beautiful."

"I'm glad you like them. Dylan and I were having a drink in the bar when you messaged."

Her sculpted eyebrows draw together, creating creases between them. "I … I hope you didn't leave early to come here … for me." Her words are stilted.

This could go one of two ways if I tell her I left Dylan behind to deal with our client when I was supposed to be there. She's either going to think I'm great for dropping everything to come here when she needed me, or she's going to catch on as to how invested I am. I want to be completely honest with her, though.

"Uh, I left Dylan to finish up. He'll be okay. All of the business stuff had already been sorted. Tonight was more about socializing."

Her eyes widen and she licks her lips. "AJ," she whispers. "You didn't have to do that. We could have done this tomorrow night."

I shrug like it's no big deal. "We can't waste any opportunities. This is important."

"Yeah, but so is your contract." She steps in, wrapping her arms around me, her eyes glassy. "Thank you, AJ. I don't know how I can ever thank you enough for what you're giving me. You left an important meeting to be here for me. I can't believe it." She drops the top of her head against my chest for long moments and I rub soothing strokes down her back because I sense she's having a moment. Having her in my arms is exactly where I want her to be, not because she's overwhelmed with gratitude, but because she wants to be wrapped up in me as much as I want to be wrapped up in her. When she pulls away, she sniffles and steps across to the coffee table to grab a tissue and I miss her immediately. She dabs at her eyes and wipes beneath her nose as she walks back into the kitchen. "Well"—she gives me a shaky smile—"I have something for you. It isn't as grand a gesture, but I made you some cupcakes."

I smile widely and rub my hands together. "Oh yeah! This is my lucky day." This explains the delicious smell which greeted me the minute I stepped inside.

She steps toward me with a plate of incredible-looking cupcakes. "I remembered you said you love apple pie, so I made you apple pie cupcakes." I flick my eyes between the cupcakes and Sarah's face, which is full of expectation. Surely she's not worried I won't like them. "They're not true cupcakes because they have no cake, but how cute are these?" Her eyes widen and meet mine as she finishes.

"They smell incredible and they look fantastic. Do you mind if I have one now?"

"Of course. I made them for you. You can take what's left home with you."

She picks one from the plate and passes it to me. Instead of taking it, I lean forward to take a bite; careful of her fingers but manage to brush them with my lips. Her eyes widen and her pupils dilate. My eyes drop to the pulse point at the base of her throat and I'm pleased to see it hammering as quickly as mine. Good to know I have some impact on the woman.

The sweet but tart flavor explodes on my tongue as the spicy apple scent fills my nose, and I close my eyes to fully appreciate it. When I open them again, Sarah's watching me closely, her lips slightly parted.

"You are a master. This is so good! Have you ever considered going into business and opening a cupcake shop? People would be beating down your door to get their hands on these." I take the cake from Sarah and take another bite, holding my hand beneath my chin to catch the crumbs.

Sarah chuckles. "Nah, that would take the fun out of making them."

I finish the first one, then take another cupcake and make short work of that one too. "I don't know if I can stop at two, but I probably should." I pat my trim stomach. Sarah's eyes drop to watch the action, and I don't think she realizes but her breaths are shallow. It's good to know I have some effect on her because God knows I can't stop thinking about her.

We chat for a while. Superficial talk about how she's been and what I've been up to. I get the impression Sarah wants to keep things shallow between us, not wanting to delve into deeper, more meaningful conversations. I'm happy to play along for now, but I'll slowly work out her code.

There's a lull in the conversation, so Sarah stands. "I have everything set up in the bathroom ready for you. You may as well get started since we both need to get up for work in the morning."

I stand too. "Okay." I step past her and pause in the doorway to the bathroom. "Wish me luck."

"Good luck," she chirps.

I close the door and lean my back against it. I've given up trying not to think about Sarah when I do this. It seems to be my default setting and thinking about her and what she looks like naked is a surefire way to get things happening quickly. I move over to the vanity and grip the edge, studying myself in the mirror. I want her to get pregnant, I do, but once I do, I won't see her again. I'm certain of it. Her walls won't allow her to see the potential of the two of us in a relationship that's more than donor and recipient. I sigh and spin around, grabbing her shampoo out of the shower and flipping open the lid. It smells like Sarah; that gorgeous scent reminds me of a field of spring flowers. I inhale deeply, filling my lungs and my cock wakes.

I unzip my pants and drop them to the floor then remove my boxer briefs, my semi-hard cock dropping into my hand. I sigh. I'd much rather have Sarah's pussy tightening around my shaft … I'd even settle for her hand at this point.

Washing my hands, I open the package containing the collection condom. With my cock in hand, I stroke loosely, bringing him fully to life, then roll on the condom. Resting my hand on the vanity, I drop my head and close my eyes, bringing forth an image of Sarah in her teal bikini. Tightening my grip, I replay the image of her adjusting the straps, making her tits jiggle, and scan my eyes down her soft stomach, to the triangle of fabric between her legs, then down her thick thighs, which I can't wait to have wrapped around my head. I widen my stance and tug on my cock, using my other hand to massage my heavy balls, then slide my fist up and down my length in quick, smooth glides, rolling my fist over the head, careful not to dislodge the condom. I repeat the process several times, my breaths coming sharper, and do my best to hold in my moans.

Doing this myself certainly doesn't give me the level of satisfaction I enjoy when I'm inside a woman, but I'm here to get the job done, not for the enjoyment of the act. I keep stroking to thoughts of Sarah, feeling the fire building through my body until it can no longer be contained and I blow into the condom with a moan, which was probably louder than it should have been in this small apartment. It's not like she doesn't know what I'm doing in here anyway, so long as I don't call her name out loud and make it completely weird between us. My knees weaken and I reach out to support myself on the vanity as I regain my composure. My breathing slowly returns to normal and the haze across my vision clears.

Once I'm back to normal, I carefully remove the condom, balancing it in the sterilized cup Sarah always provides, ensuring I don't inadvertently lose any swimmers. If there's one thing I've learned about the woman is that she's thorough in her planning and extremely organized. I wash my hands and rinse my softening cock, then tuck myself away and redress.

With a cursory check in the mirror, I make sure I look presentable, ensuring my zipper is done up, and step out of the bathroom. Sarah freezes and her head snaps up to my face, her eyes wide and waiting for me to speak.

"All done," I say, forcing brightness into my tone, raising my eyebrows to add to the excitement I don't feel. Don't get me wrong, I'm happy to help, but I would prefer the experience if we were actually getting naked … together.

Sarah's body softens and a smile touches her lips. "Thank you. I feel like those two words aren't enough."

"You don't have to thank me every time we do this. Let's hope we get you pregnant this month." Who am I kidding? I don't want her to get pregnant this month because that'll mean I won't get to see her anymore and I definitely don't want that. I didn't think my feelings would get so damn complicated. "Well, I guess I'll leave you to it." I head for the door.

"Hang on. Don't forget your cupcakes."

"Oh right. Thanks for these," I say as she hands me a Tupperware container full of mini apple pies, which taste like heaven.

We awkwardly say goodbye at the door, and I hear Sarah engage the locks, then I make my way home to my empty warehouse. As soon as I get in the door, I take a minute to download an app to help me track Sarah's cycle. That way I'll make sure I'm always available when she needs me.

ME

Did everything go smoothly?

I grab a beer out of the fridge while I wait for her response.

SARAH

I don't know how to tell you this, but I dropped the cup and lost everything on my hardwood floor

I read the message again and again, as I head back out of my front door. With almost zero traffic on the road, it doesn't take me long before I'm knocking on Sarah's front door for the second time tonight.

"Hello." Sarah's voice is unsure and muffled through the door.

"It's me." The locks immediately disengage and a wide-eyed Sarah stands before me in pajama shorts and a camisole, sans bra. My cock immediately wakes at the sight. Fuck! It looks as though she's been crying.

"You didn't have to come back," she whispers.

I can't console her because that will mean touching her and I'm barely holding onto my control, so I step past her. "I know, but you only have a limited window, and I didn't want to waste an opportunity. Do you have another condom?" I have to keep moving and not linger because if I look at her in her current state, I may throw caution to the wind and take her to bed.

It must finally register what I'm here to do because she closes the front door and walks into the bathroom. She efficiently sets everything up and then stops for a moment. "Thank you so much." She swallows and I can see her eyes becoming glassy. "I can't believe you came back." Her whispered words are heartfelt and I hope she's beginning to realize I would do anything for her.

I can't resist any longer and cup her face in my hands. "I'll always come when you need me, Sarah." Her bottom lip trembles and I press my thumb to it before I press my lips to it. "Now, let's get this done, so you can do your thing." I wink at her and press a light kiss on her forehead.

Stepping back, she nods and says, "Okay," as she closes the door behind her.

I blow out a long breath and drop my eyes down my body to the bulge behind my zipper. I sigh heavily and get down to business. I don't need to imagine Sarah in her bikini because I have new material to work with now. Those pajamas were something else. My cum fills the condom, and I carefully prop it up in the cup, then clean myself up. Stepping out, I'm disappointed to find Sarah's covered herself with a wrap thing that women wear.

"Done." She jumps up from the couch and wraps her arms around me, her soft breasts pressing against my body, thanking me again. I get that she's grateful, but the constant gratitude is unnecessary. Returning her embrace, I kiss the top of her head. "You're welcome. How about I stick around to make sure everything goes smoothly this time?"

She takes one step away from me and I'm left feeling bereft. I much prefer to have my arms around her, her scent filling my nose, and her hair tickling my chin. "Okay. Good idea." She thumbs over her shoulder. "I'll just grab the condom. Make yourself comfortable on the couch, I'll see you soon."

CHAPTER 17

—sarah—

AJ's been incredible each time he's come over this past week to donate his semen; twice the first night, after leaving an important meeting and jumping on a plane to get to me. Not gonna lie, he almost broke through my walls, but I remained strong—*barely*. It's been much more comfortable doing it in my home than in a hotel, not to mention it's saved me some money, which I can put toward expenses for when I get pregnant and have the baby.

We have the process down to a fine routine now. He comes over, I feed him dinner, we chat a little, he steps into the bathroom and does what he needs to do while I pace, then he leaves so I can do my thing. An hour later, I always get a text from him asking if I'm okay and if everything went well.

If I'm being completely honest, it's a certain kind of torture. He's patient and reliable and he's happy to support me through this process for as long as it takes. I think he would be perfect for me. That we'd be perfect together. I'm not sure when he plans to settle and start a family, but whomever he ends up with will be an extremely lucky woman.

If only that could be me.

Why couldn't I have met him under different circumstances instead of being some desperate woman who wants to have a baby? Life is so unfair sometimes.

Stop it, Sarah! Geez, I've avoided sex with AJ at all costs, and yet my heart is still fighting to be involved. I may as well have sex with him at this point.

No. I wave my arm in the air. Nope. Not going there. I don't think I would survive.

Now to finish decorating Kenny's birthday cake for tomorrow. I can't believe she's six. I was planning to make her a princess cake, but she insisted on a Black Widow cake. I study the image I saved on my phone and add the blue pin striping carefully, ensuring I keep my hand steady so the lines are straight. I lift the piping bag away once I've finished, admiring how it's coming together when there's a knock on my door. Glancing at the time on the microwave, I realize I've lost track of time. AJ's here.

Butterflies erupt in my stomach as I call out, "Coming!"

"I will be too," he immediately returns, making me giggle as I wash my hands.

I answer the door with a smile, shaking my head. "Anyone tell you that you should have been a comedian?"

He laughs as he steps inside, carrying a gift box, and lays a peck on my cheek. Something he started doing every time we meet. His citrus scent wafts around me and I draw in a deep breath. He looks incredible as always with a simple T-shirt showcasing the union jack and cargo shorts. "Not today," he shoots back. I close the door and follow him further into my apartment. "You've been baking."

"Yeah. Remember I told you it was Kenny's birthday the other day? We're having a family party for her tomorrow, and I'm the designated birthday cake maker of the family."

He wanders into my kitchen, studying the half-decorated

cake on the counter. He raises his eyes to me as I stand opposite. "This is amazing. You made this?"

"Yeah. I love making fancy cakes for the kids."

"Do you have photos of other cakes you've made?"

"Yeah, hang on. I have photos on my phone." I grab my phone and open the folder where I keep photos of the cakes I've made over the years.

"Holy shit! These are incredible. That Spider-Man is awesome! He's, uh, he's actually my favorite Avenger." Oh my gosh, how cute is that? He has a favorite Avenger.

"Is it because he can climb?" I joke.

"Huh." He looks thoughtful. "I never really thought about why I like him the best, but maybe that's it." He shrugs and then hands me the gift box. "This is for Kenny. If you wouldn't mind giving it to her when you see her tomorrow, I'd appreciate it since I won't."

"Would you like to come?" The words tumble out of my mouth before I can even think to stop them. It's so unlike me to be spontaneous. I haven't even checked if it would be okay with Emma and Theo, but I'm sure they wouldn't mind; she was smitten with him and Kenny loved him too. "That's if you don't already have plans. I know I've already taken up a lot of your week." I rush to add.

"I don't have anything going on. Are you sure it would be okay?"

"Pretty sure. I can double-check with Em and Theo, but I don't see a problem with it."

"Well yeah, I'd love to." I mentally jump up and down on the inside that I get to spend more time with AJ, but then I remember I should be avoiding the guy at all costs except for our essential donation requirements. *Damn it!* "Or, I don't have to come. You look worried."

I give him my best smile and wave him off. He's going to

think I'm some nut job if I tell him I've changed my mind. "It's all good. I'll message Emma."

ME

> Hey, would it be okay if AJ came to Kenny's party tomorrow?

I place my phone on the counter and clean up some of the cake-decorating mess to make room for dinner. I frown. "I thought you were bringing dinner with you?"

AJ grasps the back of his neck, treating me to the visual feast that is his tensing bicep. "Uh, yeah. About that. I thought maybe we could go out and grab a bite to eat."

Huh.

"Or, we could order in if you don't want to go out," he offers.

Does that make it like a date if we go out? Or is it pretty much the same thing as eating in? I'm not dressed to go anywhere. Or should I say I don't want to go out?

His rough hands land on my shoulders, his heat searing my skin. I'll be surprised if he doesn't leave char marks behind. He bends at the knees, so his eyes are level with mine, trapping me in their warm gaze. "Talk to me, Sarah. What's going on in that busy mind of yours?"

My phone buzzes with a text, so I grab it, thankful for the distraction.

EM

> Of course AJ can come tomorrow, Kenny loved him. You know what she's like, she collects people. *laughing emoji* Theo and Lachlan also want to show him the progress they've made with the climbing frame, so it all works out perfectly

I glance up to find AJ looking at the screen, a smile lifting the corners of his perfect mouth. I wave my phone between us. "You can come to Kenny's party."

"Great. I'm looking forward to it. Now tell me what's going on up here?" He taps the side of my head, and I blow out a breath.

"Nothing. Everything's great. I was thinking I need to change if we're going out to dinner." I force an upbeat tone into my voice to cover my confused thoughts.

"You look great. Come on, let's go." His hand slides down my arm to grip my hand, sending goosebumps racing across my body.

I chuckle. "Hang on. I can't go out in these leggings and tank. I'll change. I'll be quick. I promise."

He releases my hand, and I head toward my bedroom. "Okay, but I think you look great as you are." I glance over my shoulder, to answer him, only to find him staring at my ass. I stop and raise my brows at him, waiting for his eyes to make their way back up to my face. "Sorry. As I said, you look great as you are."

I chuckle and step into my bedroom, closing the door between us. I lean my back against the cool surface and blow out a long breath. Can I do this? Can I go to dinner, then come back here and wait for him to do his thing in the bathroom so he can give me his swimmers? The thing that started all of this. I'm getting attached. As I pull out my denim shorts and a silky tank, I reinforce the walls around my heart. I need to make the damn thing impenetrable. Dressing quickly, I release my hair from my standard ponytail and slip my feet into my Roman sandals, zipping up the back of each one. "I'm ready."

AJ's eyes snap up from his phone, then trail down my body and I feel his gaze as though his fingers are slowly caressing their way down my curves. Grabbing my cross-body bag, I pick up my phone and keys and head straight for the door, trying my best to ignore the wetness in my panties. His hand finds its way to my lower back as we make our way to the elevator.

"Is there anywhere around here in walking distance that's good?"

"Yeah. Do you like Mexican?"

"I absolutely do."

I point down the street. "*Los Burritos* is a fifteen-minute walk that way."

"Perfect." He takes my hand in his and we head off to grab dinner. I glance between us, my heart pounding behind my ribs and tingles racing up my arm. He's holding my hand … and it feels … natural.

The heat from the sidewalk radiates up and I wish I'd left my hair up in a ponytail. I don't even have an elastic handy on my wrist. "The place doesn't look all that great, but the food is authentic and the guys get it to you fast."

AJ nods as we step inside and once my eyes adjust, I mentally pat myself on the back. The place is packed, but I notice there are two empty stools down the back. I point toward them and we make our way through the busy hole in the wall. I can't possibly confuse this with a date. It'll be just like me and Mel grabbing something to eat. I should be able to keep myself in check.

"What's good here?" AJ asks as he sits.

I tuck my hair behind my ear and sit. "Everything. I promise you can't go wrong. The serving sizes are generous too."

"What do you usually get?"

"I usually get the chicken burrito on the spinach wrap. If you want to order yours, I'll hold our seats, then I'll order when you get back." If I pay for my dinner, it's definitely not a date. Right?

He nods. "Sure." I watch him walk toward the counter, admiring his broad shoulders which taper into narrow hips.

The man is certainly built without being bulky. He glances at me and I quickly look away, hoping he didn't catch me staring at him.

I feel him, rather than see him sit back down. "I've ordered for you, but I wasn't sure what you'd like to drink, so I grabbed you a Mountain Dew. Hope that's okay."

"That's fine. Thank you. I was going to order mine."

He studies me closely and I have to stop myself from squirming under his gaze. "It's not a problem. You've been feeding me this week. It's the least I could do."

"I'm feeding you because it's the least *I* can do since you're donating to the cause and all." I chuckle softly.

AJ's name is called over the speaker system and he collects our food and drinks, bringing them back to our seats. It smells delicious and my stomach growls in response. AJ peels away the foil, and I watch him closely as he takes his first bite. His eyes drop closed and a deep moan escapes as the flavors burst on his tongue. I watch him chew and swallow, paying close attention to the bobbing of his Adam's apple.

Why is a guy's Adam's apple so damn sexy? Actually, everything about AJ is sexy. I can't believe the guy's single. There has to be a catch.

"Sarah! This is incredible. The flavors …" He mimes a chef's kiss. "So damn good. Thank you for bringing me here."

I smile as I unwrap my burrito. "You're welcome. I come here with Max sometimes."

We both get stuck into our meals, barely speaking until we each take our last bite. "That was so good. I'm going to have to bring Dylan here. He'll love this place."

The place was busy when we arrived, but it's crazy now. "We should probably head out and let someone else have our seats."

"Sure." AJ helps me down from my stool and we make our

way outside where it's slightly cooler after being crammed into the small restaurant.

I force myself to relax as we stroll back to my place hand in hand. This time I try not to think about how right it feels to be this close to him, holding his hand in mine, heading home so we can work on my dream. This will be our sixth time doing this and I don't think I feel any less awkward about it.

"You're quiet." AJ breaks into my thoughts.

I glance up at him, then quickly turn my eyes forward again. "Just mentally running through what we're going to do when we get back to my place." *Oh God, Sarah! Really?*

He squeezes my hand. "Hopefully, in a couple of weeks, you'll know if it's worked or not."

"Hopefully." Sadness swiftly fills my body with the thought of not seeing AJ again. He said he wanted to stay friends, but what does that mean? I'll be busy getting fat with a baby and then I'll be busy looking after said baby. I can't imagine an attractive, single guy wanting to 'be friends' then. I should be filled with happiness at the thought of our efforts coming to fruition this month, not sad. This is something I've wanted for what feels like my entire life.

When we approach my building, AJ releases my hand to open and hold the door for me, his hand then taking up residence on my lower back again as we make our way to the elevator. The butterflies in my stomach have taken flight and I remind myself to take proper breaths as we wait for it to arrive.

We're both quiet as we make our way upstairs, lost in our thoughts. When we get inside my apartment, AJ stiffly thumbs over his shoulder toward the bathroom. "I guess I'll get started. Are the collection condoms still under the vanity?"

"Uh, yeah."

He nods and backs away from me toward the bathroom and closes the door behind him without another word spoken between us. I wonder what he does to get himself worked up.

Does he have Pornhub loaded on his phone ready to go? Or is there someone he thinks about? An ex-girlfriend who got away? My heart clenches at the thought of him pining for someone.

I need to keep busy, so I wash my hands and start where I left off with Kenny's cake. It's almost finished, I just need to work on Black Widow's cuffs and belt. She's looking great so far. The cuffs are easy enough to make, I roll the gray icing flat and cut the appropriate lengths, adding the detail and setting each one on her arms. This is good. I'm not thinking about AJ and his strong hand stroking his cock while I'm doing this. Good one, Sarah, now I'm thinking about it again. I drop my head back in frustration, rolling my eyes at the ceiling. I'm hopeless. Really, I am. I chuckle a little at myself.

"What's so funny?" I startle at AJ's voice right behind me. I didn't even hear the bathroom door open.

"Wow, you were quick." I blush when I realize how that sounded. "Sorry. I'm sure you last longer when you're doing the real thing." I snap my mouth closed because that was even worse.

AJ drops his head forward and chuckles as his hands land on his hips. "I promise, I'm not that quick when I'm doing the real thing." He opens his mouth to say something else, but I see the moment he changes his mind and closes it tight. I don't dare ask what he was about to add because I think it may be too much at this point. "Anyway, I'm all done."

"Thanks again, AJ. I don't know how I can properly thank you for all of this." I step into his body and wrap my arms around him in gratitude. I feel like all I do is say thank you to the guy and yet it never feels like it's enough.

His arms come around me and he pulls me in close. His warm breath touches the side of my face as he whispers, "It's my pleasure. No thanks necessary." He places a gentle kiss on my jawline slightly below where it meets my lobe and I shiver.

Did he feel it? He had to feel it.

Mortification fills me and I pull back, putting much-needed space between us. I suck in a deep breath to recalibrate and grab the gift he brought for Kenny to put something physical between us. "Here, you can bring this with you tomorrow."

He takes it. "Did you want me to pick you up?"

I mentally berate myself when I almost agree. That wouldn't be a good idea. If my family notices us arriving together, they'll think there's more going on than there really is. It's bad enough I've invited him. I wish I had a time machine to go back and keep my lips sealed. "I'll be going a little earlier to help set up, so maybe you can meet me there. I'll text you the address."

His smile drops and his eyes skate away from mine. "Sure. Whatever's easiest. See ya tomorrow." He leans forward to give me a brief kiss goodbye and then he's gone. I sag against the closed door and chastise myself for getting too caught up in him. He only wants to be a donor. He's not looking for a life partner. I'd do well to damn well remember that.

I head into the bathroom to wash my hands and collect the condom and syringe. Then I set about doing what needs to be done. After the first day where I battled with myself to not think of AJ when I came, I've given up and given in. He's now my go-to thought. Imagining his strong fingers working me over along with his tongue, pushes me over the edge quicker than I've ever known before. I figure I may as well go with it.

CHAPTER 18

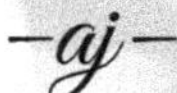

I couldn't believe my luck when Sarah invited me to Kenny's party today. I was stunned but there was no way I was going to say no. Even though I had a group climb planned today, I begged off saying I had an urgent matter I needed to take care of. When I bought Kenny a birthday gift, I never imagined it would earn me an invitation. I could tell by Sarah's shocked expression she hadn't meant to invite me, but I wasn't about to give her the opportunity to change her mind.

I wipe my sweaty palms as I take my first steps toward Emma and Theo's home and I look around at the other homes on the street. Is this what Sarah will want once she has her baby? I could easily sell my renovated warehouse; Dylan and I can rent office space somewhere and then I'd be able to buy a house with a white picket fence, fancy porch, and a backyard for our kids to play.

The screen door flies open and out runs Kenny. "You're here! I thought you'd never get here. I've been waiting for ages. Why didn't you come with Aunty Sarah?"

Woah!

"Kenny! What have I told you—" Theo's voice booms as

he flies onto the porch. "Oh, hi, AJ. Kenny, just because it's your birthday party, it doesn't mean you get to forget the rules. Okay?"

Sheepishly, Kenny turns back toward her dad. "Sorry, Daddy. I was excited and I forgot."

He steps down from the front porch and straightens her crown. "I know you're excited, Munchkin." They both walk toward me, Theo holding out his hand in greeting. He doesn't squeeze quite as tight as he did at the beach. I'll take that as progress.

"Is that for me?" Kenny's wide blue eyes snap up to my face.

"It sure is." I hand her the gift, though seeing her already wearing a crown, maybe I should have bought her something different.

"What do you say, Munchkin?" Theo reminds the little dynamo.

"Thank you, Uncle AJ." She gestures for me to bend down, so I do, then she shocks the hell out of me when she plants a gentle kiss on my cheek.

My stomach flips at her easy acceptance of me into her family unit. If only it was as easy to win over her aunt. "You're welcome. I hope you like it." She takes off inside, leaving Theo and me on the front sidewalk.

"We'd better get inside. Lachlan and I have been working on your nephew's climbing wall. We'll show it to you later."

"Thanks. Colton's gonna love having a designated space to climb where he won't get into trouble."

We climb the steps to the front porch and I freeze when I see Sarah standing with the screen door open, waiting for us. Theo steps past her, leaving the two of us in the doorway.

"Hey." It's the only word that will come out. She looks gorgeous in a red sundress that leaves her shoulders bare and hugs her magnificent tits. I tuck my hands into my pockets in a bid to disguise my rising cock.

She smiles at me, and I swear the world around me stops. I'm not usually such a sap, but when she's around, I don't see or hear anything else but her. "Hey. You found it okay?"

"Yeah." I take the steps up to her and I can't stop myself from swiping my lips across hers. She gasps lightly and I draw back. "It was easy enough to find. How are you feeling?" I study her face closely.

Her eyes grow soft and she gives me a tender smile. "I'm feeling okay."

"You're not overdoing things, are you?" I want to pull her into me and wrap her in my arms while we have this conversation, but I can't. It'll be too much for Sarah.

"It's really sweet how you keep checking on me, but you need to stop worrying so much." She chuckles. "Come in. Kenny's already announced you're here." She takes a step inside then stops abruptly, spinning around to face me as I close and lock the screen door. "A quick word of warning. Please ignore anything and everything my mom may say to you. She has no filter. And I mean that. She'll say whatever's on her mind."

I chuckle. "It's okay." I glide my fingers along Sarah's hairline, tucking the loose strands behind her ear because I can't resist touching her any longer. This close I see her hazel eyes have a touch of blue in them today. "I promise I don't scare so easily."

"Okay. Don't say I didn't warn you." She steps back but takes my hand in hers, and I feel as though I've just dragged my body over the topmost edge of El Capitan.

When we turn to head further into the gorgeous home, a woman is standing just inside the open doors which lead out to what looks like an amazing deck. She has her hand pressed against her chest and she's wearing a soft smile. She has to be

Sarah's mom, the resemblance is impossible to miss—it's like I'm looking at my future. I smile at her as we come to a stop.

"Mom, this is AJ. The man who's helping me. AJ, this is my mom, Sally."

I hold out my hand to greet her, but she presses into me, wrapping me tightly in her embrace. She pulls back after a moment, holding onto my biceps as she looks at her daughter. "Oh my, he's so handsome." She squeezes my arms. "Fit and healthy, too."

"Mom!" Sarah scolds as an older gentleman steps inside and gives the woman a look borne from years of marriage. Sally releases her hold on me and smiles at Sarah.

"Sally. Leave the poor boy alone." He kisses her temple and then holds his hand out to me. "Hi. I'm John, Sarah's dad."

I shake his hand. "Hi, John. Nice to meet you both."

Sarah takes hold of my hand. "Come on, everyone's out back."

I nod to Sarah's parents and as my foot lands on the back deck, I hear Sally speak to John. "You should have seen how he was looking at her and stroking her face when he first arrived. There's more going on there than Sarah's told us."

"Leave them be. They'll work it out without you meddling," John says in a firm but kind manner.

"Hmph. You spoil all my fun." I glance over my shoulder to catch John wrapping his arms around his wife as he presses a kiss to her temple. Her arms come up around his back to hold him close as she smiles up at him. It's beautiful to see a couple who have obviously been together for a long time still so in love. My parents aren't demonstrative with their affection, so it's a little foreign to me.

Sarah pulls me toward a tall guy standing next to a blonde woman. He has the same eyes as Sarah and Emma, so he must be Max, her brother. "Max. Molly. I'd like you to meet AJ."

Max's hard gaze traces me up and down, a look of

distrust obvious by the narrowed eyes and tick in his jaw. Molly smiles at me, showing off deep dimples. She reminds me of a princess with her almost-white hair, gray eyes, and dimpled smile. She's tall too. Only a few inches shorter than me. She holds out her hand. "Hi, AJ. It's so nice to meet you."

"Hi. Nice to meet you too. Congratulations on your marriage."

"Thanks."

I hold out my hand to Max and his eyes drop to it, then rise back to my face. "What type of guy offers to get a stranger pregnant with no commitment?"

Molly's head snaps up to her husband as Sarah slaps his arm. "I can't believe you asked him—"

I cut Sarah off with a shake of my head. "It's okay, Sarah. It's a fair question and I'll share my reasons with Max in private, so we don't spoil Kenny's party." I finish with a tight smile at my future brother-in-law. Lifting my hand, I hold it out to him again with a raised brow. "Nice to meet you, Max."

He eventually relents and slides his hand against mine. We shake, both holding firm. I feel as though I can't show any weakness with this guy. The handshake feels as though it's never-ending, neither of us wanting to be the first to give in.

"Hi, AJ." Lachlan breaks the tension. "You should see the climbing wall we're building for Colton."

Max's head snaps to his nephew and his eyes flick between me and Lachlan with interest.

"Hi, Lachlan. Yeah, Theo said it was coming along nicely. You'll have to show it to me."

"Sure." He looks at his uncle with a frown. "Why are you holding AJ's hand?"

Max glances down, only now realizing we're still shaking hands. He releases me abruptly, taking a step back. "We were saying hello."

Lachlan takes my hand. "Come on, I'll show you what we've done so far."

Sarah gasps as he pulls me forward, collecting Theo on the way, and we head toward the enormous workshop at the bottom of the backyard. Theo swings the door open and switches on the light.

"It's over there." Lachlan points to the opposite side of the space.

"We've done the frame, now we need to add the planks for the walls. Do you think it will be big enough?" Theo asks.

It's larger than I imagined, but it's amazing and will allow me to attach a range of different holds to give Colton a variety of climbing experiences. I run my hand over the smooth timber frame in awe. "This is incredible. It's bigger than I thought it would be. I think Colton will love it."

Lachlan smiles, his body seeming to expand with pride, as Theo responds. "We can make it smaller if you want."

I immediately shake my head. "No, this is great. I'll be able to attach more holds for him. It will make it more engaging and hopefully keep him out of trouble."

"How will a climbing wall keep Colton out of trouble?" Lachlan asks.

"Well, you see, he loves to climb, and he keeps climbing on stuff inside that he shouldn't be climbing on and it's a little dangerous. His moms are worried he's going to hurt himself or break something. They don't want him to stop climbing, but they want him to be able to do it safely," I explain.

Theo looks at me with approval. "We should be finished by the end of the week."

"Great. Then I'll have to work out how to get it to my sister's place."

"Not a problem. We'll deliver it on the back of my truck." Considering the guy didn't seem to like me when we first met, he's being very generous now.

"Thanks, man. I appreciate everything. Let me know how much it all costs and I'll transfer the cash for you."

"It'll just be for the materials. I'll work it out and let Sarah know."

"What about labor?"

He waves his arm through the air. "Don't worry about it. It's been a great summer vacation project for me and Lachlan." Wow.

"Thank you. I don't know what to say."

"You already said thank you. That's all you need to say." Lachlan looks up at Theo. "Right, Theo?"

Theo runs his hand over the top of Lachlan's head. "Right, buddy."

Sarah steps inside. "Are you guys coming out? Lunch is almost ready."

We move out of the workshop, Theo closing and latching the workshop door, then we head to the deck, my hand at the base of Sarah's back. An older gentleman is standing at the grill and another couple has arrived. The woman has the most amazing red hair I've ever seen and the guy beside her is intimidating as fuck.

Sarah clears her throat and introduces me to everybody. No wonder the guy looks intimidating, he's Oliver Stone, the billionaire. Grandfather rents a floor in his building in the city.

I reach out to shake the older gentleman's hand. "Cristo. One of my favorite places to eat is a Greek taverna named *Cristo's*." I chuckle.

He laughs, loud and boisterous. "Ah, it's always good to meet a fan."

My eyes widen and I'm sure my mouth drops open a little. "You're Cristo?"

"Yes. Next time, you must come and say hello! I'll give you my best table," he offers.

I glance at Sarah. "Wait until I tell Dylan. That's our go-to restaurant."

Cristo chuckles. "Bring all your friends. Bring my pretty Sarah here. I do not get to see her enough."

"Oh, I definitely will."

"Here, Dad. You can put the meat on this tray." Emma slides in next to Cristo, handing him a large platter.

"Thank you." He takes it from her and begins to stack the barbecued meat and vegetables. It looks heavy, so I take it from him to hold it with two hands while he finishes placing the food, then I carry it to the table and place it in the middle.

"We'll serve the kids first and then the adults can dig in," Theo announces.

The spread of food looks amazing and I feel obliged to try a little of everything, so I take small scoops from each dish, loading up my plate. Sarah leans in and whispers, "You know you can go back for seconds." She chuckles close to my ear, her warm breath tickling my cheek.

I turn to look at her, our lips mere inches apart. Her eyes drop to my mouth and I'm tempted to lean forward and close the distance. But our first proper kiss will not be in front of her family at a child's birthday party, so I refrain. "I know. It all looks so delicious, and I couldn't decide where to start, so I figured I'd have everything."

Conversation flows easily around the table and I'm happy to sit back and observe the family dynamics. This is obviously a family who are close and enjoy being in each other's company. Not once have I heard anyone shush the kids or remind them of their place, which is a stark contrast to my upbringing and the expectations at our family get-togethers.

Once everyone's finished eating, Theo rises and collects the empty dishes. I stand to help and so does Max. We make several trips back and forth from the table to the kitchen until everything is cleared away. Theo works on packing away the leftovers and I decide to start washing the dishes. Max moves beside me to dry the dishes as I place them on the rack. My muscles tense as I wait for him to strike up the conversation he wanted to have earlier.

He clears his throat. "So, about my question. You want to explain to me why you would offer to get my sister pregnant?"

Theo laughs and I glance at him over my shoulder. "You had to expect this question from her brother." He focuses his attention on Max. "I asked him the same thing when we spent the afternoon at the beach."

"Where the fuck was our invitation to the beach?"

"It was the day after your wedding. I'm assuming you were occupied with your wife." Theo raises his brows in humor.

Max's body relaxes. "Oh right." A smirk tips up on one side of his mouth.

I turn back to my task. "I'll tell you what I told Theo, but it has to stay between us. I don't want to ruin what Sarah and I are only now beginning to build." He raises his eyebrows but gives me a stiff nod. "I saw her when a friend and I were at *Club Rumors*. Not gonna lie, I thought she was stunning." I think I'll leave out the part about her curves. No brother wants to know some guy finds his sister hot. "When I overheard her speaking with her friend about wanting a baby, I thought I'd take the opportunity to speak with her about it. I know she's way out of my league and I'm pretty sure she wouldn't look twice at me if it weren't for my…" I wave my hand in the general area of my dick. "I helped my sister and her wife get pregnant, so I knew I could help her." His body relaxes slightly and his eyes become softer, less like he wants to strangle the life out of me. "I'm hoping if Sarah spends enough time with me, she'll get to know me and want to stick around. I don't want to only get her pregnant, Max. I want to be around for all of it. But I'm having a hard time getting through her fortress. She keeps a damn wall between us." I stand stock still waiting for his response.

He glances at Theo for a long moment, seeming to have a silent discussion. Theo raises his eyebrows and tilts his head to the side without saying a word. Max's head begins to move up and down slowly, his eyes coming back to me.

"A word of warning. You have to move slowly with Sarah. She overthinks and over plans everything. She doesn't like change, so she doesn't generally deviate from her plan."

I blow out a breath and the tension releases from my body. "I figured that much out. That's why I'm not pushing her or trying to move forward at the pace I would prefer. I don't want her to bolt."

He nods again and smiles this time. "Second warning. Don't fucking hurt my sister."

I hold my hands up in surrender. "I have zero intention of hurting her. I promise. I would rather eat my own arm than hurt Sarah."

"Good to hear."

"How are you guys doing in here? Kenny's bursting to have her birthday cake," Sarah says as she steps inside. Thank God she didn't step through the doorway a couple of minutes earlier.

"We're almost done. If you want to take out the plates, we'll be ready in a minute," Theo tells her.

She glances between Max and me, silently asking me if I'm okay. I nod and she collects the plates, heading back out to the deck.

"You do realize you two are already holding conversations without words, right?" Max asks. "I think she might be coming around, brother." His hand lands heavily on my shoulder and he squeezes.

Well, at least I seem to have her family on my side. Now to get Sarah on the same page.

We're all sitting around the table outside when Sarah walks out carrying Kenny's birthday cake. Kenny squeals with delight as Sarah places it on the table in front of her niece. "Aunty Sarah, it's beautiful. Thank you so much!"

Cristo and Theo are watching her with loving eyes and clear adoration for the little dynamo. Sarah explained to me that Emma lived in the house next door and that's how she met Theo and Kenny. Theo's technically her uncle but became her guardian when he lost his sister to breast cancer. It made me stop and think about Hayley, Lisa, and Colton and how much I love them; how devastating it would be to lose either of them.

We all sing happy birthday to the girl of the moment and the cake is cut and distributed after Kenny is certain Emma took enough photos so she never forgets what the cake looked like. Sally and John make coffee and tea for the adults and bring them to the table and conversation resumes.

"AJ, what is it you do for work?" John asks.

I wipe my mouth with a napkin. "I'm actually a computer hacker. My friend, Dylan, and I started our company after we finished college. Companies engage us to test their systems for security. We investigate and report any flaws we find and work with them to improve and tighten up their security."

"Oh, wow. That's very impressive," John praises.

"I'm fucking terrible with computers," Max grumbles.

"Max!" Sally chastises.

"Shit! Sorry," he mumbles as his shoulders hunch forward, and everyone bursts out laughing.

"Uncle Max, you're so funny!" Kenny giggles.

"Thanks, Munchkin." He smiles at her and Molly kisses his cheek with a grin, chuckling silently.

I can't believe he swore in front of the kids. I find it impossible to imagine anyone in my family speaking like that, let alone in front of kids. I mean, I'm no angel, I swear but I temper my language in mixed company. It further highlights the differences between Sarah's family and mine. I'm sad to say that I prefer hers.

"Do you have a business card?" Oliver asks. Oliver *freaking* Stone wants my business card! "I wouldn't mind having you take a look at our system sometime."

I could kick my own butt right now. "Sorry. I don't carry them on me to events like this."

He leans forward, grabbing his wallet out of his pocket. He deftly pulls out a card and hands it to me. "Contact Jase, my assistant. He'll set up an appointment."

I take the card from him. "Uh, sure thing. Any particular time?"

"Call him sometime this week. I'll let him know to expect your call. Let's see what we can set up."

I can only nod, trying to contain my internal fist bump at gaining the attention of one of the richest men in America. Wait until I tell Dylan. The accounts we're winning lately are really putting us on the map.

The kids move onto the grass to play and conversation is easy around the table. Max constantly has some part of him touching Molly and Theo and Emma are the same, as are Kate and Oliver. I hope there comes a time when I can openly show Sarah the affection I feel for her. For now, I'll settle with pressing my leg alongside hers beneath the table. She hasn't pulled away, so I'll take it as a win.

—sarah—

I can't believe how well AJ fits in with my family. I thought my brother was going to have a problem with him, but throughout the afternoon, they've been talking easily.

All of the guys have decided to play a game of soccer on the grass, leaving us girls enjoying a peaceful cup of coffee on the back deck. I'm surprised Max, Theo, and Oliver were able to tear themselves away from their ladies. I'm thrilled about my siblings' happiness even if I'm a little sad for myself.

"I have to say, Sarah, AJ is a lovely young man. And so handsome, too," Mom blurts.

The other three women hum in agreement. "Yeah, he's one of the good ones, that's for sure," Emma states.

"You think so?" I ask.

"Absolutely. And genetically blessed too. Your baby is going to be gorgeous," Molly adds.

"Well, so long as my baby is healthy. That's all that matters to me."

"Of course."

"Oh, are you two trying to have a baby?" Kate asks, her denim eyes sparkling in the late afternoon sun.

I glance around the table. It's one thing for my family and close friend to know about our arrangement, but it's another for someone I barely know. Emma helps me out. "Sarah's ready to start a family but she doesn't have a boyfriend. AJ's her donor." She says it as though it's a common everyday occurrence for women to hang out with their donors on the weekend.

"Oh right. Good for you. You definitely have yourself a fine specimen there," Kate says as she fans herself and I feel my cheeks heat. He *is* a fine specimen.

Mom leans across the table, her eyes scanning the area. "Have you noticed the way he looks at Sarah?" Mom whispers.

"Mom. He doesn't look at me like anything. Don't start with this. There is nothing between us other than maybe the start of a friendship."

"I wouldn't be so sure about that, Sis."

"Oh, I agree. I think he's in deep with you already, Sare," Molly adds.

I shake my head. "No, he's not. He said he considers us friends. He's helping me with my pregnancy plan *until* I get pregnant. Nothing more."

"We'll see," Emma states with a soft smile and a look in her eye like she knows something I don't.

"Yeah, I wouldn't be so sure about that," Kate whispers. "I had no idea he was only your donor. He seems like so much more than that."

We fall into silence and Emma watches Theo with her boys wearing a contented smile as he supports Lachlan.

Molly's eyes are glued to Max. "You know, if things don't work out with AJ, you should come down to Max's Monday night soccer games. Some of his friends are pretty good-looking."

I chuckle. "You don't think I didn't crush on some of his friends. Aaron, Finn, and Lincoln are h-o-t! But to them, I was always Max's annoying little sister. I soon grew out of my infatuation." I nudge Emma. "I always thought Lincoln had a crush on you."

She laughs. "I don't think so. Remember, I was single for a long time after my divorce. He never showed the slightest interest."

"Yeah. I guess." I sigh as I turn my gaze back to the men, particularly AJ. The way he moves so fluidly for a guy who spends hours behind a desk is impressive. I guess the climbing keeps him pretty agile and fit.

Kate sighs. "It's so good for Oliver to have fun like this with other guys. His life revolves around work … and me. Which I am totally grateful for, don't get me wrong, but I love seeing him having fun like this."

"You guys should come over more often. We have regular family afternoons like this. You're more than welcome to join in," Mom says.

"Thanks, you're so sweet."

The afternoon wears on and the sun begins to drop below the horizon. The guys have cleaned up, so there's no excuse to linger any longer. I need to get home and plan my wardrobe for my work week and make my salad jars. I ran out of time this morning because I wanted to get here and help Emma set up everything. AJ and I say goodbye to everyone and walk out to our cars at the same time, his Jeep parked behind mine on the street. I guess he needs a Jeep when he goes out to climbing locations.

"Thanks for the invite. I had a great time." He glances at Em and Theo's house. "You have a great family, Sarah. Really close."

I follow his gaze and notice Em, Mom, Molly, and Kenny duck away from the living room window and roll my eyes. "Thanks for coming and yeah, I love my family and how close we are. Kenny loves to be surrounded by people, so the more people at her party the better."

"She's a little dynamo, that one." He tugs on the back of his neck. "I think Colton would really have fun with Em and Theo's kids. He doesn't get to spend much time with other children."

"Oh." I don't like the idea of Colton missing out on fun. "Maybe we could organize an outing with all of the kids. Molly found this great park near a lake on the outskirts of the city. Leave it with me and I'll see what I can do."

And there I go making plans to combine our families. We're not dating, Sarah! Get that through your thick skull.

"That'd be great. Thank you. He'll love that."

I widen my eyes and raise my brows. "So, Oliver Stone wants you to hack his company."

"Hell, yeah. Never in a million years did I ever imagine I'd have his business card in my pocket." He pats the pocket of his shorts. "Dylan's gonna be ecstatic when I tell him tomorrow. Actually, he probably won't believe me." AJ chuckles.

"Well, good luck with it. I guess … I'd better be going. I have stuff to do before work tomorrow."

"Uh, yeah, sure, of course. Thanks again. I had a great time." He leans forward and presses his lips to mine and I freeze. He usually pecks my cheek, but this is the second time he's gone straight for my lips.

Does that mean something? Could the girls be right with their idea there's more between us? He pulls back and opens my car door for me.

"Thanks. I'll let you know when we can take the kids to the park. Bye, AJ."

"Yeah, bye." He closes my car door and stands in place as I pull out and drive away. I lose sight of him as I turn the corner and my mood immediately sinks. I hate that my relationship with him is contingent on my cycle and me getting pregnant. I sigh heavily into the silent car and contemplate how things might have been different if I hadn't met AJ under the circumstances I did.

Would he even consider dating me if he wasn't helping me to have a child? And while he's helping me, he's missing out on the opportunity to meet the woman of his dreams. Will he resent me if this goes on for too long? Will he want out?

Mel drops into the seat opposite me with a sigh.

"Hey, Mels Bells, what's up?"

"Just tired. I worked a double yesterday and I was on nights last week. It always throws my body clock out of whack and my sleep schedule is all off." Her eyes are glassy as it all comes tumbling out.

I reach across the table and lay my hand on hers. "Why on earth did you agree to meet for coffee if you're so tired you're almost in tears." Mel has never coped well when she's sleep deprived. I'm not sure why she went into nursing when nurses are possibly the most sleep-deprived people on the planet.

She pouts adorably. "I miss my best friend, Sare Bear."

I giggle at her use of her childhood nickname for me. "Well, today is my treat. You deserve it." I raise my brows. "The usual?"

She lifts my hand and kisses the back of it. "You're an angel. Yes please."

"Okay. I'll go order."

She smiles at me and then lays her head on the table, closing her eyes. I'll bet anything she's asleep by the time I get back to the table. While I'm waiting in line to place our order, my phone buzzes and my smile is immediate. I bet it's AJ checking on me. He does it at random times of the day now, instead of in the evenings. He said he wants to keep me on my toes. I liked the predictability of his text arriving in the evening, but I have to admit the randomness of his messages makes things more interesting.

AJ

How are you feeling?

My smile widens. Even though he's mixed up the times he sends his message, the actual message remains the same.

ME

I'm fine. Nothing's changed since yesterday

AJ

That's great news

I'm not sure what he thinks is supposed to be happening at this point in my cycle. It's not like I'm going to know anything until I get or skip my period.

AJ

Have you spoken with your sister?

Shit! Is something wrong with Em? I know Theo and AJ exchanged numbers last weekend to organize the delivery of Colton's climbing wall but has something happened?

ME

Not today. Why what's happened?

AJ

Nothing. I'm going there this afternoon to attach the climbing holds to the wall

I was wondering if you were going to be there

Hmmm. Maybe I should message Em.

ME

Hey, what time is AJ coming over?

EM

Hey. I'll check with Theo, hang on

I move to the front of the line and place my order and then head back to my table while I wait for Em's text. Sure enough, my best friend in the entire world is sound asleep. Her cute little snores are a dead give away and I chuckle. I'll let her sleep until our order arrives.

EM

He's coming around 2. They have some stuff to attach to the wall, then they're going to take it to his sister's place

Thanks

Are you coming over?

ME

Maybe

EM

You should. It's pretty hot outside, the guys may have to remove their shirts while they work *winking emoji* *hot emoji*

I giggle.

ME

Okay, you've convinced me. I'll come over

EM

Great. See you then

I flick to AJ's messages.

ME

I'll see you at my sister's

AJ

How about I pick you up?

Oh God! I don't know how I'll manage being trapped in a confined space with the man and his sexy scent.

AJ

We could maybe grab some dinner after we drop off the climbing wall for Colton

It would be a good opportunity for you to meet Hayley and Lisa

Shit! Is this weird? Maybe it is, but I'd like to meet his family, especially now he's met mine.

ME

Okay. That sounds like a plan

AJ

Great. I'll pick you up at 1:30

ME

See you then

"Here's your order." The waitress gains my attention.

"Thanks." I clear my half of the table so she can place the items.

"Enjoy!" she says brightly, then spins on her heel and heads back to the counter.

I smile at her retreating back, then look at my friend. I feel bad I have to wake her, but she could probably do with this. She never gets a chance to eat properly when she's working, not that this is proper food. I don't know how she maintains her slim figure.

I reach across and gently push the mass of blonde curls away from her face. "Melly Belly. It's time to wake up."

She twitches her nose. "Just a little longer."

"Your food is here," I coax. Her head rises sleepily. "Oh my God, Mel. We could have caught up another time. Seriously, let's have this and then you need to go home to bed."

She flicks her wrist between us. "I'll be good to go now. I've had a power nap." She smirks as she drags her coffee and devil's chocolate mud cake toward herself. "I only seem to see you when my shift aligns with your volunteer shift lately and I miss you. There's no way I'm going to miss out!"

And that's exactly why we've been friends for most of our life. We love each other and genuinely miss each other when we can't catch up regularly. "I miss you, too."

I drag my decadent triple chocolate flake cake toward myself and lean down to take a long whiff of the rich chocolate scent. This is always my favorite cake when we come here. It starts with stunning flakes of chocolate on top of a white chocolate layer of cake, the next layer is milk chocolate, then finally dark chocolate at the base, because you can never have enough chocolate. We each take a bite of our treats and moan at the same time.

"So good!" Mel says as her eyes roll back inside her head.

"I know, right? It's been a long time since I indulged myself like this."

Mel nods and we're both silent except for the occasional moan as we dig in. The cake is so rich, that I have to slow down once I reach halfway, so I take a sip of my coffee. "Anything interesting happening in your life?"

She scoffs. "You're joking, right? I feel like all I do is work, go home, eat, sleep, repeat!"

"You need to get a work-life balance before you burn out."

"Yeah, I know. I'm not sure how to achieve it, though."

I slump my shoulders forward. "Yeah. I don't know how you can either. What do the other nurses and doctors do?"

She shrugs. "We're all in the same boat. Why do you think so many doctors end up hooking up with nurses." She smirks. "They're the only ones who understand the craziness that is our life." We both take another bite of our food. Mel looks at me pointedly as she chews her food. Once she swallows the cake, she asks, "So how are things going with the baby daddy?"

I choke and half of my drink comes out of my nose. Grabbing the napkin quickly, I wipe my face. "Oh God, Mel. Don't call him that." I snicker.

She shrugs and leans forward. "Tell me you've at least screwed him. You're not still using the collection condoms."

I shake my head. "Sorry, I can't tell you that."

She groans, dropping her head back. "You know, this could be your last opportunity to have hot sex for a while. Once you're a mom, you'll be too busy to date. You should be using this as an excuse to be jumping that guy's bones any chance you get."

I huff out an extended breath. "Oh, Mel." I sigh. "I already like him too much for that. I don't know what I'm gonna do when this is all over and he doesn't need to come over anymore. You know, he sends me a text every single day, without fail, to check on me."

Her eyes go soft and dreamy and she reaches across the table to brush my bangs out of my face. "Oh, Sare. Maybe you could try with this guy."

I take a moment to gaze around the coffee shop, giving myself time to collect my thoughts. "I'm too scared," I whisper as I bring my eyes back to my long-time friend.

"Oh, Sare."

"I thought Michael was the one. I thought we were meant to be together forever, but he chose his career over me and I guess I chose my career, family, and friends over him. But he was the one who left. And then look at Preston. He didn't stay with Emma, and they had two kids together. If that couldn't make him stay, then what would?"

"You know they're not AJ, though, right? You don't know if he would do that. And you won't know if you never open yourself up to the chance. Maybe Michael wasn't your one. Maybe he had to leave to make way for someone so much better. Maybe AJ is your one."

My defense dies on my tongue. I'd never thought about it like that.

"And look at Emma now. She's so much happier with Theo, so Preston obviously wasn't her forever person."

Well, that's true too. Trust Mel to give it to me straight.

"Shit! Stop making sense, Mel. How are you making so much sense when you're sleeping on your feet?" I chuckle as does she.

"All I'm saying is that maybe you could relax a little and see how things go. Don't close your heart to the possibility of something amazing growing between you and AJ … and I don't just mean a baby. Maybe you could be a family." She squeezes my hand to punctuate her sentence. "I know that's what you truly want … deep down."

"I know. The problem is, though, he keeps referring to us as friends and saying he'll be around *until* I'm pregnant. I assume that means he'll move on and I don't want to fall on my own."

"I dunno, Sare. I got a distinct vibe that he was interested in more than getting you pregnant." She wiggles her eyebrows up and down. "Just promise me you'll think about it. Okay?" She raises one finely sculpted brow at me.

"I promise." Her smile is wide, showing her beautiful teeth as a result of two and a half years of braces from the time she was seventeen. "Thanks, Mels Bells."

"Any time, Sare Bear."

CHAPTER 20

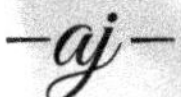

Pulling to a stop in front of Sarah's building, I find a parking space on the opposite side of the street easily enough and climb out of the Jeep. Sarah's voice stops me as I'm closing the car door.

"Sorry, I wanted to be down here waiting for you so you didn't need to park." She's slightly out of breath as she apologizes, her breasts rising and falling, capturing my attention.

A car speeds past us, and I pull Sarah in close to keep her safe. She lands against me, her hands resting on my pecs. With her this close, I can't resist greeting her with a kiss. I press my lips to hers and feel her lips spread in a smile. We both pull back, our eyes tracing each other's faces. Mine drop to her mouth, dying for a longer taste—a more *intimate* taste. Maybe one day soon. She didn't gasp or pull away from me this time. Bit by bit, I think I'm working my way around her defenses.

"That's okay, I'm a little early." I couldn't wait to lay eyes on her. I drop my hand to her hip and guide her around to the passenger side. Opening her door, I wait for her to climb in, then ensure she's safely tucked inside by pulling the seatbelt across her body. The strap settles between her breasts, accentuating them. I tear my eyes away from the soft pillows and smile at the woman I can't stop thinking about. "You look gorgeous."

"Thanks. I wanted to dress as cool as possible today because it's so hot."

"Fair enough." I close her door and make my way around the back of my Jeep, so she can't see me adjusting myself in my shorts and climb in, then pull onto the street swiftly. "I can't believe how quickly Theo and Lachlan finished building the climbing wall."

"Lachlan's on vacation, so they have plenty of time to do the work. Theo has all the specialty tools, so it means they can work quickly."

"Right. That makes sense. I forgot about school vacation. Colton's too young to go to school yet, so it's not something I think about."

"Yeah, I probably wouldn't be keeping track of it if it weren't for the fact my sister's a teacher and her kids make a big deal about being on vacation while I still have to work." She chuckles.

"I know I've been checking in on you each day, but seriously, how have you been feeling this week? You haven't been overdoing things?" I'm genuinely concerned that she's not resting enough.

She turns her head to look at me and I fight to keep my eyes on the road where they belong. "I promise, I'm feeling fine and I'm not overdoing things. Thank you for always checking on me, it certainly wasn't part of our arrangement."

"You're welcome. As I said before, at the very least, I consider us to be friends."

"Well, you're incredibly sweet. Your future wife will be very lucky to have you." Her voice drops on the last part and she gazes out of her window as she figuratively takes five steps back from me and slams the door in my face. Just when I think I'm getting somewhere, that we're moving forward, she retreats.

"I guess so."

The rest of the ride to Em and Theo's home is made in silence, the tension inside the Jeep stifling. I guess I have to keep showing up and showing her that I'm not going anywhere.

As soon as I pull into the driveway behind what must be Theo's truck, Sarah has her seatbelt off and she climbs out. Once I collect the holds I need to attach to the climbing frame, I catch up to her at the bottom of the porch steps, confused as fuck with her change in mood. She knocks once on the screen door and then tries the handle, but the door is locked. Emma comes to the door, unlocking it quickly with a smile.

"Hey, you two. Come in." She leans forward, embraces her sister, then kisses my cheek. "Theo's out back. He's ready to help you with the finishing touches."

"Thanks, Emma. I guess I'll leave you two to catch up."

I move through their quiet home and step onto the back deck. The completed wall is sitting in the middle of the back-yard beneath the shade of a tree, but Theo's nowhere in sight. He must be in the workshop. Standing at the open door, I spot him wrapping his tool belt around his hips.

"Hey, Theo. The wall looks fantastic."

He spins around to face me. "Oh, hey. Yeah, it turned out pretty great. Lachlan and I are thinking of making a couple more to sell."

"Good idea." I hold up the box containing the holds. "I can show you how the holds work so you know how best to attach them."

"That'd be great."

We step out of the hot workshop and head over to the climbing wall. I place the holds out on the ground in what I think will be a good layout, explaining the different holds to Theo as I go. I make some final adjustments and Theo helps me attach them to the timber. It's so freaking hot, we've both taken off our shirts as Theo drills and I attach each hold where I want it to go.

The ladies are sitting on the back deck, enjoying a cool drink. Now and then, loud laughter fills the backyard, but still no kids. "Where are the kids?"

"Em's ex has the boys this weekend. He was supposed to have them last weekend but with Kenny's birthday, he didn't mind swapping it around. When the boys are with their dad, Kenny stays with my dad. It gives me and Em some time together on our own once a month. But boy do I miss the kids when they're not here."

"So, Sarah and I are intruding on your couple time. I'm sorry, man. I'm sure there are better things you could be doing with your wife than helping me. This could have waited another week. There's no rush."

He waves me off. "It's okay. This is only a couple of hours and then I'll have my girl all to myself." A smirk crosses his lips as he glances at Emma.

"All right. Well, let's get this finished, so you can get back to your lady."

We get back to the task, quietly working together and before I know it, the job's finished. "All right, let's load this bad boy onto the back of my truck. I'll grab the dolly."

Once we have it loaded onto the back of Theo's truck and secured, I grab Theo's bank details and transfer the funds across immediately, with some extra to account for the time he and Lachlan spent constructing the wall. Even though he said he didn't want to charge me for their time, I feel it's only fair. He can't do anything about it now the money's in his bank account. I smirk to myself.

"Come and have a cool drink before you guys head off," Emma calls out.

Theo comes out of the house holding a couple of small towels. "Here, this'll help you cool off." He tosses one over, and it's freezing cold, I look up at him in question. "I put them in the freezer before you got here."

I rub the icy towel across the back of my neck and down my torso. "Aww, man. This feels sooooo good."

Sarah steps outside with two large glasses of what looks to be iced tea. "Here ya go, boys. I think you've earned these." Her eyes rake up and down my body, following the towel as I wipe away the sweat, and she gives me a wink. Talk about mixed messages.

"Thanks." I take a long gulp, the cool liquid soothing my dry throat. "I needed that."

Emma steps out with a tray holding four glasses. "I figured one glass wouldn't be enough. Here ya go."

She places the tray on the table and Theo goes straight for his wife and kisses her forehead. "Thanks, Peaches."

We all sit around the large outdoor table, which I'm guessing was made by Theo, enjoying our cool drinks under the shade of the deck.

"The climbing wall looks great. Will your nephew be safe climbing it?" Emma asks.

"Yeah. I'll teach him the correct holds and I have a couple of padded mats to put at the base in case he falls. He's pretty agile, though. I organized this for him because he's climbing on everything inside the house and my sister and her wife are worried he'll get hurt."

Emma smiles brightly. "Austin could have done with one of those. That boy used to climb everything." She looks at Theo with a mischievous glint in her eye. "Remember when he climbed up the side of my house to rescue his parachute Avenger?"

Sarah gasps. "Oh my gosh. How could we ever forget? He sprained his wrist. Poor little man."

Theo chuckles. "Yeah, if I remember rightly, we had a few

words that day." There's a certain nostalgia in his gaze as he reminisces.

"Oh my. Yes, we did." She shakes her head with a smile. Obviously, the event holds some good memories for these two.

I glance between them. "Does Austin still like to climb?"

"Yeah, I guess so. There isn't anywhere for him to climb unless we go to the park," Emma responds.

"I'd be happy to take him to my climbing gym sometime. I could show him the ropes, so to speak," I offer.

Emma flicks her eyes to Sarah and then back to me. "I think he'd love that. I'll ask him."

"Great. Let me know and we can set up a time."

"I will. Thanks, AJ."

I feel good that I may be able to give something back to this family since they've been more than welcoming toward me. I finish my drink, remembering I'm taking up valuable alone time. "Well, we should hit the road and get outta your hair so you can enjoy what's left of your afternoon."

Sarah climbs to her feet, collects the glasses, and places them on the tray. I take the tray from her and head inside to wash them. "You're very domesticated." Sarah chuckles behind me.

I shrug. "I guess it comes from living on my own. If I don't do the dishes straight away, I have to do them later. No one else is going to do them for me."

We work side by side, her wiping the glasses and putting them away where they belong. Emma and Theo step inside. "Am I following behind you two, or are we all going in my truck?"

I glance at Sarah. "You can follow behind. That way you can come straight home and I can spend some time showing Colton how to climb safely."

"That makes sense." He turns to his wife. "Did you want to come too? We shouldn't be that long."

"I'll stay here and get the laundry folded so we have no interruptions to our afternoon." She winks at him and Sarah groans.

"Okay, you two. Can you at least wait until we're out of here before you start?" She chuckles.

Em and Sarah hug goodbye. "Say hi to the kids. I'm bummed I missed them today, but it was nice having some sister time."

"I will. Bye, AJ. Great seeing you again. I'll let you know what Austin would like to do."

I wave over my shoulder as Sarah and I head to my Jeep and reverse out of the driveway. I wait until Theo's behind me and then lead the way to my sister's place, making sure I don't leave Theo behind.

CHAPTER 21

—sarah—

Nerves have taken over my body and even with the air conditioning in the Jeep, I'm sweating more than I should, and I can't stop my leg from jiggling up and down. I'm worried his sister and her wife won't like me and they'll tell AJ he shouldn't help me. Ultimately, the child I'll be bringing into the world will be Colton's half-sibling. What if they change AJ's mind? I don't think I'd be lucky enough to find someone else as amazing as him.

I glance across at him, watching the muscles of his forearm tense and flex as he rests his hand on the steering wheel. What is it about muscular forearms that's such a turn-on? I'd never really thought about it before I saw AJ's perfectly muscular arms. I'm not into guys who look like they go to the gym seven days a week and are bulky like the Hulk but AJ's muscles are perfect. Masculine. Sexy.

He *only* sees you as a friend, Sarah! Stop thinking about his damn muscles.

Then why does he keep kissing you on the damn lips?

Good point. Why does he do that? Does he kiss all his friends on the lips? Surely not.

"So, do you have many female friends?" *Oh shit!* I can't believe I just blurted that out. "Sorry. It's none of my business," I rush to add.

He grins at me. That sexy grin which causes crinkles around his eyes and deep lines to bracket his mouth. "Let me think about that for a sec." He puts on a big show about tilting his head this way and that. "Nope. Can't say I have any female friends."

My body deflates as I release the breath I was holding while I waited for his answer. "Oh." *Oh,* Sarah? Really? That's the best you've got.

Silence fills the cab of the Jeep as we make our way toward his sister's house. It's not long before we're parking in front of a quaint cottage-style home. The garden reminds me of a *Home Beautiful* spring garden spread. I'm not sure how they've managed to have so much greenery in the middle of summer. "Your sister's home is gorgeous."

He looks out of his window at the property as Theo pulls around us and into their driveway. "Yeah, it's really nice. Lisa has a green thumb. If it were up to my sister, everything would be dead." She sounds a lot like me. I struggle to keep plants alive. Living in an apartment suits me for that very reason.

We both climb out of the Jeep and AJ opens the back door, pulling out two canvas mats so I move closer to help him. "I've got this. You probably shouldn't be lifting heavy stuff."

I smile at him. "I don't even know if I'm pregnant yet. It won't hurt me to help you."

He studies my face closely and eventually nods. "Okay, but be careful."

We work together to lift the mats out of his car and carry them up the driveway as Theo releases the straps securing the climbing wall. Two gorgeous women step outside, one holding the hand of a gorgeous little boy. I can easily pick his sister with her dark curls and chocolate-colored eyes. She has the same coloring as her brother and her son.

The little boy breaks away with an enormous smile. "Unca AJ!" he squeals, with his arms held up. AJ crouches down and catches the little bundle of energy easily. "Is that my climbing wall?" He studies it closely with wide eyes.

AJ stands with Colton secured in his arms, walking him closer to Theo's truck. "It sure is. What do ya think?" They study it closely.

"It's so big!" Colton stretches his arms out wide.

AJ laughs and jiggles Colton in his arms. "Hey, Colton. This is my friend, Sarah." Colton looks at me, then tucks his face into AJ's neck, hiding from me. "Don't pretend you're shy because we know you're not." AJ chuckles, but Colton buries in further.

I move closer. "Hey, Colton."

"Hello," he whispers shyly, tilting his head toward me.

The women make it to us with chuckles. "He's always so happy to see you." His sister presses up on her toes to kiss AJ's cheek.

"And so he should be. I'm his favorite uncle."

Theo and I both laugh. "We've heard that before. My brother, Max, says the exact same thing."

Hayley steps toward me. "You must be Sarah. I'm Hayley." She thumbs over her shoulder at AJ. "I'm this one's sister, and this is my wife, Lisa."

Lisa steps closer. "Hey, Sarah. Great to meet you." She turns to AJ. "This looks … big!" Her eyes are wide as she studies the climbing wall on the back of the truck.

"Great to meet you, too. This is my brother-in-law, Theo. He and my nephew built the climbing wall."

"Hi, Theo." The women say at the same time. "This is incredible. Thank you so much, and please thank your son."

Theo wipes his hands on the back of his shorts and holds

out his hand to shake hands with the two women. "I'll pass on your thanks to Lachlan. He'll be thrilled you were so happy with it."

AJ and Theo work together to get the climbing wall down off the truck and located under the shade of a tree in the backyard, which is as impressive as the front yard.

Colton reaches up for Hayley and she picks him up. "Mama, look at my climbing wall." He points across to where Theo and AJ are working.

"I know. You're a very lucky boy." He glances at me, then nods slowly as he buries his face into Hayley's shoulder.

"I'm not sure why he's being so shy today. He's not normally like this," Lisa tells me.

I chuckle. "It's probably because I'm a stranger."

Colton climbs down and races over to his uncle, leaving me with Hayley and Lisa.

"You have a gorgeous garden. My sister would be impressed." Emma's always prided herself on keeping her garden looking nice. It was tougher when she was a single mom and had to do everything for herself, but since she met Theo, she has more time to enjoy it.

"Thanks. It's all Lisa. She's the gardener." Hayley snickers.

"If it were up to her, everything would be dead." Lisa nudges Hayley good-naturedly.

I nod and grin. "Same. I live in an apartment, which means I don't need to worry about trying to keep plants alive. My sister's tried time and again to turn me into a gardener, but no dice." Shit! Maybe I shouldn't have told them I can't keep plants alive. They might think I won't be able to keep a human alive either. Oh, God. There go my chances.

Hayley laughs. "We could be sisters! Come inside, I'll get some drinks for everyone."

She tilts her head toward the back door and I follow her. They don't have a deck, but they have a really sweet outdoor table and chairs under a gazebo between the house and the tree.

"It looks like Colton enjoys playing outside." Between the swing set and the climbing wall, he's going to be a busy boy.

"Oh, he loves it. And that climbing wall couldn't come soon enough. Did AJ tell you about Colton's penchant for climbing?"

"Yeah, he did. He sounds like my nephew. He was always climbing everything too. Drove my sister crazy."

"Kids, huh?" Hayley comments as she pulls out glasses and a jug of juice to place on a tray.

"Yeah." My voice has a wistful quality to it as I think about life with a child in the picture. I can't wait. I glance around their home. It's nothing extraordinary, but it has a really lovely, homely feel about it. Their home reminds me of a cottage I'd find in a tiny beachside town.

When we step back outside, Theo and AJ have already placed the mats at the base of each side of the structure and Colton's already halfway to the top. AJ's behind him, guiding him with a careful explanation as to where to put his hand and foot next.

Theo spots me. "I'm gonna head home." He kisses the top of my head in much the same way Max does. "See you tomorrow?"

"Definitely."

He turns to Hayley and Lisa with a smile. "I'll see you both another time."

"Thank you, Theo. Colton loves it so much," says Lisa.

"Yeah, thanks, Theo." Hayley's eyes widen and she holds up a finger. "Hold on. Before you go, would you mind looking at something inside?" she asks as she places the tray of drinks on the table.

"Sure."

She gestures for Theo to follow her inside.

Lisa moves closer to me, leaving AJ with Colton. "I bet she's asking him about building her a new bookshelf. The woman buys paperbacks like they're going out of style."

"Oh, well, Theo does beautiful work and at a reasonable cost too."

"He did a fantastic job of the climbing wall." I nod in agreement and we watch AJ and Colton in comfortable silence.

Theo and Hayley return a few moments later. "I'll call you with a price on Monday."

"Thanks, Theo."

"Bye everyone," Theo calls as he waves over his shoulder, heading for the side gate with Lisa.

Lisa comes back around to us. "I'm just gonna grab some snacks. Colton will be looking for something to eat soon."

Hayley watches AJ and Colton with a smile on her face. "He's gonna make a great dad one day." I nod silently. I think my ovaries exploded when I watched him with Colton out the front when we first arrived, and again now, wow. He has such a lovely manner with the little boy, who is so much more than just a nephew to him. "I'm sure AJ's explained his true relationship with Colton, but he doesn't look at him as his son. Though, their bond is so much more than an uncle has with his nephew."

I turn my head toward Hayley. "Yeah, he explained the situation. I think it's amazing he could help you and Lisa to have your babies."

"Yeah. He's been incredibly supportive of me and Lisa. Unlike some family members." She mumbles the last part. "We're grateful he stepped up and suggested he be the donor for our baby when he didn't have to."

"Oh, I didn't know he suggested it. I figured you guys had asked him to do that for you."

She huffs out a quiet laugh. "Nope. Lisa and I hadn't even considered him a candidate." She smiles at me. "You'd think he would have been the first person we would have asked, but he wasn't even on our radar, and I'm not entirely sure why. We were signed up to use a stranger as our donor."

"It makes sense, though, right?"

"Oh, definitely. I love that Colton has some of me in him."

"Are you kidding? I don't think he has 'some of you' in him, he looks exactly like you," I tell her.

She smiles widely, her eyes twinkling. "And isn't that the kicker for Lisa? She carried him for nine months and had to go through the whole morning sickness thing and delivery and he comes out looking just like me!"

We both chuckle. "So unfair!"

"Lisa doesn't mind. She loves that he looks like me because she thinks I'm the most beautiful woman in the world." She flutters her eyelashes.

Awww. "That's so sweet."

"Mama! Look at me!" Colton calls out.

We both look over at the little ball of energy. He's straddling the peak of the climbing wall, both of his hands reaching high into the air.

"Colton. Remember you're supposed to have three points of contact at all times. You need to put one hand back on the wall." AJ explains calmly.

"Sorry, Unca AJ." He drops one hand, holding onto the top of the frame. "Mama! Look at me!"

Hayley moves closer to him. "Look at you! You're at the top of the mountain, looking oh so tall!"

Lisa comes back outside and moves next to Hayley, dropping her arm around her shoulders and pulling her back into her body as best she can with her baby bump. She kisses the top of her head, and Hayley glances up and smiles at her. I feel as though I'm surrounded by loved-up couples, and I should tear my eyes away from them to give them the courtesy of privacy but they're too sweet.

AJ coaches Colton as he carefully descends the other side of the wall, while his moms watch him with obvious pride. After a short while, Lisa turns to me. "Come and sit over here. AJ will keep Colton busy for a while."

I follow the women to the outdoor setting. My skin feels prickly as I realize I don't have anyone as a buffer while AJ's busy with his nephew. Lisa offers me a snack, while Hayley pours the juice.

I take a slice of apple and cheese for something to do, chewing slowly as I try to think of what to talk about.

"AJ was telling us you're trying to have a baby," Hayley's the first to break the silence.

I swallow the food in my mouth, but it gets stuck in my suddenly dry throat. Coughing, I try to dislodge the food as gracefully as I can. Lisa pats my back as Hayley hands me a glass of juice, both women watching me with worried eyes.

"Are you okay?" asks Lisa.

I manage to get myself under control so I can answer. "Yeah." My voice doesn't come out quite right, so I take another drink. "Sorry about that."

"That's okay. Hayley's not really known for her timing." Lisa smirks at her wife and Hayley lightly pushes her.

I look at Hayley, trying to portray confidence I'm sorely lacking. "Yeah, I am. I had two attempts through the fertility clinic, but neither were successful."

"We know how disappointing that can be." The two women glance at each other.

I nod. "Yeah. It costs a lot of money, so it meant I had to put any further attempts on hold until I could save for another round."

Both Lisa and Hayley nod. "We hear ya. It's not cheap."

"It took us about six months to get pregnant with Colton. So don't give up," Lisa shares. "AJ was patient with us. Never missed a single appointment."

I glance over at AJ. "He's been amazing so far. I was incredibly lucky when he offered to help me."

Hayley nods. "He's a good guy." She glances at Lisa and takes a sip of her drink. "Can I ask you a personal question?"

Here we go. "Sure." I try not to let my nervousness show in my voice.

"We know AJ is a great guy, but you didn't when you first met him. Why would you take up the offer of help for something like this from a complete stranger you know nothing about?"

"I'm hungry, Mama!" Colton interrupts as he climbs up onto a chair.

"Hey. You need to wash your hands first, little man! Come on, let's go." AJ holds his hand out to his nephew, giving me a subtle nod, checking I'm okay. Once I respond, he takes Colton inside and the three of us resume our conversation.

The interruption gave me a second to gather my thoughts. "That's a fair question. I debated with myself before I contacted AJ after he offered to help me. He put me at ease straight away because he was happy to answer any of the questions I had for him and he seemed kind. The thing that sealed the deal for me, though, was that he'd already helped you guys." I take a small sip of my drink. "Did he—"

"My hands are all clean!" Colton barges out the back door waving his hands in the air as he runs for us.

"Great job," Hayley praises as Lisa gives him a plastic plate.

He situates himself on a seat and selects a few different items, then makes himself comfortable as he nibbles on a cracker. AJ joins us at the table, grabbing a slice of cheese as he sits in the chair next to mine. I'm not sure if he realizes his leg is pressing against mine; the same as it was at Kenny's birthday. He leans forward to grab his drink, pushing his thigh harder against mine. He winks at me as he sits back. He has to know he's touching me and I take another drink for something to do.

"Thanks so much for organizing that amazing climbing wall, AJ," Hayley says.

"It turned out so much better than I imagined. Theo and Lachlan did an incredible job."

Lisa nods. "How old is Lachlan?"

AJ looks at me. "He's ten," I tell them.

Hayley's eyes widen. "Oh, wow. I'm impressed."

"I'll be sure to let him know. He only discovered he has a talent for working with wood when Theo moved next door to my sister when Lachlan was eight. He loves it."

AJ's attention moves to Lisa. "How have you been feeling?" He looks at me. "Lisa's had trouble keeping food down."

"I'm slowly managing to eat small amounts and keep it down. So I'm improving."

AJ nods then drops his hand across the back of my chair and collects my ponytail, twisting it around his hand. "That's great. Hopefully, you'll get back to your usual self soon." He tugs on my ponytail. "What were you guys talking about?"

I glance at the girls. "Hayley and Lisa were asking me why I accepted your offer of help when we were complete strangers. I was about to tell them about our meeting in the café."

His head snaps to the other two and creases form between his brows. "Does it matter? I offered, and Sarah accepted."

Hayley's the one to answer. "We were just interested. It's our way of getting to know Sarah as a person. After all, we'll all be connected when she has her baby."

I drop my hand on top of AJ's firm thigh. "It's okay, I don't mind. As I was saying, AJ and I met in a café and he was happy to answer my questions."

AJ chuckles under his breath. "She had this long-ass list with a million questions on it."

I scoff. "There weren't a million questions. Less than twenty."

He shrugs. "Twenty. One million. There's not that much difference."

We all laugh. "I tried to replicate the questionnaire the fertility clinic used. Then AJ kindly offered his semen analysis, which was stellar, by the way." He puffs up with pride and waves his hand across the table between Lisa's stomach and Colton with eyebrows raised. "Yeah, yeah, I get it," I say through my smile and gently push against him. He wraps his arm around me and pulls me back against him playfully as we both laugh.

I catch Lisa and Hayley giving each other a certain look and pull away, straightening up.

"What's semen?" Colton asks when his mouth is empty.

I glance at AJ. "It's the stuff that helps to make a baby," he tells Colton without missing a beat.

"Okay." Colton takes another cracker.

We spend the rest of the afternoon talking about lighter topics, which don't make me feel as though I'm tiptoeing through a minefield. Time passes quickly, and I grow more comfortable with AJ's family as the afternoon wears on.

AJ stands, collecting the dishes and loading them onto the tray. "I'll do these and then we can head off."

Lisa and Hayley glance at each other. "Did you want to stay for dinner? We were thinking of ordering Thai."

AJ looks at me. "I'm happy to stay, but it's up to Sarah."

Oh yeah, lay the decision at my feet. I mean, we were going to have dinner together anyway and I guess with his family present, it might help to have that barrier. The more time I spend on my own with AJ, the harder it is for me to remember we're only friends. He's generously offering me my dream on a platter, and I refuse to put it at risk by falling any further than I already have for the guy.

I shrug. "Sure. That sounds great."

"We usually order a variety of dishes and share them. Will that work for you, Sarah?" Lisa asks as she stands.

"That's perfect." AJ smiles and heads inside with the dishes. "I'll help AJ with the dishes." I thumb over my shoulder, then spin on my heel to follow him inside.

"I guess dinner's sorted."

AJ turns toward me, his posture a little stiff. "Are you okay with staying for dinner?"

"Of course. It was unexpected, so it took me a little by surprise." I don't feel comfortable when plans change at short notice, but since spending time with AJ, I'm beginning to learn to be a little more spontaneous.

AJ visibly relaxes and he smiles at me. "We don't do this very often. I would say they invited us to stay for dinner because they like you."

My cheeks heat and my stomach flips. "Really?"

"Yeah. Why are you so surprised?"

Should I tell him about my worries before we arrived?

Oh, what the hell, I decide to be honest. I drop my eyes to the floor between us, too embarrassed. "It was important to me that your sister and Lisa liked me. I didn't want them to think I wasn't good enough and I was worried they'd stop you from helping me. If I get pregnant—"

"Okay, I need to interrupt you there." He steps into my space, using his fingers to gently tip my chin up, so I can't hide. "I have a couple of issues with your thoughts. First, what's not to like? You're a great person, Sarah. Second, it's not up to anyone but me whether or not I help you." He raises an eyebrow and I try to interrupt, but he shakes his head. "Third, it's not *if*, it's *when* you get pregnant," AJ states firmly as if it's a sure thing I'll get pregnant. I hope he's right.

I smile and roll my eyes. "Okay. *When* I get pregnant, I imagine there will be times when we get together so the kids have regular contact with each other. I wanted those times to be comfortable, so it was important to me that Hayley and Lisa liked me."

He leans in close and kisses my forehead. "As I said. What's not to like? You're a great person, Sarah, and they would have worked that out very quickly."

CHAPTER 22

—aj—

I HAVEN'T SEEN NOR HEARD FROM SARAH SINCE WE SHARED dinner with Hayley and Lisa, apart from her brief responses to my daily texts to check on her. Some days, all I get is a thumbs up, as though she can't even be bothered to type a few words. Every time I think I'm moving forward with the woman, she steps back inside her fortress and slams the damn door. I've constantly run over our conversation from that day and can't figure out what I said or did wrong to make her withdraw from me.

I check the app on my phone which tracks her cycle. She's due to get her period today if she's not pregnant. I'm tempted to skip the message and turn up on her doorstep after work. I huff out a breath.

"What's up, man?" Dylan asks as he leans around his monitor to look at me, creases across his forehead. "You've been huffing and puffing and checking your phone all morning. I don't think I've ever seen you this agitated."

"Nothing."

"If you say so. It doesn't seem like nothing to me, though." He stands. "I'm making a fresh coffee. You want one?"

"Yes, please."

I glance back at my phone and spin it around on the smooth surface of my desk. What to do? It's not like I haven't been to her place before. My lips lift at the corners as I remember her expression when I turned up unannounced after she didn't respond to my messages. She took it pretty well that I'd used my skills to find out where she lives.

I give in and unlock my phone.

ME

How are you feeling today?

Same message every single day. Let's see how long it takes for her to respond. I'm not sure how I'm expected to concentrate while I wait for her answer. Dylan steps back into the office with two cups, placing mine next to me.

"Here ya go." He takes a careful sip of his hot drink and sits at his desk. "So, how are things going with Sarah? I'm assuming she's why you're so bothered."

I blow out a long breath. If I can't talk to my best friend about her, who can I talk to? "I dunno, man. I feel like I take two steps forward with her and five steps back again."

"What do you mean? You're only trying to get her pregnant, right?" The confusion on his face would be comical if it didn't match mine.

"Yeah, that's how it started and what was supposed to happen, but … we've spent a bit of time together and I … well, I really like her. I'd maybe like to see where things could go between us."

"Right. Well, that's unexpected."

"I know. It wasn't the original plan. I thought I'd get a few months of guaranteed sex, but it hasn't been like that. I don't want to share too much because it's personal, but I've developed strong feelings for her … and we haven't actually … uh been intimate."

Dylan begins coughing; choking on the coffee he just swallowed. "Shit, man. Give a guy some warning." He wipes his mouth. "So, how in the hell are you supposed to knock her up?"

"We've been doing it like they would at the clinic. It's all been very clinical so far. And as much as I want to help her have a baby and fulfill her dream, I don't want her to be pregnant yet, because I need more time with her." I pause, shaking my head. "Fuck, I'm an asshole."

Dylan rolls his chair around to my side of the desk. "You like her that much?" I nod. "Have you told her?"

I shake my head. "I can't tell her. She has so many damn walls up, that it's almost impossible to break through. Every time I think I've made progress, she throws up another wall and I feel as though I'm back at the beginning."

"You know as well as I do, there's always a way in. You just have to find the weakness."

My phone vibrates and we both glance down. Dylan's eyes rise back to mine and a smile spreads. "Speaking of the woman of the moment."

I snatch up my phone like my life depends on it.

CUPCAKE

I'm sorry to tell you it didn't work again

I got my period *crying emoji*

My expression must give away my thoughts. "What's wrong?"

"She's not pregnant."

Dylan's expression turns somber. "Sorry. But I guess it means you'll still get to see her, right?" He widens his eyes and raises his eyebrows. "Just like you wanted."

I blow out a harsh breath, rubbing my hand across my

mouth. "Yes and no. I want her to get pregnant, but I don't want to stop seeing her." My phone buzzes again.

CUPCAKE

I'm sorry. If you want to rescind your offer, I completely understand

I must have taken too long to respond and she's taking it as a lack of interest.

ME

I'm not going anywhere until you're pregnant

"That's where you're going wrong, AJ," Dylan states adamantly as he points to my screen.

"What do you mean?"

"You just told her you're not going anywhere *until* she's pregnant." He studies me closely, but I'm still lost. He shakes his head. "When you say it like that, it sounds like you only want to be involved *until* she's pregnant, and then you're done. No wonder she's as closed off as she is. She doesn't think there's a relationship between the two of you. Well, nothing beyond getting her pregnant."

Shit! "I thought I was doing the right thing because she doesn't seem to want a partner, only a donor."

"I think you might need to have a chat."

I nod. "Yeah. I think you might be right."

CUPCAKE

Thank you. I'll let you know when I'm ovulating again

ME

I have a tracker on my phone. I know when you're due to ovulate but I think we need to talk

The dots bounce up and down. They stop. And it takes so long for something to happen that my screen locks.

"Well, that's not good. I say we need to talk and she disappears."

"She probably thinks it's weird that you're tracking her cycle, man." He scoffs.

I frown. "What's weird about it? I needed to keep track if I'm going to help her properly. Last month I was out of town and had to fly back. I'm trying to avoid those situations."

"I guess so. But it's a bit weird."

CHAPTER 23

—sarah—

HE WANTS TO TALK. *SHIT!* I RUN MY HANDS THROUGH MY HAIR, grasping the strands tightly on either side of my head.

Does he want out of this arrangement?

Calm down, Sarah. He also said he wasn't going anywhere *until* I was pregnant. The muscle in my chest spasms at the thought of getting my dream but not seeing the man I spend way too much time thinking about.

The man I'm falling for.

But when your boyfriend, not that he's my boyfriend, says we need to talk, that never bodes well. I stand from my desk and pace down the hallway, making a loop around our floor. I can't sit still as I try to figure out why he suddenly needs to 'talk.'

"Hey, Sarah. Do you have a minute?" Lucy asks as I walk by her desk.

"Uh, sure. What is it?"

"Do you think I could take Friday off from work? I want to spend the day with the kids before they go back to school."

We always check with each other when taking planned leave because we usually step in and do the other's work when they're away. She'll divert her phone and emails to me for the day, so nothing gets missed. When I'm away, I do the same.

"It shouldn't be a problem. I'll be here Friday, and it's always quiet by the afternoon. Enjoy the day with your kids."

Her smile is instant, the relief obvious. "I feel as though I've hardly seen them."

"No problem. Just let Jeff or Frank know in HR." I tap my fingers on her desk and keep walking.

As I make my way down the other hallway back to my desk, I think about how I'm going to manage to work full-time with a baby. Obviously, I'll need to take some time off at first and I'm sure Eric would let me work part-time from home. Hang on. Eric won't be my boss by then. His grandson, Adam, will be. I wonder if he'll be as flexible as Eric. Shit. My plan to have a baby couldn't have come at a worse time with Eric retiring.

"What's that sigh for, Sarah?" Eric startles me as I take my seat back at my desk. He knows I'm trying to have a baby. Even though he thought it was unacceptable for a single woman to be trying to get pregnant on her own, he still gave me his blessing and promised to accommodate any changes I would need to make to my work schedule. There's a daycare center in the building I've looked at. I'll need to put my name down for a place the minute I know I'm pregnant.

"Nothing. Just thinking. Did you need something?"

His eyes soften. "You're worried about something. I can see it. We haven't worked together all these years for me to not recognize the signs." I slump my shoulders. I shouldn't put my concerns on Eric's shoulders. He's my boss and he has enough going on with getting the company ready to hand over. "Talk to me," he prompts.

"I'm a little worried about my plans to have a baby. What if your grandson isn't as accommodating as you?"

"Oh." He waves his hand through the air, swatting away

my worries. "I'll have it written into the changeover documents. You don't need to worry about any of that. I promise he'll take good care of you."

"It seems a lot to ask a new boss when he'll need me to show him where everything is and help him get used to how this place runs."

"Don't worry about it, Sarah. It will all be okay. I know how much you worry when things change, but I'm hoping this transition will be seamless." He can hope all he likes, but that doesn't mean it'll be that way.

"Oh, Lucy asked for Friday off. I didn't think it would be an issue since there's barely anyone in on Fridays."

"Of course. The kids will be back at school soon, and she's barely had any time to spend with her children. They need to have their mother around more." His forehead wrinkles as he contemplates. "Maybe we should introduce some kind of policy that allows mothers to have the ability to work from home during school vacation."

I widen my eyes. "You could make the policy to include fathers. I'm sure they'd like to spend time with their kids during their vacation too."

He slashes his hand through the air. "No. That sort of thing really should be left to the mother." He spins on his heel and heads back into his office mumbling something.

I love Eric. Working for him has been wonderful for me but he's a little old-fashioned in his views. Maybe his grandson will be more of a forward thinker in terms of gender roles. We only have two women on staff here and both of us hold secretarial positions. I remember there were a handful of women who applied for the Vice President position when it was available and Eric and Johnathon, the previous Vice President, dismissed them outright without even reading over their applications. Perhaps it'll be good to have a change in leadership around here, because I get the sense Tony likes to keep women in their place, too.

My phone catches my attention and I realize I haven't responded to AJ's message. What does he want to talk about? Is he not happy with the arrangement? He has a goddamn app tracking my cycle for goodness sake. He seems pretty serious about following through with my pregnancy plan. But things change. I did say we would reevaluate if he met someone he wanted to pursue. Oh my God. Has he met someone? Is that it?

I pick up my phone and unlock the screen, reading back over our chat thread. The words are typed as clear as day that he's not going anywhere until I'm pregnant.

Until I'm pregnant.

That doesn't mean he'll be around after. I know it was the original arrangement, but things have changed for me. I know I wasn't supposed to catch feelings for the guy, but how can I not? He's amazing. Any woman would be lucky to have him. *Just message the poor guy, Sarah.*

ME

Okay. When would you like to talk?

I place the phone back on my desk and try to concentrate on the email I'm supposed to be drafting, but my eyes won't stay on the computer screen, instead skipping back to my phone. It lights up and I almost jump out of my skin.

AJ

How about tonight? I can bring dinner

and chocolate

He remembered I crave chocolate when I get my period. My heart expands, thumping heavily in my chest.

ME

Okay, but I can cook and I have chocolate already

AJ

I insist. Save your food, my treat

ME

Thank you

As expected, this afternoon dragged and I couldn't concentrate for the rest of the day. I may as well have gone straight home after AJ's message. My mind kept running in circles of *what-ifs* —making me almost dizzy as I leave for the day. The humidity is shocking as I step from the air-conditioned building onto the sidewalk. I stop at the liquor store and grab a couple of craft beers I know AJ will enjoy. Even though I'm not drinking, there's no reason for him to miss out and even though I'm careful with my money, he deserves a treat.

I walk through the door of my apartment and immediately slip off my shoes; as cute as these shoes are, by the end of the day, they pinch my feet. I glance at the clock and decide I have time for a shower so long as I don't linger.

At six-thirty, there's a knock on the door. My stomach immediately rolls with anticipation for our 'talk,' and my palms are instantly damp. I draw in a deep breath in the hopes of calming myself and answer the damn door. My heart skips a beat as I lay eyes on AJ in a navy and white striped V-neck T-shirt and navy shorts. His warm brown eyes lock on me and his lips slowly tip up. He holds up the food, which is dangling from two fingers, making his bicep bulge. I drag my tongue across my bottom lip. *Stop it!*

His smile drops and I'm certain he moans low in his throat, but I can't be sure. He swallows and I watch his Adam's apple bob. So damn sexy. Everything about this man is like he was made to my exact specifications. Frown lines form above his brows. "Sarah?"

I realize I've been standing in the open doorway looking at him like he's a piece of meat. *Good one!* I quickly move into action, stepping out of the way so he can pass through. "Sorry."

He leans in, landing a kiss on my lips but doesn't linger. His scent surrounds me, overwhelming my senses like it always does. "Are you okay? And don't tell me you're fine if you're not. You can be honest with me."

"I'm fine. Honestly. Nothing a delicious dinner won't fix, followed by some chocolate, Midol, and a heat pack."

He places the food on the counter and steps back into my space. He gently cups the side of my face and I barely resist the temptation to press into his large hand. His eyes slowly trace every single inch of my face. "Your eyes are incredible. The way they're always changing color. I hope our baby has your eyes." I suck in a sharp breath. He said, *our baby*. Not *your* baby but *ours*. Does that mean something or am I getting carried away as usual?

"Th-thank you. I have the same eyes as Emma and Max, which we get from our mom." Great Sarah. He's paying you a compliment, not seeking a family genetics lesson.

He smiles. "Well, you're all very lucky." He points to his warm chocolate eyes. "Mine are boring. Always the same color, day in, day out."

"I don't know about boring. You have warm eyes, caring and inviting." I slam my mouth closed. Now I've said too much.

"You think so?" I nod. We stand silently, trapped in each other's gaze for I don't know how long. He swallows again and my eyes drop to watch the action and unbidden, I mirror him. He reaches up and slides a lock of my hair through his fingers, his eyes dropping to watch, then lift back to mine as he releases the strands. "I guess we should eat before the food gets cold."

I take a step back and chuckle nervously. We just had a moment, right? I wasn't imagining it. "Good idea." Trying to lighten the tone, I rub my hands together. "What delicious treat did you bring with you tonight?"

"Vietnamese. I hope you don't mind."

"Oh, I don't think I've eaten Vietnamese food before."

"Well, you're in for a treat. The freshness of the flavors is something else."

He moves around my kitchen with familiarity and busies himself dishing up plates of food, while I pull out a beer for him and pour myself a glass of filtered water. When he places our dinner on my small table, his eyes snap up to mine. "You didn't have to get me beer."

I shrug. "I figured it's the least I could do since you were bringing dinner. I bought a six-pack, so you can take home whatever you don't drink while you're here."

"I can leave it here for next time." He sits, not realizing the impact his words have on me. I guess that means he's not telling me he needs to stop helping me with my pregnancy plan.

I take my first bite of the rolls AJ put on my plate and the fresh flavors burst across my tongue. "Mmm, you weren't kidding. This is delicious."

He nods at me with a mouthful of food, his eyes smiling. He chews and swallows. "Right?"

We continue to eat as he fills me in on the meeting he had with Oliver over the phone today. He asked him and Dylan to test out the system for the *Parkerville Project*. Apparently, the *CornerStone Foundation* supports it by providing the majority of its funding. They had money stolen a couple of years ago, and

Oliver wants to ensure their system is secure and there is no possibility of it happening again.

"So, if we do a good job on that project, securing their systems to prevent possible future fraud, he said the next job we do for him would be to check over *Stone Corporate Investments*." AJ's excitement is palpable, and I can't help but get caught up in it with him. "This is a huge coup for us. With the job we recently won, then the one from Vegas, and now this one, big business will be beating down our door."

I lean forward, awkwardly engulfing AJ in a hug. "Congratulations. I'm so happy for you guys."

"Thanks. Dylan and I couldn't be happier with how our business is growing. We may need to take on another team member, which would be incredible."

"Oh, wow. That *is* a big deal."

We finish eating and AJ collects the plates from the table. I beat him to the sink and fill it with soapy water, so I can clean up before he does. He's always cleaning up and I don't think it's fair since he provided the meal.

"I was going to do the dishes," he tells me as he tries to work his body into position in front of the sink.

I turn my head, not realizing how close our faces are, our lips only inches apart. I raise my eyes to his and wish we were in a place where it would be okay to steal a kiss whenever I pleased. His warm breath brushes across my cheek and I quickly snap my head forward and wash the dishes. "Nope. I'm doing them tonight. You're always cleaning up after everyone. It's my turn since you brought dinner."

"And you're probably beginning to feel uncomfortable and should sit. Come and put your feet up."

"I'm okay. I can manage." It astounds me how in tune AJ already is with me, considering we haven't lived together or spent all that much time together. Michael never knew when I was getting my period or considered I might be experiencing discomfort at this time of the month. He wouldn't have had a clue when I was ovulating or what was going on with my body. I glance at AJ out of the corner of my eye, checking to see if he's real.

We work in comfortable silence until the job is complete and my nerves start getting the best of me again. I'm guessing he'll want to have the 'talk' now. I pull up my big girl panties and ask, "Did you want to have that talk now?"

"Yeah, sure. Let's get you comfortable on the couch and I'll grab a beer." He takes over, guiding me to the couch, then returns with chocolate, Midol, and a heat pack as well as a fresh beer. It feels strange to be cared for in such a way but when I think back over every interaction I've had with AJ, I realize he's been doing it from the very beginning. He sits beside me on the couch, handing me my current project. I think he's figured out I'm better at communicating when my hands are busy.

"Thanks. So, what did you want to talk about?" Let's get started.

He twists his body so he's facing me directly. "I hope you know I would never share anything truly personal with anybody outside of our relationship."

Relationship. He used the word, relationship.

I scrunch my eyebrows together because I'm not sure where he's going with this. "Um, yeah?"

"In saying that, I was agitated at work this morning and Dylan was asking me what was wrong. Then in between, you and I were texting. He saw the texts as they came through."

My cheeks heat with embarrassment at Dylan knowing I got my period today, not that it's anything out of the ordinary, but it's not something I normally share. I only shared it with AJ so he knew I wasn't pregnant this month. "Oh." But then it registers he said he was agitated at work *before* my messages. "Is everything okay with you? Why were you upset at work?"

He blows out a heavy breath. "Yes and no. I … uh … I felt as though I said or did something which upset you on Saturday."

I rack my brain, running through our conversation from Saturday, and shake my head. "I can't remember being upset with you on Saturday."

"It sort of felt like we were getting along okay and then suddenly you pulled back from me, which made me think I'd done something to upset you. Then today, Dylan saw the messages and he thinks he knows what I may have said to upset you."

"Oh. And what does he think you've said?"

"He thinks when I say things like 'I'll be around *until* you're pregnant,' it may be upsetting to you. That I'm implying we won't see each other once you're pregnant." My eyes widen. Dylan must be incredibly intuitive to pick up on that type of thing. I don't know too many guys who would be so switched on. AJ smiles and tips his head down, then looks back at me. "That's it, isn't it?"

I nod slowly, embarrassed. "It's okay, AJ. That was our arrangement, remember? There won't be any need for us to see each other once I'm pregnant. You have your life, and I have mine and they'll be quite different once I have the baby. I won't have as much time to spend with friends, especially in the early months; having to get up for feedings and diaper changes throughout the night. I'm betting on the weekends, I'll be a zombie and won't be pleasant company." I chuckle.

"But you see, the thing is, Sarah, I've grown to really like you. I enjoy your company, and I would hope once you're pregnant, you'll still allow me to drop around occasionally with dinner. Or, you know, I could watch the baby while you have a nap or something. I don't want to lose the friendship we have."

Friendship. That dreaded word.

"Oh, well, we can definitely do that if I have the time. No

expectations, though. I'm sure you'll be sick of seeing me by then, anyway." I try to make my voice as upbeat as possible because the thought of not seeing AJ regularly hurts my heart.

I've fallen for this guy and it was the last thing I was supposed to do.

"There was something else I wanted to talk with you about. I have an idea and I want you to hear me out before you shoot me down." He widens his eyes, waiting for my agreement, which I give. "I think we need to try a different approach to getting you pregnant. I don't think the collection condom/syringe combo is working."

Dread fills me but I turn my body to face him more directly. "What would you suggest we do?"

"Hear me out, okay?" I nod. "I think we should have sex. Old-fashioned, missionary position, with the cushion under your butt, sex. Or maybe doggy style. I read that's pretty good for what we're trying to do. Cut out the middle-man, so to speak."

I'm frozen. Paralyzed where I sit. All of the air has been sucked out of my apartment.

"Sarah? Cupcake? Are you okay?" He places his hand on my shoulder, squeezing firmly to gain my attention. "Sarah. Take a breath."

Oh, God! He wants to have sex to get me pregnant. I can't do that! I'm already halfway in love with the guy.

"Sarah! Take a breath."

He shakes me and I snap out of my shocked state with a gasp. "I … I … can't … breathe." I manage to get out. I flap my hand in front of my face.

"Jesus, what do I need to do?" He stands, pulls me to my feet, and drags me to the window, opening it and pushing the top half of my body outside. I draw in gasping breaths, filling my lungs with each suck in and blow out. "Shit! Are you okay?"

I turn to look at him for the first time since he dropped his helpful suggestion, but my vision is fuzzy. I think his eyebrows are furrowed over his eyes and even though I can't see him properly, his worry for me is radiating from him in waves. It's almost stifling. I draw in deep breaths and try to regain my composure. That was possibly the last thing I imagined when he said we needed to 'talk.' And I'm not sure why it wasn't something I even considered a possibility.

"Are you okay?" He helpfully rubs his hand up and down my back, sending my body haywire. He has zero idea of the impact his touch has on me. How his concern affects me, my heart.

Without making eye contact I nod. "Yeah. Sorry about that. I'm not sure what happened."

"I think you had a panic attack. You ever had those before?"

I shake my head. "No. I don't think so," I whisper. Well, not that severe, anyway.

"Was it the idea of having sex with me that set you off?" My eyes snap up to his, my cheeks heating in embarrassment. I want to lean forward and erase the frown lines between his eyebrows but I daren't.

I nervously laugh. "Uh, what … no … of course not," I scoff. My heart beats an erratic rhythm and I'm worried I'm having a heart attack now. I'm too young to have a heart attack, right?

"Then what set you off?"

Oh, God! I can't tell him I've fallen for him and if we actually have sex, I'll be asking him to marry me. He'll think I'm a fruit loop and run for the hills, never to be seen again. He only agreed to be my donor, not tie himself to me for life. I step away from him to get some space and air that's not filled with his citrus scent, which is an aphrodisiac for me. "It … it's just that was never part of my plan. I don't like it when plans change suddenly and I'm unprepared." There, that doesn't sound too crazy. I hope.

He chuckles mildly. "I've sort of picked up on that trait of yours. I'm not saying we should have sex right now. You have time to get your head around the idea." He digs his phone out of his pocket and checks something. "You have ten days to get used to the idea."

My mouth drops open. "You really do have an app to follow my cycle."

"Yeah. I told you I did."

The tension I'd been holding in my body releases a little. "I was worried you wanted to talk about ending our arrangement because maybe you'd met someone." I point toward his phone. "But you're taking this seriously." I step closer and lay my hand on his forearm. "Thank you. And I'll think about the next step."

He grabs the back of his neck and looks down at the floor between us. "I have … uh … met someone."

I remove my hand from his arm as though I've been burned. "Oh."

"I'm taking it slow. I'm not sure if she feels the same for me as I do for her, and I'm trying my best not to rush things because I don't want to scare her off."

Well, if anyone knows how that feels, it would be me. I smile at him, but I'm certain it looks forced. "Are you sure you want to move forward with my pregnancy plan? She might not appreciate you spending time with me, to uh … you know, get me pregnant."

CHAPTER 24

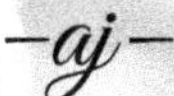

DAMN IT! I'VE SCREWED UP. I SHOULDN'T HAVE TOLD HER I'D met someone. She's going to assume it's someone else, and I can't tell her it's *her*.

"Oh yeah. I made a promise, and I intend to keep it."

"Well, I definitely don't think we should have sex then. That's not fair to the woman you're seeing." She's pulling away again. Me and my stupid mouth, but I didn't know what else to say to throw her off.

"It's okay. Honestly. I think it's all one-sided. An infatuation. It's not like we're dating, or anything. I made a promise to you first and I always follow through with my promises." I step back into her space. "I think you should give my suggestion the consideration it deserves. It'll be more efficient. It's the method that's worked for thousands of years."

She chews on her bottom lip and drops her eyes to the floor. Uncertainty is written all over her face. "I don't know if it's such a good idea. I don't want feelings to get involved for either of us or your lady to get hurt."

She doesn't want feelings to get involved. See, dickhead, it's all one-sided. You're way over your head here. My heart constricts. How is it I find the perfect woman and she only wants me to be her donor? She's so determined to stick to her plan that she doesn't see me at all. But I made a promise, and it's not her fault I've fallen for her when it was never part of the plan. I lower my voice. "Don't worry. Feelings won't get involved. I promise."

She nods slowly, her eyes become glassy, but she blinks quickly, then turns her face away from mine as she swallows. "Okay."

My eyes widen in surprise. Okay? Did she just agree to try my idea? Or was it okay because there won't be feelings involved?

I run my tongue across my dry lips. "Great. You can come to my place next Thursday night." Sarah nods. I think I should leave before the conversation gets any more complicated and I say more shit I shouldn't say. "All right, I'll head off and leave you to your evening. Are you gonna be okay? Do you need anything?"

She smiles and her entire face changes. Gone is the worry, replaced by a lightness I'd like to always see. I don't like that I've upset her. "I'm okay. Stop worrying about me. I promise I've managed just fine on my own."

I want to tell her that she no longer has to manage on her own, that I'm here now and I can help her, but we've just gotten back onto steady footing and I don't want to mess that up again.

"Okay. Call or text if you need anything. I'll see you in ten days unless you're free to get together before then." I lean into her and lay a soft kiss on her jawline near her ear, and she sucks in a sharp breath. I know she's somewhat affected by me, but she's bound and determined to resist it every step of the way for some damn reason.

"Take," I call down to Dylan. I needed to climb today. The excess energy in my body is driving me crazy the closer the clock ticks down to our arranged dinner date.

Not a date.

Stop thinking of it as a date. For fuck's sake. It's an impregnation session. Yeah. That's what I'll refer to it as in my head so I don't get too carried away. I don't want to scare the woman away. I think I'll be walking a fine line tonight.

"Are you ready to lower?" he calls back.

"Ready to lower."

My feet land on the mat and Dylan loosens the rope. "You're climbing like a machine."

I'm distracted in my reply. "Yeah. Thanks."

His hand lands on my shoulder and I look up at my long-time friend. "Hey. You okay?"

I blow out a breath. "Yeah. Just have a lot of nervous energy I need to burn."

"What has you so nervous? Is it because of the inevitable phone call from your grandfather tomorrow morning?"

My grandfather. The current bane of my existence. I'm going to drag that man into the twenty-first century kicking and screaming if I have to. He'll give the damn job to Mom or Hayley by the time I'm finished with him. "Nah, I haven't really thought about him, but I am getting ready for a face-to-face meeting. I've put together a slideshow of all the women who fill CEO roles in big business as well as their achievements and what they bring to the table." Dylan snickers. "Sarah's coming over tonight." I don't need to say anything more. Understanding washes over his features.

"You've got this. Just keep doing what you're doing and she'll come around. How can she resist you? You're perfect boyfriend material." He squeezes my shoulder then we release our ropes.

"Thanks, man. And thanks for coming with me this afternoon. I needed this."

"No problem." We both collect our bags and go our separate ways in the parking lot.

I walk in the door and head straight to the shower with thoughts of what's going to happen in a few short hours. Not gonna lie, I've been dying to get my hands and mouth on her sweet body. I can't count the number of times I've rubbed one out in the shower to thoughts of touching that smooth skin, running my hands over her killer curves—and there I go again. My cock grows and throbs.

"You're gonna have to wait a little longer, buddy. I don't want to waste a single drop of my swimmers today. They're all for Sarah." My dick taps against my stomach at the thought of filling Sarah with my cum, seeing her round with my baby. I blow out a breath and turn the water to freezing, trying to think of something else that will help my body calm down. Ignoring my dick, I wash my hair and my body, then step out and dry off.

I've noticed Sarah seems to like it when I wear my Henleys, so I choose a black one and pair it with my favorite jeans. I make sure the bathroom's tidy and do the same with my bedroom. I don't live like a slob, but I don't want Sarah to step in here and see any mess. I need everything to go perfectly tonight. I give one last cursory look to make sure I haven't missed anything and then head downstairs to make sure the living room is tidy.

Once I'm happy with everything, I grab the ingredients I need and start preparing dinner. I can't cook it in advance, but I can have everything on hand ready to go. I slice the chicken and peel the shrimp, then prepare the vegetables according to the instructions. Glancing at the time, I still have twenty minutes and too much nervous energy, so I grab a beer and head upstairs to my outdoor deck. I watch the traffic in the street as I lean on the glass and try to settle my thoughts, but they land back on Sarah like they always seem to do.

I get that her high school boyfriend hurt her when he took the promotion and left for Australia without considering her, but I wonder why she's so determined to do this baby thing on her own. Am I hoping for something that'll never happen between us because she only sees me as a donor and nothing more? How can I make her see me as something more? Can I make her fall for me, the way I've fallen for her?

I take the last sip of my beer as I see her teal Yaris park in front of my place. It's showtime.

CHAPTER 25

—*sarah*—

Our lack of success for the last two months has landed me on AJ's doorstep, promising him that I'll try this *his* way. I'm not so sure it's a good idea when he's interested in someone else. And wasn't that a stab to my already tender heart, finding out he's interested in someone. I don't know how I'm going to survive this experience with my heart intact.

I like the guy.

Really like him.

But he likes someone else. I need to remember that.

I *was* hoping it wouldn't come to this. My stomach rolls and my heart knocks rapidly against my ribs as I contemplate what's about to happen. Raising my shaky hand, I press the doorbell and try to draw enough oxygen into my lungs so I don't pass out. Imagine that, AJ opens the door to find me collapsed on his stoop. I spin on my heel to face the street as a distraction and focus on gaining my self-control while I wait for him to answer the door.

Within less than a minute, the sound of the door opening has me turning around to face the man who has infiltrated my thoughts at every turn. Starting at the floor, I take in his bare feet, torn jeans, and black Henley.

Shit! I'm in so much trouble. I'm a sucker for AJ in a Henley.

This is going to be tougher than anything I've ever done. But if this works and I get pregnant, then all of this discomfort will be worth it. With a bit of luck, I'll be pregnant this time next week and I can put all of this behind me and focus on the future. And he can work on building his relationship with someone that's not me. I could cry at the thought.

His lips spread in welcome and he steps back, making room for me to enter his home for the first time. "Hey, Sarah." He leans forward, his warm breath ghosting across my skin as he presses a tender kiss to my jaw near my ear, and my flesh burns at his touch. It's not the first time he's kissed me there, and my reaction this time is no less potent than it was then.

"Hey." I try to make my voice light so he doesn't pick up on my nerves. His place has an industrial feel to it with a combination of rough brick and smooth concrete walls, as well as large factory-style windows. It should feel cold and sterile, but it feels warm and inviting. I would never have guessed this was a home from the outside because it looks like a factory with a roller door at the side of the building. I was expecting it to be dark and dank on the inside. I couldn't be more wrong. Even though the space is large and open, it has a certain homeyness to it. My entire apartment could probably fit inside his living room space. "You have a beautiful home."

"Thank you. It took a bit of work to get it to where I wanted it to be, but I'm happy with the outcome." I nod as he leads me deeper into his home and across gorgeous hardwood floors. "This is the kitchen, which is probably obvious." He half chuckles. *Is he as nervous as I am?* "And the space at the back of the house is my office. Dylan and I work here." He slides open a huge barn door to reveal the most incredible computer setup I've ever seen outside of the office. "All of the bedrooms are upstairs." He points to the ceiling.

"Wow. This is impressive." I'm genuinely impressed as I'm sure he can tell by my wide eyes as I take in everything.

"Thanks. Would you like a drink or anything?"

Since my tongue is stuck to the top of my mouth, I figure it may be a good idea to have a drink. I swallow around the dryness. "I wouldn't mind a glass of water if you don't mind."

"Of course." He deftly reaches up to grab a couple of glasses, exposing toned ab muscles just above the top of his jeans. I quickly tear my eyes away and watch the play in the muscles of his forearms as he releases the lever on the filtered water tap to fill them. His hand is steady as he passes a glass to me, and I take it, trying to hide the tremble in mine. His eyes rise to mine and a comforting smile touches his lips. "Are you nervous, Sarah?"

I half-laugh with embarrassment. "Yeah. How could you tell?"

He moves into my space and his scent surrounds me, comforting me, making me feel safe. From the first instant I met AJ, I felt completely safe in his company. He takes my free hand in his and my eyes drop to watch his much larger hand surround mine. "Your hand is shaking and your voice has a slight tremor that would be unnoticeable to most people unless they were paying attention."

My eyes snap up to his. I swallow. Has he moved closer? The lighter flecks of caramel in his chocolate eyes are impossible to miss with him this close to me. His other hand rises and he tucks a lock of hair behind my ear, then strokes his knuckles gently down the side of my face to my chin. He raises my face to his and I swallow the excess saliva that's decided to multiply in my mouth. "You don't need to be. We'll do everything at your pace. If you feel uncomfortable at any time, just say so.

Okay?" He crouches down so he's at eye level, raising his brows in question on the last word.

How can he be so calm about this? *We're about to have sex!* It's not a date, where one thing leads to another and we *may* end up in bed together. This is *planned* sex and it feels terribly awkward.

I nod silently and his eyes follow the movement. One side of his mouth tips up and he moves closer, pressing his lips to mine tenderly. They're warm and soft, and I would give anything to be able to return his kiss, but I can't.

I need to keep myself in check.

He's doing this to help me get pregnant.

He's not in love with me.

He doesn't want a future with me. He wants someone else.

The reminders run through my head on a loop and I draw back, putting much-needed space between us. If he's disappointed he doesn't show it. "I thought we could eat dinner upstairs on the deck. How does that sound?"

He's acting normal. Like tonight's no big deal, so I follow his lead. If he can do this, so can I.

"That sounds nice." I hold up my sweater. "I have this if it gets a little cool." I set my purse and sweater on a stool and wash my hands at the kitchen sink. "Anything I can do to help?"

"Nope. You sit there"—he points to a stool situated at the counter—"and look beautiful."

I get comfortable on the designated stool as my cheeks flush. While he cooks dinner for us, I take a sip of my water and run through everything I've seen so far of AJ. He helps clean up whenever he's at someone else's home. I look around his neat home and decide he must do a decent job with housework, and now I find he cooks. He's fantastic looking. Is sweet and thoughtful, as well as generous with his time and his … uh sperm. He runs his own successful business and defies gravity by climbing rock walls. I can't find any faults with the man.

He holds up a plate with shrimp, snapping me out of my head and back to his kitchen. "You okay with these? I can leave them out."

"No. I'm all good. I'm not allergic to anything that I know of. Are you?" Do allergies get passed down through the genes? I should probably look that up. I take another sip of water.

"No, nothing that I know of." He turns back to the wok and continues preparing the delicious-smelling meal.

"What are you cooking?"

"Char Kway Teow. It's a Malaysian noodle dish. I hope you like it."

"It smells divine, I'm pretty sure if it tastes half as good as it smells, I'm gonna love it."

He scoops out two healthy servings and holds the bowls up in front of him. "Would you mind bringing up the drinks and cutlery?"

"Sure." I grab them and follow him upstairs. A gasp leaves me at the unexpected space I would never have imagined when I looked at the building from the street. "This is gorgeous. What an amazing space. The view is spectacular."

"Thanks. I like it up here." He places the bowls on the low table and takes the glasses from my hands, his fingers making contact with mine.

We both take our first bites of food. "Mmm." With wide eyes, I look at AJ. "This is divine. Thank you for making me dinner."

"You're welcome. I enjoy cooking."

"Ugh. I do my cooking on Sunday mornings for the week. I try to do all my food prep then so I don't have to worry about it when I get home from work. Some days, I don't leave the office until six. If I didn't have my meals already prepared and waiting for me, I'd be too tempted to buy takeout."

"I'd noticed all of your labeled meals in your fridge. That's a practical approach."

We spend the meal chatting, but there are also comfortable moments of silence. I could imagine spending evenings on this deck, enjoying a glass of wine, and watching our toddler play in a kiddie pool. I freeze. What the hell, Sarah? Stop it already! What am I doing sitting here like we're on some kind of date, fantasizing about a future that will never be? I stand abruptly, stacking the dishes. "I'll clean up since you cooked dinner, then we can … we can, uh … get started. I'm sure you have plans and don't need me taking up your entire evening."

"I don't have any other plans but we can get started. I can do the dishes later." Those words have to be the sexiest form of foreplay on the planet but I need something to do.

"I insist." With everything in hand, I make my way downstairs to the kitchen and set about washing the dishes. AJ works alongside me, drying them and putting them away. The task doesn't take long and I'm now wishing I'd dragged it out a little since there's nothing else to do but have sex!

With AJ!

Oh my God.

How am I going to get through this? I'm pretty sure my panties are already wet after being in his company, and this isn't about pleasure. It's about getting pregnant. I blow out a long breath. "I guess I'm ready."

He chuckles softly. "Anyone would think you're being sent to the gallows. It's just sex, Sarah. People do it all the time. I promise it won't be so bad."

Embarrassment floods me and my palms sweat. I drop my gaze to the floor and discreetly wipe my hands on my dress. I'm such a fool. I'm acting like a thirty-four-year-old virgin who's never been touched by a man. I've had sex plenty of times. The problem is it means so much to me. It's personal and private and when I have sex with a partner, I'm giving them a personal, private part of me I don't give to anyone else. It's why I confuse sex with love, even though I know the two don't always go hand in hand. I'm terrified this experience with AJ is going to show him how much I already care for him. Finally, I nod and grab my purse. "I know."

He takes my hand and leads me through his home to the stairs, which lead to the bedrooms. His grip is sure and strong, confident. I don't sense any jitters or nerves from him. My pulse increases and I have to remind myself to take measured breaths. I made sure to wear a dress, so I don't have to get completely naked, using the clothing as the barrier I need between us. I'm certain he's going to think I'm a weirdo, but it's the only way I could think to reduce the intimacy of our situation and send the correct message to my heart.

We cross the threshold into AJ's masculine bedroom. Hardwood floors and concrete walls complete with enormous floor-to-ceiling windows provide an impressive space for the king-size bed which is quietly intimidating in this situation. Holding my purse against my body like a shield, AJ leads me further into the room, which has his personality all over it. That quiet masculinity he wears so easily which appeals to me on a fundamental level.

Tugging me around in front of him, he studies my face closely, then takes my purse from me and places it gently on the nightstand. He brings his hand up to cup my face, his fingers sliding into my hair and I desperately want to press into his warm touch. With his eyes locked on mine, he moves in closer, his breaths licking across my lips.

He's going to kiss me.

He's going to expect foreplay and while I know I need to get him aroused, I've brought lube for myself. Though, I don't expect I'll need it if he starts kissing me and paying attention to my body in a way I know, just know will be incredible. I don't think the chemistry between us is in my imagination but I wonder if he feels it too.

AJ presses his lips to mine and for a moment I allow myself to enjoy the pleasure—the feel of his soft lips against mine, his tongue tracing the seam. I open with a sigh and he surges in, his tongue stroking along mine with confidence. This is a man who knows how to kiss. My body sags into his and his fingers slide further around to the back of my head. He grasps the strands of my hair firmly, tilting my head where he wants it, then proceeds to deepen the kiss in a way that leaves me breathless and my legs trembling. My shallow breaths speed up and my heart pounds a fast rhythm against my breastbone. He presses his body tight against mine, squashing my boobs between us and I can't miss the hardness in his jeans.

A tiny moan escapes and AJ groans in response, pressing his pelvis further into my stomach. My panties are soaked.

This can't happen. It will be disastrous for me.

I pull back swiftly and AJ's hand drops from my hair, a puzzled expression taking over his face. "What's wrong?"

"Uh, nothing. I didn't want to get carried away." I step back and without showing all my business, I drag my panties down my legs, scrunch them into a ball, and tuck them in my purse—heaven forbid he sees my underwear. He's about to put his penis inside me—I internally roll my eyes at myself. I point to his bed. "Do you mind if we pop one of your pillows beneath my butt?" I glance around the room, noticing an ensuite. "Damn it, I should have brought a towel with me, so there isn't any mess."

He shakes his head with a smile. "You can put a pillow anywhere you need and don't worry about the mess, I'll aim to get everything inside you. We wouldn't want to waste any." He chuckles mildly as he winks at me.

"Oh, right. Of course." I move the pillow to where I need it, slip off my shoes, and lay down, positioning my hips on the pillow so they're raised. The websites say you don't need to do this, but I figure I may as well give myself the best possible chance of this working. "I'm ready," I tell AJ with a bright tone as I lie stiffly on top of his covers.

"You don't want to kiss or have foreplay? Or get naked?" He rests his hands on his hips, looking positively puzzled.

"Uh no. I don't think it's necessary." I glance down at his jeans which still show the outline of an impressive erection. "I'm wet and you're ready. I think we're good to go." He seems reluctant, but he pulls his shirt over his head in that sexy way that guys do, grasping the back collar. He's so defined and this close I can see the details of the tattoo around his bicep. A rope with some kind of intricate knot—makes sense since he loves to climb.

Hang on. He can't take his shirt off, I need the barrier of our clothes. "You can put your shirt back on if you like and keep your jeans on too."

"What?"

I wave my hand around the area of his groin. "We just need the essentials to be bare. That'll do the job."

"The job?"

"Yeah."

"I'm not sure I can … uh … perform under these circumstances, Sarah." I glance back down at his zipper. It still looks impressive, so I don't think he has performance issues. But I can help him out if needed.

"Oh. I can help you." I sit up and reach for him, ready to help him but he pulls back.

"So, you'll help get me hard, but I can't help get you ready for me?"

I chuckle nervously. "You don't need to worry about that. This is for reproductive purposes, not for enjoyment." His eyebrows shoot up.

CHAPTER 26

—aj—

I can't believe this. I've never had sex under these circumstances, and I'm not sure I'll be able to do what needs to be done. For some reason I have no hope of comprehending, she wants us both to stay almost fully clothed, but I refuse to put my shirt back on. I'll keep my jeans on and drop them just below my ass if it helps Sarah feel more comfortable, but that's my limit.

She spreads her legs wider and the skirt of her dress slides down her thick thighs. I climb onto the bed, kneeling between the thighs that have starred in many of my fantasies since I first met her, and get my first glimpse of her pussy. I want to dip down and taste the silky flesh, so I do.

As my tongue makes first contact with her lips, her thighs slam shut around my head.

"What are you doing?" she gasps and her hand presses against the top of my head, pushing me away.

"I need to get you ready for me." I tilt my head down to my cock, but she's too flustered to look for herself. "I'm not a small guy. I don't want to hurt you." My cock grows thicker, as though he's showing off.

Without glancing down, she gives me a tremulous smile. "I'll cope. Just go slow at first." She drops back to the pillow, tension still filling her body and creases marring her beautiful forehead.

I reach forward and gingerly swipe my fingers along her lips, finding them dry. I need to work her over and build her up. I dip my finger inside her tight opening and she tenses.

She raises her head. "What are you doing now?"

Surely she knows. "Getting you wet."

She pushes up on her elbows and points to her purse. "I brought lube with me. If you can just grab it out of my purse, I'll be good to go."

Lube. Of course, she brought lube. Because she planned to keep this as impersonal as possible. I climb from the bed and grab the lube from her purse. I dribble some on her pussy and spread it with my fingers in the least sexual way I can. I grit my teeth and try to focus on the job at hand, not that my fingers are gliding through Sarah's pussy. This certainly isn't how I imagined our first time together.

After applying lube, I slowly edge my way forward and push inside Sarah's silken sheath for the first time. Gritting my teeth as she holds her body stiff, I push her legs open wider to help open her up for my cock, then apply more lube to my shaft to help me slide in more easily. I've never had to use lube before because I've usually been able to engage in foreplay with my partner. Sarah's aversion to anything remotely personal is messing with my head, but sliding inside her feels so damn good.

I drop my head forward and open my eyes to check on her. Her eyes are squeezed closed and her lips are pressed together in a tight line. "Sarah. Cupcake," I murmur. "Look at me."

She shakes her head slightly, keeping her lids locked tight and I sigh as I pull out of her glorious heat, gritting my teeth. Her eyes fly open as I rest my ass on my heels.

"What are you doing? Why'd you stop?" Her words tumble out in a panicked rush as she pushes upward, pulling her skirt down to cover herself.

"This isn't going to work if you can't even look at me while we're having sex. What's the problem?" She looks everywhere around the room and I guide her face back to me with my fingers gently cupping her chin.

"What does it matter if I look at you or not? This is about impregnating me, not an emotional connection."

I sigh heavily. She's fighting this for some reason. Obviously, I need to go slower and make her forget about the process, so we can move forward. "Okay. Sorry." I guide her to lay back against the pillow and shuffle forward, nudging my cock at her entrance, and press inside her welcoming heat, her pussy walls tightening around my shaft. Her mind may be fighting whatever this is between us, but her body is certainly happy to have me inside as her walls grip me. With my hips pressed all the way forward, my shaft is buried deep inside Sarah's warm heat and I wrap my hands around her thighs, pulling out slowly only to thrust back inside.

"Hold your legs open wide for me," I tell her, then drop down over her when she complies. I press my lips against hers, needing intimate contact, but she draws her head back, breaking the connection. I huff out a breath, making the loose strands of hair across her face move. I gently stroke them out of the way so nothing is impeding my view of her stunning face. Sarah holds her body stiff as I drag my cock out of her welcoming heat.

"Are you ready," I whisper lowly against her ear, noticing the thrumming at her pulse point.

"Yeah. Ready whenever you are." Her voice is breathy.

I push in and Sarah opens her legs wider still, ensuring that my hips have clear access without touching them, so I glide my hand down her silky thigh and grasp her ass cheek in my hand, squeezing as I draw back out. Sarah's breaths coat the side of my face as I push my cock slowly inside and glide back out. It's fucking incredible to be inside the woman who has stolen all rational thought from me since the moment I laid eyes on her in that damn club. I scan her face, noticing the frown lines between her brows and the tightness around her eyes.

This certainly isn't the way I anticipated our first time together. I never imagined I'd be having sex with a partner whose body language is screaming that she doesn't want any part of this, but contrary to those thoughts, my body is building closer to release.

It feels wrong.

As much as it pains me to do, I stop and withdraw, resting my ass on my heels again. Her lids fly open and she pushes up. "I'm sorry. I can't do this," I whisper, dragging Sarah's skirt down to cover her modesty. "I'm not built to have sex with someone who's so obviously opposed."

A pink stain coats her cheeks and she reaches forward to grasp my hand. "I'm sorry. Please don't stop. I'm not opposed to this, I promise," she says, panicked. "I'm trying to keep myself in check," Sarah whispers.

With my free hand, I rub her thigh tenderly. "Why do you need to keep yourself in check? Why can't you relax and enjoy the experience?"

She shrugs. "It's how I'm built."

"What, so you don't enjoy sex?" I'm honestly puzzled.

Creases form between her brows. "Of course I do." She glances out of the darkened window. "When I'm in a relationship, I love having sex with my boyfriend. This is different." She squeezes my hand. "I'll try to relax a little more. I'm sorry I'm being difficult."

"You're not being difficult, but I feel as though I'm forcing you and that doesn't sit well with me."

"You're not." She lays back and tugs her skirt up, revealing her pussy, and gives me a timid smile. "Please, AJ," she whispers.

The 'please' does me in and I stroke my softening cock back to life. I want to kiss her. Desperately. Dropping over her, I rest on my elbows and cup my hands around her head, stroking her silky hair. Locking my eyes on hers, I lower my head until our lips are a mere inch apart. Her warm breath is coming in pants while her lips separate slightly. I close the distance and swipe my tongue across the supple pillows and moan at her taste. Her lips part with a sigh, and I push my tongue inside to tangle with hers. This. This is what it's all about. The connection, the intimacy. I probably sound like a chick, but guys need to feel this too. Angling my head, I kiss her deeply, stealing her breath as I notch my cock at her entrance.

Sarah raises her hips, signaling she's ready for me to move, so I do. Inch by magnificent inch, I slide inside her inviting heat, her walls tightening around my shaft as I suck her tongue into my mouth. It feels incredible. Her body arches and I drop lower, pressing my body into hers, flattening her gorgeous tits, which are sadly covered. Maybe next time she'll let us get naked, so we can do this properly. At this point, I'll take her kissing me back and moving rather than laying stiff as a win. It's progress I wasn't sure we'd make.

Moving her hips in time with my thrusts, we begin to build a solid rhythm. The sensations building in my body are explosive and I know if Sarah ever allows her walls down and lets go, we'll be dynamite together. My body heats, sweat forming down my spine, while I slide in and out of her heat, her walls fluttering and tightening, causing my entire focus to narrow to a singular point.

Sarah's hands wrap around my forearms and her short nails dig into my flesh, sending ribbons of my cum into her without warning. Fuck! I grunt through my release and hang my head in shame. She's going to think I'm a goddamn two-pump chump. She didn't have an orgasm, not even close.

"I'm sorry."

She releases her grip from my forearms, her eyes opening as she presses her hips into the mattress, disengaging from me. She immediately grabs the pillow next to her and I take it from her and place it on top of the first pillow as she lifts her hips. The second pillow ensures her hips are tilted higher. Sliding it beneath her ass, my eyes drop to her pussy and I notice some of my cum leaking out, so I scoop it up and push it inside.

Sarah's eyes widen. "What are you doing?"

"Trying not to waste any of my cum." I keep my eyes on her center as I push my fingers in and out of her opening under the pretense of pushing my release inside.

She attempts to close her legs, but she can't because I'm in the way. "I'm sorry I came before I could get you there," I whisper, ashamed of myself.

"Oh, that's okay. I'm not here for the orgasms, remember." I huff and move my thumb over her clit, making small, tight circles around the bundle. "I'm sure it's all inside. You can stop now."

I glance up at her rosy cheeks. "I need to give you an orgasm to help my swimmers get to where they need to go. Remember?"

Her cheeks flush further and she looks stunning. "I brought my bullet for that. If you wouldn't mind stepping out, I'll do what needs to be done, and then I'll be out of your way."

I shake my head and hold out my hand. "Give me the bullet."

"No. I can do it." Her voice is sure and strong. Stubborn.

"Why won't you let me help you? Look, I'm sorry I came before you did. That doesn't usually happen to me. My only excuse is that it's been a while and despite your obvious aversion to having sex with me, you felt so damn good. But I never leave my partner unsatisfied."

She pushes up, bringing her face closer to mine, her eyes finally making contact. "It's okay. Honestly. I don't expect orgasms out of this. You're helping me to get pregnant and it's more than I ever expected from anyone. Now, if you wouldn't mind stepping out of the room, I need to …" her eyes widen. "And if you don't mind, I like to lie still for about half an hour. Then I'll be out of your space. I'm sure you have other things you need to do."

I study her eyes closely. This is genuinely how she wants, *or maybe needs*, things to be between us, so I relent—reluctantly because I respect her. I don't want to force her or make her feel uncomfortable or she might decide to go back to how we were doing things before. At least this way, I get to be inside her regularly over the next week and I can work on getting her to forget and loosen up a bit—make it enjoyable for her and hopefully make her fall for me. More importantly, make sure she comes before I do.

I nod and move out from between her legs. "Okay. Uh, take your time." I grasp the back of my neck and Sarah's eyes drop to my bicep as they usually do, so I tense it. "There's no rush. I don't have anywhere I need to be."

I tuck myself away and collecting my shirt, I back out of my bedroom slowly, keeping my eyes on Sarah as I do. Closing the door quietly, I lean against it and blow out a breath, feeling like a failure. She's bound and determined to keep distance between us and I'm not sure why that is, but *I'm* bound and determined to erase every single inch of that distance and make her mine.

She steps into the living room, her hair slightly mussed and her eyes glassy. I bet she looks fucking stunning when she comes. "Uh, thank you." She thumbs over her shoulder toward the front door. "I'll … uh … get outta your hair."

I quickly stand. "I ordered dessert. It should be here any min—" The doorbell rings at that exact moment, and I refrain from tipping my head back and thanking the heavens for their impeccable timing. I stroll past Sarah and open the door.

"*Japanese Dessert House* delivery for Jackson?"

"Yep, that's me. Thanks." He hands over the desserts and spins on his heel, returning to his car. Closing the door, I make my way past Sarah and toward the couch. "Come on, let's eat." I drop the dessert onto the coffee table and make my way to the kitchen as if it's a given that she'll stay. "What would you like to drink? I have soda, juice, sparkling water …" She's frozen to the spot, holding her purse to her body as though it's a life preserver and she's adrift in the deepest ocean. "Come on, Sarah. Don't make me eat this alone."

The indecision on her face is plain for anyone to see. Even if I didn't know her, I would be able to see how torn she is between staying and leaving. She takes a timid step toward the couch, her shoulders dropping slightly. "Okay."

I duck back behind the fridge door to hide my grin and blow out a breath. "Great. Now, what would you like to drink?"

"Water's fine. Thank you."

I grab a beer for myself and water for Sarah and head back to the couch. The coffee table is too far away, so I slide it forward and open the dessert containers. "I didn't know what you liked, so I ordered one Ferrero Crêpe Cake and one Hokkaido Crêpe Cake."

She smiles at me, picking up a fork. "I've never had either before, but they look delicious."

"We can share both."

"I don't often treat myself to stuff like this because of my saving plan," she tells me.

"Fair enough. I don't eat dessert often either, but I figure it's okay now and then." She nods. "So, how did it go in there?" Good one, dickhead, you just got her to relax and now she's going to be all stiff and distant again. "Sorry. None of my business." I take a bite of crêpe cake to keep my mouth busy so I don't say more stupid shit. I hold in a moan when the lightness of the crêpes melds with the sweet tartness of the strawberries on my tongue.

She chuckles, but it's awkward and stilted. "Good. I guess. Hopefully, it works this time. I'm sorry it's taking so long for me to get pregnant." Her cheeks flush and she drops her eyes to the table.

"No need to apologize, Sarah. It takes as long as it takes. We didn't put a time limit on this, remember." The longer it takes, the better my chances of winning her over. And doesn't that make me the biggest asshole around.

A tight smile forms on her delectable lips, the ones I desperately want to kiss again. The small taste I had earlier wasn't nearly enough. "I know," she whispers. "I … I just feel terrible that I'm taking up so much of your time, and now I'm also invading your home … and you've met a woman you'd like to date. This isn't conducive to starting a relationship with someone. You've been incredibly kind and generous." She glances away then back to me. "I'll be forever grateful to you, AJ. I hope you know that." I knew I'd fucked up when I mentioned I'd met someone, now it's like I have a guillotine waiting to be released on my neck.

"I do." The mood has grown heavy and it's the last thing we need. "You wanna watch this Discovery show I recorded? It's about the most extreme places in the US."

She shrugs and agrees. "Sure."

I pull up the program and settle back into the couch,

inching closer to Sarah, and press play as she settles in, making herself comfortable. I scoop a forkful of cake and offer it to her and she distractedly opens for me. I slide the food into her mouth and she closes her lips around the fork, giving a small moan as the flavors burst on her tongue. I scoop myself a mouthful of cake as we get caught up in the program.

"Hmm. I always thought Chicago was the windiest city," Sarah speaks for the first time as we've learned about the deepest lake and the quietest place in the US.

"Yeah, I thought that too. I love watching shows like this. I always learn something new." I chuckle.

"I think I could become a convert. I'm enjoying this more than I thought I would." She turns back to the television and I watch her for a few more moments. She's enthralled by the information being shared and I'm thrilled she's still here. My eyes snap back to the television when she points toward the screen. "That looks amazing. I wonder if they do overnight camps there? Not that I camp, but that night sky looks incredible."

"I could find out if you like." A perfect opportunity to steal her away for a couple of days.

She spins her head toward me. "Oh, you don't have to do that. I've never camped. I'm sure I'd be terrible at it."

"You'll never know if you don't try. I happen to love camping so I could teach you. I sometimes do an overnight trip when I climb."

"Really? I just figured you climbed close by."

"I do, mostly. But sometimes I like to get away for a weekend. I can let you know next time I'm going and you could come along if you like."

"You don't need to go to any trouble for me."

"It's no trouble at all. It'll be fun."

We spend the rest of the program learning about the highest and lowest places in the US, the coldest and the hottest, the driest and the wettest. When the credits roll, my stomach sinks because I know it means the end of my time with Sarah for tonight. My spirits lift when I remember that she'll be back here in forty-eight hours.

"Thanks for tonight, AJ. For everything. Honestly, you've been amazing," she says as she stands, collecting the empty dessert boxes.

I force out a laugh and stand too. "I wouldn't say I was all that amazing in there." I tilt my head toward the stairs and my bedroom, taking the boxes from her.

"We got the job done, right? That's all that matters." *Job.* It's not meant to be a job.

I dump the boxes in the kitchen and come back to the living room, where Sarah's edging her way toward the front door. "I guess so, but I promise it'll be better next time."

"As I said, I'm not here for the orgasms." She gives me a tight smile. "You delivered what you promised, and that's the main thing." She tugs her purse straps over her shoulder.

Pressing my hand to her lower back, I guide her to the door. I'd dearly love to guide her back upstairs where I can show her I'm not a thirty-second lover. That I know how to please a woman, but I know she won't stay. I'll have to show her next time. "Let me know you got home safely."

She nods. "Well, anyway. Bye. Thanks again." She leans forward to peck my cheek and scurries toward the street and her car before I can respond. My lips tip up at the fact she laid a kiss on me ... *willingly.*

CHAPTER 27

—sarah—

WHAT A DISASTER! WELL, NOT A COMPLETE DISASTER. I *DO* have his semen inside me.

I climb into my car and pull onto the street, drive for a bit until I'm far enough away from AJ's place, and then pull over. Tears burst from my eyes and I drop my head into my hands.

That was the most difficult thing I've ever done and he probably thinks I'm some frigid touch-phobic crazy woman. My phone lights up on the passenger seat, Em's name on the screen. I press the green button because I selfishly need my sister right now.

"Em," I sob.

"What's wrong? Where are you? What happened? Why are you crying?" Her questions tumble out one after the other.

"We h-h-had s-s-ex, and it was awful, and now I'm a mess and I'm parked on the side of the road!"

"Sheet! Can you get home safely? I'll come to you." I nod, the tears streaming down my cheeks. "Sare? Can you get home?"

"Y-yeah."

"Okay. I'm on my way." She disconnects the call and I wipe my eyes and draw in some measured breaths.

I go to pull back onto the street when a horn blares and I slam my foot on the break—my heart pounds and my hands shake. "Shit! That was close." I pause and make sure I'm focused, then double-check the street is clear so I can pull out. Keeping my eyes trained on the road, I drive home cautiously, park, and make my way up to my apartment.

When I get inside, I drop my purse and head straight to the bathroom. Switching on the light, I step in front of the mirror and cringe at my swollen eyes, red nose, and blotchy cheeks. I wash my face, splashing cold water on it repeatedly, hoping it calms down before Em arrives. When I look up to check, my eyes catch on my sister leaning against the doorframe, a startled yelp escapes and I jump a little. I wasn't expecting her so soon. She must have walked straight out the door after our call. Her eyes are full of worry and I break down crying again, so I cover my face with my hands.

"Oh, Sare." Her arms wrap around me and she pulls me in tight and strokes my back soothingly. She's always taken her role as big sister seriously. Once I catch my breath, she leads me through to my bedroom. "How about you get changed? I'll make us some hot chocolate and we'll meet on the couch."

I nod. "Thanks."

We separate and a few minutes later I'm flopping onto my couch. Emma places two cups of hot chocolate on the table, then pulls my phone out of her pocket to hand it to me. "It's been buzzing. It's him."

I take it from her like it's a ticking time bomb. "He wanted me to let him know I got home safely."

"Well, you should let him know you're home." She sips her drink, watching me over the rim of her cup.

Glancing at my phone, I find three text messages.

AJ

Are you home safe?

Sarah?

I'll come over there if you don't answer me

Shit! That's all I need. I don't want him to see me like this, so I quickly respond.

ME

I'm home safe. You don't need to come here

AJ

You're lucky, I was about to walk out the door

Are you okay?

ME

I'm fine. Thanks for tonight

AJ

I promise next time will be better

Ugh! Tonight was crappy because of me. Nothing he did. I can't even think about next time.

ME

We got the job done. That's what's important

I tuck the phone between the cushion and the arm while Em waits patiently for me to spill. I take a sip of my drink and try desperately to gather my thoughts.

"So you had sex with AJ?" she says slowly and I nod. "And it was terrible?" She widens her eyes and raises her eyebrows. I nod again. "What was so terrible about it?"

Where do I start? How do I explain?

"Talk to me, Sis."

I blow out a breath and start from our two months of failed attempts and AJ's suggestion that we try having *actual* sex.

"Oh no."

"Yeah. You know that's not gonna end well for me, Em. I already liked him more than I'm supposed to—"

"What do you mean…?" she asks gently.

"Well, he offered to be my donor, not my lover, not my boyfriend, not my life partner. And … and he told me he's met someone he really likes. How's that gonna work?"

"Oh, Sare."

Tears trickle down my cheeks. "It's so not fair. Why couldn't I have met him without all this donor stuff between us? He's perfect in every way." My tears increase and my sister becomes blurry.

I feel the couch move as she shuffles closer and wraps her arm around my shoulder. "Sometimes we don't get to choose when we get to meet our person. Sometimes it happens unexpectedly. You can't plan everything, you know that, right?"

I tip my head back and blow out a breath. "I know."

"What was so bad about the sex, apart from knowing he likes someone else?"

How do I explain the disaster to my sister? "Just to be clear, I find everything about AJ sexy." She nods. "And I'm desperately trying to not fall in love with him. Though, that's not working out so well for me."

"Mhm." She nods again.

"He kissed me, Em." She raises her eyebrows. "It was everything." The edges of her lips tip up. "Before I went there, I knew I was in trouble, but when he kissed me, I *knew* I was in trouble."

"Mhm."

"So, I refused to get naked and told him to keep his clothes on too. I figured if I had a physical barrier between us, it would help."

"Did it?"

"Not really. He took his shirt off."

"Oh my."

"Right? So there went that plan." I tell her how I held myself so stiff and still with my eyes and mouth squeezed shut tight to try and limit the overwhelming sensations. "I shut down so well that he had to use lube. Lube, Em!"

She squeezes me tight. "Oh, Sare."

Tears form again. "He wasn't going to go forward with the plan because he felt like he was forcing me. I convinced him and let him kiss me and worked on relaxing and engaged a little, but I had to focus on everything else, so I wouldn't come. I … I couldn't be that vulnerable with him, Em. Anyway, mercifully, it was all over and done with pretty quickly. I'm not sure I could have held out much longer. He felt amazing but I'm reasonably certain he thinks I hated every single moment of it." I sob. "Then he left me to do my thing and he ordered dessert! Dessert, Em. Who does that after the woman laid there like a dead fish? AJ does. Because he's so damn sweet. And now I can never see him again, which means my dream to become a mom is over!" Tears flood down my cheeks.

As I cry, Em tucks my head into her shoulder and strokes my hair while whispering soothing words like the amazing big sister she is. The silence is broken when Em's phone buzzes.

THEO

If he's hurt her, I'll grab Max and we'll pay the asshole a visit, just get his address from your sister

With wide eyes, I look up at Em. "Oh my God. I love your husband."

A slow smile spreads. "Me too." She looks at me. "He knew you were seeing AJ tonight because I told him earlier. Then when I called you, I told him I needed to get to you as I was grabbing my car keys because you were upset."

A giggle escapes which makes Em smile. "You can tell him he can put his white horse and sword away."

She chuckles as she texts him back.

THEO

Only if you're sure. I don't mind

Em shows me the screen before she responds, then tucks her phone away. "Now, what are you going to do? Because avoiding him isn't going to help you make your dream come true."

Sighing heavily, I comb my fingers through my hair. "I know."

"Maybe if you were honest with him about how you're feeling and your tendency to confuse sex with love it might help him to understand. He might surprise you."

"How awkward would that be? *Oh yeah, I know you're into someone but I'm into you. Oops.* Yeah. I don't think so."

"Hmmm, I guess so."

"I think I'm gonna have to skip the rest of our insemination plans this month and put some distance between us. I'll use the time to recalibrate and strengthen the walls around my heart. That should work."

Em nods thoughtfully. "I'm not convinced you can switch off your feelings like that, but it's worth a shot. Step away this month and see how you feel."

"Yeah. It's worth a shot." That's what I tell myself anyway.

"What are you gonna tell him?" I frown at Emma. "He'll need a damn good reason from you for not following through this month. You'll need to be convincing."

"Hmmm, true." I think for a moment, running through different scenarios. "I've got it." I go on to explain my plan.

Em looks impressed. "That should work."

"I'll text him tomorrow." We spend a little more time talking about the kids and then she leaves to head home to her hunky Greek husband and gorgeous kids. Sigh. One day, that'll be me. Well, the gorgeous kid, singular, and not the hunky Greek husband either.

CHAPTER 28

—aj—

I HOLD MY PHONE AWAY FROM MY EAR. THIS HAS BECOME MY regular Friday morning, listening to my grandfather dictate my future with no regard for what I want. Or that we live in the twenty-first century where women run corporations all the damn time. A text lights up the screen.

CUPCAKE

I just found out I have to go to a conference

Flying out this afternoon

Won't be back until Wednesday. Raincheck?

I frown at the screen, my eyes narrowing. *What?*

"Grandfather. I need to go." I disconnect the call without waiting for a response and read Sarah's message again. My gut tells me this is a ruse. That she's not really going anywhere. That she's building her damn fortress after last night. Dylan's not here today, so I can't get his take on this latest development.

ME

Tell me where. I can book a ticket and meet you. I can work from anywhere while you're at the conference and we can work on your pregnancy plan at night

I press send, satisfaction filling my chest. Let's see what she comes back with. I stare at my phone, waiting for her response. Tapping my fingers on my desk, my phone remains dark. I push away from my desk and head upstairs to my deck for some fresh air while I wait for her answer. An hour later and I still haven't heard from her. I could hack into the airline servers to find her and meet her at her conference, but I feel like that's maybe taking things too far. Not to mention, if I get caught hacking into airline servers, which is highly likely, I'll probably end up behind bars, which doesn't suit my plans.

Finally, my phone buzzes.

CUPCAKE

You don't have to do that. You've already been so generous plus I'm away for work and I like to be professional

There are social expectations for the evenings anyway

See you in a month *smiling emoji*

What the hell? If she thinks she won't be seeing me between now and her next ovulation cycle, she's sorely mistaken. For one, I wouldn't be able to survive that long without seeing her. And two, she's not going to get rid of me that easily.

ME

No

CUPCAKE

What do you mean ... no?

ME

I mean I won't see you in a month. I'll see you
when you get back from your work thing

CUPCAKE

There's no need. Spend the time with your
new lady

My heart spasms. That damn mistake is going to keep biting me in the ass. After a few minutes, I reluctantly text back in defeat.

ME

Okay

CUPCAKE

Great. Good luck with your lady

ME

Thanks. I'm gonna need it

CUPCAKE

Nah. She'll love you

Well shit! If only she did.

ME

I'm not so sure about that

CUPCAKE

Sure she will. What's not to love?

Apparently, my semen is the only lovable part of me.

CUPCAKE

Sorry, gotta go

I can't shake the feeling she isn't going anywhere, that she's making an excuse to avoid me. I know my performance was shit last night, but I know I can do better. I've never, in my life, since becoming sexually active, left my lover unsatisfied. Last night was an anomaly and I want the chance to show her what it would be like between us if she just let down those damn walls of hers.

Standing outside the hospital doors, I'm trying my best to appear casual—I'm anything but. My pulse pounds in my ears as I repeatedly swallow the excess saliva being produced by my nerves. The more I thought about Sarah's sudden need to attend a conference, the more my gut told me she was putting up her walls again. So here I am, leaning against the garden wall opposite the doors to the maternity wing of the hospital. I know this is her Saturday to volunteer. Glancing down at my phone, I check the time. She should be out in another ten minutes. I got here early to ensure I didn't miss her. I can't wait to see her face and hear her excuses.

My phone lights up as I'm about to put it away.

HAYLEY

Hey, when are you bringing Sarah around again?

ME

I don't know. I'm working on it

HAYLEY

Well, don't take too long. Colton loved her

ME

He's not the only one

HAYLEY

Oh, do tell, little brother *winking emoji*

ME

Next time we catch up

HAYLEY

Okay. Have you heard from Grandfather?

I roll my eyes.

ME

Only every single Friday for the past year

HAYLEY

I'm sorry you have to deal with him

ME

Me too, but I'd rather take his anger than you
or Mom having to deal with it

HAYLEY

Love you xx

ME

Love you too xx Give Colton and Lisa a hug
from me

See you soon

HAYLEY

I will

I tuck my phone in my pocket and when I look up, my eyes instantly lock on Sarah. I feel vindicated that my gut was right, but I'm also devastated she felt the need to go to these lengths to avoid me. She hasn't noticed me yet because she's busy waving goodbye with a wide smile to the staff. Her gorgeous eyes are probably sparkling with happiness like they always do whenever she talks about her time cuddling the babies.

She pulls her purse strap higher over her shoulder and as she steps through the doors, she looks up. Her ever-changing eyes land on me and she freezes. The glass doors are stuck open because she's rooted to the spot in front of the sensor.

I step forward. "Sarah." She swallows but still doesn't move. "How's the conference going, Cupcake?" I take her hand in mine, linking our fingers together. "I think we need to talk."

She blinks at me and nods slowly. I tug on her hand gently, encouraging her to move out of the doorway and she comes with me. Without words, I guide her to my Jeep, open the passenger door and help her inside, ensuring she's safe by engaging the seatbelt. I climb in and start the engine.

"My car," she says vacantly as we pass it on the way out of the parking lot.

"It'll be okay here. We'll come back later and collect it."

She nods and we make the drive toward *The Riverside Café* through Saturday morning traffic in silence. Mom and Dad used to bring Hayley and me here now and then. It's one of the best places in the city to enjoy brunch while relaxing by the river. I thought it would be the perfect place to chat, so I booked a table.

"I'm sorry," Sarah whispers and I nod to let her know I heard her apology, but keep my eyes forward.

I pull the Jeep into the parking lot and climb out of the car. Sarah opens her door before I can make it around to her side. Linking my fingers through hers, we make our way inside the busy café and are promptly escorted to a table with the perfect view. We place our order and the waitress leaves us alone. Sarah fidgets in her seat, glancing around the café and out of the windows which overlook the river where several kayakers are paddling, avoiding my gaze at all costs.

She's not going to talk, so I draw in a breath, gather my thoughts, and start. I need to be soft with her. There's no point showing her how upset and hurt I am because she'll clam up. "Want to talk about it?"

Her eyes drop to the table where she's tracing the wood-grain pattern. "I needed some space."

I nod. "I figured as much."

"How did you know?" She finally looks at me, her eyes wary.

I reach across the table and take her hand, linking my fingers through hers. Her touch settles me somewhat. "I know you. Well, the parts you let me see and the parts I've observed." She nods. "Talk to me, Cupcake."

She slumps and blows out a breath as she glances out across the river. Keeping her head turned away from me. I decide it's best if I wait her out. "I … I don't know where to start."

The waitress delivers our food and I release Sarah's hand so she can eat. She looks down at her plate but makes no move to pick up her cutlery. "Eat," I point to her food with my fork. We're quiet for a few minutes. She needs the time to gather her thoughts and I need to give her that even though every cell in my body is demanding answers. My need to understand wins out.

"Can you explain why you felt the need to lie to me?"

"I needed the space. It's a little embarrassing," she mumbles the last part as she scrunches up her face adorably.

"You don't need to be embarrassed with me. I won't judge you."

She's quiet for long moments and then she huffs, sadness oozing from her. "The thing is, I've broken our agreement. I know our arrangement is only meant to involve you being my donor to get me pregnant, but I've grown to like you." Well, this is a step forward. I work to keep my expression blank because I want her to keep talking. My eyes drop to her throat as she swallows. "I like you more than I should and there's something else," she rushes to add, so I nod for her to continue. She swallows again and licks her lips. The lips I want to taste properly; take my time with and devour repeatedly. I watch her closely as she drops her eyes to the table. "I … uh … have a habit of confusing sex with love," she whispers in a rush. I'm pretty sure my eyebrows jump to my hairline. "So you can see my dilemma. Especially now you have someone you're interested in pursuing."

"You're going to need to explain this dilemma to me, Sarah. Because I don't see the problem here."

"What don't you understand? I've fallen for you and you've fallen for someone else," she huffs, hiding her eyes from me.

I collect her hand in mine and squeeze lightly, taking a moment to absorb her confession, which was completely unexpected. "Cupcake, can you please look at me?" I wait for what seems an eternity, while my heart tries to beat its way out of my chest, for her eyes to meet mine. "The woman I said I was interested in … she's you." Sarah's eyes widen. "I too have a confession. You see, I've also broken our agreement and fallen for you. As much as I want to help you get pregnant, each month that we've been unsuccessful I've been grateful I get to spend another month with you. I know it makes me an asshole, but I'm being honest with you here."

She smiles and blows out a breath, then proceeds to start chuckling. Slowly at first, then her chuckles turn into full-blown laughter. "Oh my God. What a pair we are."

It's amazing to see her demeanor change so drastically. She's always been so confident, but it was missing on Thursday night and this morning. At least now, I sort of understand these walls she's been working hard to keep in place. "So where do we go from here?" I ask.

She shrugs. "I don't know."

She's still holding back. Even though she knows I've fallen for her, she's still closed. "Would there be anything wrong with us seeing where this leads? I want to be with you." I can't be any clearer about my intentions.

"Uhm, I still want to have a baby. It doesn't seem like the best way to start a relationship."

I shrug. "It's worked for us so far. It may not be the norm, but who says we have to follow society's expectations? So what if that's how we start out? Why can't we do things the way that works for us?"

"I guess so."

She's not convinced. "What else is holding you back, Sarah?"

Creases form between her sculpted brows and I lean forward to stroke my finger over them, wanting to erase her concerns. If only it was as easy as erasing some creases.

"What makes you think something else is holding me back?" She swallows. Awkwardness has replaced the lightness which was there mere moments ago.

I tilt my lips up slightly. "As I said before. I've gotten to know you a little. I've felt the more time we've spent together, the higher you've built your walls. And even now that we both know we've fallen for each other, you're still throwing up barriers. I can sense them." She nods slowly, her eyes tracking around my face. I can see a war going on inside her; she's not sure if she wants to open up completely yet. "Come on. Let's lay it all on the table, so to speak. Then we can move forward."

She studies me closely as if trying to work out if I'm genuine. She must see what she needs. "If I'm going to be completely honest with you, my priority is starting my own family. I'm happy to do it on my own because it's not guaranteed the father will stick around. The number of relationships that fail outnumber the relationships that work and I'll need to make my child my number one priority. Their safety, happiness, and well-being are what will be most important to me and I can't risk starting a relationship only for it to fail."

Woah. I didn't realize her views on love and relationships were so negative. There's a lot of love in her family, so I'm not sure where this is coming from. "No relationship is guaranteed. You know that, right?"

I watch her cement another brick back in place. "Yeah, I know. I've watched more relationships fall apart than stay together. It's made me wary, I guess."

I frown. "But your parents are happily married, and so are your brother and sister." I don't get it.

"Yeah, but Em's first marriage fell apart. They had two kids together and that wasn't enough to make Preston stay. My ex, Michael, chose a promotion over our relationship and we'd been together since high school. Mel's dad walked out on them when she was five. Men don't stick around. Not generally."

And now we're finally at the crux of the issue. I choose my words carefully. "I understand what you're saying. I've also witnessed many failed marriages and I honestly wouldn't say my parent's marriage is a great example either. But when I say no relationship is guaranteed, those words are true to some extent. However, there are things that couples can put in place to ensure they have a better chance at success. Couples need to *choose* each other every single day. It must be a decision each and every day to stay with your partner, to show them how much you love them, appreciate them, and adore them. It's not always going to be easy and as I said, I, like you, have been witness to marriages and relationships falling apart. But when I think about them, when I pick apart their relationship, I don't think they chose each other every single day."

Sarah nods and after a long moment, she finally responds. "I guess so. That makes sense."

"I'm asking for a chance, Cupcake. Let me adore you." I hold out my hand, hoping she'll take it.

"You don't think it's too much that at the beginning of our relationship, I'm trying to have a baby?" she asks, still unsure.

"*We're*"—I widen my eyes and wave between us—"trying to have a baby, and no I don't." She still looks uncertain. "Share the day with me. Let's have some fun and spend time together that's not about getting pregnant, but just hanging out." I lift my eyebrows with a hopeful expression still waiting for her to place her hand in mine.

Her lips tip up at the corners and she begins to nod meekly, gradually increasing in confidence. "Okay." She finally places her hand in mine and I feel as though I've cracked the greatest firewall on the planet.

"Okay?"

She giggles. "Yeah, okay."

I throw my fist into the air. "All right!" I lean across the table and plant a light kiss on her smiling lips. "Let's get outta here!"

I pay for our meals, keeping Sarah's hand in mine. Not far from the café is a guy renting side-by-side tandem bikes, so I drag Sarah across to him. She giggles the entire way, making me feel lighter than I have in months. "Let's go for a ride."

She points to the yellow one. "On that?"

"Yeah. It'll be fun." I sign my life away, then hand over my credit card and we're free to climb onto the bright yellow bike with a white and yellow striped canopy. It's a gorgeous day, the ideal temperature, with the sun shining down on us. It's like today knows this is a new beginning for us; the start of something beautiful.

As we ride along, we take turns pointing out pelicans and various other birds soaring above the river or floating on its shimmering surface. Sarah shares her easy smiles with me and my mood soars with the birds. The breeze has caused some strands of hair to come loose from Sarah's ponytail and she's battling to keep them out of her face as her eyes sparkle in the sunshine.

She looks beautiful. I've thought she was beautiful from the get-go, but today, there's a lightness about her that's been missing. The weight of her self-imposed safety net has been lifted and she's more carefree than I've ever seen her.

With our legs working together, I take her hand and rest it on my thigh, keeping mine on top to hold hers in place. I like this. The simplicity of spending this time with her without any pressures or worries. I like it a lot. It gives me a glimpse into our future. I only hope Sarah's seeing the same as me.

"This is fun," Sarah says simply, mirroring my thoughts. "I should bring the kids down here and do this with them. They'd really like it."

"We should make a day of it and include Colton, too."

"Definitely."

Our designated time is almost up, so we make our way back to the bike rental place to hand over the bike. Heading back to the parking lot, holding my girl's hand in mine, I tug her around to face me once we arrive at my Jeep. I glance between her eyes, which are bright like springtime grass, and her mouth. She licks her lips and I move in slowly, waiting for her to pull away once she reads my intention, but she moves forward, meeting me halfway. My hope soars that this is the beginning of our forever.

Her warm breath brushes over my lips as we make first contact, my heart beating a heavy rhythm, and my breaths seizing in my lungs. Under the bright, warm sun, with the breeze blowing at my back, I kiss Sarah the way I've wanted to since the night I met her. I bring my hand up to cup her face with reverence, while I wrap my other around her waist, tugging her body snugly against mine. Her soft curves press against my hard muscle like we were always meant to be together in this way. One pass, then two, my tongue darts out for a taste; teasing and tempting. Delicious. My cupcake sighs against me and I take the opportunity to slide my tongue inside against hers. Blood rushes in my ears and to my cock. Sarah presses tighter against me, her fingers sliding into my hair as I deepen the kiss, trying to reach all the way to her soul. I need her to feel my unfettered desire for her, to understand how much I want her. That this kiss isn't about anything other than enjoying her, connecting with her, appreciating her. As our tongues tangle and explore, our bodies pressed tight, and our hearts pound in a rapid rhythm against the other.

"Yeah, baby! Stick it to her!" shouted from a passing car rudely tearing us apart.

I chuckle as I press my forehead to Sarah's, taking pride in the fierce flush on her face. "Sorry, I got carried away." I press a light kiss to her lips. "Actually, I'm all about honesty today. I'm not sorry I got carried away, at all."

Sarah chuckles, her body shaking against mine. "If I'm being honest, I'm not sorry either."

CHAPTER 29

—sarah—

AJ'S PHONE BUZZES AND WHEN HE ANSWERS IT, THE VOICE ON the other end sounds panicked. He listens for a moment, then responds, "We're on our way." He tucks his phone away. "That was Hayley. Lisa's parents have been in an accident and are being taken to the hospital. I need to pick up Colton."

My heart races. "Of course."

He links his hand with mine and quickly helps me inside his Jeep and we head to the hospital. The cab is silent, filled with tension as AJ navigates early Saturday afternoon traffic through the city. Even though he's clearly upset and in a hurry to get to his sister and her family, he drives cautiously.

I lay my hand on his thigh. "I'm sure they'll be okay." I know they're empty words because I have no idea how serious the accident was, but I need to offer some comfort.

He glances at me, his jaw tight. "They're good people, so I hope they are."

We pull into the parking lot and we spot Hayley and Colton straight away. AJ parks and we both jump out quickly. Colton leaps for AJ as soon as he's close enough, with Hayley close behind. "Unca AJ!"

"Hey, little man." His voice is calm as he lands a kiss on Colton's nose. That's something I've noticed about AJ; he seems to keep his cool.

While they're busy, I hug Hayley. "Hey. You okay?"

"Yeah. I'm worried about Lisa. She was really upset. They're a close family, and she's an only child."

I nod. "Hopefully everything will be okay. Please tell her I'm thinking about her and her parents." Hayley nods gratefully, squeezing me close. "Is there anything you need? Anything I can do?"

"Thanks. I'll let you know if there's anything."

"Aunty Sarah!" Colton sings, reaching for me. I take him from AJ and he immediately wraps his little arms around my neck. I can't believe this is the same shy boy I met three weeks ago.

"Hey, little man." I squeeze him close and step away from AJ and Hayley so they can talk without little ears. "You're so lucky, you get to hang out with your uncle."

"Yeah." His cheeks split in a wide grin. "And you, too."

"Yeah, and me too." I smile at him, jigging him in my arms. I tell him all about our bike ride along the river and promise that we'll take him one day.

Colton's booster seat is switched to AJ's Jeep and his backpack is placed on the back seat. Hayley hugs and kisses Colton goodbye, then disappears into the hospital, leaving us in the parking lot. We work quickly to situate Colton in his booster seat, and I kiss him goodbye.

His bottom lip trembles. "I want to play with you."

Glancing over the door to AJ, he shrugs. "How about you come back to my place? We can order pizza for—"

"Yay, pizza!" Colton shouts.

AJ and I chuckle. "Dinner and hang out," AJ finishes.

"Please, Aunty Sarah," Colton pleads with puppy dog eyes and it's impossible to refuse his cute little face.

"Okay. But I'll follow you." I thumb over my shoulder toward my car on the opposite side of the lot.

"All right. See you at home," AJ whispers. Pulling me in close he drags his bristly cheek along mine to plant a kiss on my lips. His body presses against mine, reminding me of our kiss earlier, but this time we have little eyes watching, so I pull away.

I follow behind the guys, with Colton waving to me every so often, and when we pull up to AJ's home, he opens a garage door that has space for two cars. He points at the space, indicating I should park inside, so I do. While AJ's helping Colton out of his booster seat, I grab his backpack and we head inside with Colton holding my hand. It's hard not to skip ahead into the future and imagine us coming home from a day out as a family.

Geez, he kissed me and I already have our future mapped out. *Slow down, girl!*

AJ hands Colton his backpack. "How about you take this upstairs to your bedroom?"

He has his own bedroom here? I shouldn't be surprised since they're so close.

"Okay." Colton grabs the bag and heads upstairs.

"I usually have Colton overnight once a month to give Hayley and Lisa a break," he explains. "Though, it's probably been closer to six weeks since he's been here. I'm not sure how that happened." I can see AJ working through his memory trying to figure out why it's been so long.

He sets about washing his hands and preparing a healthy snack for his nephew, then rolls a cart full of Duplo blocks, books, and toys out from beneath the stairs. It's only now I notice there are several cupboards, each of which must pull out. What an ingenious use of space.

We spend the afternoon creating questionable buildings, reading stories, and playing hide and seek with Colton, who obviously adores his uncle. AJ's a natural with him. They share a level of comfort that is plain to see. Being fortunate enough to spend this time with them is giving me an insight into AJ as a father and my heart skips as I watch him with his nephew; he's going to make a great dad one day. Perhaps to a child we create together if what he confessed is true. I squeal a little on the inside as I think back to earlier. It was scary to open up to him and share my honest thoughts and feelings, but he didn't balk at all. He was open and willing to lay my fears to rest.

"Okay, little man. Time for me to order our pizza. Shall I get our usual?"

"Yeah!" Colton shouts excitedly.

"I should go and let you guys enjoy your evening."

"No, have pizza with us." Colton grips my hand, preventing my retreat and I glance up at AJ.

"Stay. Eat with us. Once he's in bed, we can take up where we left off earlier." He winks. Now that's an invitation too good to refuse. How things have changed in less than forty-eight hours.

I glance between the two and relent. "Okay."

Colton cheers loudly, jumping around the room as though his favorite TV characters have stopped in for a visit.

"What pizza do you like? We usually have Hawaiian because Colton loves picking off the pineapple."

"I love anything. But I especially love Hawaiian pizza. You might want to order double pineapple." I giggle.

AJ pulls me in close, his sexy scent surrounding me and sending my senses haywire. "You're made for me, Cupcake," he whispers and I chuckle. I guess he's happy I like pineapple on my pizza.

AJ makes the call to order the pizza, and we continue to play while we wait for it to be delivered. As soon as it arrives, we wash up for dinner and dig in.

"This is great. I have to admit, it's been a long time since I've indulged in pizza."

"Me too," says Colton, and I chuckle because he sounded like an old man.

The evening moves swiftly once dinner is finished and Colton's bathed and tucked into bed after two stories and several hugs, leaving AJ and me to our night. Anticipation for what's to come fills my body and the ache that AJ stoked in me earlier today, returns. I make a bathroom stop and when I return downstairs, soft music is playing over the speakers and the lights have been dimmed. AJ waits for me in the middle of his living room with his hand outstretched. Butterflies erupt in my stomach as I step toward him, appreciating his masculinity. He gives me one of his signature smiles and tugs me into him the second my hand connects with his, holding it between our bodies.

We dance to the soft music, his other hand on my ass, holding me firmly to him and scorching my skin through the flimsy fabric of my dress. "Thanks for helping me with Colton," he whispers against my ear, sending goosebumps cascading over my skin. I wrap my free hand around the back of his neck, sifting the soft strands at his nape through my fingers.

"You didn't need my help. It was so sweet watching you guys together. He idolizes you." AJ's warm breath coats the side of my neck with his chuckle.

"I idolize him too. He's such a smart kid." I nod in agreement, then rest my head on AJ's chest.

This is nice. Moving slowly together without an agenda and enjoying the moment rather than planning everything down to the smallest detail. Soft lips press against my temple and I breathe deeply, taking in AJ's addictive scent. His strong heartbeat increases in tempo and his hand glides up my spine to grasp the back of my neck. His grip is sure as he tugs my head back, our eyes instantly finding each other in the dim light. It's hard to tell, but I'm certain his pupils are dilated to match mine. The ache from before has returned in full force now, and I desperately want him to kiss me.

To touch me.

To make me his.

Everything falls away as we both move forward to meet midway.

The first press of his warm lips against the corner of my mouth has a sigh escaping.

The gentle swipe of his tongue across the soft pillows of my lips has me sinking into him.

His breath blending with mine has me opening to him eagerly.

He draws my bottom lip between his, then pulls away, returning moments later to tease me again. Finally, he delves his tongue into my mouth and we explore and taste, tempt and tease as I press into AJ's firm body, ensuring every inch of me is touching every inch of him. His hard cock presses against my soft stomach, promising things yet to come. I slide my other hand around AJ's torso, grasping the back of his T-shirt, then drag my short nails down the planes of his back. Our kiss deepens, heightening my senses and making my skin acutely sensitive to his roaming touch. Having his hands on me and being able to fully enjoy the experience is unreal and I relax.

Relax into AJ, into this moment, into his kiss.

He pulls away and places teasing kisses, biting my bottom lip before returning to a full-on assault. My temperature rises and my breaths are becoming labored, yet I need more. I need to feel his skin. Sliding my hands down his trim body, I locate the bottom of his T-shirt and slide my fingers beneath the fabric, making contact with his heated flesh. He moans and goosebumps erupt beneath my touch.

"Cupcake," he whispers against my lips with a pant, his eyes heavy with need. "I want you so bad."

"Me too." Our lips connect again, deeper, more insatiable. Months of built-up desire finally have an outlet. AJ smooths his hand up my back, twisting in my hair and tugging the strands, sending fire licking through my scalp. "Mmm," I moan into his mouth. He presses his impressive cock deeper into my stomach, making my clit pulse and I grasp the sides of his T-shirt to hold him to me.

He pulls his lips away, his eyes locked on mine as he slides his hands down my arms to collect both of my hands in his. "Let's take this upstairs."

I nod and follow him willingly—quite the turnabout from Thursday night. Was that only two nights ago? And while this may seem sudden, it's been a long time coming. After many self-induced orgasms to thoughts of the man currently leading me into his bedroom, I'm going to finally get to experience him firsthand. Thursday doesn't count because I was doing my best *not* to enjoy our time together—one of the most difficult things I've ever done. My nerves shoot through the roof when I finally realize the reality of what we're about to do.

I'm going to have sex with AJ.

For real.

And not because I'm trying to get pregnant—though, that would be a great side-benefit—but because we're hot for each other.

He closes the bedroom door and immediately pushes me up against it, where we resume our kiss. Our hands explore, gliding beneath fabric and roaming over heated flesh. His kisses make me dizzy with lust and I'm certain my panties are drenched. He slides his thigh between my legs and I use it to quell the ache in my pussy. His fingers trace their way up the zipper of my dress and he tugs the slider slowly downward, loosening the fabric. The straps fall from my shoulders, exposing the tops of my aching breasts. His eyes drop, quickly followed by his head as he kisses each mound in turn; lavishing my sensitive flesh with much-needed attention. I push my chest forward and his hands come up to cup each breast firmly, pushing them into his mouth.

"God, I love your body," he moans, laying kisses across from one boob to the other. "Every single curve and dip. And I plan to explore them all tonight." I sigh, holding his head to my heaving breast. His mouth feels amazing, the softness of his lips so different from the roughness of his end-of-day scruff. His tongue darts out, blazing a path across my flesh and I shiver. I wonder if I could come from this? His eyes dance up to mine from his position, and he gives me a devilish smirk as his thumbs rub back and forth across my peaked nipples. He knows exactly what he's doing to me as I grind down on his thigh again.

Raising his hands, he kisses each shoulder softly as he slides the straps of my dress down my arms, making the fabric fall to the floor, leaving me in my matching lace teal panties and bra. I thank the heavens above I wore my matching set this morning. I was feeling low, so I thought I'd wear my best underwear to improve my mood. It always works. Sexy underwear beneath my clothes will always give me the lift I need.

He takes a step back, breathing heavily while his eyes scorch a trail over every inch of my body. I'm on the curvier side, but unlike Emma who was always self-conscious of her curves, especially after Preston's constant put-downs, I'm proud of my shape. It's feminine and sexy. AJ bends his knees and tips his head back with a groan, then drops his eyes back to me.

"Fucking stunning. I knew you would be and when I saw you in your bikini, it only confirmed what I already knew to be true. I can't believe how lucky I am to have you standing in my bedroom like this." With the tip of his finger, he tilts my chin up and takes my lips in a searing kiss I feel all the way to the tips of my toes. I press up and wrap my arm around his neck, holding him in place while I devour him as much as he's devouring me. He walks backwards to the bed, his hands holding my wide hips, without breaking the seal of our lips.

Now that we've decided to try a relationship, I'm all in. I no longer need to fear the consequences of having sex with AJ, because I know we're on the same page. I *do* need to be careful not to blurt the 'L' word, though. That wouldn't be prudent the first time we have sex. *Really* have sex. I'm not counting Thursday night's fiasco. It's probably best to wipe that experience from the memory banks.

I feel the clasp of my bra release and the cups give way, so I scoot back and slide the bra from my arms. And yeah, the girls don't look so perky now because they're definitely on the voluptuous side, but I don't think AJ is going to complain about that with the way he's scooping them up and pressing them together. He nuzzles his face into my cleavage, then glances up at me with a sexy glint in his eyes. "I'm gonna fuck these beauties once you're filled with my cum." My entire body shivers.

So hot!

He lowers his mouth, taking one nipple inside and sucking —hard. It feels divine and a low moan escapes unbidden. He switches over, paying the same attention to my other nipple, while his fingers twist the nipple he just released, then he kisses his way down my soft stomach to my panties. Burying his nose in my pussy, he draws in a deep breath. "Mmhm." His tongue pokes out and he glides it around my clit through the lace. Unable to keep still, I squirm under his ministrations and drop my hands to his head as I press my pussy against his face. He kisses me thoroughly through the soaking lace, moaning with pleasure. He tucks his fingers into each side of my underwear and slides them down my legs, tapping each foot in turn so he can remove them completely. I'm totally and utterly bare to him, while he's still fully dressed.

So unfair.

"AJ," I murmur with a moan as his tongue circles my needy clit. My hands slide through the strands of his hair, pulling him away to allow me to see his eyes. "I need you naked, too," I pant.

He quickly stands and using one hand he drags his T-shirt over his head, discarding it carelessly to the floor. I reach forward to trace the trail of dark hair—so damn sexy—leading from his navel down to the waistband of his jeans and disappearing behind the denim. Unsnapping his button, I release his zipper, pushing his jeans past his hips. Gravity takes care of the rest for me, thank God. I press my hand against the significant bulge trapped behind his boxer briefs, noting the wet patch near the band. He groans at my touch and his cock throbs beneath my palm. When I seek out his eyes, they're half-mast, watching me rub his erection through the fabric. I drop my gaze down his strong thighs, appreciating the sheer masculinity of his form. He certainly is an impressive male specimen.

"Take it out, Cupcake." His voice is gruffer than I've ever heard and it sends heat flaring to my needy clit. I do as he asks, his briefs falling to the floor. He steps out of them while I wrap my hand around his hot length. Steel wrapped in velvet, the head red and throbbing, leaking precum. I drop to my knees so I can have my first taste. With the gentlest of touches, I touch the tip of my tongue to the very tip of his cock and it thumps against his defined abdomen. I swirl my tongue around the crown and then through the slit, ensuring I clean up every drop of his musky precum. He moans, sliding his fingers through my hair, but instead of holding me in place, as I anticipate, he pulls my head back roughly. "Nope. Every single drop of that needs to be inside your pussy, not down your throat." He tugs my hair. "Stand up and lie on the bed."

He helps me stand and while I position myself as he wants, I allow my eyes to roam his physique. "You have an amazing body, AJ." I glance up at his face to find his carnal gaze gliding over my curves.

"Ditto, Cupcake." I smile at his term of endearment. He strokes his cock several times, then climbs onto the bed between my legs, his muscles shifting and moving. "My turn for a taste."

He reaches for a pillow to prop under my ass, then pushes my legs wider apart, so I'm splayed open to his liking. His eyes drop to my pussy and his lips tip up in a delicious smile. "I've been waiting so long to do this," he whispers, then he dives in. Literally dives in, swiping his tongue up my seam without prelude. He's not messing around. My back arches and I suck in a sharp breath. He nips my clit and then repeats the process over and over. Each stroke is incrementally firmer than the last.

"Ohhhhh," I moan, my stomach muscles quivering.

He positions my legs over his shoulders, then his thumb connects with my clit and he draws tight circles around the bud as his tongue delves into my opening. I drop my arm over my mouth to stifle my cries. The last thing we need is to wake Colton and have him stroll in here wondering what's going on.

"Let go, Cupcake, give me your first one." He replaces his tongue with his capable fingers and rubs that magic spot inside of me, which sets off my body. Lights explode around my vision and my heart seems as though it wants to escape the confines of my chest with the way it's hammering against my ribs. My legs involuntarily tighten around his head and I'm worried I'm going to suffocate the poor guy. Death by oral fixation. *Ha!* No, that's not even funny, Sarah. I release my legs with a sigh as the tremors ease from my body, and a sense of satiation takes the place of the tight muscles from a moment ago.

CHAPTER 30

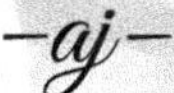

"Fucking stunning." I knew she would be. With flushed cheeks and her mouth dropped open in an O, she's so damn beautiful.

Keeping her legs draped over my shoulders, I slowly make my way up her body, kissing, nipping, and licking a path to her magnificent tits. Even though Sarah's voluptuous body shape is my ideal, I've never been fortunate enough to be with someone with her shape. It's like a playground designed just for me. Lavishing her breasts with the attention they deserve, I rub my bristly cheeks across them to add to the marks caused by my sucks and bites. When I shift back to study my handiwork, my inner caveman beats on his chest with pride. I line up my cock with her entrance and slowly slide inside her silken sheath.

Pure and utter decadence.

That's what this experience is. I groan as I bury myself to the hilt, pausing to absorb the moment.

Sarah moans and glides her fingers through my hair, gripping the strands and guiding my mouth up to hers. We hungrily connect, our tongues lashing against each other. She tilts her hips up. "Please move, AJ," she says with desperation.

With her legs over my shoulders, I slide out and back in slowly, teasing both of us to the brink. In this position, I can push in deep, which is perfect for what we're trying to achieve. With both of our bodies coated in a sheen of perspiration from our exertion, I change my position slightly to ensure I hit that special place inside. I wrap my arms around Sarah's shapely legs and draw out and then snap my hips back in, my eyes on her heavy tits as they move with the force of my thrust. Her back arches as her head tilts back with a low mewl and I repeat the action over and over until I'm not sure I can last much longer.

Sarah bites her bottom lip as our eyes remain connected, tethering us to each other. This is everything I've ever wanted with her. It's more than I ever imagined that night in the club.

Sarah's pussy walls tighten around my cock, and I almost see stars, pushing me closer to the point of no return. I refuse to come before her ever again so I use my thumb to circle her clit lightly, sending her flying. The top part of her body lifts off the bed, while high-pitched pants leave her gorgeous lips and her body shudders with her release. I lose my fight to hold on and it seems every cell in my body is focused to a singular point as my balls draw up tight and my release shoots into Sarah. I press my hips tight against her pelvis to ensure I'm as close to her cervix as possible, giving us the best chance of getting pregnant. We're each lost in our moment as we come together for the first time. It's a time I'll always remember because it means Sarah's finally dropped her defenses.

Keeping my dick inside Sarah's sweet pussy, I lower my head to take her lips in a slow, luxurious kiss. With panting breaths, our tongues slide against each other sensually, completing the intimate moment. I lower my chest to Sarah's, pressing every hot, sweaty inch together. Her heart hammers against my pecs and brings me a sense of satisfaction and pride I'm not sure I've felt before. It hasn't been easy getting Sarah to this point, but it was certainly worth every ounce of my patience. Slowing the kiss, I tease her lips with light pecks and nips, then pull back enough so I can scan her features. Flushed cheeks, a satiated grin, heavy lids, and sweaty hair indicate a job well done and I only hope I redeemed myself somewhat after Thursday's disaster.

Leaning closer, I rub my nose against Sarah's with affection and her lips widen as her arms wrap around my neck. "That was …"

"Incredible," I finish for her. "We were so in tune."

She nods, her eyes twinkling. "Yeah." The word almost comes out as a sigh.

Pushing up, I keep my cock inside as I rest my ass on my heels while Sarah's butt rests on the pillow and my thighs. I rearrange her legs, so I can hold them up against my chest, rubbing soothing strokes up and down her thighs. With her body elevated like this, I'm hoping my release can get to where it needs to go. My bedroom is silent since our breathing has returned to normal, neither of us feeling the need to fill it with noise. I'm happy to be in Sarah's company in silence, watching television, enjoying a meal, or defiling her body. As long as she allows me the privilege to be with her, I'm a happy man.

Sarah's shoulders shake. "You don't have to hold my legs up, you know."

"I know," I answer flippantly. "I like that I can do this for you. It gives me an excuse to keep touching you."

Sarah's body sinks further into the mattress. "You don't need an excuse," she whispers. "I'm pretty sure we're past all that now." Something inside me shifts with her words. A sense of relief fills the deepest parts of my body. Fuck, I hope we're past all of that. She wiggles her legs. "I think that's long enough. I carefully disengage from her and move out of the way to lay her legs down, then lie beside her so I can tug her in close and kiss her forehead. "Do you think it worked this time?" she asks, her voice small.

I move my head back slightly, so I can see her face better and gently stroke her hair away. "I hope so, but just in case, I think we should do it again." I nudge her with my hips. "I need a minute and then I'll be ready to go."

I feel her chuckle against my body, rather than hear it as she tucks her face into the crook of my neck. "Have I released a beast?" I glide my hand down the side of her body, following the dips, and make a path to her delicious ass, squeezing one lush cheek in my hand as I pull her forward to feel my growing erection. She throws her leg over my hip and her face snaps up to mine. "Oh."

I kiss the tip of her nose. "Yeah, 'oh.' Up on your hands and knees. You're gonna take it deep from behind, so I can watch my cock disappearing between these luscious ass cheeks of yours." I slap the cheek I was holding and then release her, so she can do as I said.

Sarah scampers to her hands and knees without question, her tits hanging low. They're gonna look fantastic swinging as I thrust into her from behind. I crawl in behind her and swipe my tongue from the top of her slit to her opening and press it inside. She tastes like a combination of me and her—my new favorite flavor. Sarah drops her head to the pillow with a gasp, drawing her pussy out of my reach, then looks over her shoulder at me, her eyes full of heat.

Gorgeous.

"Stay still." I grasp her hips firmly and pull her back to my face. Licking and stroking my tongue in and out of her soaked pussy; her legs quiver as she sighs, moans, and mewls. I love that she's not afraid to make a little noise as she pushes back into my face.

When her opening flutters around my tongue, I remove it and replace it with my cock in one hard thrust, pushing her up the bed. Sarah's back bows as she cries out. Her tits swing forward as I hoped they would. With my fingers digging harshly into her hips, I push in and draw out of her opening, each time going harder than the time before. She switches her hold, gaining better purchase on the headboard, her spine making a beautiful curve as I continue to fill her and retreat.

"That's it. Take my cock the way you were born to." The sound of skin slapping against skin and the view of my cock disappearing between her cheeks is erotic as hell and my cock swells and throbs, ready to release a second time. "Play with your clit, Cupcake," I demand between harsh pants, my voice low and gruff. The musky smell of sex fills the air as we both build closer to our release.

"Oh my God!" Sarah cries out, her back bowing while her walls strangle my dick. Working her through her orgasm, I incrementally slow my movements to prolong the experience. Reaching around, I grasp one of her tits, rolling her nipple between my fingers to heighten her orgasm. The rippling of her walls around my cock has me close to coming for the second time tonight, but I want to see if I can take her into another orgasm. Leaning over her body, I nibble on the lobe of her ear, then kiss my way down the column of her neck to suck on the pulse point, tasting the saltiness of her exertion while still holding my dick inside her body. I'm dying to come, barely balancing on the edge. Her breaths pick up again as I play with her nipple and suck on her neck, so I take that as a sign to start moving again. I rear up, balancing on my knees, and pull Sarah back on my cock.

"Use my dick, while I play with your pretty clit."

"I … I don't think I can come again," she whispers with a harsh pant.

"Of course you can. Ride my dick."

"Mmhm." She drops her head and pushes back, connecting her ass with my thighs, and slamming those delectable cheeks against me. Her cheeks jiggle as I massage her clit and grasp her tit. The sight is so fucking hot, my balls draw up tight to my body and that telltale tingle moves down my spine as what feels like electricity makes its way from my fingers and toes, through my limbs to my balls, and I shoot my load, my cum pulsing deep into Sarah's body.

Her walls flutter and contract around my dick with her orgasm, and we both moan in between panting breaths. "Fuu-uck!" I grit my teeth and hold myself still, ensuring I spill every last drop inside her. I don't want to waste a single swimmer.

As sated as I feel right now, I know I'm going to need her again tonight. I'm never going to get enough of her.

Sarah flops forward onto her stomach, collapsing beneath me. I drop on top of her, keeping most of my weight on my arms, our sweaty bodies fighting to catch each breath. She must feel my heart hammering against her back as it fights to burst out of my body and climb into hers.

She chuckles. "Wow. I don't know why we didn't just start with that instead of my asinine approach to getting pregnant."

"I would have been on board with that." I kiss my way along her damp shoulder.

The shakes in her body increase and she turns her head to the side. "I'm sure you would have." The sparkle in her eyes is so damn sexy, I lean forward to take her lips in a fiery kiss, spearing my tongue inside. She welcomes me readily, giving me the same level of fire as I'm giving her.

I roll to the side taking Sarah with me, so she's tucked in as close as possible, and drag the covers over our cooling bodies. Our lips unite again and we lose ourselves in a lingering kiss; neither of us is in a hurry for it to end.

Eventually, we pull away and Sarah buries her face in the crook of my neck. "Thank you," she whispers, her hot breath brushing across my pec. She traces her finger around my nipple, causing it to bead, then leans forward to swipe it with her tongue.

I slide my fingers through the silky strands of her hair, a shiver racking my body. "Stop thanking me, Cupcake. We're in this together, both hoping and wishing for the same outcome." I use my fingers to gently guide her eyes to mine. "Okay?"

She nods slowly, a smile tipping up the corners of her mouth. "Okay."

And I feel as though I've demolished one of the most powerful firewalls on the planet. This is exactly what I was hoping for. My dream woman opening her heart to include me in her plans to have a family. A family we can make together. A family which will be happier than my own. The child we'll create will be allowed to be a child and have fun, just like Colton. Just like Kenny, Austin, and Lachlan.

CHAPTER 31

—sarah—

THE END OF THE MONTH IS ALWAYS BUSY. ERIC LIKES TO finalize projects and insists on meeting with each staff member to ensure they're on target to achieve the company's short- and long-term goals, as well as to make sure everyone's still happy and experiencing job satisfaction. So work was crazy today and traffic coming home was even crazier. I close myself inside my apartment and blow out a breath as I lean back against the front door. A smile forms unbidden as I run my mind back over this past month. It's definitely been a whirlwind of emotions— from the lows of trying to keep my walls intact to the highs of letting AJ in. I still can't believe it.

I move further into my apartment, my smile widening when my eyes land on AJ's business shirt draped over the dining chair. Picking it up, I bring it to my nose to inhale his yummy scent, then run my fingers down the front, noting the missing buttons. When I saw him in his suit last night, I got carried away and tore his shirt away from his body in a bid to get him naked as quickly as possible. I felt it was only fair to offer to repair the damage.

My mind slides back to last night and the way he caressed

my body, worshiping every single inch of me as though it would be the last time he got to put his hands on me. I rub my thighs together as the memories assault me and notice the wetness there. My heart drops to my toes and the lust I was feeling vanishes into thin air. Disappointment rushes in, filling every cell in my body. When I hadn't gotten my period by lunchtime today, I was … hopeful. God knows I've had enough sex this month that I should be pregnant. My eyes sting and as much as I blink to hold back the tears, they still fill my eyes and drop over my lashes. For fuck's sake, Sarah, don't be such a crybaby. Just because you want it to happen, doesn't mean it's going to happen on your timeline.

I drop AJ's shirt back onto the chair and semi-stomp my way into my bedroom to grab clean underwear and step into the bathroom. I may as well have a shower and get into my PJs. It's not like I'll be going anywhere tonight and I need to be comfortable. Standing under the warm stream of water, I permit myself to let go. With tears hidden by the spray, I rub soap across my stomach, wondering how I can feel as though I've lost something I've never had. Why do I feel so empty?

Maybe I'm not meant to be a mom? Maybe the universe is telling me I'd be terrible at it, so it's not giving me what I want? Maybe I'm not worthy? Maybe I've left it too late?

I stand under the spray until the water turns cold and then finally step out of the shower to dry off, feeling detached from my body. I work on autopilot as I dress and dry my hair. My mind remains blank and numbness settles over me. Grabbing what I need from the kitchen, I skip dinner and curl up in bed, hugging my pillow, tears soaking the fabric.

It's dark when I wake, and I immediately know I'm not alone.

"You okay?" My sister's voice whispers in the dark. With the light from the living room spilling into my bedroom, I can make out her silhouette but not the details of her face. But I don't need to see her face to feel her concern for me. The fact she's here, laying opposite me tells me everything.

"I got my period."

She lifts her hand and strokes my messy hair out of my face. "I'm sorry, Sare."

"Maybe the universe is telling me I'm not fit to be a mom," I murmur.

She blows out a breath. "To use your own words, that's the bullshittiest bullshit I've ever heard. You're gonna be a great mom." She kisses the top of my head. "The best."

I burst into tears at her heartfelt words, and I feel her move close, then her arms come around my body, tugging me in tight. I bury my face in her chest and let it all out. I'm not sure how long we lie together while I work to compose myself.

"How did you know to come over?"

"AJ called Theo when you wouldn't answer your phone or the door."

"Oh my God," I whisper.

"He's waiting on your couch."

"No."

I feel her head nod. "Yeah." She smooths her hand down my arm and squeezes my hand. "He's really worried about you."

I sit up, brush my hair away from my face, and lean over to turn on the lamp. Squinting in the brightness, I turn back to Emma. "I don't want him to see me like this."

She sits up, glancing over my shoulder as the bed dips behind me. AJ's scent surrounds me as his arm wraps around my middle and he pulls me back against his hard body. "Cupcake," he whispers, then places the softest of kisses on my shoulder. My lids drop closed with appreciation for his tenderness and I feel the bed move. When I open my eyes, Emma's standing.

"I'm gonna go and give you two some space. If you need anything, let me know, okay."

I nod, and as Emma passes by me, I reach out and grab her hand. "Thank you."

She bends down and kisses it. "Anytime." When she stands, she pats AJ on the shoulder. "Take care of her."

"I plan to." Em smiles and takes her leave. The front door opens and closes, leaving me alone with AJ. "Why didn't you call me, Cupcake?" I can't answer him, so I shrug. "We're in this together and I don't want you upset and alone. You fucking broke my heart when I saw you curled into a ball in the middle of your bed." He lands another gentle kiss on my shoulder and I shudder beneath his touch.

AJ moves into the middle of my bed and then pulls me into him until I'm cradled between his legs, facing him. He wraps his arms around me and I have no escape; not that I would want to leave the safe cocoon he's created for us. "I'm sorry." I drop my forehead to his chest in shame.

His arms tighten around me, banding around my middle and his hand strokes leisurely up and down my spine. I slide my arms around his waist, holding him close and we sit in silence. AJ kisses the top of my head now and then, reminding me he's here, and I soak in every touch, his warmth, every breath as it puffs across the top of my head, and every beat of his heart as it thumps against my cheek. He's quickly become my person.

"What time is it?" I ask without lifting my head from my favorite spot.

"After nine." His hand slides up my back, gripping the back of my neck. "Have you eaten?" I shake my head. "You need to eat. C'mon, I'll feed you."

I shake my head. "I don't wanna move." I band my arms

tighter and a puff of air rushes across the top of my head from his chuckle.

"We can come back to bed once you're fed." He taps my ass and I grumble as I shuffle from his lap. He climbs off the bed and then helps me stand. "How're your cramps?"

I melt. Literally, melt. "They're not too bad. I took some Midol before."

He guides me to my couch and gently pushes me down, hands me my crochet and the remote for the TV, and leaves me with a kiss. I find the latest baking show and work on my latest project while he heats the dinner he brought with him. Once it's ready, he brings it over to the couch and we sit together to eat as though we've always been together. These last few weeks with AJ, since our relationship has moved from the donor/recipient mode to relationship mode, have given me an insight into my future with him. This thoughtful, kind, and caring man. The one that's put me and my needs first since we met. As usual, once we've finished, AJ cleans up, then returns to me. He props himself in the corner of the couch, then encourages me to sit so I'm leaning against him. His hand comes around the front of me, and he holds it on my stomach, his thumb rubbing back and forth in soothing strokes.

And I decide … *this is nice.*

Turning my head to the side, I press my lips to AJ's and he immediately returns my affection. His hand slides up my body to cup the front of my throat as we deepen our connection. The light pressure turns me on and I twist so I have better access. I moan when his hands cup and squeeze my ass, pressing me into him, his hard length unmissable. AJ uses his hold on my ass to rub my clit against his dick—it feels amazing and pressure quickly builds in my core.

"Are you gonna use my dick to make yourself come, Cupcake?" he whispers with harsh breaths against my ear. He drags his scruff down my neck and bites my collarbone, drawing a moan from me.

"Yeah," I tell him, softly. One hand slides inside my sleep shorts, heading straight for my clit and the move is enough to break the spell. Pulling my body away, I quickly sit back as though a bucket of iced water has been poured over me.

"What's wrong?"

What's wrong? I widen my eyes at him. "I have my period. You can't put your hands down there."

"Yes, I can. You know orgasms help with cramps, right?" He winks at me and shuffles closer and I shuffle back, but I can't go any further because the arm of the couch prevents my escape. "Don't be shy. Not with me."

"I've never done it before when I have my period. Isn't it messy?"

"Not as messy as you would think, but there are ways around it if you're interested." His expression is hopeful. Since we had sex the first time—for real—I haven't been able to get enough of him, nor him me. He must sense me wavering from my initial stance because he stands and holds his hand out to me. I slide my palm against his roughened fingers and he tugs me to my feet, presses a kiss to the corner of my mouth, then swipes his tongue across the seam. His hands come around me, linking behind me as he deepens the kiss. The man is a master kisser and he easily drags me out of my head and into the moment. My hands slide up his back, gaining purchase as I cup his shoulders, holding us together as he tangles his tongue with mine for long moments.

AJ slows the kiss and pulls away, stepping backward toward the bathroom, and tugging me with him. He strips out of his clothes and then helps me with mine. As he tucks his fingers into the waistband of my panties, I grasp his hands to stop him, imploring him to give me a moment. "Let me deal with this part, okay?"

He nods, then steps out of the bathroom in silence. I blow out a relieved breath that he let me do this part in private. I know it's silly since he's kissed and caressed every part of my body, but my head is overruling my lust. I take care of the tampon and start the water, then open the door. The sight that greets me has my lust returning like a tsunami. His hand is wrapped around his thick length, stroking it slowly. His breaths are choppy and his eyelids are at half-mast. A slow, devious smile tips his lips, creating those deep creases to bracket his mouth.

I reach out and drag him into me, wrapping my hand over his to help him work over his cock. His answering groan sends pulsing waves directly to my clit. Using my hold on his cock, I walk us backward and into the shower.

"Are you wet for me, Cupcake?" he whispers against my ear, his hot breath tickling my flesh and sending goosebumps radiating outward.

"Mmhm." I nod, biting my bottom lip in an attempt to be seductive.

He wastes no time pressing my back against the cold tile and dropping his mouth to my boob. He sucks the nipple into his warm mouth, swirling his tongue around the sensitive bud. I slide my fingers into his wet hair to hold him in place, while he lavishes attention on my breasts. I love having his attention on my boobs and he loves giving it. His hand slides up my thigh, tracing the crease where it meets my body toward my clit which is in desperate need of attention.

His kisses start moving lower, down over my soft stomach and the action jolts me out of the moment because I know exactly where he's heading. I'm not ready for it. This is already out of my comfort zone. I use my grip on his hair to stop him and he peers up at me, not removing his lips from my body. I shake my head, pleading with my eyes. "Please don't do that. I'm not ready." He must recognize my discomfort because he gives a simple nod and works his way back up to my breasts.

"Maybe another time." The relief filling me with his ready acceptance of my limits is instantaneous and I quickly drop back into the moment, knowing I'm always safe in his hands. He lifts his lips from my boob for a moment. "Spread your legs for me, Cupcake." Expecting me to do his bidding, he returns to his ministrations and I spread my legs. Closing my eyes, I lean my head back against the tile as his fingers connect with my sensitive bud, sending a shiver through my body. I can't hold back the moan his touch elicits. I feel his lips spread against my flesh and he increases the pressure of his touch, alternating between circling my clit and sliding his fingers through my pussy lips. He dips his fingers inside and I hold my breath as he fingers me with first one finger, then two. It feels unreal; more sensitive than usual.

"Mmhm. Don't stop. Please don't stop." I tighten my grip on his hair. My breaths are mere shallow pants and my heart pounds as though it's trying to escape its confines, my legs shake and my internal walls tighten around AJ's fingers—everything's happening at once, overwhelming me. "I'm so clo—aaaah!" I cry out, using my grip on his hair to pull him up to my mouth. I attack his lips with a fierceness that surprises me and as I come back into my body, I realize I've been holding his cock this entire time and haven't been paying it the attention it deserves.

After tearing my mouth away from AJ's, I smile at him. I'm sure it looks stupid because I'm drunk on my climax. With what I'm hoping is a sexy wink, I push him back and then switch positions so his back is against the same wall I was using to hold myself up. I kiss him again, then glide my hands down his ripped torso and drop to my knees on the hard tile, ensuring I keep my eyes locked on his.

His brows furrow and his Adam's apple bobs with his swallow. "Cupcake?"

I wink at him, then swallow his shaft in one long glide. "Oh, fuck!" He closes his eyes and drops his head back against the tile, and his Adam's apple bobs again. So sexy. I trace my finger down the trail of hair from his navel, around the base of his shaft, and cup his heavy sac. He won't let me do this to him during my ovulation period, using the excuse that he needs to save all his swimmers. Even when I'm not ovulating, he still won't let me do this. I'm surprised he's letting me suck him off now. "You're so good at sucking my cock." I moan around his shaft as I take it deep, massaging his balls. Slipping my finger back further, I locate his taint and rub it with tight circles. A long, low groan echoes in the shower stall and he drops his eyes to mine as he thrusts his hips gently. His nostrils flare as he watches his cock disappear into my mouth. "I don't want to cum down your sexy throat. I want to paint your tits."

Oh my God. His mouth is so damn hot. I swear he could talk me to an orgasm. My clit pulses and I double my efforts. AJ's hand tightens in my hair and his shaft pulses against my tongue. He drags my mouth from his dick, and I move back slightly, so he can cum over my breasts like he wants. A couple of firm strokes by his own hand and ribbons of cum shoot across my breasts. Using the palm of my hand, I spread his orgasm over my breasts, massaging them seductively, and AJ's eyes flare wide.

"Fuck, yeah! Spread my cum over those gorgeous tits." His voice is rough and raspy, and I happily oblige. He uses his grip on my hair to tug me to my feet, switching our positions again and pressing me against the tile. He dips his head and licks his cum from my breast and it's the dirtiest, most erotic thing I've ever seen. Pressing his semi-hard cock, which seems to be growing harder by the second, against my stomach, he moans against my breast and the vibrations echo through my body.

Bending his knees, he notches the head of his cock against my entrance. "You ready for me, Cupcake?"

"Oh my God, y—" He thrusts into my body roughly before I can finish, stealing my breath. Our mouths lock, melding together as he builds a fast, rough rhythm. Fucking me into the tiled wall, our bodies slipping and sliding against each other. Sighs and moans echo off of the walls as the warm water cascades over us.

High-pitched moans escape each time AJ hits deep inside me, my walls tighten around him, trying to hold him inside. "Fuck, you feel so damn good."

"Not as good as you," I pant. My vision goes hazy and my legs shake as I edge closer to the precipice of my release.

AJ sucks on my lobe and then bites his way down the tendon in my neck, and it's enough to set off the fireworks which have been building. His talented cock throbs inside me and he groans through his release, holding himself deep inside me. Wrapping his arms tight around me, he buries his face in the crook of my neck, and I slide my hands soothingly up and down the muscular planes of his back, while we both work to catch our breath.

CHAPTER 32

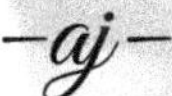

"I haven't been to this lake for years," I comment as we pull into the parking lot. Now to find a parking space.

"Really? We only discovered this place in May when Molly organized a surprise birthday party for Max here. The kids loved the nature playground and I thought Colton would love it too." She was adamant about inviting Hayley and Lisa to her family's Labor Day get-together, so Colton could meet and play with Emma's kids.

I pull into a spot and turn off the engine, then angle my body toward Sarah. "Thank you for including my family." I take a lock of hair between my fingers, appreciating the silkiness of the strands, and tug her to my lips. I hope my kiss conveys exactly how grateful I am for her thoughtfulness.

We pull away, our lips only an inch apart. "You're welcome," Sarah murmurs, her breath skating across my lips. She lays another quick peck, then we climb out of my Jeep and collect our picnic stuff out of the back.

Heading toward the picnic tables, we locate the last empty one at the far end. Even though it's busy, it seems our plan to arrive early paid off. Working together, we set everything up and wander to the lake's edge to watch the kids playing in the water while we wait for our families to arrive. Sarah has her hands wrapped around her middle as she watches parents play with their children, the longing she has for a child of her own obvious. I move in behind her, wrap my arms around her and encourage her to lean back against me.

After laying a tender kiss on the top of her head, I murmur, "We'll have that soon. I promise." I'm not sure I can keep the promise but I damn well intend to do my best to make her—*our*—dream a reality.

She spins in my arms, looking up at me. "What if I can't? I mean all of the tests I had to do with the clinic showed there was physically no reason for me not to get pregnant, but what if I can't?"

I dip down and kiss the tip of her nose, squeezing her tighter to me. I skate my gaze between her mouth and her eyes. "If we can't do it this way, then we'll work out another way to make you a mom. Don't give up, Cupcake."

She smiles softly and drops her forehead against my chest. "How did I get so lucky?"

"I'm pretty sure I'm the lucky one here, Sarah." I finish with a kiss on the top of her head.

"Unca AJ!" A little voice shouts from behind me. Sarah steps out of my embrace and we turn to find Colton running toward us as fast as his little legs can carry him. He bypasses me and heads straight for Sarah, crashing into her legs with a force that makes her take a step back. She giggles as she bends down to scoop him up. "Aunty Sarah!"

"Colton, my little man." She rubs his nose with hers, her eyes sparkling in the warm sunlight. Her easy acceptance of him in her life makes me fall harder for her. Watching them together when Colton spent the night with us made me long for our own family—nights enjoying a movie and playing games together and mornings where we share sleepy smiles and breakfast.

Hayley and Lisa make it to us and after our usual greetings, I take their picnic stuff from them and set it up at the table we procured.

"Can I go for a swim, Mommy?"

"In a little while. Let's wait for everyone else to arrive first."

"Okay." He helps me lay out the blankets next to the table, while the girls set out their picnic.

"Aunty Sarah!" I lift my head to see Kenny running straight for us, her smile a mile wide. "Uncle AJ!" She throws herself at me in my crouched position and I fall backward, landing on my ass with a chuckle.

"Kenny!" Theo calls to her. "You can't run off like that, Munchkin." He turns to me. "Are you okay?"

"Yeah, I'm fine."

"Sorry, Daddy." Theo musses her hair, then holds out his hand to pull me up.

Emma arrives, chuckling. "Are you okay, AJ? That was quite a landing."

"Yeah. I should have prepared myself for the attack." I wipe the grass from my butt.

We introduce everyone and Austin and Kenny take Colton into the fold with ease. Lachlan stands a little away, something I've noticed he does. Sarah explained to me he's on the spectrum and he takes a little while to warm up to new people. Molly and Max arrive and the introductions start all over again.

"Okay, where should we start? On the playground or in the water?" Sarah asks the kids.

"In the water!" Kenny and Colton shout.

"On the playground!" Lachlan and Austin call out at the same time.

"Oh no! Okay, how about this? Let's start with the water

because you won't be able to swim with full bellies after lunch. Then after lunch, we can play on the playground," Sarah offers.

"Yay!" Kenny pumps her little fists in the air.

"Yes, let's do that!" Lachlan says, nodding his head.

We get the kids ready for a swim and head toward the water. The water only comes to above our knees this close to the edge, so Sarah's tucked her dress up into her panties to keep it dry. We toss a ball around the group, keeping the kids entertained until Colton complains he's hungry. Piling out of the water, we set about unpacking the coolers and serving the kids their lunch, closely followed by the adults.

As we dig into the salads and sandwiches, chatter starts up. Emma and Lisa have common ground with their teaching backgrounds, so they talk about the areas lacking in the curriculum and how she and Hayley hope to fill some of the holes with their computer games. I think maybe they've won Emma over to incorporating the use of their games in her program. Hayley updates Theo and Lachlan on Colton's progress with the climbing wall they built and Lachlan and Theo share that they've built and sold another one and have another order to make. Considering Theo is Lachlan's stepfather, they are incredibly close.

The thing that becomes obvious to me as the day wears on is how well our families integrate and knit together. The picnic has been easy and comfortable. Kenny and Austin have spent the day fussing over Colton, ensuring he's not left out, and Colton has soaked up every minute of the attention from the older kids.

As we're packing up to head home, Hayley stops next to me. "Sarah has a lovely family."

"I know. Her parents couldn't make it today, but they're equally as warm. So different from ours."

"Yeah. It seems everyone's family is more loving than

ours." Sadness fills Hayley's eyes. I know what she means. It's something I'm adamant to change in my family with Sarah.

"How are Lisa's parents recovering from their accident?"

"They're okay. Her dad was being stubborn, trying to do everything for himself. But a broken arm does slow you down. And her mom finally accepted our offer to pay for a food delivery service for her while her broken collarbone heals. Slowly but surely, they're improving."

"Give them my best. Do they need me to cut their grass or anything?"

"Oh, would you? That'd be great."

"Sure. No problem." I can't believe I didn't think to offer sooner. I've been so wrapped up in Sarah, I haven't been paying attention to anything outside of our bubble.

Emma comes to hug me goodbye after my family leaves. "How is she?" she asks as her eyes find her sister, talking to Molly and Max.

I glance at my future. "She's okay. She picked herself up and dusted herself off." I tuck my hands into my pockets. "We'll keep trying until she gets pregnant. And if that doesn't work, we'll find another way. There are plenty of ways to make Sarah a mom."

Emma reaches forward, squeezing my forearm. "Thank you for supporting her through this. It's been something she's wanted for such a long time and I'm glad she met you, AJ. You're one of the good ones."

"You don't have to thank me, Em. It's my privilege to be with Sarah." I look across to find her watching me. I raise an eyebrow and give her a smirk. "I don't plan on going anywhere. She's it for me."

The happiness in Emma's eyes tells me she liked my answer. She leans in to hug me goodbye, and we all make our way to the parking lot to head home.

CHAPTER 33

—aj—

THE MINUTE WE WALK THROUGH THE DOOR OF SARAH'S apartment, I grab her hand and spin her around, then take her lips in a fierce kiss. When we eventually pull apart, Sarah looks dazed, and I decide it's my favorite look on her, apart from how she looks when she falls apart beneath me. That would be my most favorite.

"What was that for?"

"Thank you for organizing today." I kiss her again, keeping it light.

"You're welcome. Colton had such a great time with the kids and they loved having him to play with." Her eyes light up with happiness that the afternoon was such a success.

I press her back against the door, kissing her deeply, my tongue sliding against hers, making my breathing erratic. I slide my hands up the side of her thighs, drawing the skirt of her dress up as I go, then dip my fingers into each side of her panties to slide them down her legs. Releasing them, gravity takes over and they drop to the floor. Sarah sucks on my tongue in response, and I swipe my fingers through her folds, groaning at the wetness there. "You're always so ready for me, Cupcake."

"Mmhm," she responds, chasing my lips to resume our kiss. Her hands slide up my arms to tangle around my neck.

Dropping her skirt, I take her hands and raise them above her head, pressing them into the door. "Keep them there, okay?" I raise my brow while I wait for her to answer me.

"Okay," comes her breathy acquiescence. So fucking sexy.

Dropping my eyes from her face, they get caught on her breasts which are heaving with her panting breaths. She's so damned turned on. This woman was made for me. "That's a good girl."

Her eyes flare and her mouth drops open in an O. She likes that.

Good to know.

Kissing my way down the side of her neck to her collarbone, I nip her pulse point, then move to kiss her tits over the top of her dress. Lowering to the floor, I gather the skirt of her dress in one hand and duck closer to swipe my tongue through her pussy lips and up to her clit, where I roll the sensitive bud with my tongue. Sarah moans, dropping her head to watch me. "AJ," she whispers. "Do it again. Please."

I don't need to be asked twice, so I press in, teasing and biting her clit in between licks and sucks. I push my fingers into her opening and massage her front wall; the area I know sends Sarah flying. Her legs shake as she takes panting breaths in between her cries of pleasure. Her hands drop to my head, grasping the short strands and I immediately stop what I'm doing.

Her head snaps down, her eyes narrowed at me. "Why'd you stop?"

"Put your hands back where I told you to keep them."

"Oh my God, so damn bossy," she huffs out.

I wink at her. "You'd better believe it, Cupcake." I tip my chin up. "Go on."

She pretends to be put out but returns her hands into position, and I get back to work. It doesn't take long before she breaks apart beautifully beneath my touch, chanting my name repeatedly. I think my favorite thing to do is to make her come. Watching her fall apart is equally as beautiful as watching any sunrise.

"You're so damn good at that."

I stand and hold my fingers to her lips, painting the soft pillows with her release. Her tongue darts out, following the path. My cock, which is already fighting for space in my shorts, grows further, pressing against the zipper. I wouldn't be surprised if I don't have zipper marks on the damn thing.

"Get naked, beautiful," I tell her as I pull my T-shirt over my head and drop my hands to the button and fly on my shorts. Biting her bottom lip, she does as I ask, never tearing her eyes away from my body.

"I love your body, AJ," she tells me, her voice dripping with lust.

"Ditto, Cupcake." I lift my chin toward her. "Now get naked." She moves into action, removing the dress, and leaving her in only her bra and sandals. Once I'm naked, I drop down and remove each sandal carefully, ensuring Sarah doesn't lose her balance and she removes her bra. I point to the table. "Bend over the table for me. I need to bury my cock in your pussy."

She bends over the table, her full breasts squishing against the surface, giving me a spectacular view of her swollen pussy. I swipe the head of my cock through the glistening slickness and Sarah pushes back against me. "Hurry up. I need you."

I grunt as I notch my head against her opening and push inside in one swift thrust. We both moan at the beauty of our joining. I throw my head back and press in as deep as I can, holding still until I'm in control. If I start moving straight away, I'm not gonna last, and I never want this to end.

Sarah turns her head, watching me over her shoulder. "Are you okay?"

"Yeah. Just need a minute," I grit through clenched teeth. Rubbing my hands up and down her smooth back, to her neck, and down to her ass cheeks, I leave a trail of goosebumps in my wake. Her body shivers beneath my touch, and I feel like the king of the world. Once I'm certain I won't come in two strokes, I separate her ass cheeks and slide out.

"Oooooh," Sarah moans.

I slide my hands around to her hips, gripping tight, and begin to pump steadily, ensuring I hit that special spot each time I push inside. Small grunts leave Sarah's lips every time I bottom out, making my cock infinitely harder. Dropping my eyes to Sarah's ass, I admire the movement every time my hips slap against her and groan at the sight of my glistening cock sliding out of her heat.

"This is quite the fucking sight. I wish you could see this." I wonder if she'd let me record this sometime? My phone is completely secure, so the videos and images would be one hundred percent safe.

As I pick up speed and power, the table edges across the room with each thrust, adding to the obscene sounds of skin slapping against skin and the squelching sound Sarah's pussy makes every time I push back in. A sheen of sweat is gathering down her spine, and I run my hand down the dip to the crack of her ass. Separating her ass cheeks, my cock pulses at the view of her oh-so-tempting tight hole. Dragging my fingers along her sensitive area, I wet my thumb and then trace circles around the hole. Sarah freezes. "It's okay. I promise it'll feel good, Cupcake. Trust me."

Her body relaxes and she nods. Her trust is a gift and shows me how far our relationship has come. Rubbing around the tight hole, I dip back down to collect more of her lubrication, then carefully breach the ring of muscle eliciting a gasp from Sarah. She pushes back against me, panting, her legs trembling.

"Oh, God. That feels so good. I … I'm so close." I slide my thumb out and back in, matching the action with my cock. The pressure feels incredible as her walls tighten like a wave around my length. "Aaaagh!" Sarah shouts.

Her release sets off mine, and stars dance around the edge of my vision, my lungs trap my breath, and electricity shoots from the furthest parts of my body to one singular point—my cock. My balls draw up and my cum explodes in ribbons into her. "Fuuuck!" I moan while I bury my cock as deep as I can—my dick pulses, emptying everything I have into the woman I love.

Love!

I'm pretty sure I fell in love with her the first night we met, and my feelings for her have only grown deeper, more complex.

Draping my torso over her body, I keep my dick inside her as I kiss my way down her spine, running the palms of my hands down each side, tracing the valleys and curves. We're both panting heavily, working to catch our breaths when Sarah turns her head to the side and smiles sleepily at me. I move so I can meet her lips with mine. We connect in a lazy kiss as we come down from our high. Sarah wiggles her ass, and I take the hint that she probably needs me to climb off of her. I help her up, then carry her into her bedroom and position her ass on my thighs so I can hold her legs up.

She chuckles. "I'm not ovulating yet, we don't need to do this."

"Don't care. We may as well get started. Just in case." I

wink at her, rubbing my hands up and down her legs. It's then I notice the red marks where her hips were probably connecting with the table. I run my fingers over the redness. "I'm sorry. I got a little carried away."

"You never have to apologize to me for getting carried away when I'm on the receiving end of it." She wiggles her eyebrows up and down, smirking at me.

And just like that, I'm hard again. Still holding her legs upright, I open her to me and slide my cock into heaven and proceed to defile her all over again.

Lying on my back with Sarah draped across my chest, her leg thrown over both of mine, I trace patterns up her arms. The room is considerably darker than it was before as day turns to night. We've pretty much had a sex-a-thon since arriving home this afternoon. "I think you should move in with me."

Sarah's head snaps up. "What?" At least she hasn't gone into a panic attack like she did when I suggested we have sex to get her pregnant rather than using the collection condom and syringe method.

"Hear me out. If you move in with me, we can have sex every morning and night. Surely, that'll get you pregnant. None of this every other day stuff only when you're ovulating."

"I'm pretty sure we were doing it more than every second day during my ovulation period last month," she sasses back.

"I want you with me," I murmur. Gliding my fingers through her messy hair, I watch her closely as she runs through the pros and cons. My Sarah is an overthinker, which is probably good because she balances out my spontaneity. And while my suggestion for her to move in with me may seem out of the blue, it's something I've been thinking about since we first decided to see where this relationship could go. I don't expect her to make a decision tonight, but I'd be thrilled if she did so we can move her things straight away.

Her eyes come back to mine and her lips slowly spread, her eyes twinkling in happiness. She begins to nod slowly, gradually picking up speed while her smile grows wider. "Okay."

"Okay?" Surely it's not that easy.

She chuckles. "Okay."

CHAPTER 34

—sarah—

I WAKE TO BUTTERFLY KISSES BEING PRESSED ALONG MY SPINE, sending goosebumps radiating out from the middle of my back through my body in waves. A tiny moan leaves my throat and I feel AJ's lips smile against my flesh.

"Happy birthday, Cupcake," he says, his voice gruff from sleep.

"It certainly is." I turn my head toward the window, noting it's not quite morning, and sigh. This has been my life since I moved in with AJ. He wakes me before dawn to ensure we have plenty of time to start our day right before we need to get ready for work. I've had so much sex these past weeks, I'm surprised my pores don't ooze semen.

He moves up my body, using his forearms to balance over me, and kisses the corner of my mouth which immediately tips up. Using his tongue, he traces the seam of my lips, and I lean forward slightly to nip it and suck it into my mouth. He groans and uses his knee to push my leg upward, positioning his cock at my opening. I love having him inside me, filling me up, knowing I'm the last woman he'll ever be with like this. I push my hips back, encouraging him inside until he's deep and every thick inch of him is buried inside me. Without taking his lips from mine, he moves his hips slowly but surely, languidly making love to me, no dirty talk, just pure physical connection. The way he fills my body is the definition of divine. Deep moans resonate from AJ, sending my pulsing clit into overdrive. Panting breaths brush across my cheek as the tell-tale tremors of my impending orgasm barrel down on me. Pushing my hips back to take AJ's cock as deep as I can, I cry out as I break apart, every single atom which makes up my body flying into space.

"Happy birthday, Cupcake," AJ breathlessly repeats, pressing another scorching kiss against my lips as I piece myself back together. Without removing his still-hard dick from me, he hoists up my hips and starts all over again, this time, his talented fingers work over my clit, while his dick hits my G-spot in the most delicious of attacks. "Feel your pretty clit putting on a show just for me."

My panting breaths and AJ's groans fill the silence of the room as I quickly build toward my second release. I probably won't be able to walk today and I'm more than okay with that. AJ's cock pulses inside me as my walls clamp down on his length. A long, low "fuuuck" leaves his gorgeous lips as he holds completely still inside of me. His harsh breaths carry through the room and mingle with my fast pants.

"This has to be the best start to a birthday I've ever had." My body shakes with my chuckle.

"Fuck. Don't do that when I'm still inside you," he grumbles harshly.

I turn my head to look at him. Adorable creases are prominent between his eyebrows as he pulls out and carefully rolls me over to my back. Resting my ass on his thighs so he can hold my legs up, his roughened fingers glide up and down my heated flesh in a smooth caress and I smile at him.

"I love how you do this for me every time we have sex."

"I want this to work as much as you do. You know that, right?"

I nod dreamily. "Yeah."

He kisses the back of my knee, sending a smattering of goosebumps across my leg. Leaning back slightly, his eyes drop to my exposed pussy. The next thing I know, his fingers slide through my slit to my opening and push inside me. This is the other thing he always does. He scoops any cum that slides out of me back inside with an impressive level of diligence. At first, it was shocking and embarrassing, but now I'm used to it.

AJ has been the most unexpected surprise throughout this entire journey. His eagerness to comply with whatever I've needed from him from the very start has been ongoing. He's made me feel completely comfortable throughout the process, even through the bumps in the road caused by my insecurities. I couldn't have asked for a better boyfriend if I'd made a list of what I was searching for. I close my eyes and sigh, thanking whomever it is I need to thank that my self-sabotage didn't scare him away.

"That was a big sigh. What's going on in that head of yours?"

"Just thanking the higher powers that be for bringing you into my life. I'm incredibly thankful you sat in our booth that night and were brave enough to approach me."

Still holding my legs up, he moves out from beneath me, bringing his face close to mine. "I'm the one who's thankful, Sare," he whispers against my lips, soulful brown eyes locked on mine. God, I hope our child has his gorgeous eyes, so warm and inviting. When he presses his lips to mine gently, I raise my head to deepen the kiss. I need to show him how much he means to me. I'm not ready to say those three little words yet, but I can show him.

Our kiss builds quickly, as it always does, going from a spark to a full-on inferno in mere seconds. He ignites a passion in me that's foreign and has been out of reach until him. A sharp smack to my ass has me jolting away from him. "What was that for?"

He tilts his head to the side. "No reason. I just love your ass. And I'm gonna love seeing my handprint on it when you climb out of bed." He smacks me again, lightly this time. "Come on. I want to make you a decent breakfast before you go to work."

We climb out of bed, and shower together, which leads to me dropping to my knees and him returning the favor. Oh yeah, three orgasms before breakfast! I'll definitely be walking into the office with a spring in my step this morning.

AJ makes breakfast burritos while I dress and then tells me he booked a surprise for my birthday over the next long weekend. He's not giving me any hints either, taking great joy in my incessant guesses which he says are way off base.

I kiss him goodbye for the day, and he reminds me of the dinner reservations he made for tonight; we'll be headed to *Cristo's* with my family for my birthday.

The second the elevator doors open, I spot my best friend speaking with Joe, still wearing her scrubs with baby penguins decorating the pink fabric. I run toward her as fast as my fitted skirt and heels allow. When she spots me, she breaks away from Joe and runs toward me with her arms open wide, wearing a broad smile on her gorgeous face. God, I love her. We collide with giggles. Just like the gif with the two little boys running toward each other on a sidewalk.

"Happy birthday, Sare Bear!"

"Thanks, Mels Bells."

She grips my hand. "Let's grab lunch. There's no time to waste."

We walk, arm in arm, toward the sushi train not far from my building. Grabbing two seats facing the train, we both make our first selection.

"Oh my God, this is so good!" Mel exclaims after taking a bite of her California roll.

"So good. Thanks for meeting me for my birthday."

"Always." She drags an envelope out of her purse. "I got you something, too."

I love presents. I mean what girl doesn't? I open the envelope and slide out a gift card for a nail pampering session at my favorite salon, *R&R Nail Salon*. I lean across and hug my long-time friend. "Thank you so much. I hope you're coming with me."

She reaches back into her purse and pulls out a second envelope. "You betcha! We just need to coordinate our schedules."

I always love spending time with Mel, she's the best friend a girl could ask for. "You seem less tired today."

She chuckles. "I'm on days this week, so I'm getting proper sleep. It always helps." She scans me up and down. "You look as though you're glowing and I don't think it's just because it's your birthday." She wiggles her eyebrows up and down.

I sigh with what I'm sure is a dreamy look on my face.

"Oh yeah, clearly lover boy is doing a good job at keeping you sexed up!" Mel chuckles.

"Oh my God, Mel. I've never had so many orgasms in my entire life. The man is a master." I chuckle. "But that's all the information you're getting out of me on that front."

"Boo! What sort of friend are you if you're not gonna share the deets with your bestest friend in the whole entire world?" She nudges me with her shoulder. "Only kidding. I'm happy to see you happy, my friend. You deserve it."

"You deserve it, too, you know," I tell her and she shrugs.

"So, do you think you're pregnant yet?"

My mood drops like a lead balloon. "I don't know. I should be for the amount of sex I've had this month." I shrug. "But who knows."

Mel places her hand softly on my forearm. "It'll happen. The universe knows what a great mom you'll be, so you *will* have a baby. You'll see." She squeezes my arm gently.

I'm glad she's feeling so positive about the whole thing. I'm honestly beginning to doubt if I'll ever have my dream. And will AJ want to stick around if I can't get pregnant? Or will he decide it's best to move on with someone who *can* have a baby? Is our relationship wholly contingent on us getting pregnant and having a child together?

Thankfully, Mel senses the drop in my mood and changes the subject to lighter topics; sharing stories about the girls she works with. Some of them sound a little unhinged which is surprising since they always seem so put together whenever I've volunteered, but Mel says they're great girls. I'll take her word for it. And they can't be too bad, they spend their days and nights caring for incredibly sick babies.

"Shit, I need to get back." Mel stands, tossing her purse straps over her shoulder. I stand too and we head for the pay station. "My treat today, since it's your birthday." She gives me a side hug.

"Thanks, Mel, and thanks for meeting me today. I love seeing your face."

"Me too. I mean, I don't love seeing my face, I love seeing *your* face." We both chuckle as we leave the restaurant and walk back toward my building arm in arm. We hug goodbye and I head back upstairs.

"Honey, I'm home," I call as soon as I enter AJ's home. Even though he's made me feel completely welcome here, I still think of it as his home. Everything's quiet. AJ and Dylan must still be working. I head toward their office at the rear of the house.

"Okay, I'll see you on the seventeenth!" AJ snaps harshly. I've never heard him raise his voice.

Dylan steps out of their office and smiles at me. "Is everything all right?" I ask and his head tilts to the side in question. I point at the open barn door. "AJ sounds pissed at something."

"Oh that. It's nothing, just some family drama." He steps closer and wraps his arms around me, lifting me off of my feet. "Happy birthday, Sarah."

I chuckle. "Thanks."

When he places me back on my feet, we both walk inside their well-appointed office. AJ has his back to the doorway, his hands resting on his hips, and his head dropped toward the floor. His shoulders are rising and falling with heavy breaths. I don't think his call was 'nothing,' he seems upset.

"Look who's home!" Dylan calls.

AJ spins on the spot and his entire demeanor changes when his eyes land on me. In three long strides, he has his arms wrapped around me, repeating Dylan's action by lifting me off of my feet. "Hey, Cupcake." He presses his lips firmly against mine and we go from zero to one hundred in five seconds flat. His yummy scent wraps around me, making me feel calm and steady. That's what he does for me. He steadies me, calming my overactive mind.

"All right, I'm outta here. Enjoy the rest of your birthday, Sarah."

By the time I manage to tear my lips away from AJ's, Dylan's gone. I wrap my legs around AJ's hips and study his face closely. "Is everything okay?"

Creases form between his brows and his hold on me tightens. "Yeah, why?"

"I heard you on the phone. You sounded pissed." His body tenses. "I'm just checking on you. That's what girlfriends do, you know." A smile tilts up the corners of his mouth.

"Yeah, everything's fine. Just some family stuff I should have taken care of ages ago."

"If you need to talk about it, I'm here."

He kisses the tip of my nose. "I know, but I promise, it's nothing. It'll be sorted out in the next few weeks."

His grip drops to my ass and he grabs a cheek in each hand, squeezing. I grind against him, feeling him harden against me. "You want my dick?"

"Yeah," I respond breathily. *Is that even my voice?*

His lips crash onto mine and I kiss him back hungrily, and I realize I never seem to get enough of this man. I'm turned on as soon as I'm in his vicinity. He doesn't even need to do anything and when I stop to think about why that could be, I come back to the fact that apart from being utterly sexy, he steadies me. He gives me a safe place where I don't need to think of every single scenario because I know he's got me. That we'll figure out whatever it is, *together.* I deepen our kiss, grinding down on his cock. I feel us moving, and then my butt lands on the cold surface of the kitchen counter. I immediately drop my hands to his belt and drag the leather through the metal buckle, then release his button and zipper.

"You're so fucking perfect," he groans into my ear, his hot breath skating down my neck adding to my arousal. "I bet you're already soaking for me."

Moaning at his words, I push down his pants and boxer briefs and wrap my hand around his engorged length. Hot and silky to the touch, it's heavy in my hand as I stroke it, then I swipe my thumb across the top, collecting his precum which I lick from my thumb with a moan. At the same time, AJ pushes up my skirt and slides my panties to the side, stroking his fingers through my pussy. "You're so fucking ready for me and I haven't done anything."

"I'm always ready when you're in the room. I can't help it," I murmur.

He groans, dropping his head back, before returning his heated gaze to me. His dark eyes are intense as they skate around my face. I line up his cock with my opening, and he thrusts inside without preamble making us both groan. I'm worried I'm turning into an addict for his cock. The more he's inside me, the more I want him inside me. I can't get enough and AJ's the same.

All of my focus narrows to where we're intimately joined and it's no longer just about making a baby, it's also about connecting with a man who's grown to mean everything to me. The sex is incredible, but it feels more like making love and building our connection the more we come together. He sets my body and my soul ablaze with every thrust of his hips and swipe of his tongue.

The erotic sounds of our coupling fill the space, echoing through the large, open room as our heavy breaths mingle with grunts and moans. I use my hold around his neck to pull him tighter to me and he picks up speed, his panting breaths blowing across my sweaty cheek. "Harder," I cry out between thrusts. "Please, AJ."

"I'll get you there, Cupcake," he breathes harshly. His hands tighten on my hips and I know I'll have his marks there. I love seeing the evidence of our joining in the various shades of bruises that seem to be constantly on my hips. His movements become harder, deeper, reaching that special place inside of me.

AJ slides his hand around the front of my body, and his thumb circles my needy clit, setting off an explosion of light behind my eyes while tremors rack my body from the tips of my fingers to my core and everywhere in between. My grip on him tightens as I break apart, shattering into a million pieces.

"Aaaah," I cry out, dropping my head onto AJ's shoulder as he buries himself deep inside me, his cock growing and pulsing with his release.

"Fuuuck!" He shouts as his body locks tight. The room is suddenly quiet as we both fight to catch our breath.

My lips widen against his hammering pulse point and I nip it lightly, then lick the saltiness of AJ's exertion. "I've turned into a limp noodle." I slide my fingers through the short, sweat-slicked strands of dark hair resting at his nape.

AJ chuckles. "That means I did my job." He strokes his hand lovingly along my thighs to my hips, which he rubs sooth-ingly. Using his fingers, he grips my chin tenderly and raises my face to his. Gently, reverently, he takes my lips in a slow, lazy kiss. It's deep and soul-stealing and it's everything. He strokes my tongue with his in such a way that tells me he feels the same for me as I do for him. His hips begin to mimic the action of his tongue and with leisurely movements, he slowly builds the inferno once again, taking us both to completion.

CHAPTER 35

–aj–

I'VE BEEN FLOATING ON A HIGH ALL WEEK, AND IT'S NOT JUST because of all the sex I'm having, though I'm sure it's a contributing factor. Dinner at *Cristo's* with Sarah's family on Monday night was incredible. It was the second time Sarah and I have spent time with them since we decided to build a relationship, and her family is genuinely happy for us. Apart from Theo and Max laying down the law, which I understood, the Stanfields have made me feel welcome from the beginning, but on Monday there was a deeper level of acceptance I'm certain I wasn't imagining. I felt as though I belonged.

Heading upstairs, I go in search of Sarah. I noticed her car in the garage, but she never came to say hello, which is something she always does. "Sarah," I call out as I enter our bedroom. Checking the walk-in closet, I find the space empty. She wasn't downstairs and I'm puzzled as to where she could be. Maybe she's on the deck. As I step around the bed on my way out to check, a sob catches my attention, and I backtrack to the ensuite. Another sob sounds.

My heart sinks. Breaking and bleeding.

I drop my forehead to the wooden door, closing my eyes as

my heart drops to my toes, leaving a bloody mess. I listen to her sobs through the door, feeling my heart crack for her, for both of us. Because even though this started as her dream, it quickly became mine as well. Placing my open palm to the surface, I whisper, "Sarah? Cupcake?" The sobs stop but she doesn't answer me. "Can I come in?" Still no answer, so I try the door but it's locked. "C'mon, Cupcake. Let me in. You don't have to deal with this alone. Let me hold you."

Silence fills the room for long moments before I hear shuffling from the other side of the door and the lock disengage. The second the door opens, I step inside and gather my girl in my arms. No words are spoken; none are needed. I know she's devastated as am I. My cupcake buries her head in my chest, her hands gripping the side of my shirt, and she lets go, releasing her pain and disappointment. Her body shakes and I tighten my hold on her, laying kisses on the top of her head and stroking her silky locks in long, soothing strokes.

I feel so fucking helpless.

I desperately want to give her what she wants and for the number of times I've been inside her, I was sure we'd made a baby this month. Her hands slide around to my back and she presses tighter against me as her sobs slow. "I'm so sorry, Sarah."

She mumbles something against my pecs I can't understand so I bring my hands around to cup her face, tilting it up to mine. Red, swollen eyes and blotchy cheeks greet me, breaking my heart further. I kiss her forehead, nose, and each eyelid. "What did you say, Cupcake?"

"I'm the one who's sorry. You have these super sperm, so I must be faulty."

Her words are like a red cape to a bull. I tilt her head back further. "Don't ever, and I mean ever, call yourself faulty. You're fucking perfect in every way." As she opens her mouth to argue, I drop mine over hers and kiss her in a way I hope shows her how perfect I think she is. How much I love her. Not that I've said the words yet. Sarah likes to do things slowly and at her pace, so I'll hold onto those three words until I'm certain she's ready to hear them, and now's not the time. I kiss her like it's the last time I'll ever get to kiss her and I do my best to take away her pain and piece her back together.

When we pull away to catch our breath, I drop my forehead to hers. "What if I can't get pregnant, AJ?"

"Then we find another way to make our dream come true." Her eyes widen and her mouth drops open in a small O.

"Our dream?" she whispers.

"Yeah. *Our* dream. You know I'm in this as deep as you are." I rub my nose along hers.

She nods slowly. "Thank you."

She seems to forget we've had this conversation before. I gently brush her hair away from her face, tucking the silky locks behind her ears. My eyes dart between hers. "You don't need to thank me, Cupcake. I'd do anything for you."

She smiles at me and a portion of the crack in my heart repairs. I want to make her smile all the time. I don't want to see these tears—this sadness. Without words, I undress her and turn on the shower. Slowly, I guide her beneath the fall of the water and make love to her. No words are spoken, they're not needed as our bodies move with synchronicity. Hands stroking and mouths teasing, we come together beautifully, Sarah's cries and my grunts echoing off the tiled walls.

I kiss her slowly as we both come down from our high, my softening dick sliding out of heaven. Still keeping my hold on Sarah, I step back slightly and grab the soap to wash her body. With careful strokes, I wash every inch of her, then start on her hair. First with shampoo, then conditioner, just the way she showed me. I massage her scalp with firm fingers, eliciting moans from my girl. "If you keep making those noises, I'm going to have to fuck you again."

She chuckles. "Like that's a punishment." She pushes her ass back, connecting with my growing cock. It's always like this with her. I'm addicted to her pussy, but more than that, I'm addicted to her.

"Where are you taking me?" Sarah chuckles as I manhandle her out the door. I packed our stuff while she was at the hospital for her volunteer shift and now we need to get moving if we're going to make it to the airport on time.

"You'll see when we get there. It's your birthday surprise."

"But I didn't pack anything. How do I know if you packed everything I need?"

I smirk at her. "I've got you covered. I used to be in the Scouts."

Her feet lock in place and she looks at me. "Really?"

"Nah, just kidding. But I have everything you need. I promise." I kiss the tip of her nose and drag her to my Jeep.

On the way to the airport, Sarah's questions don't stop. "Can't you give me a hint?"

"Nope." I pop the p like a teenager with attitude and grin at her as she huffs.

"I don't feel like I can relax and enjoy the experience without knowing where we're going or what we're gonna be doing?" And there she is, my overthinking cupcake.

I figure I'll throw her a bone. "I'm taking you camping. Well, sort of."

Her head snaps toward me and with wide sparkling eyes, she asks, "Really?"

"Yeah."

Her smile is wide. "I've never been *sort of* camping before."

I collect her hand and place it on my thigh, leaving my hand resting on top of hers. "It'll be fun."

We pull into the airport parking lot and find a parking space, then make our way into the terminal. "Where on earth are we camping that we need to catch a plane to get there?" Sarah giggles.

Sarah spends the flight updating me on the babies in the NICU. She practically vibrates with joy when she shares her excitement at getting to meet the parents of a baby she cuddled last time and how grateful they were she was there to love on their baby when they couldn't.

The off-road RV I organized is waiting out front of the terminal when we arrive and we waste no time in getting on the road to our final destination for the next two nights. Sarah's eyes almost pop out of her head when she realizes where we're headed. "I've never been here before. Have you?"

"I haven't, so it will be a first for both of us." I glance across at her.

Her answering grin and whispered words, "I like that" make me feel as though I'm standing atop El Capitan.

Once we arrive at Stovepipe Wells, we grab our camping site, and I make us a bite to eat from the supplies in the fully stocked kitchen. Because it's almost late afternoon, we decide to check out the nearby Mesquite Sand Dunes for some fun and then we'll have a picnic dinner to watch the sunset. I specifically brought Sarah here because, while it's not considered the darkest area in the United States, it's rated pretty high by the International Dark Sky Places Program. And I remembered her saying she would like to experience this when we watched the documentary about the most extreme places in the US.

We climb out of the RV, and as Sarah and I scan the area, the vastness of the dunes steals our breath. "Oh my. It's gorgeous," Sarah whispers reverently.

"Yeah." I grab our sand boards, which were kindly supplied, and hand in hand, Sarah and I begin our trek through the dunes. The number of footprints in the soft sand is incredible, but what's surprising is that some parts are dry and cracked like a dried-up lake bed. Obviously, it hasn't been too windy the last couple of days to erase the footprints covering the dunes.

Sarah points far off into the distance. "Look at that one. It must be enormous, it juts out so much higher than the others."

"Shall we check it out?"

"Yeah. But let me carry one of the boards."

"I'm okay. If they start to get heavy, you can carry one."

We climb over each dune, past dead gnarly trees, taking the time to snap some shots of the magnificent backdrop with our phones. Sarah photobombs some of my shots so I make sure to return the favor, pulling funny faces as I leap across in front of the lens.

As the sun crosses the sky, we finally reach the highest dune we were aiming for. We must have walked about a mile. Nobody else is here and we're both hot and sweaty from the workout of climbing dunes in soft sand. Panting, we both drop to our asses.

"Shit, that was quite a workout!" Sarah exclaims through panting breaths.

Sitting beside her, I raise my knees and clasp my hands around them loosely. "I'm gonna need a minute before we take these bad boys to the bottom." I tip my chin to the boards beside me.

"I can't believe I was sitting in the NICU this morning and this afternoon I'm sitting atop the tallest dune here." Her eyes are full of wonder as she takes in the incredible landscape, and I take the opportunity to sneak in a photo. Her skin looks golden with the reflection of the late-afternoon sun casting across the dunes.

"Are you ready to ride the dune?" I ask, wiggling my eyebrows.

Sarah chuckles. "Of course. Let's go."

We situate ourselves on our boards and push off at the same time, ensuring we're a safe distance apart. Sarah screams on the way down, holding onto her board for dear life, while I laugh at her, ensuring I don't fall off my board. When we get to the bottom of the dune, my board stops, but the momentum of the slide means I keep going forward, rolling in the deep sand. I manage to close my eyes, but my mouth fills with sand. Once I come to a stop, I spit out as much sand as I can as Sarah comes running over to me and drops to her knees.

"Are you okay?" I can't make out her face with the sun shining behind her, but I can tell by her tone that she's worried.

I begin to laugh and reach forward to pull her down on top of me. "I'm fine," I tell her through the grit stuck to my tongue. Our water bottles are at the top of the dune along with our shoes, so I'll have to wait until I'm at the top before I can rinse out my mouth. "That was so much fun. I wanna do it again and again and again."

She chuckles as she props herself up on my pecs. "Me too!" I push up and press my lips to hers chastely, then we climb to our feet and begin the trek back to the top. The afternoon passes by as we slide, climb, and slide again until our legs won't carry us any further. "I think my legs are gonna fall off. I don't think I can climb it again *and* have enough energy to walk all the way back to the parking lot."

"Let's head back then. I have a picnic dinner waiting for us and we can watch the sunset."

"You've thought of everything." I hope I thought of everything. I wanted to make this getaway memorable for her.

I pull her into me, holding her hands behind my back, making her body flush with mine. Lowering my head, Sarah presses up on her toes to meet me halfway and our lips collide.

Our kiss is deep and bruising. Rough and explorative as we connect. I love how we can go from laughing our asses off, sliding down a dune, to sharing passionate kisses which leave me breathless.

Sarah pulls her lips away, her eyes glistening in the low light. "I felt like a kid again. Sliding down the dune was exhilarating." She squeezes my hands. "Thank you for planning this. It's the best birthday present I've ever been given."

"Anything for you, Cupcake."

Sarah sets up the outdoor camping chairs while I collect our picnic dinner and we both put our feet up while enjoying the feast as the sun disappears below the horizon. She points toward the dunes. "Look at how the colors are changing with the waning light." She takes a drink of her soda. "Stunning," she whispers.

"Yeah." I couldn't care less about the colors of the dunes because I can't tear my eyes away from my girl.

She notices I'm not looking at the dunes. "Look. You don't want to miss it, we only have a sliver of sunlight left."

At her insistence, I turn my head and my eyes catch on the almost glowing amber dunes under the waning light. I reach my hand out to grasp Sarah's, and I picture us doing this when we're much older and we've lived a long and happy life together. The way her face lights up with an appreciation of the spectacular show nature is putting on for us is something I'll file away and remember for the rest of my days.

We clean up from dinner and lock our RV, then head back into the dunes with a blanket tucked beneath my arm. "Thank goodness for the full moon. It's making it easy to see where we're going."

"Yeah, it worked out pretty well for my plan." When we're far enough away from the parking lot, I lay out the blanket and invite Sarah to join me. Lying on our backs, we look up at the night sky. At first, the stars aren't all that clear. I turn my head toward Sarah. "It'll take about twenty minutes for our eyes to adjust from the light of the RV to the darkness, so we can see the stars clearly."

She turns her head toward me with a smile. "Whatever shall we do to fill the time?" she asks all innocent-like. We're the only ones out here tonight, so I roll on top of her.

—sarah—

When AJ rolls on top of me I can't contain my giggle, until he drops his lips to mine. That shuts me up quickly. I adore the way he kisses me. I sigh as he places a soft kiss on my bottom lip, then traces his tongue along the seam where my lips meet. "You're so beautiful, Sarah. And I'm not just talking about how you look. You have a beautiful heart," he murmurs against my lips, sending my heart somersaulting.

My hands grip his sides as I press up to capture his lips. He opens and slides his tongue into my mouth without hesitation. As our tongues dance with each other, I slide my hands along the hard planes of AJ's back, feeling the play of his muscles as he holds his body weight off me. I press down, encouraging him to close the distance between us. I want to feel him on top of me, be trapped beneath his strong, hard body. He takes the hint and drops so his chest is pressing against mine, his pelvis cradled between my thighs. I wrap my legs around him, locking him to me, and push up against his steely shaft trapped behind his zipper. He grinds down and it's amazing, sending sparks flying through my body. Gliding my hands to his shoulders, I trace his muscles down his arms and back again, finally sliding my fingers through the short strands of hair at his nape.

My heart pounds in a fast rhythm, as our kiss continues, deepening, becoming more intense. He's making love to my mouth under the full moon in the middle of the sand dunes and I want this moment to last forever. I want to burn it into my memory banks and remember it when I'm old and gray. With confident movements, AJ removes every stitch of clothing from my body and his and makes love to me beneath the starry night sky.

With glistening skin, we lay on the blanket catching our breath, wrapped in each other's embrace. I gasp when my eyes land on the night sky and the billions of stars twinkling above us. "This is gorgeous, AJ." I turn my head to look at him. "Thank you for bringing me here."

He presses a kiss on my lips. "You're welcome, Cupcake. Happy birthday." I shiver. "Are you cold?"

"A little."

"Let's get dressed, then." We both quickly dress, curling back around each other to enjoy the starry night for a while longer. As our eyes grow heavy, we decide to make our way back to the RV in the dark. "I thought we could sleep here tonight." AJ presses a button and the roof shade slides back, exposing the night sky through a moon roof. The perfect name since we now have a spectacular view of the night sky while laying on our soft bed.

"Oh my God, this is amazing!"

AJ locks the door and climbs into bed beside me, he places his hands beneath his head, and a proud smile fills his face. "I'm glad you like it."

"*Like* it? I freaking love it. It's incredible." I snuggle into his side, and he wraps his arm around me, tugging me in tight to his body where I know I'll always be safe.

I wake to the early rays of dawn streaming down on me, wrapped in AJ's big spoon. I press back into him, enjoying his warmth and he kisses the back of my head. "Morning." His voice is gruff from sleep, and my body immediately responds. "I should have closed the roof last night," he grumbles.

I turn over within his embrace. "I'm glad you didn't. I want to watch the sunrise with you."

His lips tip up and he kisses the end of my nose. "We could make that a thing you know. Watching the sunrise together. We're both early risers."

"I like the sound of that," I whisper. AJ's fingers glide lazily up and down my spine, following the curve from the base of my neck to the top of my ass as the cabin fills with golden light to start a brand-new day. We lay in silence, my mind quiet while I soak up this moment, both of us happy to absorb each other and our uninterrupted time together. "We should get up and watch the sun touch the dunes."

AJ taps his fingers on my hip and climbs out of bed, helping me up. I throw on one of his T-shirts, and he pulls on a pair of gray sweats, leaving his magnificent torso bare. My breath gushes out of me as my feet touch the cold gravel and my eyes land on the golden dunes. AJ's arms wrap around me from behind and he walks me forward, his breath warm against my neck. He rests his chin on my shoulder, and I bring my hands up to cover his, tucked beneath my breasts.

My gaze skates across the dunes, appreciating their beauty, so different from yesterday. "How is it that the same landscape can look so different in a new light? This has to be one of my most memorable moments," I breathe.

Cataloging the changes to the landscape, I have a sudden epiphany. I think Mel was right. Michael and I had to fall apart to make room for AJ to come into my life. When I think back to the years I spent mourning the loss of that relationship, I wish I could go back and change my perspective now I can see things in a new light.

I feel AJ nodding. "Definitely. I know I'll never forget it."

Once the sun rises, we get dressed and eat breakfast, then AJ proceeds to spoil me with adventure after adventure. I can't believe he planned all of this for me. When we weren't doing the touristy thing, AJ was inside me, blowing my mind and loving on my body. The memories we've created during this trip will stay with me forever and I let a future with AJ wash over me. Trips together, exploring, growing together, and raising a family … *together*.

As I place Eric's morning pot of tea on his desk, he smiles at me. His demeanor has been more relaxed over the last couple of weeks. He tips his chin toward the seat opposite his desk. "Please sit, we need to discuss a few things."

"Do I need my tablet to take notes?"

"No, you'll be fine." I take a seat, ready to listen. It's been great to have the old Eric back, the office is back to its usual relaxed atmosphere. Eric straightens and folds his hands one on top of the other on his desk. A smile forms and his eyes glisten. "My grandson will be coming in next Monday."

My heart skips a beat. I know this is what Eric wants, what he needs, but I can't help the selfish side of me that doesn't like change. I squeeze my hands together to stop myself from fidgeting. "That's wonderful, Mr. Wainwright. I can't wait to meet him." Hopefully, my smile looks genuine and I make a mental note to prepare a special batch of cupcakes in an attempt to impress my new boss.

"Yes, it's been a long time coming. He's moving from New Jersey as we speak, and I couldn't be happier to have my grandson home." He blinks his eyes rapidly and moves his gaze over my shoulder. I barely resist turning around to see what's caught his attention.

"I bet the entire family will be happy to be reunited with him. I can't imagine my mom being too happy if one of us moved that far away from home." Another reason why I let Michael go all those years ago.

"Well, yes." He tugs his collar away from his neck and smooths down his tie. "We need to ensure all of our handover documents and the updated policy handbook are completed. Can you make them into those fancy books you do?"

I nod. "Of course. I noted a couple of things you need to take a closer look at, then I can make those adjustments and print it. Did you want copies for all staff, or only for Adam?"

"Since it's been updated, let's make enough policy handbooks for each staff member, but only Adam needs the handover documents. Book a staff meeting on Friday morning, so I can deliver the updated policy handbook and let everyone know Adam will be in first thing Monday morning. I don't want people poking their heads out of offices wondering what's going on."

"Okay. Will that be all?"

"For now. Thank you, Sarah."

"No problem. I'll work on the documents today and tomorrow and get them printed and bound, ready for Friday."

Collecting the handover document with my notes, I take it to Eric and explain my thoughts. He agrees with my suggestions and I return to my desk to make the necessary changes. I spend the rest of the day formatting the files, which requires minimal concentration on my part. Exactly the sort of work I need. My mind won't stop racing, imagining how things around here might change under the new boss. Will he be as good to the staff as Eric is? Will he still allow for flexible working hours? I know a lot of people here rely on that flexibility to work around school drop-offs and pick-ups for their kids. How will it impact the leave I was hoping to take if I ever get pregnant?

Eric seems to have a lot of faith in Adam, so I should trust his judgment, but my anxiety is growing by the minute. My stomach rolls at the thought of not seeing my long-time boss every day. I glance across at the window between my space and Eric's office. Someone else will be sitting behind that desk, and it doesn't feel right.

—sarah—

"Joe! Hold the elevator, please." I quicken my steps to make it to him as fast as possible, nausea making it difficult—damn anxiety. He smiles at me and presses the button to hold it. "Thanks, Joe. I can't believe I'm running late. Of all the days."

"You're welcome, Miss Sarah."

I hold up the Tupperware container of cupcakes. "I'll save you one."

"Thank you. I'll look forward to it!" Joe smiles as he pats his stomach.

I quickly step inside, then glance at the other occupants, my eyes landing on AJ. The surprise of seeing him makes the nerves that were overwhelming me moments ago dissipate and I smile as I move closer. He hasn't noticed me because he's frowning at something on his phone. He said he had an important meeting this morning. One that was going to be difficult but I had no idea it was in this building. I bump my shoulder into his arm to catch his attention. His eyes snap away from his screen to me and his entire face relaxes; a smile immediately forming.

"Sarah," he breathes. That single word makes my heart pound faster and my stomach flip.

"Hey." He leans down, pressing a kiss to my lips and I melt. I was naked with this guy yesterday morning, yet that simple kiss has butterflies filling my stomach. "I missed you last night. How are your parents?"

"They're slightly better today. I can't believe they were both so sick at the same time. I don't think it's ever happened before. I was up most of the night checking on them. Molly's spending the day looking after them, so I could come to work."

"You work in this building?" I guess I've never told him where I work, only that I worked in the city.

"Yeah. Is this where your meeting is today?"

"Yeah."

The elevator stops and people step out, while others step in.

"I'm running late. I think I dozed off in the early hours of this morning and slept through my alarm after not getting a lot of sleep during the night. I hate being late." I huff. "But I have cupcakes!" I raise the container for him to see.

He reaches toward the container with a cheeky grin. "Can I have one?"

I snatch it back. "Nope, they're to impress my new boss. I'll make you some when I get home."

AJ's eyebrows dip causing creases between them. "That's today?"

I nod and draw in a shaky breath. "Yeah. And I'm feeling so crappy."

He places the back of his hand against my forehead. "You don't feel warm, but you look pale. Should you even be at work today? Maybe you caught the virus your mom and dad have?"

The elevator comes to a stop and more people step in.

"I don't think so. I've been anxious about meeting my new boss, and it's causing an upset stomach. I'll be okay."

He gives me a soft smile, tucking my hair behind my ear. "Your new boss will love you. You don't need to be nervous."

The elevator stops at my floor. His meeting must be with Oliver Stone. His floors are the only ones above ours. "Anyway, this is my stop. Good luck with your meeting. I hope it's not too tough." I press up on my toes and peck his cheek.

AJ glances up at the floor number, a puzzled expression on his face. "This is my floor, too."

We both step out of the elevator and the doors close, leaving us standing near the front reception desk of *FutureTech* —the only company on this floor—and Lucy.

"Really? Are you here to check our systems? I didn't have anything about it on my calendar for today?" I'm confused. I keep track of everything that goes on because I have to keep abreast of everything for Eric. But maybe it slipped my attention because I've been so stressed about today. "Who are you meeting with?"

"My grandfather. Eric Wainwright."

No. My legs shake and the room spins. Suddenly, there's no air and I can't seem to catch my breath.

"Morning, Sarah. Are you okay?" Lucy steps from behind her desk. "You look pale."

AJ takes the container of cakes from me and grasps my bicep, leading me to the nearby chairs. "Would you mind getting Sarah a glass of water?"

"Sure." Lucy disappears down the hallway and I'm left alone with AJ.

My gut rolls and I have a sinking feeling. "Adam?" I whisper.

"Yeah."

Shit!

Only me. This shit can only happen to me.

The stranger who offered to help me have a baby.

The man I've fallen for even though I wasn't supposed to.

The guy I'm living with is going to be my new boss.

This is the crappiest of crappy situations ever. AJ pushes my head down between my legs as my breaths grow choppier.

"Are you my new boss?" I ask from my position between my legs.

"Fuck!" I hear him shuffling. "I'm hoping I won't be. I haven't agreed to take the position. I'm trying to convince my grandfather to give the company to Mom. She wants to run the company and she'd be damn good at it. But he's an old-fashioned misogynist and he doesn't believe women can be successful in high-level positions."

I sit up and twist in my chair, facing him directly. "But Eric said you lived in New Jersey. He said you only moved here last week, that you had to finish your work and it had taken longer than expected. I don't understand. You said you've always lived here." He couldn't have lived in New Jersey, because I met him back in June and have been living with him since September.

AJ takes my hand in his as Lucy returns with a glass of water for me. I take it gratefully, my hand shaking. "Thanks, Luce."

"You're welcome." Her forehead creases in confusion as her eyes dance between me and AJ. I tip my head to the side and pointedly look at her desk, hoping she gets the hint to leave us alone. Thankfully she does and steps away.

"I *have always* lived here. Look, I don't understand why my grandfather told you I lived in New Jersey. I've never lived anywhere but here. I've never lied to you; I promise. My relationship with my grandfather is"—he glances away from me, grasping the back of his neck—"complicated. It's a long story, and I'll be happy to fill you in later, just not here." He huffs out a breath and shakes his head, tension and anger emanating from him.

"Adam!" Eric's voice booms from down the hallway and I carefully slide my hand out of AJ's hold, shifting in my seat to put as much distance between us as possible. Eric's eyes catch on me as he steps closer. "Sarah, are you feeling okay? You don't look well, my dear."

"Uh, yeah, I'm okay. I just met"—I glance at AJ with a tight smile—"Adam in the elevator and felt a little dizzy. He was kind enough to help me sit so I can catch my breath." I hold up the glass of water. "I feel better now." I force myself to make eye contact with AJ … *Adam*. "Thank you for your help." I climb to my feet, hoping my shaky legs hold me. AJ stands too, his hand reaching out to support me, but I take a step away and force a smile to my lips. "I'm sorry I was late this morning, Mr. Wainwright. I'll go and set up for the day. Let me know when you're ready for me to join your meeting."

Smoothing down my skirt, I step away from the man who's been like a grandfather to me and the man I was beginning to believe I could have a future with. I don't know how I make it to my work area, but I do. I tuck my purse in the cupboard behind my desk and turn on my computer as usual, then head straight to the bathroom. In my need to escape, I push the door open too hard and it bangs loudly against the wall. Trying to catch it, so I can close it quietly, I push it shut with a quiet snick. Leaning against the vanity, I look up at the ceiling. "Why?" I roll my eyes and huff out a breath, then study myself in the mirror. Everyone's right. I do look pale. I don't feel so good and the connection I've just discovered isn't making my anxiety and nausea any better. Dipping down, I splash some cool water on my face and take measured breaths to regain my composure. I need to get to work and act like the professional I am. I've already got off on the wrong foot with my new boss!

Ugh! Boss.

Fuck my life.

I blow out a heavy breath and head to the kitchen to make a pot of tea for Eric and coffee for … Adam. God, it's going to be so hard getting used to calling him that.

As I'm making the drinks, I work through my memory for signs I must have missed that AJ is Adam. But I don't think there were any to miss. AJ and I hadn't talked about work very much and not once did he mention he was expected to take over the family business. Plus, Eric said his grandson lived in New Jersey. How would I have possibly thought AJ was Adam? None of it makes sense. AJ's been here the entire time I've known him whereas Eric said Adam only moved here last week. My head hurts trying to piece it all together.

Lucy steps into the kitchen with my container of cupcakes. "Here ya go. I thought I'd bring them down before I ate them all." She chuckles and leans her hip against the counter. Raising her eyebrows, she fans her face. "The new boss is pretty hot. Too young for me, but ideal for you."

Saliva pools in my mouth and I choke on air. I snap my head around, checking there's no one in earshot. "You can't talk about our new boss like that, Luce," I whisper-shout at her. "Plus, do you remember the updates to the handbook? No fraternization between employees."

She shrugs with a smirk. "At least we'll finally have some eye candy in the office." She chuckles as she walks toward the door to leave.

"Stop it!" I hiss and then hear her chuckle from the other side of the wall.

I blow out a breath and add some cupcakes to a plate, then place everything on a tray with shaky hands. I guess AJ will get a cupcake after all. I fortify my shaky legs and carry the drinks and food to Eric's office. The door's closed, so I place the tray on my desk and raise my knuckles to knock, only to be startled by Eric's shout.

"She's a woman! And not fit to run this company." My eyebrows almost shoot to my hairline. I had never heard Eric raise his voice, but over the past few months, he's done it a lot. I glance through the gap in the closed blinds to see a red-faced

Eric leaning over his desk in a most intimidating way. AJ is still seated, looking as calm as anything.

Since there's a lull, I knock on the door and open it, pasting on my best smile. "I brought you both a drink and some cupcakes. Do you need anything else?" I look at Eric, then glance at AJ to check if he's all right after his grandfather's outburst. He nods his head slightly and I turn my attention back to my current boss.

He smiles at me, straightening his tie and returning to a seated position. "That will be all for now. Thank you. I'll let you know when we're ready for you."

"No problem, Mr. Wainwright." I tip my head and escape, closing the door behind me. I quickly make myself a cup of decaf coffee and get to work checking emails and updating the database—it's hard to maintain my concentration, though. Now and then Eric raises his voice, but never AJ. I'm not sure what's going on, but clearly, Eric isn't happy.

I grab my phone and shoot Mel a message.

ME

Guess who my new boss is

Forget it, you'll never guess

MEL

Is he a super stud hot model that poses in Calvin Klein underwear?

Of course, Mel has her mind in the gutter and ordinarily, I would laugh at her message, but not today. I'm too wound up at the prospect that I've lost AJ, and I've totally ruined my career by sleeping with my future boss. I drop my head to my hands. How could I mess up this epically?

ME

> Nope. I wish it were some super-hot model. That would be a hell of a lot simpler than the real answer

MEL

> He can't be that bad

ME

> Yes, yes he can

MEL

> Well, don't keep me in suspenders. Who is it?

ME

> AJ *crying emoji* *crying emoji* *crying emoji* *crying emoji* *crying emoji*

My phone instantly rings, so I jump up from my desk and head toward the reception area, the farthest distance from Eric's office as I can possibly be and remain on the same floor.

"You have to be shitting me."

I blow out a heavy breath. "Nope. I wish I was. God, Mel. How is this possible?" I pull my hair back and hold it away from my face as I pace. Lucy gives me a weird look so I lower my voice. "Why? Mel. Why does this shit happen to me? Just when I thought I could have something real and meaningful with AJ, this happens. I'm going to lose him now and I could lose my damn job."

"Calm down. You met him *before* he became your boss, surely that means it won't impact your job and you don't know if you'll lose him. Is there anything in the company policy about dating colleagues?"

I glance over, noticing Lucy leaning forward. I would take the call in the stairwell, but it's a dead zone and I can't get reception in there. I move further away and soften my voice. "Not in the original employee handbook, but he included it in the updates. What am I gonna do?"

"You're going to do your damn job because you're good at it, and then you're going to speak with AJ when you get the chance and find out what the hell's going on. I thought Adam lived in New Jersey and only moved back here last week?"

"I know, right? I'm totally confused. I know AJ hasn't lied to me about where he lives, that would be impossible. But why would Eric lie about where his grandson lives? I don't understand."

CHAPTER 38

—aj—

Fuck! Fuck! Fuck!

I felt it. I felt her shut down on me. This is the worst possible scenario. The situation with Grandfather and his company is bad enough, but now I find out Sarah's his assistant and I had no damn clue. And how would I? Grandfather never refers to her by name, it's always 'my assistant' because he doesn't deem her important. I've never called his office, so I've never spoken to his 'assistant.' Now I'm wishing I had because I wouldn't have been blindsided. She let her last boyfriend go because she loved her job … and her family … so much that she couldn't bear to leave.

What if she chooses her job over me?

Sarah steps into the room with a fake smile plastered on her face. I know it's fake because her lips are too tight. Normally, she smiles so big her lips separate and she shows her perfectly straight teeth. Her hand shakes as she places a tray of cupcakes and drinks on Grandfather's desk.

"I brought you both a drink and some cupcakes. Do you need anything else?" She looks at Eric, then glances at me. I can see the question in her eyes. She had to hear Grandfather's outburst. I nod my head discreetly to let her know I'm okay, and she returns her attention to my grandfather.

He softens his posture and smiles at her, straightening his tie and returning to his seat. "That will be all for now. Thank you. I'll let you know if we need you." He's different with her. Softer, kinder.

"No problem, Mr. Wainwright." She tips her head and escapes without giving me a second glance, closing the door behind her.

Grandfather pushes the plate of cupcakes toward me. "Sarah makes these every Friday. She made these, especially for you." He nods to the plate and I blow out a breath, then take a cupcake. I love her cupcakes, so I'm not about to say no. I'll take anything to make this situation more bearable.

"Thanks."

Grandfather takes a sip of his tea, then places the cup on its saucer. "Women don't belong in CEO roles, Adam. As much as you want to be progressive, it's not appropriate. They don't have the same level of success as men do."

"Only because they're not given the opportunity because of men like—"

"Watch your mouth, boy." Spittle flies across the desk and I'm glad it's as wide as it is or I'd be wiping it from my face.

I sit forward on the edge of my chair. "What about Diane Hendricks? Huh." I raise my brows. "She took over sole ownership of the company she had with her husband and then went on to buy out her two biggest rivals. She made history."

His face turns red. "One. One successful woman doesn't mean that all women are cut out for this role, Adam."

I pull the thumb drive from my pocket and hold it up. "I have an entire presentation I can show you, with all the facts and figures you could possibly need to be convinced to give the company to Mom."

He scoffs, rolling his eyes. "This is *my* damn company, and it's my decision whom I hand it over to. A woman will run this company over my dead body." His face is red and splotchy, his breaths becoming harsh.

I feel as though I'm going in circles and getting absolutely nowhere. This is the same conversation we've had since he got it into his head that I was the only suitable candidate to take over the company, our family legacy, so he could retire. He's always treated me like a child, so I'm not sure why he's so adamant I run things. Oh, that's right, I'm the only direct relative with a penis instead of a vagina.

He presses a button on his phone. "Please join me in my office." He lifts his finger, cutting off the call without waiting for a response. I sit back further into my seat, savoring the final bite of my cupcake while I wait for Sarah to join us.

The door opens and in strides a man I've never met. I peer behind him, hoping to spot Sarah, but he closes the door quickly and moves to take the seat next to mine. "Tony. This is my grandson, Adam. Adam. Tony, my Vice President."

I hold my hand out to greet the man. "Nice to meet you, Tony." He tips his head to me, with no move to take my proffered hand, so I drop it back onto my lap. There's a level of frostiness radiating from him that has my hackles rising.

"Adam here is still trying to convince me to give the company to his mother instead of him," Grandfather scoffs at Tony as though I'm no longer in the room, making me feel small. Anger blooms inside me, and I know I'm going to struggle to keep it contained.

Tony studies me with clear disdain. "As I've said to you before, Eric. I'll be happy to step in and run the company with you still at the helm. There's no place for a woman in the leadership role here."

Jesus! I glance around the office. Standing, I stride to the windows and peer down at the cars on the street. Finally, I check the date on my phone.

"What the hell are you doing, boy?"

"Just checking that I'm living in the twenty-first century and not the damn nineteen-fifties," I snap. "No wonder you won't budge. Your Vice President thinks exactly the way you do." I turn to Tony. "I was hoping you would help me drag him into the current century, but you're as entrenched in the old ways as he is." I refuse to allow this idiot to have any more control in this company. I turn back to Grandfather. "I'll take the damn position *and* the damn company." I glance between the two men, frustration and anger filling my body. I'm surprised the top of my head hasn't blown off. "But let me make this clear." I move back in front of Grandfather's desk and poke my finger angrily at the surface. "You will not interfere with how I run it. Once it's in my hands, I'll fill the leadership roles with whomever I see fit, whether that person is a man or a woman." I rarely lose my cool, but as I stand here with these two dinosaurs, I can no longer contain my anger.

I spin on my heel, and storm out of the office, slamming the door behind me. Sarah's head snaps up from her computer and frown lines form between her brows as she studies me closely. "Are you okay? That all sounded very intense in there."

I step closer to her desk. "I don't know how you've managed to work here as long as you have."

She leans forward, glancing behind her at Grandfather's door. "What do you mean?"

"I mean, my grandfather is a damn misogynist still living in the nineteen-fifties." I blow out a breath.

She chuckles and waves her hand in the air like she's dismissing my comment. "He's not that bad. A little old-fashioned maybe."

"You know I never knew the name of his assistant because he always referred to you as his 'assistant.'" Her eyes widen. "Yeah." I nod and hold out my hand to Sarah. She studies it but makes no move to take it. "We need to talk."

She glances back at the door as boisterous laughter comes from Grandfather's office. "Not now, I'm working," she hisses.

"When you get home, then."

Her shoulders jump up to her ears. "About that." She glances at the door again, then leans closer, dropping the volume of her voice. "I'll need to pick up my things."

"No!" I shout, then lower my voice. "I know what you're gonna do and I won't let you."

"This is my job, AJ."

The muscle in my chest pounds heavily and I search for something to say. "And I'm your boyfriend."

She shakes her head. "You can't be. You're gonna be my boss," she whispers, her shaky hand coming up to push a lock of hair roughly behind her ear.

I lean over her desk, closer, locking my eyes with Sarah's, imploring her to listen to me. "I don't give a fuck if I'm going to be your boss. I'm not letting you go. Not now. Not ever. Don't throw away what we have for this." I drill my finger into her desk.

She presses forward and my eyes drop to her cleavage as her top gapes open. "It's okay for you to expect me to give up this job, you have your own company and then you'll have this one," she hisses. "How will I support myself? This is one of the best-paying assistant jobs around."

"I can support you, Sarah. You and our baby when we have one. You won't need to work."

She huffs out a sarcastic chuckle. "So, you're like your grandfather then. You think women should be at home with the children, not in the workplace."

What the fuck?

I draw my head back as though she slapped me. "No. Of course not. How can you say that? All I'm saying is you don't need *this* job. You've got me." I jab my thumb into my chest. "But maybe you don't want me. This only ever started with you wanting a donor. Is that all I'm good for, Sarah?" Her eyes widen and her mouth drops open. I snap my mouth closed and hold my hands up in surrender. "I'm sorry. I shouldn't have said any of that." My anger at the situation and fear of losing Sarah has crumbled my usual control.

Grandfather's door opens, catching Sarah and me staring at each other in disbelief that we've just fought. If I was worried I'd lose her before, then I'm pretty sure I just hammered the nail in our coffin. "I thought you'd left." He steps to the side of the door, waving his arm inside. "Come back inside, we'll hammer out some of the details."

My eyes bounce between Sarah and Grandfather, and I grasp the back of my neck and squeeze it tight. "No. I can't. I have a project I need to get done today." Without another word, I spin on my heel.

"Are you okay, Sarah? You don't look so well," I hear Grandfather say. Every molecule in my body is telling me to stop. To go back. To make things right. To check she's okay. But I can't. I've said too much and crossed too many lines today. I need to regroup.

I climb into my Jeep and slam the door, then thump the steering wheel. I start the car and drive. I need to think and I need to calm the fuck down. I never lose my cool like that, but the fear of losing Sarah was overriding my common sense and I couldn't seem to shut my damn mouth. It felt as though a knife stabbed me in the chest when Sarah chose her job over me. I knew it was coming the second I realized she worked for my grandfather, but I had hoped that she loved … no, cared for me enough that she would choose our future together over her position in the company. A company that doesn't even respect or value her.

Glancing at the back seat, I check if I have my climbing bag in the car and I do. I turn right instead of left and head toward the gym. I can't sit in an office with this pent-up frustration inside of me. I need to burn some of it off.

Grant does a double-take when he spots me walking through the door. "You're not usually here at this time of day."

"Need to expend some energy. Is it okay if I climb?"

"Go for it. You know you're always welcome here. I can come and belay for you in a minute, once I finish updating my books."

"Thanks, Grant. Appreciate it, man." I head to the locker room to change and start with some basic bouldering while I wait for Grant.

Taking a few deep breaths, I focus my attention, pushing this morning to the far recesses of my mind. It won't do me any good to be unfocused while I'm climbing. Grant's changed the holds since I was here last, something he does regularly to keep the climbs fresh, making it easier to narrow my focus from one hold to the next.

"Looking strong there, AJ."

"Thanks." I make my way to the other end of the wall easily and climb down to the mat. Grant's waiting ready to give me a high-five. Chalkdust flies in the air and we make our way over to the rope section.

I spend most of the day climbing, using the ropes when Grant's available, and bouldering when he's not. I direct all of my focus toward climbing the route better than the previous time, using faster more efficient moves. My muscles burn and cramp and my stomach feels as though it's going to revolt. I've experienced this before when I've pushed myself too hard—I need to stop.

I climb down carefully and drop onto the mat, exhaustion

taking over my body. Sucking air into my lungs, I shake out my arms and legs. Dipping down to my bag, I grab my water bottle, coming up empty. Damn it. I didn't have one with me. I spot the water fountain and make my way over there slowly. Pressing the button, I gulp the cool water like my life depends on it and this is the last of the available water on the planet. Lowering to a nearby bench, I drop my head into my hands. I could climb all the way to the top of Mount Everest, but it won't help me keep Sarah. I should be devising a plan to make her see reason, rather than escaping up a damn wall.

Collecting my bag, I check my phone. Missed calls and messages from Hayley and Dylan fill the screen. Nothing from Sarah. I blow out a breath, my heart feeling heavy in my chest. I wave at Grant on my way out and make the drive home.

The instant I open the door, I know something's not right. "Where the hell have you been?" Dylan barks at me.

"I need to have a shower." I walk past him and head straight for the stairs up to my bedroom.

"Sarah was here." He pauses. "She packed her stuff and left in tears."

My feet freeze on the step and that heavy feeling in my chest implodes and shatters. My nose tingles and eyes prickle and I keep my back to my long-time friend. Nodding my head a couple of times, I take the stairs slowly, leaving shattered pieces of my heart behind, and close myself in our bedroom, leaning my back against the door. I squeeze my eyes tight because I can't bear to see the room without her things in it, but it's futile because her springtime scent still fills the space. I kick the heel of my foot against the door and run my hands through my hair. "Fuck!" I was hoping she would at least talk this through and try to work out a solution. I'm not a violent man, but I have an overwhelming desire to punch something.

I had no idea Saturday night would be the last night I got to spend with the woman of my dreams. If I'd known I would have never let her leave this room and then we wouldn't be in the mess we're in. I head for the shower, noting the shelf is void of Sarah's stuff, except for the pink razor she uses to shave her legs.

Dylan's waiting outside my bedroom door with two beers when I open it. He nods his head toward my deck and makes his way outside. I follow behind because I need someone to talk to right now and it may as well be him.

"Did Sarah say anything to you before she left?"

He shakes his head, his lips pressed tight.

I blow out a breath, then start at the beginning, telling him about seeing Sarah in the elevator, finding out she's Grandfather's assistant, to our argument at her desk.

"Fuck, man," he whispers. "What are you gonna do?"

I shrug. "I was hoping we could talk it through and work out a way forward, but it makes it damn hard if she's running in the opposite direction." I take a drink of my beer. "She chose her job … and her family and friends … over her boyfriend four years ago, and they had been together since high school."

"Shit, man. I don't like your chances."

Yeah, thanks for the vote of confidence. "Me neither."

CHAPTER 39

—sarah—

"THANKS FOR LETTING ME STAY, MEL. I DIDN'T HAVE anywhere else to go," I sob as I wipe the tears that won't stop away from my cheeks. I could have gone to my sister's but he knows where she lives and I wouldn't put it past him to turn up there. I needed somewhere he didn't know and couldn't find.

"You know you're always welcome here, Sare." She wraps her arm around me and tugs me inside her apartment which is even smaller than mine. "Even though I only have a pull-out sofa." She steps back into the hall and grabs my suitcase, bringing it inside and putting it next to the other one. I drop my overnight bag from my shoulder and it thumps as it lands heavily on the carpeted floor.

Mel guides me to the couch and sits me down, then heads for her tiny kitchen. I grab a tissue from the coffee table while she fusses for a few minutes, before returning with two steaming cups of hot chocolate. Ordinarily, this would be wine or something stronger, but she knows I've been avoiding alcohol since I started trying to get pregnant. Though, maybe I could have a drink. It's not like I'm pregnant or have any prospect of getting pregnant in the near future. She drops to the cushion beside me, curling one foot beneath her butt, and resting her drink on her raised knee. "So … AJ is Adam."

With gut-wrenching sadness, I nod. "I can't believe it. Of all the people."

"It was certainly unexpected. I can't imagine the shock you're feeling. What are you gonna do now?"

"I can't afford to lose my job, Mel." I explain how AJ … *Adam* … expected me to give up my job and said he would take care of me and our baby. Not that there's a baby.

"I don't see the problem with that, to be honest. It'll give you time with the baby when it's born and during the early formative years."

I nod because deep down I love the idea of having that time with my baby in the early years. It's something I can't afford to do if I'm on my own. "I'm not even pregnant." More tears stream down my cheeks at the reminder that I got my period again this month, though it was lighter than usual. I've been stressed about meeting my new boss and my body's trying to cope with my sky-high anxiety. It's probably why I'm having trouble getting pregnant—too much stress.

Mel places her cup on the coffee table and moves in closer to embrace me, letting me sob into her shoulder. My tears are filled with pain for the loss of AJ and my dream of a baby. A baby with him. Creating a *real* family with the man of my dreams.

"I don't understand why it has to be an either-or situation. Why can't you stay with AJ *and* keep your job?" She rubs her hand up and down my arm in a soothing motion.

"How would that look?"

Mel's face scrunches up. "Who the fuck cares how it would look, Sare? You were with him *before* either of you knew … he didn't know you worked there, right?"

I shake my head. "No. Apparently, Eric always referred to me as his assistant, never by name."

"What?"

"AJ said he's a misogynist and doesn't deem me worthy of using my name. Which was completely shocking to me because I've never found Eric to be like that. He's a great boss. Fair and flexible with the staff. Admittedly, there are only two women in the company and both hold secretarial-type positions."

"Sounds like he might be to me."

"But then AJ wanted me to give up my job to raise our baby, doesn't that make him the same?"

Mel shrugs. "Depends what his reasons are and why he said it. To me, it sounded like he was saying it to give you options. He probably knows you well enough and realized you'd break things off with him to keep your job. But think about this, Sare. If you break things off with AJ to keep your job and he becomes your boss, you'll have to work with him every single day. Will you be able to do that? Knowing what the two of you share and what you've given up, could you be happy seeing him every day and not be able to touch him?" She chews on her bottom lip. "How will you feel if he starts dating someone else?"

I drag my hair around to one side and fiddle with it, feeling sick to my stomach at the thought of AJ with someone else, while I think about Mel's questions. She's right, dammit. This is why I love her. She knows me so well that she knows exactly how and why I respond to things the way I do. "It'll kill me," I finally whisper.

"Then why can't you have the man *and* the job?" She squeezes my arm. "He obviously adores you, Sare. Why would you give that up? Jobs come and go, but love … true, deep, lasting love, that's not so easy to find."

Tears burst forth again, pouring over my lashes and down my cheeks. "Oh my God, I've made a terrible mistake, Mel." I press my face into my hands. God, I'm stupid. As if a job is worth more than AJ. "It was a knee-jerk reaction to hold onto my job. I'm so used to having to take care of myself and plan for my future."

I'm not sure how long we sit in silence on Mel's couch before her stomach growls loudly, breaking through my haze. I look at my best friend: sitting beside me, comforting me, giving up her sleep for me. I have to be the luckiest girl in the world to have Mel as my best friend. I pat her leg and climb to my feet, shaking out the pins and needles in my left foot so I can put it on the floor without tipping over. "How about I make us something to eat and you can shower and get ready for work?"

She shows me her gorgeous straight teeth and nods. "Sure, that'd be great."

She heads off to her bedroom, and I step into her kitchen, ready to look after my best friend. Opening her fridge leaves me scratching my head. It's pretty bare, but I think I can make us both an omelet. By the time she comes out, dressed in her cute pink scrubs with baby elephants on them, I have two omelets plated and ready to eat. I quickly pour Mel a coffee and we sit at her two-seater dining table pushed against the window to eat.

Mel moans around a forkful of food. "Delicious, Sare. I always love your cooking."

I chuckle. "Only because you don't cook. Your fridge looks like it belongs in a bachelor pad."

She shrugs. "I'm not here all that much. The food spoils if I have too much stuff." She takes another bite and then swallows, locking her gaze on me. "What are you going to do?"

"I'm going to sleep on it tonight because I need to plan how I'm going to apologize properly to AJ. I need to be clear about what I'm going to say. I'll talk with him after work tomorrow. Hopefully, he's the forgiving type and won't hate me too much for my behavior today. I only wish I respond better when I'm blindsided like I was. I'm not proud of my actions,

Mel. I'm ashamed of myself. He's been nothing but supportive and caring toward me."

"We all make mistakes, Sare. You're not the first and you definitely won't be the last. It's how you take responsibility for it that matters."

"Thanks, Mel." I lean across and hug my girl, then shoo her out the door for her shift. "I'm sorry you didn't get your sleep today."

"That's okay. I'm glad I could be there for you. I probably won't see you tomorrow. So, good luck."

"Thanks." We hug goodbye. She heads to work and I clean up from our meal.

After minimal sleep last night because I was missing AJ so much, work was awful today. It felt like it was never going to end, and all I wanted to do was get to AJ. I'm so churned up about seeing him, that I couldn't bear to eat anything for fear it would make a reappearance. This whole situation has me questioning everything. AJ hasn't messaged me and I'm second-guessing my plan to go over to his house to apologize. Maybe he's thankful he's finally free of me. After all, I was just a stranger he offered to help.

I take a deep breath and reach up a shaky hand to press AJ's doorbell. The sound is empty, reminding me of how I feel knowing I've hurt AJ. I spin on my heel to peer down the street while I wait for an answer. I can't hear anyone making their way to the door, so I ring again and wait.

No answer.

I have a key I could use, but it feels all kinds of wrong to walk inside his home after the way we left things and I packed up and moved out. I'm kicking myself for my overreaction yesterday. If I'd only taken a moment to think things through properly. He must think I value my job more than I value him and the relationship we were building.

When there's still no answer, I wander around to the side entrance, the one he uses for the business. I knock on the door and I don't have to wait long before I hear footsteps moving close. It swings inward, revealing Dylan. He tips his chin at me and steps back inside, leaving the door open, I assume so I can follow him.

"Hi." My voice comes out shaky.

"Hey. AJ's not here." Dylan's frosty greeting adds to my anxiety about speaking with AJ. He leans against a desk, crossing his arms over his chest and his feet at his ankles. His stance is one of careless relaxation, but there's an undertone of annoyance.

"Oh. Any idea when he'll be back?"

He shrugs. "Nope. He said he needed some space, so he's gone camping to climb."

Shit! That's not good. I was hoping to sort this out today. "Do you know where he went?"

"Nope. And I've tried to call him, but he's out of range."

Panic quickly fills my body. "Is that safe? What if he has an accident or something? How will he get help?"

"He knows what he's doing, and it's really none of your concern anymore, is it?"

I prickle at his tone. "What do you mean? I still care about him. I don't want him to get hurt."

He chuckles, but it's completely fake. "You already hurt him, Sarah. That's why he took off."

My eyes prickle and a boulder quickly forms in my throat knowing I've hurt AJ. I try to swallow, but it's stuck. I glance around the room, trying to fight off what's happening inside my body, but I can't catch my breath. I bring my palm up to my throat and pat the base, trying to dislodge whatever's trapped in there, but nothing happens. I can't breathe and my heart races. Panic overwhelms me and the more I try to suck in air, the less air I'm getting. Everything's starting to spin when strong hands grasp my biceps.

"Sarah!" I'm shaken, but nothing helps, I can't get any oxygen into my lungs. My legs tremble and I'm sure Dylan's grip on my arms is the only thing keeping me standing. "Sarah!" he shouts, shaking me more vigorously. "Fuck!"

I feel him push me into a chair and fold me almost in half so my head is down between my legs. This keeps happening to me and I'm sick of it. I need to learn to manage my emotions better.

"Sarah, I want you to take deep breaths with me. Okay? Breathe in, one, two, three. Hold it. Breathe out, one, two, three." I focus on his deep, calming voice and follow his instructions. He repeats the process several times, kindly stroking his hand soothingly up and down my spine.

When I feel I'm finally back in control, I sit up and wipe my face with shaky hands. Finally, my heart feels like it's slowing to normal speed and my lungs don't feel as though they're on fire. "Thank you," I murmur. I'm so damn embarrassed. I push my sweaty hair away from my face and give Dylan a timid but grateful smile. "Sorry about that."

He leaves the office and comes back with a glass of water. Handing it to me, he studies me closely, creases between his blond eyebrows. "Does that happen often?"

"Uh, when I'm super anxious about something it can sometimes happen." I shrug and take a sip of the cool water. It seems to be happening a lot lately.

"Are you gonna be all right?"

"Yeah. But could I ask you a favor? I know I have no right, but if you hear from AJ, can you please let me know. I need to know he's okay. I'm sorry I hurt him, and I came here to apologize and ask his forgiveness. I was hoping we could put it behind us."

He nods, studying me like I'm some sort of alien being. "Sure. Give me your number and if I hear from him, I'll let you know."

I smile gratefully. "Thank you." I give him my number and stand to leave.

"You're not gonna stay here?"

I tuck my still-damp hair behind my ear. "No. I don't think it's right for me to stay until I know he's forgiven me." Dylan nods. "Thanks for taking care of me."

"No problem. Take care, bye."

CHAPTER 40

-aj-

Without Sarah beside me, sleep was impossible to come by last night, so I decided to pack and come to one of my favorite climbing spots for a few days. It's not too far from the city, but far enough away that I can leave everything behind. Dylan understood my need to take a few days when I told him I'd be back by Friday. I just needed enough time to clear my head and work out if there's any way I can move forward with Sarah. She made it pretty clear her job is more important than me or a relationship with me. Not gonna lie, that fucking stung. I thought we were building something real, but clearly, I was wrong.

I look up at the rock face, studying it and planning my route. There's a buttress to the right, but it's a little off the path that looks safest. The climb isn't that high, only about thirty feet, but I'll be free climbing it on my own, so I need to ensure I take the safest path possible. Attaching my chalk bag, I rub the ball of chalk between my hands ensuring I have decent coverage. Testing the rock, I make my first hold and follow with my feet, testing the stability. I'm only a foot off the ground, but it feels great to have the sandstone beneath my fingers and the sun on my back. I work my way up carefully, following the path I mapped out visually before I started.

When I'm about fifteen feet from the ground, a bird swoops low, landing on a ledge just above me. It peeks over the edge like it's watching what I'm doing. I smile at it, contemplating how brave it must be to come so close to a human. Returning my focus to the rock face, I grumble when I notice the distance to my next suitable hold. It didn't look that far from the ground but I'll need to stretch wide and push hard with my legs if I have any chance of reaching it. I take a deep breath and push up with my legs and stretch out with my arm, but miss and at the same time, the rock beneath my other hold gives way.

"Oh shit!"

My heart falters as I begin to free fall. My head connects with something hard and pain shoots through my skull.

Everything goes black.

Pain radiates through my body and I try to open my eyes. The heaviness of my body is foreign to me like my limbs are weighed down by heavy boulders. A woman's voice sounds far in the distance and I'm cold all the way to my bones. Shivering hurts. *Everything fucking hurts.* I groan. Well, I think I do.

"Sir. Sir." Hands squeeze my shoulders. "My name's Violet. Help is on the way. We've got you. You're going to be okay." I think I nod if the throbbing in my head is anything to go by. I've never felt agony like this before. It's too much so I stop moving, hoping this is a bad dream.

Blackness infiltrates from the outer edges of my mind, swamping me, taking me under again.

Jostling and pain. I think I'm moving. Levitating over the ground.

Voices fade in and out.

Pain. So much pain.

The throbbing in my head pounds like a jackhammer and my need to vomit is strong. Bile moves up from my stomach, burning through my body.

Tight. Everything's so tight. I can't move. I'm trapped. The contents of my stomach explode out of my mouth.

I'm swimming in blackness.

Loud noise. Jostling. Voices. Throbbing. Cold air. Agony. Darkness.

CHAPTER 41
—sarah—

It's mid-afternoon and my phone rings with an unknown number. I'm always reluctant to answer calls I don't recognize but I'm hoping this is Dylan with an update on AJ. I need to see him and tell him how sorry I am. I need his forgiveness. The whole thing's been eating away at me. I need to tell him I'm prepared to find a job somewhere else, so we can be together. I've already applied for a couple of positions this morning on the other side of town. It's just a matter of time before the applications close and I'll know if I have an interview.

With trembling fingers, I press the green button and hold the phone to my ear. "Hello, this is—"

"Sarah." The male voice is panicked, sending my pulse skyrocketing. "It's Dylan." Blood rushes to my ears because I know from his tone that something terrible has happened.

"Wh-where is he?" I stammer.

"Mercy Vale."

"Oh my God. This is all my fault. I'm on my way." My legs shake as I stand, my breaths coming fast, and grab my purse, heading straight for the elevator.

"Sarah!" Dylan almost shouts down the line. I forgot I still had him on the phone. "Don't drive. I don't want you having an attack like you did yesterday while you're driving. Fuck, I should have come and picked you up. Stay on the line with me. I've already called AJ's family."

"O-okay." I get to the reception desk. "Lucy." She snaps her eyes to me. The tone of my voice has her eyes widening in alarm. "C-can you please call me an Uber? I n-need to get to Mercy Vale Hospital. I'll wait downstairs." I can't believe my shaky legs are holding me up and my heart is still inside my chest.

"Is everything okay?" Her eyebrows are scrunched low over her worried eyes.

"I do-don't know." Shit, I should probably tell Eric.

I take my first step toward Eric's office when he comes barreling toward me. "I need to go. My grandson's been in an accident." He tosses at me as he passes.

I pick up my pace and follow him. "Can I come with you?"

"What's going on, Sarah?" Dylan's voice calls out and I remember I still have him on the phone.

"AJ's grandfather is on his way to the hospital and I'm asking if I can go wi—"

"Who are you speaking with, Sarah?" Eric interrupts.

"Dylan, AJ's best friend." Creases form between his brows momentarily but waves me forward to follow him. As I pass Lucy, I tell her to cancel the Uber and follow Eric into the elevator. His driver is waiting out front and we climb straight in. "Dylan. I'm in the car with AJ's grandfather. We're on our way. Where can we find you?"

"Emergency. Come straight to the Emergency Room. We're all here."

"Okay." Ending the call, I turn toward Eric. "We need to go to the Emergency Room." We make our way toward the hospital in silence, both of us lost in our thoughts. My leg bounces involuntarily and the nausea I haven't been able to shake since Monday morning threatens to escape. Squeezing my hands together in my lap, I try to keep my thoughts positive and in the moment, so I don't have another panic attack—it won't do me any good to fall apart. I monitor my breathing carefully, making sure I take measured breaths in and out. I need to keep it together.

For AJ.

God, I hope he's going to be okay. I can't lose him.

Glancing at Eric, I find him gazing out of the window, but I doubt he's seeing the traffic. He looks vacant. "He'll be okay," I tell Eric, but the affirmation is more for myself than for him.

Eric huffs. "Why was Dylan calling you?"

I squeeze my hands together, twisting my fingers. "Uhm …"

Eric turns his head toward me, his eyes searing into the side of my face. "Sarah?"

"Uhm … I …" I swallow the sudden build-up of saliva that's pooled in my mouth. "We … uh …" Damn it, just spit it out, Sarah. "AJ and I were living together."

"What?" He spins in his seat, facing me properly and I drop my gaze to my lap, so I don't have to meet his narrowed eyes and downturned mouth. "Explain."

We're probably another fifteen minutes away from the hospital at this point. I start at the beginning when I met AJ at *Club Rumors* at the beginning of June. I explain how he offered to be my donor and how our relationship changed and grew into more. I mean, I leave out the intimate details because he doesn't need to know all that. The expression on his face filters through various emotions, the last one being guilt. He must know that I know he lied about his grandson.

"If you want me to resign from my position, I'm happy to do that." I rush to add.

He swipes his hand through the air. "There's no need to make rash decisions."

Finally, we pull into the hospital parking lot and I jump out of the car and head straight to the emergency doors, barreling through like my life depends on it. I head straight to administration. "Hello. I'm here for—"

"Sarah!"

I spin on the spot at the sound of my name to find Hayley hurrying toward me. I race to her, embracing her tightly. "Do you know anything?"

She shakes her head, tears gliding down her cheeks, her nose red. "Nothing yet." She pulls away and takes my hand, leading me toward Lisa, Dylan, and an older couple I'm guessing are AJ's parents. They look exactly the same as they do in the photograph on Eric's desk, only older. "Sarah, this is our mom and dad, Elaine and Adam. Mom. Dad. This is Sarah. AJ's girlfriend." Hayley mustn't know about our argument.

Their eyes widen, obviously unaware that AJ had a girl-friend. Not that I'm certain if we're still a couple or not. AJ's dad is the first to reach his hand forward. "Nice to meet you, Sarah."

His mom steps forward with a shaky smile. She's obviously been crying if her red-rimmed eyes are any indication. "It's lovely to meet you, Sarah. I only wish it were under better circumstances."

I swallow the lump in my throat carefully—so I don't choke—and take her hand in my shaky one. This is not how I imagined I'd meet AJ's parents. Thank goodness I've already met Hayley, Lisa, and Dylan. "Nice to meet you both."

Dylan comes over and embraces me, then steps back, holding my shoulders. I read the unspoken question in his eyes and give him a shaky smile. "I'm okay. Holding it together the best I can."

"Father." Elaine walks with quick steps toward Eric.

"How is he? Any news?"

She shakes her head. "Nothing."

"Well, that's not good enough." He stomps over to the registrar, demanding answers. The woman behind the desk remains calm, obviously used to dealing with anxious family members. He steps away from the counter, shaking his head, his face red.

"Mr. Wainwright, why don't you come and sit with your family? We may have to wait for a while. I'll go and get you a cup of tea from the cafeteria." Look at me being all cool, calm, and collected. If I stay busy, I have a better chance of holding myself together. He smiles softly at me, nodding as he takes a seat next to his daughter, who is looking at me as if she's trying to solve a puzzle.

Hayley flicks her eyes between me and her grandfather. "Do you know each other?"

I glance at Eric and before I can open my mouth to answer, he does. "Sarah's my assistant."

Everyone's eyes widen; everyone except Dylan. I'm assuming AJ told him who I was before he went climbing. Hayley's mouth drops open and she comes to stand next to me, leaning in close. "Oh my God, how have you managed to work with him? He's intolerable," she whispers. She links her arm through mine and then turns to her family. "I'll go with Sarah to get drinks for everyone. I think we're gonna be here a while."

We head off in search of the cafeteria, leaving everyone behind, and weaving down hallways until we find it. All the while my heart hammers wildly in my chest and I'm concentrating hard to control my shakes. I need to know AJ is going to be okay. I need to apologize, beg for his forgiveness, and then I need to tell him I love him. I was holding back before. Too scared we were moving too fast and worried things wouldn't work out. But I might not get the chance and that thought devastates me. I don't want to lose the best thing that's happened to me in a long while—if ever. I can't believe I thought it would be better to hold onto my job instead of him. I must be the world's biggest idiot.

While we're waiting for our order to be filled, Hayley turns to me. "Did you know Grandfather and AJ were related? AJ never mentioned anything and I had no idea you were Grandfather's assistant. He's never even mentioned your name." AJ said something similar and it doesn't sting any less, considering I've worked for Eric for more than ten years and I thought we were close.

I shake my head. "No. Neither of us had any idea and Mr. Wainwright only just found out on the way here that AJ and I are in a relationship." Or should that be past tense? I shake my head. "We didn't have time to unpack the situation properly."

"This is crazy. Did you know Grandfather wants AJ to take over *FutureTech*?"

I nod, feeling like a bobble doll. "I've known for a while that Mr. Wainwright wanted his grandson, Adam, to take over, but I never put two and two together because I've always called him AJ. I didn't know AJ's name was Adam." I raise my eyebrows at Hayley.

"Yeah, it reduces the confusion with Dad and AJ having the same name." She shrugs.

"Also, Mr. Wainwright told me that Adam moved here last week after living in New Jersey since college."

"What?"

I nod. "Yep. There was no way I'd ever connect the two being the same person or that I was dating him."

"Yeah, I can see how you wouldn't make the connection. I wonder why Grandfather lied about AJ living in New Jersey? Maybe he was trying to save face because AJ kept holding off on taking the position. He doesn't want it."

"Maybe. I don't know." We collect our order and make our way back to the waiting room. Hayley and I distribute the drinks and sit. I lock my gaze on the doors which I assume a doctor or nurse will come through to tell us any news. We each sit in silence, the hard plastic of the chairs uncomfortable even for my padded butt. One would think the damn chairs would be more comfortable since people have to sit in them for hours on end. People come and go as the light outside the windows wanes.

"What the hell is taking so long?" Eric huffs as he climbs to his feet to pace.

His wife, who arrived not long after we were all settled with warm drinks, stands. "Eric. Calm down and have some patience. Come and sit back down." She coaxes him back to his seat and I smile at how sweet they are together.

A woman in scrubs steps through the doors and I straighten. Waiting. "The Jackson family." *Finally.*

We all jump to our feet, quickly making our way over to the woman. "We're Adam's parents."

She directs her attention to Elaine and Adam. "Mr. and Mrs. Jackson." She smiles. "Your son had a nasty fall, and from what we were told, rock debris also landed on him. He's currently in recovery. He hasn't woken since he arrived and from reports, he was in and out of consciousness during his rescue this morning."

Why is it taking her so long to tell us if he's all right? "Is he going to be okay?" Shit, it's not my place to ask, so I slam my lips closed.

She smiles at me. "He's going to be okay."

We breathe a collective sigh of instant relief and Dylan's arm comes around my shoulders, squeezing me to him. I glance up and give him a relieved smile.

"He's not out of the woods yet, though. As I said, he hasn't regained consciousness since arriving here. We've done a scan of his head, which shows swelling indicative of a concussion." Elaine gasps and my heart lurches. "He has a contusion and fifteen stitches where he hit his head. He was possibly unconscious before he hit the ground. He has an open fracture of the lower leg, both the tibia and fibula were broken, and we've realigned them with screws and plates which will remain permanently in place. He will need a cast for several weeks, followed by physical therapy. As one would expect, he also has lacerations, bruising, and swelling."

"Can we see him?" Elaine asks.

"Soon. A volunteer will come through to collect you once he's settled in his room."

"Thank you. And thank you for taking care of our boy." Adam reaches forward to shake the doctor's hand.

"You're welcome. We have another scan scheduled for the morning to keep an eye on the swelling and concussion." She spins on her heel and disappears back the way she came.

Elaine and Adam hug as do Lisa and Hayley and Eric and Anne. The relief is palpable among our little group. I turn into Dylan, holding onto him like a lifeline. "Thank you for calling me. I know AJ and I hadn't left things on great terms, so I appreciate you including me."

He scans my face. "He would want you here." I nod, giving him a shaky smile. "And, Sarah. This wasn't your fault. None of it. I shouldn't have said you're the reason he took off. That was part of it, but it was also because of his grandfather." My eyes sting and I blink to hold back my tears. I've kept it together this long, I can keep it together a little longer. Dylan tightens his hold, squeezing me, then lets me go, taking my hand to keep me steady.

"Thank God he's going to be okay, Adam." Elaine sobs and Adam rubs her back soothingly. I can see why AJ's family calls him AJ instead of Adam. Things could easily get confusing.

"Of course, he's going to be okay. That boy is as stubborn as they come." Eric states.

Elaine pulls away from her husband giving Eric a pointed look. "He gets that from you, Father."

Anne chuckles while Eric sputters his denial. We all move back to our seats, slightly more relaxed than we were before, knowing he's going to be okay. Lisa says her goodbyes to everyone so she can collect Colton from their neighbor, who kindly offered to watch their little one at short notice. They've been messaging back and forth, checking on him, but it's late and way past his bedtime.

This afternoon has felt as though it's been the longest of my life. Every minute has dragged beyond belief. My feet are aching and so is my back and as my anxiety settles marginally, the come down from the burst of adrenaline has left me exhausted. Finally, a volunteer steps through the doors. "The family of Adam Jackson?"

We all stand. "We're his family," Adam informs the woman.

She smiles at us. "Please follow me." She heads back through the doors with the seven of us hot on her heels. The hospital smell of disinfectant and sterile rooms hits me as we stride through the halls, into an elevator, and down a few more hallways. She stops outside of a room and waves her hand out. "He's in here but he's not awake from his surgery yet. You're welcome to have short visits, only two at a time, though. There's a family lounge at the end of the hall where you can wait."

My heart rate picks up at the news he's still not awake. AJ's parents go in first while the rest of us make our way to the end of the ward. It seems to take forever for them to come out so AJ's grandparents can see him. I stand to pace, unable to keep still while I less than patiently wait for my turn. When they finally return, Hayley turns to me and Dylan.

"Do you two want to go in next?"

I glance at Dylan. "If you don't mind, I plan on staying. So you and Dylan can go in next."

Hayley nods and I notice out of my periphery that AJ's parents and grandparents are speaking quietly between themselves. Dylan and Hayley head toward AJ's room and I take the few steps over to the window. It's dark out, and the streetlights are on, shining the way for people to head home.

When Hayley and Dylan return to the family, Hayley steps into her mom's arms and they both break down in tears. My heart thumps heavily in my chest and my worry increases exponentially as I fear what I'm about to see.

Dylan wraps his arm around my shoulder. "Are you going to be okay going in there on your own?"

I nod slowly, building my resolve. AJ needs me to be strong for him and that's exactly what I'm going to be. "Is he awake yet?"

He shakes his head. "Nope and he's pretty banged up. You need to prepare yourself."

I swallow, my mouth suddenly as dry as the dunes AJ and I climbed. My heart pounds and blood rushes to my ears, but I refuse to allow my body to shut down on me. I draw in measured breaths and push my shoulders back. I've got this. I say my goodbyes to AJ's family and Dylan and head down the hallway alone to AJ's room on rubber legs. The hallway seems longer than before, each step filled with dread as I imagine AJ's broken body lying still on a hospital bed. The man who is so full of life and vitality.

As I reach the doorway, I pause and suck in much-needed air. You can do this Sarah. He needs you. It's your fault he's lying in the damn bed, broken and battered. I cover my mouth to hold in my sob and steady my shaky legs, then push open the door to his room. Machines beep a steady rhythm in the low-lit room and I urge my feet to move me forward. Air gushes out of my lungs as I lay eyes on the man who's only ever been kind, generous, and patient with me.

His head, wrapped in a bandage, is the first thing my eyes latch onto, before slowly cataloging the rest of his face, noting every scratch and bruise. A gasp escapes and my eyes well as I take in his bruised and battered features. "I'm so sorry, AJ," I whisper to nobody.

Pulling over one of the two chairs in the room, I gently take his hand in mine, keeping my eyes firmly locked on him for any change or movement.

CHAPTER 42

—sarah—

Soft touches glide through my hair, waking me from a fitful sleep. It takes me a moment to figure out where I am, and when I sit up, a pinched pain in my neck pulls me up short. Rubbing the area, I glance around the hospital room, memories of yesterday afternoon and last night assaulting me. I'm unsure how I managed to sleep with the constant sound of beeping machines and the dim light the nurses kept on so they could see what they were doing each time they came to check on AJ. I made myself as comfortable as I could on the plastic chair, leaning my head on the side of AJ's hospital bed because I couldn't bear to leave him.

The guilt swamping me about his accident and how I responded on Monday were eating at me, making me feel like throwing up. He's lying in this bed, broken, because of me and my shitty response to our new reality. I wish I could go back in time and change everything that happened.

"Sarah." AJ's raspy voice captures my attention and I snap my gaze to his face.

His eyebrows are scrunched low and there's tightness

around his eyes. "AJ," I breathe. "Do you need me to get a nurse?"

He nods, then winces. "Please."

I stand, smoothing down the skirt I wore to work yesterday —*was that only yesterday?*—then head out to look for someone to help. I find a nurse stepping out from behind the desk. "Hi, my boy— … uh, Mr. Jackson in room five two seven is awake and in pain."

"Sure. I'll be there shortly. I just need to give these to another patient." She holds up a tiny cup with some tablets.

"Thank you." I spin around and rush back to AJ.

A glass of water with a straw rests on the side cupboard, so I offer him a drink while we wait for the nurse. I stroke my fingers down the side of his face, cataloging each cut and bruise so I don't hurt him worse than he already is. His usual five o'clock shadow has become more of a fuzz since I saw him on Monday. I lower my face to his and kiss his temple with the lightest of touches, cupping the opposite side of his face gently. "I've been so worried about you."

He presses into my touch. "Sorry."

"You don't need to apologize. I'm the one who's sorry." I draw in a deep breath of hospital air. "I'm so sorry. I'm just glad you're okay. I couldn't bear to think of a world without you in it. That I never got the chance to tell you I love you." One of my tears lands on his cheek and he reaches up slowly, wiping beneath my eye with his thumb.

He slides his fingers through my hair, cupping the back of my head and bringing me down to his mouth, pressing his cracked lips to mine. "I love you, too. So much." His warm breath brushes my lips, and I lightly press my palm against his heart, reminding myself he's here and he's going to be okay, if not a bit banged up for a while. My eyes dance between his, noting his sincerity and exhaustion.

He loves me. He said he loves me.

His words bathe me from head to toe in warmth and lightness that's been missing since Monday. I could float on the clouds with relief.

Squeaky footsteps break our moment, and I look up to see the nurse I spoke with in the hallway. "Nice to see you awake, Mr. Jackson. I'm Adele, and I'll be your nurse. I believe you're in pain." She presses her fingers to his wrist and watches her fob watch. "On a scale of zero to ten, zero being no pain and ten being the worst pain you can imagine, what would you rate your pain level?"

"Maybe a seven or eight."

I wince. Here I am confessing my love for him, and he's in terrible pain. He probably won't even remember this conversation or that he told me he loves me. Maybe it's the drugs in his system doing the talking?

"Okay. I'll grab your meds." She records information on her tablet after checking over the machines, then leaves us alone again.

"Do you remember what happened?" He nods and groans. "Stay still."

"I remember looking up for my next hold and realizing it was farther away than I originally thought it would be. I knew I'd have to push hard and stretch long to reach it but I don't remember doing it." His eyebrows slash low over his eyes and I watch him as he works through his memories. "Or falling." The beeps on the heart monitor change; increasing in frequency. "I can't believe I fell."

I take his hand in mine and slowly stroke my thumb back and forth across his knuckles. "Don't worry about that now. You're going to be okay." He shakes his head and groans. "Stay still, AJ. You're going to hurt yourself and getting upset won't help anything. You're going to be back to your usual self in no time." I lift his hand to my lips and lay a soft kiss against the back of it, trying to settle him.

His eyes skate around my face, drifting down to my clothes. "You're in your work clothes."

I glance down at my creased skirt and blouse. "Yeah. I came straight from the office yesterday when Dylan called. I haven't been home to change. I didn't want to leave you here on your own."

His body visibly relaxes and he melts into the mattress. "Thanks for being here."

I squeeze his hand, careful of his grazes. "I wouldn't be anywhere else, AJ. I needed to be here with you. I needed to know you were okay. I needed to tell you I love you," I tell him softly, hoping he realizes how important he is to me. "I've done a terrible job so far of showing you how much I value you and how much I love you. My dismissal of you on Monday was awful and hurtful, and completely unacceptable. I'm so sorry. I only hope you can forgive me." I bring his hand to my lips and press another kiss to his knuckles. The need to kiss him and make him feel better is overwhelming. "I promise to do better."

"Good morning." AJ and I turn toward the woman's voice. "I'm Doctor Fieldman. I believe you're experiencing a fair amount of pain. Let's take a look." She checks AJ over from head to toe, explaining his injuries to him as she works. "Do you know what day it is?"

He looks at me. "Uh, Tuesday"—he glances out of the darkened window—"night?"

Doctor Fieldman glances at me. "It's actually very early Thursday morning. You were found and rescued mid-morning yesterday by Parks and Wildlife and brought here immediately. We operated on your leg and head wound yesterday afternoon."

AJ's eyes widen. "But I was climbing on Tuesday. That's when I fell." He shakes his head and groans. "I can't believe I fell. I never fall."

Shit! That means he was lying unconscious exposed to the

elements overnight before he was found. I snap my head back to the doctor, waiting to hear her thoughts on that.

Doctor Fieldman purses her lips and makes some notes. "You were very lucky then, Mr. Jackson. The temperature was fifty-nine on Tuesday night. I'm surprised your condition wasn't worse when they brought you in."

I glance at AJ, thanking whoever above that he was brought back to us. "He's going to be okay, though, right?" I'm doing my best not to panic.

"Oh, absolutely. His leg and head will heal nicely, and he'll be as good as new with some physical therapy." She turns her attention back to AJ. "You'll have a nasty headache, bouts of confusion, and extreme fatigue for a few days as a result of the concussion. Make sure you rest and don't put pressure on yourself to be at full capacity right away. We'll keep a close eye on you while you're here." She raises an eyebrow at AJ and he nods slowly.

"I'll make sure he rests."

She turns her focus to me. "Good. I'll leave you to it and send a nurse in with some pain medicine."

"Knock, knock." The three of us turn toward the door, finding Hayley standing on the threshold. I'm not surprised she's here at the crack of dawn, she was reluctant to leave the hospital last night. Hayley makes a beeline for her brother, and I step out of the way so they can reunite. Her body shakes and AJ does his best to stroke his hand up and down her back, but the angle is awkward.

I thank Doctor Fieldman, while AJ and Hayley embrace, stepping off to the side to give them some privacy. Maybe I should leave? I'm sure his family will be coming to visit and they don't need me hanging around. Eric gave me the day off to be with AJ, but perhaps I shouldn't intrude on family time.

Hayley takes the chair I slept in as I stand beside the window to give them space. "Sarah," AJ calls my name, snapping me out of my thoughts and I turn to him. He's holding out his hand for me. "Come here, Cupcake. I want you next to me." The rigidness I was holding in my body dissipates instantly. He wants me next to him which means I'm not going anywhere, even if I have to live in these clothes for the entire time he's in the hospital. I step forward quickly to slide my hand into his roughened one and he pulls me forward. When I try to sit on the second visitor's chair next to his bed, he tugs me forward. "Sit here."

I smile at him and perch my butt on the edge of his hospital bed, careful not to bump him. "Okay." I lean down and peck his lips. He explains to Hayley about his fall, coming to the end of his story when his mom and dad walk in, closely followed by the nurse.

"Oh, you have a full house. I have your medicine here." Everyone says hello and she administers AJ's medicine through his IV. "You'll probably feel sleepy in a little while. It's the best thing you can do for your body's healing." After she checks the monitors again, she leaves the room and AJ's parents fuss over him, his mom sobbing.

My phone buzzes in my purse, which is on the floor beside Hayley. "Would you mind passing my purse?"

She hands it over and I dig around with my free hand to find it. Mel's face flashes on my screen. "I'm just gonna step out and take this." Reluctantly, AJ releases my hand and I step into the hallway to accept the call. "Hey, Mel."

"Hiya. I wanted to check how you were doing. I'm sorry I'm on nights this week and haven't been around much." I burst into tears at the sound of my best friend's voice. "Hey, hey, hey. Sarah." Her voice is panicked. "Do you need me to come home?"

"I … I'm okay. I'm not at your place, I'm at the ho-hospital," I manage to say through my tears.

"Why are you at the hospital? Are you okay?" Her words tumble out quickly.

"It's AJ. He f-fell when he was cli-climbing."

"Oh shit! Is he going to be okay?"

I calm down enough to tell Mel everything, and when she offers to grab me a change of clothes from her apartment and bring them to me after her shift, I thank her profusely. When I step back inside AJ's room and return to my spot on the edge of his bed, he smiles at me sleepily, so I take his hand in mine and kiss him gently. "Sleep. I'll be here when you wake," I whisper against his lips, noting the dullness in his eyes.

"Promise?"

"Promise. I'm not going anywhere." He closes his eyes, leaving me with his family, who stay for a short while, then leave with promises of returning tomorrow.

CHAPTER 43

$-aj-$

SOUNDS OF MACHINES INFILTRATE MY CONSCIOUSNESS AND I slowly wake. I don't know what they gave me, but whatever it was knocked me out. Sluggishly, I open my eyes. Squinting, I peer around the small, sterile room. When I look to my left where Sarah was when I fell asleep, my heart rate spikes to find the chair empty.

She promised she would stay.

The disappointment of finding her gone is overwhelming. I was sure she told me she loved me, but maybe the drugs in my system had me hallucinating the whole thing because that's what I want. Maybe she was never here at all. I turn my head and stare up at the ceiling, working through everything that's happened.

I can't believe I fell. I've never fallen, even when I was starting out. I run through the last moments before I knew I was going down. I was holding on and then I had to push up and across to reach my next hold, then … A retching sound comes from the bathroom, breaking into my thoughts and startling me. It continues for a few minutes and I would prefer to investigate, rather than lie here on the uncomfortable hospital bed, but with my leg in a cast and the pounding in my head, I'm reluctant to move so I call out, "Hello. Are you okay in there?" The retching happens again and the need to know who's being sick in my bathroom outweighs my need to remain still.

Pushing myself into a seated position, I ignore the aches and pains in my body, then twist so my legs are dangling over the side of my bed. Fighting the pounding in my head, I inch my butt closer to the edge and place the foot of my good leg on the floor to test my balance, then using the furniture, I collect my bag of fluids in one hand and drag the IV pole with me as I hop slowly to the bathroom—it's tough to balance with all the shit I'm carrying. My head spins while the pounding in my brain feels like the drummer from AC/DC is practicing a solo.

I knock on the bathroom door. "Are you okay in there? Do you need me to call a nurse?"

"I'm okay. I'll be out in a sec." That's Sarah's voice.

She *did* stay. Relief swiftly replaces the disappointment I was feeling.

But why is she sick? If she's sick, she shouldn't be here watching over me. She should be home resting. Has she even been home?

Ah, fuck! Grayness pulls at the edge of my vision and my head spins. The floor comes up to meet me and I barely get my hand out in time to stop my face from smashing into the linoleum. Shit, that fucking hurts. I grunt as I try to push up but before I can move, the door swings inward and Sarah stands in the doorway. Her face is blotchy and the loose hairs around her face are stuck to her cheeks. I can see she's been crying.

"Shit, AJ, are you okay? What on earth are you doing out of bed?" She immediately crouches down, hooking her arm around my waist to help me back to my feet. She awkwardly guides me back to bed, permanent creases marring her normally smooth forehead. She helps me sit on the edge of the hard mattress, then carefully lifts my broken leg, followed by my good leg onto the bed. "I don't think you're supposed to be up yet. And I definitely don't think you should be putting any weight on your leg," she chastises me as she covers me with the starchy sheet and thin blanket, efficiently ensuring the tubes going into and out of my body aren't twisted. I lie back on the pillow and close my eyes to catch my breath. I feel as though I've run a damn marathon with that short trip to the bathroom.

"Are you okay? You were sick." I study her closely. She looks pale beneath the blotchiness.

She waves me off. "Yeah. I've been feeling off all week. I think the anxiety of all this"—she waves her hand in my general vicinity—"tipped me over the edge. I'm sure I'll start to feel better now I know you're going to be okay." I take her hand to pull her closer, but she resists. "I need to brush my teeth. Back in a sec." She pulls her hand free and steps back into the bathroom, returning a couple of minutes later. "I hope you don't mind. I used your bathroom to have a quick shower while you were sleeping."

"Be my guest. I'm just happy you're still here, but if you need to go, don't feel obliged to stay. Shouldn't you be at work?" I figure I should give her the option since work is so important to her. Maybe she only said she loved me out of worry and she doesn't really mean it.

She frowns at me. "Are you trying to get rid of me?" I shake my head, ignoring the thumping. "Good. Because this is exactly where I need and want to be. I'm not going anywhere, AJ."

I blow out a relieved breath and hold out my hand to her. When she puts her hand in mine, I tug her forward, cupping the back of her head to pull her down to me. Our lips are mere inches apart and this close I can see the residual tears in her dull eyes. She must have been genuinely worried about me. "Trust me, Cupcake. I don't want to be away from you either, but if you need to go and rest, you should do that." I press up, ignoring the pounding in my head, to swipe my lips across hers. Closing my eyes, I remind myself she's here. She's with me and she's not going anywhere. "I missed you," I whisper on a breath, then press more firmly against the soft pillows of her lips. My arms shake as I try to hold my body up, but I'm not about to stop what I'm doing, so I hold her to me as I lower my head back to the starchy hospital pillow. I kiss her soft bottom lip, followed by the top. Sarah opens, willingly inviting me inside and I don't waste a moment, plunging my tongue into her mouth to reunite with hers, tasting the minty toothpaste. Our kiss is slow and sensual, full of apology and forgiveness, of love and passion, knitting the cracks in my heart back together.

This woman is it for me. I knew it from the second I overheard her talking about wanting to have a baby and my feelings for her have only deepened the more time I've spent with her. I've been in deep from very early on, waiting for her to join me. Even while we've been living together, I still felt as though she wasn't in as deep as I was. But this kiss is showing me she's finally caught up.

Maybe it wasn't such a bad thing that I fell after all? I always like to find the positives out of a negative situation.

"Ahem."

Damn it, between the doctors, nurses, and my family, I can't catch a break. We separate, and the dazed expression on Sarah's face makes my day. She goes to step away from me, but I grip her hand to keep her close. She'll be lucky if I ever let her go.

"It seems you're feeling much better this evening, Mr. Jackson." The doctor steps further into the room, checking the machines. I'm pretty sure it's the same doctor from before, but I can't be sure. I've been finding it difficult to keep track of things since I woke up. They said it was normal to experience some confusion and disorientation after a concussion, so I'm not too worried.

"I am, thank you."

"And your head? How are you doing?"

"Still have a bit of hammering if I move too fast, but I'm okay."

"And how's the pain level for your leg?" She asks as she squeezes each of my toes. "Can you feel that?" I nod. "Good."

"The pain isn't unbearable."

"Excellent. That'll be the pain meds doing their job."

CHAPTER 44

"Okay, Mr. Jackson," Doctor Fieldman starts as soon as she crosses the threshold into my room. "Your head scan and bloodwork have come back clear. You're managing to shower and go to the bathroom yourself, so I have your discharge papers here." She smiles at us, clearly delighted to be giving us good news. She'll probably be glad to see the back of me because I've been begging to go home.

"Already?" Sarah asks, her brow furrowing. She's in no hurry for me to leave the care of the nurses and doctors, though she must be exhausted.

"Yes. Mr. Jackson is making good progress. There's nothing more we can do for him here. There will be follow-up appointments required, and he'll need assistance at home for a while, but he's on the road to a full recovery."

After what felt like the longest week of my life, we finally leave the hospital and the fresh air feels amazing. Sarah stayed with me the entire time, only stepping out on Saturday morning for her volunteer session at my insistence. I draw in deep breaths, exchanging the stale hospital air for fresh air and Sarah pushes me toward our Uber and then helps me get in.

"*Stone Tower*, please."

"I don't want to see my grandfather," I grumble as my muscles draw tight. I'm not ready to deal with him yet.

She takes my hand in hers. "I need to collect my car. It's still parked at work."

My muscles relax and I nod. "We also need to get your stuff. You're moving back home."

Sarah grins at me. "Oh, am I now?"

"Yep." I lean across and touch my forehead to hers. "No arguing with the invalid." I may as well use this to my advantage if it gives Sarah the excuse she needs to move back in.

"Even if you weren't all broken to pieces, I'd be moving back in. I don't want to be away from you any more than I have to."

Finally.

Fucking finally she's with me.

To be fair, her sleeping in that uncomfortable chair for the duration of my hospital stay showed me all I needed to know. I did my best to convince her to join me on the bed, but she was stubborn. If she thinks we won't be sharing my bed tonight, she's gonna be sorely mistaken. I refuse to allow her to sleep anywhere else but with me.

We switch cars, stop at the drugstore for my medication and the other stuff I need, and then make a final stop at Mel's place to collect Sarah's things. Sarah kisses my cheek, then climbs out of her car. I feel like I've handed in my man card when I have to wait while she carries her things downstairs on her own, loading them in the trunk. As soon as I'm back on my feet, she won't have to lift a damn finger. I'll make sure of it.

We arrive home and Dylan comes out to meet us. "Hey. It's good to have you back." He embraces me carefully. "I'm fucking glad you're okay, man," he whispers next to my ear. When he pulls back, I can see the worry in his eyes.

"It's good to be back." He tries to help me inside, but I brush him off. "Can you please take Sarah's bags up to our bedroom? I can get inside on my own."

"Are you sure?"

"I'm okay. I can manage." Sarah grumbles as she drags one suitcase out of the trunk of her car.

I nod. "Yep. I don't want her doing the heavy lifting on her own." I lock my eyes with Sarah's, so she gets my point. "It's bad enough she had to carry them downstairs from Mel's place."

She chuckles, holding up her hands in surrender. "Okay, okay."

Good. I'm glad she's listening to me without an argument. Dylan grabs the bags and lugs them upstairs while Sarah helps me inside, settling me on the couch with my injured leg resting on the ottoman. Exhaustion is quickly taking over now that I'm settled back home.

She blows out a heavy breath. "I'm going to make us all a coffee."

Sarah disappears into the kitchen, and I rest my head on the back of the couch and close my eyes as I listen to her work. A sense of peace and calm washes over me, knowing she's home for good.

"You okay?" Dylan's voice breaks my quiet moment. Damn, I think I could sleep for a week. I'm completely shattered. Not that I'll admit it to anyone.

I open my eyes slowly and without lifting my head, turn in his direction. "Yeah. I was just listening to Sarah in the kitchen and appreciating her being back where she belongs."

"Where? In the kitchen?" Dylan jokes. "You're becoming more and more like your grandfather every day."

"Piss off." I huff. "As if. No, I mean home."

"I knew what you meant. Hopefully, she's here to stay, right?"

"Hopefully."

CHAPTER 45

—sarah—

MY ANXIETY IS FINALLY QUIET SINCE BEING HOME WITH AJ AND knowing he's going to be okay. It's all I need—well, I wouldn't mind if my upset stomach finally disappeared—because nothing else is as important as him being safe.

After helping AJ bathe away his hospital stay, I help him to bed. He looks drained after the effort it took to get him upstairs and then showered. I'm also feeling exhausted after a week of the shittiest of shit sleep in the hospital. I'm grateful Eric allowed me to work on a laptop from the hospital and has told me there's no need to rush back to work. I quickly shower and clean up the bathroom. As I open the bathroom door, my gaze catches on my man, so I lean against the door frame to watch him for a few moments while his eyes are closed. He's probably already passed out.

"Are you gonna stand there and watch me like a creeper all night?" He smirks and I walk toward him.

"Maybe," I sass.

"Come here, Cupcake. I need to hold you properly." A sigh escapes as I climb into bed. God, I've missed him. I'm not sure how I thought I'd be able to live without this man. He holds his arm out and I snuggle as close as I can without touching him. We had to swap sleeping sides so I won't accidentally knock his broken leg during the night. He sighs and drags me closer. "You can touch me."

"I don't want to hurt you. You've just had a major fall."

"You won't hurt me, Cupcake. Not being able to touch you hurts far worse than any of my injuries. Plus, I'm feeling okay." I lay my hand on his abs and settle my body so it's touching every available inch of his. His muscles relax beneath my palm and when I glance up at his face, his lips are raised in a serene smile.

I press a light kiss to his bristly jaw. "Goodnight. I'm so glad you're home safe. I love you."

He turns his head, kissing my forehead with a lingering press of his lips. "I love you. Night, Cupcake. Thanks for taking care of me."

I leap out of bed before I'm fully awake, careful not to bump AJ, and race into the bathroom to empty the contents of my stomach. I drop to my knees, the tiles digging into my flesh, retching into the toilet over and over. A never-ending, gut-wrenching purge that seems to have no end. The room spins when I finally finish, and I flush away the evidence. Closing the lid of the toilet, I fold my arms on top and rest my head on them to catch my breath, noticing some of my hair is covered in vomit—yuck. Geez, that was close. I almost didn't make it. The sound of the bathroom door opening has me looking up through bleary eyes. God! I don't want him to see me like this. His worried gaze locks on me.

"Sarah? How can I help you?" He lumbers into the bathroom balancing on his crutches, coming closer and I hold up my hand. He's getting better at moving around, even though we've only been home five days. Tomorrow marks two weeks since his fall and I'm still not over the shock of it all—ugh!

"Please stay away. I'm revolting and I don't want you to come any closer."

"Cupcake," he breathes. "Let me help you."

"No. I'm okay. I'll … uh … just have a quick shower. You shouldn't be up on your feet. Remember. You need to stay off that leg as much as possible." I point to his cast. "I can manage. Promise." I implore him with my eyes and he takes a reluctant step back, leaving me in the bathroom with a nod.

"If you need anything, just shout. I'll help however I can."

"Thanks. I won't be long."

I brush my teeth, then climb into the shower. I let the warm water beat down on me, rinsing the vomit from my hair. With my eyes closed, I let the spray rinse away the past two weeks—a time I'll never forget. The regret I'm holding onto about my reaction to AJ being my new boss, which sent him out climbing to clear his head and subsequently falling is overwhelming. A sob leaves my throat with the guilt I'm holding on to. Even though Dylan tried to make me feel better and remove some of the blame from my shoulders, it's the only place the blame belongs.

The sound of shuffling captures my attention and I open my eyes to find AJ standing naked on the other side of the glass, wearing the waterproof cast we picked up from the drugstore. I open the door and help him inside. As much as I know he shouldn't be standing unnecessarily, I selfishly want him with me. He pulls me into his body, cupping the back of my head, and my sobbing resumes.

"Shhhh, shhh. It's okay. Let it out, Cupcake." His roughened hand glides from the top of my head, down my back, and then starts back at the top, repeating the process. The action is soothing and makes me feel cherished. Something I'm not sure

I deserve after my behavior. I don't think I'll ever forgive myself.

I catch my breath and wipe my eyes, then look up into AJ's soulful brown orbs. "I'm sorry I've kept you at a distance. I was scared and wrong, and I promise I won't do it anymore. If you'll still have me, I would like the opportunity to make things right."

His eyes flick between mine as he brushes my wet hair out of my face. "I'm not sure how you missed the signs, but there's never been a question in my mind about us. I've wanted to be with you since the moment I laid eyes on you. I've just been waiting for you to catch up."

My lips tip up in relief. Somewhere deep inside, I've known it all along, but my stupid fear stopped me from seeing it for what it was. I press up on my toes and touch my lips to AJ's tenderly, aiming to keep it light but AJ wraps his hand around my hair, holding me in place, our lips a hairsbreadth apart.

His eyes dart between mine and a sensual smile forms on his face. "I need more than that, Cupcake."

I eagerly move forward, careful of his leg, and wrap my arms around his torso to cup his shoulders, as I show him how much I love him. Expressing my sorrow and begging for his forgiveness. Our tongues tangle while our teeth clash, and I whimper into his mouth when I feel his cock growing between us, pressing against my soft stomach. I can't believe that after all he's been through, he's getting hard. I pull far enough away to study his face, my eyes cataloging his features. "How are you feeling today?"

I watch him closely as he takes a moment. "I feel fine. Still have a bit of a headache, but Doctor Fieldman warned me about that. My leg aches, but not enough to stop me from coming to you when you need me." His voice has dropped low as he strokes my hair away from my face.

My heart pounds in a heavy rhythm at his subtle seduction.

I carefully guide him to sit on the ledge at the end of the shower and then lower to my knees in front of him, ensuring I don't bump his broken leg. His hands automatically cup each breast and his thumbs swipe across the sensitive nubs, his carnal gaze watching the movement.

"You have the most gorgeous breasts." His gaze flicks up to mine momentarily before dropping back. "So full and lush." He lowers his head, sucking one nipple into his mouth, while he plucks and rolls the other between his deft fingers. I moan. The feel of his warm tongue swirling around the hard bud sends an electrical pulse straight to my clit. My boobs are always sensitive to attention, but this is unreal. Not having AJ's hands on me for the last two weeks has made me more sensitive than normal. I hum my pleasure, reaching up to slide my fingers through the short strands of his hair, avoiding his stitches. He switches over, paying the same attention to my other boob, and I finally come to my senses enough to remember why I'm on my knees in front of him.

Using my hold on his hair, I pull his head away and meet his lustful gaze. "There's something I wanted to do." I press my lips to his roughly and then kiss my way along his jawline to his ear. "You make me feel so good, let me do this for you." I nip his lobe and then trail my fingers down his torso, following with my mouth. Kissing, sucking, and licking my way to his gorgeous thick cock. "I love your body. But mostly, I love *you*."

"Ditto, Cupcake."

He squeezes my left breast and I tease the tip of his cock, swirling my tongue around it like I'm licking my favorite lollipop before wrapping my hand around the engorged length to stroke him.

I move closer until AJ's shaft is flush between my breasts, then press them together, surrounding his length. When I look up at AJ's face, the heat in his lidded gaze steals my breath. I slide up and down the length, squeezing my breasts tight and when the tip of his cock slides out from between the tight space, I dip down to press a kiss to the crown. AJ's harsh whispered, "fuck" makes me smile.

He reverently cups my face, tilting it up to his. "You're so damn beautiful." He crushes his mouth to mine in a rough, messy kiss, and I lose my momentum for a moment. When we pull away, I release my boobs and wrap my hand around his hot length and slide it partway into my mouth, swirling around the tip with my tongue.

His hands find my hair and he grasps a handful at the roots, pulling me away from his dick. "You don't have to do this, Cupcake."

I smile at him. "I know. I want to. I *need* to." I implore him with my eyes and as his eyes dart between mine, he nods slowly.

"Okay." He guides my mouth back to his shaft and this time I don't mess around. I take him to the back of my throat and his hips jolt upward. "Fuuuck!" he groans. "You're so good at taking my cock. Do you like having my thick cock in your mouth? Does it make you wet?" It's my turn to moan at his filthy words. "Fuck. Do that again." He raises his hips as I moan around his shaft and I relish in the tiny bit of pain he causes as he tightens his hold on my hair.

Rubbing my thighs together, I bob up and down his length, wrapping my hand around the base to ensure I have as much of him covered as I can. The hand that's not holding onto my hair returns to my breast as he massages the globe and pays attention to my nipple—pinching and plucking it until it's sharp enough to cut glass. AJ's hips thrust gently into my mouth as he uses his hold on my hair to move me how he wants. I lift my gaze to his face and the sheer masculinity that greets me is breathtaking. The veins in his neck are protruding as his heated gaze watches his cock slide in and out of my mouth. My heart hammers sending my blood thrumming through my veins.

"Take it deeper, Cupcake, and swallow when you can't go any further. I fucking love watching my dick disappear between your sweet lips." I drop my hand between my legs and circle my fingers around my aching clit needing relief. Nothing's as good as AJ's touch, though, but this will have to do. His eyes drop lower, watching me work myself over and he groans, tugging on my hair to speed up my movements. He presses his pelvis closer to my face and pauses as his thickness grows in my mouth. "Do you want to taste it?"

I nod the best I can with a mouth full of his dick. He throbs in my mouth, growing to take up all of the available space. His mouth drops open with a groan and his release hits the back of my throat. My clit pulses and my body tingles as I detonate, sending me skyrocketing into bliss.

AJ's head bangs against the tiled wall and I quickly snap my focus back to him. Sliding his softening cock out of my mouth, I swallow his orgasm. "Are you okay? You shouldn't be banging your head against the tile; you have stitches and the tail end of a concussion." I shake my head and stand on jelly legs, feeling slightly dizzy with the rush of blood that just went to my clit. "I can't believe I did that in the shower. How damn stupid am I? I put you at risk." My drunken lust haze dissipates quickly.

Spinning to turn off the faucets, I help AJ stand and climb out of the shower. "Calm down, Cupcake. I'm thinking that was exactly what the doctor ordered. I feel great."

I playfully hit his pec as I return to him with a towel to dry him off. "I bet. But that probably wasn't a good idea for your head injury."

"I dunno. While all the blood was rushing to my cock, my head wasn't pounding so much."

I furrow my brows and narrow my eyes. "How bad is your headache?"

He softens his voice, regarding my face closely. "I'm okay. Stop worrying. That blow job made me feel amazing." AJ's lips tip up cheekily and I relax a little. "Now let's go back to bed so you can sit on my face."

"That's not even funny." I can't believe this guy.

"Remember, you're not supposed to argue with the invalid," he taunts.

I roll my eyes heavenward. "I'm not sitting on your face when you have fifteen stitches in your head and you're recovering from a concussion."

"That sounded like you said you don't love me." He pouts. He's genuinely pouting at me like a five-year-old child.

"What the hell? No, I didn't. I'm not sitting on your face *because* I love you. You're supposed to be taking it easy." I bend down to remove the waterproof cast carefully as he holds onto the vanity, his semi-hard cock right in my face. I kiss it, then stand.

"You can't tease me like that, Sarah."

"Of course I can." I lead him into the bedroom and sit him on the edge of the bed and then do my best to help him dress. He's not helping at all. "Can you help me out a little here? Please."

"Nope. I don't wanna get dressed. I want you to fuck my face."

"No." I step into the walk-in closet and dress out of his line of sight, returning to find him still as he was when I left him. "C'mon, AJ. Help me out. I promise I'll sit on your face when the doctor gives you the all-clear." I can't believe this is the conversation we're having.

His eyes light up. "Promise?"

I shake my head at him and huff out a laugh. "Promise."

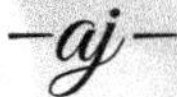

After a lingering kiss, Sarah climbs into her car and heads off to work. Having her here with me, living with me, still feels unreal. If I could walk without crutches, I'm certain I'd have a bounce in my step. It took a bit of convincing to get Sarah to return to the office, but there wasn't anything more she could do for me at home. I can manage everything and Dylan's here during the day anyway.

I pour myself a coffee and lean against the kitchen counter to enjoy the first sip of steaming goodness. Nothing beats a good cup of coffee in the morning. Well … maybe that's not quite true. I can think of several things, all of which involve my sexy girlfriend, that trump coffee. My phone vibrates in my pocket and I dig it out.

GRANDFATHER

My office. 9:30 a.m. sharp.

My eyes widen, then I frown at the message. I've been home for a week and have an appointment at one for a follow-up with my doctor. It's one of the reasons Sarah didn't want to go back to work but Dylan promised to take me and report every single detail back to her.

The large barn door to our office slides open. "Morning," Dylan calls as his footsteps get louder the closer he comes to me. I glance up at him to say hi. "What's going on?"

I hold up my phone to show him the screen. "I've been summoned by the almighty to his tower."

Dylan grabs a cup and makes himself a coffee. "Shit. What do you think it's about?"

"Really? You have to ask."

He turns, leaning his ass against the opposite counter. "You'd think he'd give you a little time to recover after your accident."

I nod. "One would think so but we are talking about my grandfather here."

"I can drive you in."

"Thanks." I tuck my phone back into my pocket and take another sip of my coffee. "Let's get some work done first."

We make our way into our office and as I'm about to sit my phone rings and Hayley's face lights up the screen. "Hey, Sis. What's up?"

"I got summoned into the office for a nine-thirty meeting."

"Shit. So did I." Dylan spins in his chair, listening to my side of the conversation.

"What do you think it's about?"

Who the fuck knows if Hayley's gonna be there? He's never deemed her worthy to talk with about business.

"I assumed he was calling me in to finalize the details of me taking over the company, but maybe that's not it if you're going to be there too."

"Hmm. I've never been to his office before." No kidding. Neither had I until the day everything went to shit.

"You want me to pick you up? I mean Dylan will pick you up since he's gonna be driving."

"How about I come and get you? Seems more efficient."

"Sure. See you at nine." We disconnect the call and I spin my chair toward my best friend, who's waiting for information. "Hayley's gonna pick me up since she's been summoned as well."

Dylan whistles long and low. "Man, I wonder what's going on?"

"Me too."

We reach the glass doors to the magnificent building, which is owned by one of our new clients, Oliver Stone. Hayley holds the door open for me and I lumber through, then we make our way toward the elevator. The same guy from last time is waiting to press the button like people aren't capable of pressing it for themselves. The elevator is as busy today as it was two and a half weeks ago.

Hayley chews on her bottom lip, fidgeting with her fingers. "Stop worrying. I'm sure it's nothing."

My phone vibrates in my pocket and I pull it out to read the message.

CUPCAKE

Your mom's just arrived

Before I can respond, the doors open to *FutureTech*. I hadn't told Sarah I had been summoned to the office, I figured she'd already know. As we step out of the elevator I tell Hayley, "Apparently Mom's here."

Her head snaps toward me. "What? This is strange."

I nod. "It's very unlike Grandfather. I wonder what's going on?"

We announce ourselves to Lucy, and she buzzes Sarah to

let her know we're here. Within moments, Sarah comes into view from the hallway leading to Grandfather's office, wearing creases between her brows I want to smooth out with kisses. She glances across at Lucy, then puts on a more professional expression.

"Good morning, Mr. Jackson. Ms. Jackson."

Hayley totally breaks protocol, not reading Sarah's tension, and moves in to hug her. "Sarah. It's so great to see you."

Sarah stutters, "Y-you too." Her wide eyes catch my gaze over my sister's shoulder as she awkwardly returns Hayley's enthusiastic embrace.

Lucy's watching it all go down as though she's at the movies. All she needs is a tub of popcorn. I know Sarah's uncomfortable about the office knowing about our relationship, but they're gonna find out sooner or later. It may as well be sooner. That's if they haven't already worked it out after Sarah left with my grandfather to race to the hospital. Sarah told me all about sharing a ride with him and having to tell him about our relationship. I felt sick to my stomach that she was put in that position.

I glance across to make sure Lucy's still watching, then I clear my throat. "Uh, Sis. You mind letting me hug my girlfriend?" I smirk at Lucy's widened eyes, then focus on moving closer to my girl.

"Uh, yeah, sure. Sorry." Hayley releases Sarah and steps out of the way, brushing her curls away from her face.

"Come here, Cupcake." Coughing sounds from behind the front desk and Sarah shakes her head at me as a slow smile forms.

She moves into me, wrapping her arms around my torso. "I know what you're doing and I'll get my revenge later," she whispers, her warm breath fanning across my ear. Between that and her words, a shiver makes its way down my spine.

"I'll look forward to it," I whisper, then pull back to wink at her.

She steps away. "Thanks, Lucy." Looking at Hayley and me, she asks us to follow her and we make our way down the hallway to our grandfather's office. My eyes drop to Sarah's ass, wrapped in a tight dark gray pencil skirt; her calves look sensational in the heels she's wearing. She knocks on Grandfather's door, then promptly opens it when he tells her to come in. "Mr. Wainwright. Mr. and Ms. Jackson are here to see you."

"Thank you, Sarah. Please show them in."

"Certainly, Sir." Maybe I *should* take the position, then she can call me 'sir.' The thought makes my dick hard. She turns back to us and we step across the threshold into Grandfather's office. "I'll bring in some drinks."

"Thank you, Sarah."

The door closes with a click and my eyes land on Mom, sitting ramrod straight opposite her father, her face pinched tight. I never wanted Mom and Hayley on the receiving end of Grandfather's chauvinistic ways; it's bad enough we have to deal with him at family events. I didn't want them to have to deal with him when he's in business mode and his misogynistic beliefs are at an all-time high.

I lean down the best I can to kiss Mom's cheek. "Hi, Mom."

She cups my cheek. She's been different since my accident. More openly affectionate and even though I'm thirty, I'm loving this side of her. It's something that's always been missing in our household. "AJ. How are you feeling?"

"I'm doing okay. I'm getting around a lot easier, even if I am a little slow with these things." I balance on my good leg and hold out my crutches to the side.

"You're looking much better. If you need anything, your father and I are only a phone call away."

"I know. Thanks, Mom." I turn my attention to my grandfather as Hayley says hello to Mom and we both take a seat. "What's going on?" I ask. Let's get this meeting underway.

He leans forward in his chair, folding one hand on top of the other on his massive desk. "Your grandmother and I have been talking. Well, she's been talking and I've been … uh … listening. She said she'd been holding her tongue for too long and it was time she told me some home truths."

Hayley, Mom, and I glance at each other, and I know we're all thinking the same thing: since when does Grandfather listen to anyone besides himself?

There's a quiet knock on the door and all eyes turn toward it. Sarah steps in with a tray of drinks, which she distributes efficiently and we each thank her. As she turns to leave, Grandfather stops her. "Please take a seat, Sarah. This meeting involves you too."

Her brows furrow, and to say I'm confused as to what's going on would be a gross understatement. "Sure. Do I need my tablet?"

"No. Just take a seat, please."

Sarah takes the seat next to mine, and I want to reach out and take her hand to calm her obvious nerves, but I know she wouldn't appreciate the gesture. I'm already going to be in trouble for what I did in front of Lucy. This would be far worse in her eyes.

The silence in the room builds and I've never seen my grandfather look more uncomfortable. He stands and walks over to his floor-to-ceiling windows, tucking his hands in his pockets with his back to us for several moments, then he heaves a loud sigh. We all look at each other. I wish he'd start talking and put us all out of our misery.

"Grandfather?"

"Give me a moment, Adam, would you?"

I lean back in my chair. And wait.

He finally spins on his heel to face us. "Adam. You've made it very clear you don't want to take over *FutureTech*. For the life of me, I can't understand why, but recent events and discussions with your grandmother have opened my eyes a little."

I nod and blow out a breath. Finally. I glance at Mom and Hayley, noticing them sitting forward slightly in their seats. I know they want to get their hands on *FutureTech*. They've discussed the possibility of bringing Hayley and Lisa's software company under the *FutureTech* umbrella, allowing them a greater reach.

Grandfather walks toward us, gripping the back of his leather chair. "Elaine."

"Yes, Father." It's easy to hear the note of excitement in her voice. I hope he's made the only choice he can make. The *right* choice.

"After careful consideration, I would like to offer you the CEO position of *FutureTech*. Along with that position you will become a fifty percent shareholder in the company."

Mom rises from her chair and I'm certain she wants to jump up and down on the spot, but years of social conditioning have her controlling her reaction. She steps around to Grandfather and wraps him in a stiff hug. "This means the world to me. Thank you for putting your trust in me. I won't let you down, Father."

He pats her back as if he's patting an acquaintance. "I hope not." And there we have it, folks. The lack of faith and acknowledgment of Mom's talents. He forgets—or fails to recognize—she was a CEO of a Fortune 500 company until eighteen months ago when she decided to retire with the hope she would eventually take over *FutureTech*.

I glance at Sarah. Her mouth is dropped open slightly and her eyes are wide as she watches their interaction. She had a taste of how cold my family is when she met them while I was recovering in the hospital. They stopped by regularly to visit, but there were no warm embraces or the general love and affection Sarah is used to from her family.

Mom returns to her seat, wearing a slight smile. I know she's holding back her joy at this new development. Grandfather turns his attention to my sister. "Hayley."

"Yes, Grandfather." She sits a little straighter.

"I know it's roughly six weeks until your little one will be born, but I would like to offer you the position of Vice President. You and Lisa can work out a system that will work best for you in terms of looking after your children and balancing work. With the role, you will receive a twenty-five percent share in the company."

She jumps out of her seat, squealing in delight. Obviously, she doesn't care for the years of conditioning. And I can understand her excitement. This means big things for her and Lisa's software company. Running around the desk, she flings herself at our grandfather, and finally, he cracks a smile as he returns her affection. "Thank you, Grandfather. I won't let you down. We're going to take *FutureTech* to the next level. You wait and see."

"We have more to discuss."

Hayley moves back to her chair, but not before embracing Mom in an excited hug. When they separate, both of their eyes are twinkling in happiness and their nervous disposition from earlier has completely vanished.

"Congratulations, Mom. Congrats, Hayley. I'm happy for you both." I look at my grandfather. "Thank you."

He tips his chin. "You're not completely off the hook, Adam. I may not have given you a role as such, but I want you involved as a silent partner. You will take the position of the second Vice President and hold the final twenty-five percent of the company's shares. Your skills and talents could be very useful here." He scans the three of us. "No arguments."

Damn it. That doesn't seem fair since I won't be as involved in the day-to-day operational side of things. I'll have to speak with Mom and Hayley about it once Grandfather steps down. I don't want to upset his good mood and bring it up now because this is the outcome I've always wanted for Mom and Hayley.

"Now, Sarah. It is entirely up to you, my dear, but I'm hoping you'll stay on to help Elaine and Hayley during the transition period and beyond. You know as much about the running of this place as I do and you will be an invaluable asset to them."

Sarah blinks a few times. She told me she offered to resign from her position because of our relationship. "I would love to stay, Mr. Wainwright. It would be an honor to assist Mrs. Jackson and Ms. Jackson as they transition into their new roles."

"Please, call me Elaine while we're in the office." Mom smiles at Sarah. "You can call me Mom the rest of the time." She winks. My mother winks at my girlfriend. Well, soon-to-be fiancée if I have anything to do with it. I feel like aliens have taken over my family.

"Same goes for me. Hayley will do just fine."

"Okay." Sarah's still trying to maintain her professionalism, but I can see the excitement vibrating beneath the surface. She turns back to my grandfather. "What about Mr. Booth?" Ah, the asshole who supported Grandfather with his outdated views. "Will he be staying on?" Sarah's stiff as she waits for an answer.

"Uh, no. I'll be informing Tony, when the time is right, that he will need to seek other employment. It's recently been brought to my attention how old-fashioned we both are"—he pointedly looks at me—"and I think it would be a good opportunity for a clean sweep. I believe these changes are exactly what *FutureTech* needs to carry it forward." He sits and places his hands on his desk. "I would like this transition to begin as soon as possible."

We all nod in agreement, the room feeling more relaxed than it was forty minutes ago.

CHAPTER 47

$-aj-$

SINCE I'VE BEEN HOME FROM THE HOSPITAL, SARAH'S THROWN up as soon as her eyes open every single morning. I feel helpless and she refuses to see the doctor about it. She says it's because of her anxiety, but I don't think it's that at all. The tracking app on my phone says she should have finished her period yesterday, but Sarah hasn't mentioned anything about getting her period this month, and I didn't find her crying in the bathroom as she has before.

I wonder if she's given up. Or maybe she doesn't want to mention it because she's trying to cope with her devastation on her own?

"Hey, Dylan. Can you help me with something?"

"Sure. What do you need?"

"I need to get some flowers for my girl and I can't drive yet. She's been through a lot of stress with trying to get pregnant, then finding out I was supposed to be her new boss, and then the fall." Fuck, that's a lot of stress in a short period. Maybe it *is* stress making her sick.

"No problem. Let's go."

I'm getting around much easier with the crutches, so it's

not long before we're on our way. We stop by one of the best florists in the city, *Blooms and Balloons*, to get an arrangement of spring flowers for Sarah. As soon as I saw the bright colors and smelled the springtime scent, I knew they'd be perfect for my girl. We stop at the drugstore to pick up a couple of items, then hit the grocery store so I can cook a meal for us tonight, instead of Sarah having to do everything when she gets home. I'm steadier on my feet, and I can sit at the counter to cut up the ingredients.

Stopping in front of my place, I turn to Dylan. "Thanks, man. If you can help me get all this inside, then we may as well call it a day."

"No problem. I might take up being an Uber driver if our business ever tanks."

"As if that's ever gonna happen. We're busier than ever with the accounts we've secured lately. Mr. Mitchell's happy with our work for *The Cardinal* and Oliver's impressed with our work for *The Parkerville Project*, he wants us to look at his business. Don't forget how happy Mr. Noble was with our work for him. These are huge fucking contracts. We won't be going out of business anytime soon." If anything, we need to seriously look at employing another member to join our team.

"Yeah, I know. I was joking around. Let's get all this shit inside. I might go for a ride since the afternoon is nice."

We make quick work of unloading Dylan's car and then he takes off. I clean up a little: wash the breakfast dishes, tidy the living room, set up the upstairs deck for dinner, and take a seat at the counter to start preparing our meal.

I'm about to set the timer on the oven for the chicken casserole when Sarah walks in the door. "Honey, I'm home!" She calls out with a smile in her voice. My lips tip up in a matching grin. Her brows furrow when she steps into the kitchen and scans the counters to see the mess I've made.

"What on earth are you doing? You shouldn't be making dinner. You're not supposed to be on your feet."

My smile widens as I step toward her, wrapping one arm around her waist as soon as I'm close enough. I love how much she worries about me. I press my lips against hers without preamble. Her body softens against mine and her hands find their place in my hair at the nape of my neck. Once I've given her a proper welcome-home kiss, I draw back slowly, keeping my lips close to hers. "Welcome home, Cupcake," I whisper, then bite her bottom lip gently because I can't resist the puffy pillow.

One side of her lips tip up and I glance at her sparkling eyes. "I missed you today."

"Not as much as I missed you." We have thirty-five minutes to kill and I have just the thing to keep us busy. I tug her hand. "Come with me, I have something to show you."

She drops her purse on the sideboard where she usually keeps it and I grab my second crutch. Sarah follows me slowly up the stairs—though I am getting faster at climbing them— and into our bedroom. A gasp escapes her and her eyes widen when they land on the flowers and gift bag. She tears her eyes away from them and steps carefully into me, wrapping her arms around my torso. I can't embrace her the way I want while I'm holding both crutches, so I drop one and wrap my arm tightly around her.

"Thank you. They're gorgeous but you didn't have to get me anything."

I kiss her forehead. "I wanted to thank you for looking after me since my accident. The flowers don't seem enough for all you've done for me."

She presses her lips together and creases form between her sculpted brows. "You don't have to thank me for anything. Helping you has given me the chance to show you how much I love you. I wouldn't be anywhere else." She rises on tiptoes and swipes her lips across mine. I slide my tongue between her lips to deepen our connection. Every time I kiss Sarah, I fall for her all over again.

She's my life, the very breath that fills my lungs, the reason my heart beats faster—*the reason it beats at all.* I'm sure it was thoughts of her that pulled me through the night I was partially buried by rockfall in low temperatures.

I soften our kiss slowly and nudge her nose with mine. "Open your present."

Her smile spreads across her lust-drunk lips. "Okay. I love presents, so I won't say no."

I chuckle. "Of course, who doesn't love getting presents? It's not much, so don't get too excited."

She smells the flowers first. "These are gorgeous."

"They reminded me of you," I tell her as I step closer.

Sarah opens the gift bag and peers inside, finding the rectangular box. Her eyes narrow as she studies it closely. "What's this about?"

I step into her body and take the box from her. "Do you know what day it is?"

"Well, of course. Do you?"

"Yep. It's Friday. I'm all good with my days now." I was getting confused there for a while.

She lifts her hand to my cheek, cupping it gently, her eyes going soft. I lean into her touch before turning to press a kiss on her palm. "Do you realize that you should have finished your period yesterday?"

Her eyes dart back and forth and I can practically see the wheel's turning in her head. She lifts her wide eyes to mine. "Do you think …"

I raise my brows and nod. "Yeah, I do."

"Holy shit." She looks at the box, covering her mouth with her palm. "What if … No, I can't say it. I probably skipped my period because of all the stuff that's been going on and my anxiety." She pushes the box back toward me. "I'm too scared to take the test. What if it's negative?"

I transfer the box to the hand holding my crutch and slide my fingers through her soft hair, tucking it carefully behind her ear. "But what if it's positive?" I whisper around the lump in my throat.

She bites her bottom lip, taking a moment to think about it. "I *have* been sick and my boobs have been super sensitive." She reaches down to take the box from me, pushing her shoulders back and her beautiful tits out. "I'll take the test. Will you take it with me?"

"I wouldn't be anywhere else." She spins on her heel and rushes toward our bathroom, and I follow behind as quickly as I can. "Hang on. I'll need to pee on the stick first. Wait out there." She points at our bedroom.

"I was wondering how long it would take you to realize you needed to pee first." I chuckle and then sit on the edge of our bed to wait.

After a few moments, I hear the toilet flush and the water run, so I climb to my feet to join Sarah in the bathroom. She spins as I open the door. "Our lives could change in a couple of minutes," she whispers with eyes full of hope. God, I hope the test is positive. I'll feel so shitty if I've given her hope where there is none.

With my heart pounding, I lean my hip against the vanity, using only one crutch to hold me up and pull Sarah in close. "My life changed the night we shared a booth in the club." Her body softens against mine. "There was no going back for me once you agreed to let me be your donor. I just had to wait patiently for you to catch up."

Sarah brings her hands up to my pecs, resting them there as her eyes flick between mine. "I'm sorry I was so blinded by my plans and I was too scared to take the leap. I wasted so much time. I love you so much, AJ."

"Love you, too, Cupcake. And it doesn't matter because we're together now." I press a kiss to her lips and drop my eyes to the white stick. My heart bursts with happiness as my smile instantly spreads and I look back at Sarah's face. "And you're stuck with me forever."

Her eyes widen and snap down to the test and the two pink lines. "Holy shit! We're pregnant." She jumps up and down, then realizes she's jostling me and freezes in place. "Shit, sorry. Oh my God! We're pregnant." She slams her lips onto mine and I bring my hand to the back of her head, grasping the silky strands at the base of her scalp to tilt her where I want her, deepening our kiss. Our tongues unite and dance with one another in celebration. Tasting and teasing. Teeth clashing and breaths mingling. I want to share these moments endlessly with her.

With the need to draw breath, we reluctantly pull apart, and I press a few soft kisses to her swollen lips. I drop my forehead to Sarah's. Our dazed eyes find each other, our smiles matching. "We're gonna be parents, Cupcake." She nods against me with an enormous grin and I drop my hands to cup her stomach with affection. I can't wait until she's round with our baby. *Our baby.*

We did it. We fucking did it!

"We are." She covers my hands and gives me the biggest smile I've ever seen. Her eyes are sparkling with delight, and she's never looked more beautiful to me than in this moment.

CHAPTER 48

—sarah—

I'M LITERALLY FLOATING ON A CLOUD AS I CARRY OUR DINNER upstairs to the deck. With only a month until winter, the evenings are cool, so AJ has turned on the outdoor heater and drawn the clear blinds to keep the area cozy. His smile is instant the moment I breach the doorway with a delicious-smelling dish in each hand. I love this space up here, but what I love more is that AJ comes with it.

"This smells divine. I think I'll keep you around since you're such a good cook."

"Yeah? And here I thought it was because of my super sperm." He winks as he takes his plate of chicken casserole from me, placing it in front of him, while I chuckle.

"Well, that too." I press my lips to his cheek as I sit beside him and take my first bite. Flavors explode on my tongue, matching the deliciousness of the aroma. "Mmmhm. So good." I quickly scoop up some more, ready to shovel it in as soon as I swallow the first forkful.

AJ nods. "Not too bad." He swallows his food. "You have your volunteer shift tomorrow. Will Mel be working?"

"Yeah."

"You gonna tell her?" Mel's been incredibly supportive through all of this, she should be the first person I share our news with, but it feels wrong not to share it with my family first.

"We probably need to get it confirmed officially first. It could be a false positive." I still can't believe the tests were positive. Yeah, tests. I had to do both of the tests that came in the box. I didn't trust the first one was accurate. After all of these months. If I am pregnant, I'd only be barely pregnant because I got my period last month, even though it was light. I shrug. "I want to be sure."

AJ reaches across and takes my hand. His warm grip is sure and strong, soothing as he rubs his thumb across my knuckles. "I understand. But I'm convinced the tests are accurate. Let's book a doctor's appointment as soon as possible so we can share the news."

I love how excited he is. When I thought I'd be going through this on my own, the unexpected happened and the perfect guy came into my life. I get to create a family with the man I love. A man whose focus is always to fulfill my needs above his own. The man who has the biggest heart and kindest nature I've ever been lucky enough to call mine. I think if I gave him the okay, he'd be on the phone sharing the news with his sister and Dylan straight away.

Squeezing his hand, I agree. "I'll call first thing and see if I can get in to see my GP after my shift tomorrow. Then we can tell everyone over the weekend."

His eyes light up. "I'm coming to your appointment. I don't want to miss a single thing."

Leaning closer, I put my mouth as close to AJ's ear as possible. "I love you," I murmur.

He rubs his scruff against my cheek, his warm breath coating my sensitive flesh. "Good." His fingers slide through my loose hair, pushing it gently away from my face, then he grasps the strands making a fist. "Because I'm never letting you go, Cupcake." He caresses my cheek with open-mouthed kisses until he arrives at the corner of my mouth.

I sigh, knowing exactly what's to come. When AJ kisses me, it's the only thing that takes up space in my mind for those moments. His kisses are all consuming and I think—not think, *know*—I'm addicted to them, addicted to him. Using his grip on my hair, he tilts my head to his liking as his tongue traces my bottom lip. I dart my tongue out to meet his softly, teasing him. The vibration of his groan resonates through my hand resting on his pecs and satisfaction fills me at the effect I have on him. I swallow it greedily and his tongue delves inside my mouth. AJ presses me closer using his grip on my hair, tightening his hold as he ravages my mouth. Heavy breaths and soft sighs escape as our tongues mingle and teeth clash.

Sliding my hand down his defined abs, I reach the waistband of his gray sweats and slip my hand inside, palming his hard cock. He increases the intensity of our kiss, so I squeeze his shaft. Suddenly he pulls away, his hands falling to the waistband of my leggings. "Take these off and climb on." He stretches out the fabric and tries to pull it over my hip one-handed.

I stand with panting breaths, willing to do as he asks because it's exactly what I want. I step back from him to give him a show, dragging my sweater over my head and revealing the cups of my lacy bra which do nothing to hide my beaded nipples. The heat in his eyes burns my skin as he reaches behind his neck, dragging his Henley off and displaying his phenomenal abs and my favorite part, the dusting of dark hair which trails from his navel to beneath the waistband of his sweats.

"As sexy as that bra is, lose it. I want those pretty nipples bare for my mouth while you bounce on my cock." I rub my thighs together at his rasped words. I quickly unlatch it and let it fall down my arms, then toss it on top of my sweater.

He raises his butt and hooks his thumbs into the waistband of his sweats, sliding the fabric down his muscular thighs. His thick cock springs free, bouncing against that sexy trail of hair I was admiring. "I love your body. It's so sexy."

"Ditto, Cupcake." I lick my lips and bend down to taste the tip of his dick, my sensitive nipples brushing the hairs on his thighs. His hand grasps the back of my neck and he drags me up for another scorching kiss. Once he's stolen all of my breath, he pulls back. "Lose the leggings, Cupcake. I need your pussy."

On shaky legs, I stand and hook my thumbs into the waistband of my leggings and panties, taking my time to drag them down my legs. All the while, I keep my eyes locked on AJ as he fists his cock and strokes it seductively. A moan leaves my lips, and I quickly remove my clothes the rest of the way. AJ crooks his finger at me, motioning me forward. As soon as I'm within reach, that same finger slides through my slit and into my opening without preamble. Not that I need any. "Fuck, you're drenched."

"Mmhm." I sweep my tongue across my bottom lip, dropping my chin to my chest so I can watch the corded muscles in his forearm flex as he teases me with his talented fingers. He applies pressure, using the finger he has inside me to tug me closer until my shins hit the edge of the outdoor lounge.

"Come and straddle me." He holds his dick straight up and there's something inherently delicious watching him handle his shaft. His fingers wrapped around the thick length, inviting me to use it for my pleasure and his.

"How can I refuse?" *And why would I want to?* I position myself, careful not to knock his injured leg, with my knees on either side of his thighs. Holding the back of the lounge, I rise ready to slide down onto AJ's shaft, but he releases his cock and grasps my hips firmly. He pulls me down on top of him and leans forward, claiming my mouth. As he fucks my mouth with his tongue, he uses his hold on my hips to rub my pussy along his length in delicious strokes. "Oh, AJ. That feels so damn good," I pant, then return to his lips.

"Hell, yeah it does. You're perfect for me, Cupcake." With his grip on my hips, he lifts me away from his body and he drops his eyes to watch. "Look how wet my cock is from your juices." His volcanic gaze lifts to mine. "Watch as I slide into your perfect pussy."

I nod, my eyes dropping to where we're about to be joined. I take my weight when he releases his grip to grasp his dick, rubbing it through my swollen lips before notching it at my needy opening. I want to drop down and swallow his shaft until I'm completely full, but he squeezes my hip to stop me. "Not so fast. Let's do this nice and slow."

"You really know how to torture a girl. You know that, right?"

His hot breath brushes my lips with his chuckle. "Only in the best possible way." He winks, giving me a sexy smirk. "Watch."

I can't argue with that, so I don't even bother. I drop my eyes to watch his dick disappear inside me, inch by fabulous inch, stretching me wide, until my pelvis is resting against his. He brings his hands up to cup my face and I drop mine to grip his shoulders. With him buried to the hilt, his eyes dance between mine. "If I could live with my cock buried inside your pussy, I would." He presses up, then winces. "I'm afraid you're gonna have to do all the work, Cupcake." He kisses my lips with a tenderness that surprises me and I press into him, my breasts crushing against his pecs. His hands glide down each side of my neck, to my collarbones, around my breasts, and trail to my hips. Grasping them, he lifts me slowly.

A moan escapes me as I take the hint and press away from AJ's body, then I use my thighs to push myself up, feeling the slide of every ridge of his shaft massaging my muscles until just the tip of his crown is still inside. I pause, peering down between us to see his shaft coated with my lubrication, and snap my eyes to his face. "That's so hot. Seeing your dick so wet from me." Using my thigh muscles, I control the drop, making sure I slide down slowly, swallowing his thick length as I take him back inside. I repeat the teasing process over and over, getting hotter with each stroke.

AJ's eyes dance between my bouncing tits and his cock, his breaths hot on my skin—sending goosebumps scattering across my heated flesh. One hand leaves my hip and reaches for my breast. He palms the mound, then scoops the peak into his warm mouth. I cry out as his tongue circles my nipple and lose my focus for a moment, remaining seated pelvis to pelvis with AJ deep inside. He tears his mouth away from my breast. "If you stop, I stop and I know how much you love it when I suck on these pretty nipples."

I'm scandalized. "You wouldn't."

He simply raises an eyebrow and it's enough to move me back into action. He resumes his ministrations, this time working over my other breast as I bounce up and down on him, building us both ever closer to our completion. High-pitched pants leave my lips on puffs of air as his other hand finds its way to my clit. Using his thumb, AJ makes tight circles around the pulsing bud, and sparks quickly form around the edge of my vision while my hair sticks to my face. My thighs are burning and my toes cramp as I grow ever closer to what I know is going to be an explosive orgasm. AJ groans when the wetness from my pussy makes squelching sounds every time I drop down his shaft.

I've never been this free and uninhibited with a lover before and I know it's because AJ makes me feel safe and cherished. Safe to be exactly who I am, flaws and all. There's nothing more freeing than that. It's a gift I'll never take for granted.

"Fuck. You know how hot it is that you get so wet for me?"

He grips the back of my neck, pulling my lips to his, smashing the pillows together. His tongue invades with rough strokes and with everything that's happening to my body, I can't hold back my orgasm. I moan into his mouth as my body tightens from the tips of my toes to the very end of each strand of my hair. "Ah, shit! Feel your pussy." He bites my neck and his cock swells inside me, a hot burst of his cum filling me up as he throbs.

On a long moan, I use my pelvic muscles to tighten around him, keeping us locked together. My breaths are choppy and my vision swims with the lack of oxygen filling my lungs. I drop against him, our sweaty bodies pressed together everywhere. He brings his arms around me, caressing his fingers up and down my spine in a calming motion. Our chests rise and fall rapidly as we try to catch our breath and our hearts do their best to beat their way out of our bodies. With the cooler evening air, despite the outdoor heater, it doesn't take long for our heated skin to cool and a shiver to slide through my body. AJ squeezes me tight, then drags the blanket we keep on the back of the lounge around me, wrapping us within its cocoon.

I bury my face in his neck and my lips naturally spread. His citrusy scent is more pronounced after our strenuous activity. It's a smell I'll always associate with AJ. With home. "I love you," I murmur against his hammering pulse point.

His hands tighten around me. "I love you, Cupcake. Thanks for letting me share your booth."

I chuckle and tip my head back to look at him properly. "Thanks for volunteering to get me pregnant."

epilogue

CHAPTER 49

—sarah—

WITH OUR HANDS ENTWINED, AJ CARRIES A STUNNING FLOWER arrangement while I carry balloons and a gift for Colton as we make our way down the hallways toward the maternity ward. We're both excited to meet the newest addition to the Jackson family. Lisa gave birth to their second son, Braden, late last night and AJ was determined to be one of the first to visit and wish them well. My thoughts race forward to the day when we finally get to meet our baby and I drop my hand to rub over my very slight bump. If you didn't know I was pregnant, you'd think I ate a big meal. I still have to pinch myself that I'm finally living my dream with my dream fiancé. That's right. Once my doctor confirmed my pregnancy, we invited everyone over to share our good news, and AJ surprised me by dropping to one knee to propose.

Our steps slow as we come to Lisa's room. Glancing at each other with matching smiles, we step through the door. The sight that greets us makes my heart sing. Hayley and Lisa are both sitting on the bed, with their new son resting across Colton's lap. The girls lift their gazes to us but Colton is too focused on his new baby brother to notice we've arrived.

"Hey," I whisper as I carefully lean down to kiss Lisa and Hayley's cheeks. "Congratulations." I glance down at Braden. "He's so handsome."

They both swell with pride. "Thank you. We're just a little in love with him. He's been so good."

"Looks like Colton loves him already."

"Yeah. He hasn't taken his eyes off him since Lisa's Mom dropped him off a little while ago."

I chuckle then move out of the way so AJ can pass on his congratulations. I place the balloons on the side cupboard, then bend down and place a soft kiss on top of Colton's head. "Hey, little man." His eyes skip up to me quickly then return to his little brother.

"Have you met my brother?" he asks.

"Not yet. You wanna introduce us?"

He nods. "This is Braden. He's my baby brother, and I'm gonna look after him and make sure he's always safe."

My heart melts. How adorable. I loved Colton already, but he's just burrowed himself deeper into my heart. "I bet you will. You're gonna be the best big brother." I smooth my hand over his dark hair.

His eyes snap to his uncle. "Unca AJ. You're here."

AJ chuckles. "I wouldn't be anywhere else. I had to meet the new guy. Is he being a good boy?"

Colton nods enthusiastically. "Yep."

"Colt, you wanna let Aunty Sarah and Uncle AJ have a cuddle?" Hayley coaxes. "They brought you a present."

His little eyebrows dip over his gorgeous brown eyes, and I can see him working through his options. He finally nods slowly. "Okay."

"Who wants the first hold?" Lisa asks.

AJ tips his chin toward me. "Sarah can have the first hold because once I have him I won't want to give him up."

I chuckle. "Okay. If I have to." I hold out my arms and

wiggle my fingers. Carefully, I lift him from Colton's lap and cradle him close to my body as I did with the baby I cuddled in the NICU this morning. I take a deep breath, drawing his newborn smell into my lungs. I love that new baby smell. "He's so tiny." I automatically sway my body gently from side to side as I kiss the top of his head.

Colton climbs across to AJ and lifts him into his arms. "Hey, Colt. How's it feel to be a big brother?"

He thinks about it for a moment. "Good so far." We all chuckle at the serious tone of his voice. AJ hands him his gift and sits him back on the bed so he can open it. He tears into the paper and reveals the gift AJ found for him. "It's Doug from my book!" he exclaims, holding the plush sheep above his head.

Braden jolts in my arms and lets out a whimper at the sudden noise.

"Sorry, Braden." Colton rises to his knees to check on his little brother, and I lean closer so he can see he's okay.

"He's okay. See?"

Once he's satisfied, he returns to his sheep, snuggling it tight and studying it closely. "Thank you, Unca AJ."

AJ musses his hair. "You're welcome. It's from Aunty Sarah too."

"Thank you, Aunty Sarah."

"You're welcome. I'm glad you love him."

We chat quietly with Lisa and Hayley, and AJ tells them about the dinner service we ordered for them for the next two months so they don't need to worry about cooking dinner.

"Thanks for such an awesome gift." Hayley climbs from Lisa's bed to hug AJ and when they've finished, I pass him the baby, so I can hug her too. "That'll be one less thing we need to worry about."

We chat for a while longer, AJ hogging the baby, and when

Braden starts fussing, Lisa tells us it's time for his next feeding, so we take our cue to leave.

"All right, Colton. You wanna hug Braden? It's time for us to go." We had already made plans with Colton that he'd stay with us for a few days when the baby was born, and he was excited about it. He's been asking when it's going to happen for weeks.

"I don't wanna leave Braden. I'm s'posed to look after him." AJ glances at me. This is new. He's always eager to spend time with us. Lisa and Hayley weren't sure how he'd respond to the new baby. They were worried he'd be jealous or feel left out. We thought if he stayed with us for a day or two, we could make a fuss over him while the girls settle their new addition at home. I don't think any of us predicted that Colton would be so infatuated and protective of his new sibling. It's endearing.

AJ crouches down so he's at Colton's level. "I understand. But Aunty Sarah and I were hoping you'd hang out with us for a little while." He glances up at his sister. "We'll only be a little while and then we'll bring you back to Braden."

Hayley nods, recognizing Colton's need to stay close. "Uncle AJ and Aunty Sarah have a surprise for you, then they'll bring you back to the hospital."

His eyes widen. "A surprise?"

I nod. "Yep. It's really cool, too. I think you'll love it."

He finally relents and we head in the direction of AJ's climbing gym. This will be his first time back at the gym since his accident. When we arrive, Theo and Austin are already waiting out front for us. Theo offered to meet us here so we didn't have to drive to the opposite side of town to pick up Austin.

The boys greet each other like they're best buddies and Colton excitedly shares how he's now a big brother.

Austin listens carefully. "You're lucky he's a boy. Little sisters can be a bit annoying sometimes." It's the first time I've ever heard him say anything negative about Kenny. "They talk a lot and they always wanna hug you. Even when you're in the middle of jumping on the trampoline." He rolls his eyes and we all laugh. He's not wrong there, Kenny's always very affectionate.

Theo rests his hand on Austin's shoulder. "If she annoys you, just tell her to stop."

Austin shrugs. "It's okay. I love her mostly and her hugs are pretty good." Theo catches my eyes, raising his eyebrows.

When we step inside the gym, Colton and Austin's eyes almost pop out of their heads. They turn this way and that, taking in the array of climbing walls, but AJ guides them straight to a section designed especially for kids.

"Can I climb?" Colton asks, his voice full of excitement.

"Absolutely. That's why we're here."

"This is the best," Austin chirps.

"It really is. I love hanging out here. So let's do some climbing." AJ claps his hands together and we make our way over to two empty spaces on the beginner's wall.

The boys cheer and AJ sets them up, explaining everything with just enough detail. Colton has a fairly good idea about the holds because of his climbing wall, but he's never used a rope before. Theo and I listen closely so we can help. Standing side by side, AJ and Theo support the boys as they climb the wall, then come back down to them only to do it all over again.

Throughout the afternoon, the boys' skills and speed increase as well as their confidence. I love that AJ wanted to include Austin. I love watching him interact with the boys as he patiently coaxes and encourages them every step of the way. He's going to be such a great dad. The afternoon flies by, and the boys are beginning to look a little tired.

"Uncle AJ, I wanna see you climb."

"Yeah, show us how you climb," Colton encourages.

"Go on. I'd love to see you in action." I wink at him. I

know he's a little nervous since he's only had two physiotherapy appointments so far, but this place is completely safe. It would be good for him.

I can see the internal argument he's having with himself but he finally agrees. The boys cheer as we move to the climbing area for adults. The array of colored holds scattered across the walls is mind-boggling. It's incredible to think that a little piece of plastic can support an adult. My eyes scan the numerous climbers in various positions up the wall. There's even a woman hanging upside down from the roof. My heart pounds as I watch her go for her next hold, and I blow out a relieved breath when she makes it successfully.

"Would you mind belaying for me? I'll only do a couple of quick climbs, then we'll get out of here."

"You would trust me to do that for you?"

He pauses and scans my face. "Of course. I trust you to be the mother of my child." He cups my small bump. "That's the most trust I could put in anyone, Cupcake." And there goes my heart, melting in a puddle at my feet. He slides his fingers through my hair and draws my face closer to his. "You're the person I trust with my heart and soul. Of course, I trust you with this." He swipes his lips across mine.

"What is it with the grownups always kissing?" Austin moans, breaking the moment and making us giggle.

Before I know it, AJ and I are connected to the ropes, and he's making his way up the wall at a steady pace but I can tell he's favoring his recently healed leg. When he makes it to the top, Colton, Austin, and Theo cheer while relief swamps me. I'm proud of him and glad he did this today while the kids were with us. I think having his personal cheer squad helped his confidence. When he makes it back to the mat, the boys race to him. Colton wraps his arms around his legs, looking up at his uncle with pride. Theo gives me a side hug and then shakes AJ's chalk-covered hand.

"You were awesome. You could be Spider-Man!" Austin tells AJ.

"That'd be pretty cool. He's my favorite Avenger," AJ tells him.

I raise my eyebrows. "You were amazing. You looked really strong, considering you've only had your cast off for a little while."

"Thanks. It felt good to be back on the wall." He leans closer and presses a chaste kiss to my lips. "When we get home, I'll thank you properly." He winks at me, giving me his signature grin.

CHAPTER 50

—aj—

Sarah's smooth tongue licking up the underside of my cock drags me into consciousness. I press my hips up and a moan escapes from the deepest part of me. When I open my eyes and trace them down the length of my body, the sight that greets me makes my cock throb. Sarah's tits hang heavy as she balances on her knees to work me over. Her eyes glance up, then pause on mine. She smiles at me, her eyes glittering in the early morning sunlight.

"Happy birthday."

I slip my hand into her hair and return her smile. "It's pretty happy so far." I raise a brow and she snickers. Raising my head, I drop my voice. "Happy Valentine's Day, Cupcake." I tug her up to my face and drag my morning scruff across her cheek until I reach her ear. "Now get on your hands and knees." She opens her mouth and I'm certain it's to argue, so I press the pad of my thumb to her lips and shake my head. "No arguments. I'm the birthday boy and I get what I want."

Her delectable mouth slams closed and she moves to the middle of the bed, holding onto the headboard, her back bows beautifully, and her fantastic ass juts out. I move in behind her, running my hand along her spine and around her waist until I can caress her expanded belly. "How's our baby today?"

She turns her head to look at me over her shoulder. "He's great."

I raise my eyebrow at her. She insists we're having a boy since Hayley and Lisa have two boys now, but I want us to have a little girl with hazel eyes and a beautiful heart like her mother. I lower myself until my front is touching the length of Sarah's back, then kiss my way down her spine, rubbing my morning scruff before sucking and licking over the redness. Her back rises and falls with her sighs, then she pushes her ass into my dick.

"Give me your big cock," she moans breathily.

My lips widen. I love how she tells me exactly what she wants, so different from how she was the first time we came together. Gliding my roughened palms up the outside of her thighs, I grasp each ass cheek and squeeze, then skim my fingertips through her pussy. "Fucking drenched," I groan.

She was made for me. Her beautiful heart, perfect curves, ever-changing eyes, and lust for my cock are everything. Not to mention how damn hot she looks carrying my baby.

She rocks back on my fingers, adjusting her angle. "AJ," she whimpers.

I kiss her ass cheek and swipe my fingers up to her already pulsing clit; so damn responsive; more so since she became pregnant. Making delicate circles around the bud, I slide one finger into her hole and pump it in and out, exchanging one finger for two, two for three; the sounds of her wet pussy make me hotter for her. She rocks her body in time with my fingers, a sheen of perspiration building along the dip of her spine. My cock juts out toward Sarah's pussy, begging to get inside her.

"Stop teasing me," she growls and I chuckle.

"So bossy." She pushes back hard, her frustration getting

the better of her. She's been so damn horny, which is perfect for me because I can't get enough of her.

I drag my fingers out and slap her ass, making her jump and cry out. My pink handprint looks fantastic on the lush cheek. I shuffle forward, notching my cock at her opening and before I can push inside her slick heat, she lunges back, taking me deep. "Fuck!" I groan with a harsh breath. Gripping her hips, I stop her from moving anymore until I'm ready. "Don't move. Not yet."

She smirks at me over her shoulder, knowing exactly what she does to me. "Fuck me, AJ. Please."

Tightening my grip on her hips, I nod and drag my cock out of her warm sheath, relishing every single perfect inch. I snap my hips forward, slapping my thighs against hers, making her ass jiggle and shunting her up the bed. "Are you ready for me, Cupcake?"

"Oh yeah." She sighs and I watch her knuckles turn white as she tightens her grip on the headboard.

Withdrawing slowly and torturing both of us, I drop my gaze to my glistening cock. "You should see how wet my cock is." I grab her ass cheeks, separate them, and snap my hips forward, filling Sarah deep. Her walls flutter around my shaft and I groan. "You feel so damn good. I think you should let me stay inside you all day as my birthday present."

She chuckles with a moan as I swivel my hips, hitting that special spot inside her. "I have to go to work."

"Call in sick."

"I'm thinking your mom might catch onto the fact it's your birthday and that I'm not actually sick." She raises one eyebrow at me over her shoulder—so damn sassy.

I groan. "Don't talk about my mom while I'm inside you." She giggles again. "Your pussy feels incredible when you laugh, but you'll make me come too fast if you keep that up," I groan again.

Enough talking. I pull out and snap my hips forward repeatedly, directing all of my focus to my cock. Her panting mewls and the tightening of her walls tell me she's getting close to her release so I move my fingers to her clit, rubbing delicate circles around the tight bud. When I pinch it, she explodes, strangling my dick and sucking me inside so I can't even see the root of my cock. It's enough to have fireworks exploding throughout my body and tension locking up my muscles. My dick swells and I quickly pull out of Sarah's heat to finish off on her ass. Stroking my cock, I watch the ribbons of creamy fluid coat her ass. Stars dance around the edge of my vision and I have to close my eyes as the tension in my body finally relents. When I open my eyes again, they instantly drop to Sarah's ass and I lay my palms over the smooth globes, spreading my release across her flesh.

"Mmhm. I love it when you decorate my skin," she rasps in between panting breaths.

See. Perfect for me.

I lean over her, wrap my arms around her middle and kiss my way across the curve of her shoulder until I reach the nape of her neck. "I think you should skip your shower this morning. That way you can smell like me all day."

I roll carefully to my side, taking Sarah with me. She snuggles her body back into mine until we're spooning. "You know, if it were the weekend, and it was just you and me, I'd totally do that." I nuzzle into her neck with a smile because I know she would. She's done it for me before. "I have a birthday present for you." She smiles, turning her head and pressing her lips to mine.

Cupping her face, I deepen the kiss and tangle my tongue with hers. I'll never tire of kissing the woman. Softening the kiss and pressing smaller kisses to her lips, I pull back slightly. "You just gave me the best birthday present ever."

Her grin is big and beautiful. She tries to wriggle out of my hold, but I tighten my grip, making her laugh, and her tits jiggle. Oh yeah! "You might have to let me go so I can get it for you."

"Don't wanna." I pout like a toddler.

She slides her fingers through my hair and presses a hard kiss to my lips. "I promise you'll love it."

I loosen my hold. "Okay then."

She climbs out of bed and heads to the bathroom to do her normal morning stuff, and I take pride in the fact that she's wearing my handprint on her ass. When she comes out, she heads to her nightstand and pulls out an envelope then climbs back on the bed. Her eyes remain focused on the white paper as she runs her fingers around the edges repeatedly.

"I had no idea what to get you for your birthday, so I hope this is okay." Her eyes lift to mine and she hands it to me with a swipe of her lips across mine. "Happy birthday, Husband" she whispers, her breath touching the place she just kissed.

That's right, *husband*. I whisked us off to *Cardinal Quarry Casino and Resort* along with our friends and family for a New Year's Day dawn wedding. I take the envelope from her and peel it open. Inside is a slip of paper. As I tuck my fingers inside to pull out the paper, she lays her hand on mine, stilling me. "This is totally for you. Don't show me or tell me what it says."

My eyes narrow, drawing my eyebrows down. Now I'm intrigued. I nod my agreement and she removes her hand. I pull out the slip of paper and open it, careful to angle it in such a way that Sarah can't see it. The word 'boy' is written across it in an unfamiliar scrawl. I snap my eyes back to Sarah. "What's this?"

"I know you wanted to know what we're having and you've been going along with my need for a surprise, so I thought I'd ask our obstetrician to write it down for you. I have no idea what it says and I still don't want to know so don't spoil the surprise for me."

My heart swells with the trust she's giving me. I tuck the slip of paper back inside and roll over to my nightstand to put it out of sight, then I pull my girl into me. Wrapping my arms around her, I drag her in tight to me and take her lips in a fierce kiss full of gratitude. Sarah's always thinking about everyone else's needs above her own. It's one of the reasons I fell in love with her so easily. Softening my mouth and slowing our kiss, I press my forehead to hers. Our eyes lock and hold, Sarah's eyes twinkling with delight. "Thank you, Wife." I'll never tire of calling her that. I press a kiss to the tip of her nose and raise a brow. "Sure you don't want me to tell you?"

She uses the hand resting on my pec to push at me playfully. "No. And you're not allowed to tease me either. That's not fair."

"But I love teasing you, and you love it when I do."

She wraps her arm around my neck with a chuckle, her stomach trapped between us. "I just love *you*."

Would you like a sneak peek into the future?
Sign up for my newsletter to visit Sarah and AJ for a glimpse into the future.
https://tinyurl.com/unexpectedkisses-bonus

Have you met Sarah's eldest sister, Emma? Find out what happens when she meets her new neighbor in **Stolen Kisses.**
A neighbors to lovers romance
A steamy, emotional, stand-alone contemporary romance about a single mom giving her all for her kids and a single uncle learning how to be a dad while coming to terms with devastating losses.
https://books2read.com/dsj-stolenkisses

How about Sarah's older brother, Max, in **Moonlit Kisses?**
An age-gap workplace romance
A steamy, low-angst, stand-alone contemporary romance about
a workaholic mechanic with a generous heart fighting his
attraction to his assistant, and a younger woman who's down
on her luck but never gives in or gives up.
https://books2read.com/dsj-moonlitkisses

pinterest

I put together a Pinterest board for Sarah and AJ's story. If you're interested, you can check it out here:

https://tinyurl.com/unexpectedkisses-pinterest

debra's books

The Summer Twins

Loving Summer | *Kate Summer & Oliver Stone*

Second Chance Summer | *Toby Summer & Cassia Phillips*

The Summer Twins | Complete Series

Spin-off Novella

Loving Roman | *Roman Armstrong & Alice Reed*

Kisses

Stolen Kisses | *Emma Miller & Theo Drivas*

Moonlit Kisses | *Max Stanfield & Molly Lewis*

Unexpected Kisses | *Sarah Stanfield & AJ*

Kisses | Complete Series

Monday Knights | *novellas*

Enemy Kisses | *Finn Brady & Harriet Dubois*

Wicked Kisses | *Lincoln Kingsley & Sophie Chalmers*

Everlasting

Everlasting Love | *Shane Sutton & Violet Jamison*

Everlasting Promises | *Hope Sullivan & Benjamin Taylor*

Everlasting Vows | *Nixon Steele & Abigail Steele*

Debra has a list of her books available on her website.

You can find them here:

https://debrastjamesbooks.com

connect with debra

stalk me

You can stalk me pretty much everywhere!
https://debrastjamesbooks.com/connect/

How about joining my Facebook group?
https://www.facebook.com/groups/DebsBibliomaniacs

newsletter

Join Debra's newsletter to receive important updates before anyone else. Newsletters will be sent once a month unless something exciting is happening.
https://debrastjamesbooks.com/newsletter/

thank you

Thank you so much for reading Sarah and AJ's story and making it through the slowest burn I've written to date. When Sarah's story came to me, I imagined her and AJ having sex almost from the first chapter since she wanted to have a baby. However, the woman had a plan and she was bound and determined to stick to it. But we got them there in the end and that's the most important thing.

As always, I would like to thank Mr. St James and our two sons for their support and patience with me when dinner was late, or I didn't listen as attentively as I should have, or I didn't want to leave my cave because I was working on this baby.

To my beta readers, Kelly, Debbie, Wendy, and Rita, thank you for your invaluable feedback. Andrea, thank you for your invaluable information regarding AJ's injuries and treatment. Your medical knowledge and advice really helped to make that part of the story realistic. And finally, Tiffany. Thank you for sharing your experience in the NICU to help make Sarah's volunteer shifts as a baby cuddler as accurate as possible.

To my online support network, you were there for me on the days when I doubted myself. Ladies, you are so very important to me. I'm grateful we connected and I can call you my friends.

To you, the reader. Thank you for taking a chance on me; for reading my book. I truly do appreciate your time. If you've enjoyed reading about Sarah and AJ, I'd love to hear from you.

about the author

Debra St James is an author of spicy, slow-burn contemporary romance that features cinnamon roll heroes who listen to their women's hearts and their words. She takes her time to weave a detailed tapestry of genuine characters, real-life struggles, love, and romance to create engaging stories that will have you so immersed in the story that you'll never want to leave. Her stories are always guaranteed to take you on an emotional journey that ultimately ends with a HEA!

Debra loves to read romance. Her family often finds her with her nose stuck in her iPad, swooning over her latest book boyfriend. She writes part-time from her Perth home, which she shares with Mr St James and their two sons, whose antics often make her roll her eyes and laugh in equal measure.

Writing a novel had never been on her radar. One morning, she was enjoying a coffee by the river and a story sprouted, seemingly from nowhere. At 51, she pulled up the Pages app on her phone and began to type, giving life to her debut, *Loving Summer*.

The rest, as they say, is history!

amazon.com/author/debrastjames

facebook.com/debra.stjames.books

instagram.com/debrastjames_books

bookbub.com/authors/debra-st-james

goodreads.com/debrastjames

pinterest.com/debrastjamesbooks

www.ingramcontent.com/pod-product-compliance
Lightning Source LLC
Chambersburg PA
CBHW060810120726
47909CB00006B/1865